Poe & I

Matthew Mercier

Let the world know:
#IGotMyCLPBook!

Crystal Lake Publishing
www.CrystalLakePub.com

Copyright 2024 Matthew Mercier

Join the Crystal Lake community today
on our newsletter and Patreon!
https://linktr.ee/CrystalLakePublishing

Download our latest catalog here.
https://geni.us/CLPCatalog

All Rights Reserved

ISBN: 978-1-964398-13-6

Cover art:
Ben Baldwin—www.benbaldwin.co.uk

Layout:
Lori Michelle—www.theauthorsalley.com

Edited and proofed by:
Jaime Powell, Theresa Derwin, and Joseph VanBuren

This is a work of fiction. Names, characters, businesses, places, events and incidents are either the products of the author's imagination or used in a fictitious manner. Any resemblance to actual persons, living or dead, or actual events is purely coincidental.

No part of this publication may be reproduced, stored in a retrieval system, or transmitted in any form or by any means, without the prior permission in writing of the publisher, nor be otherwise circulated in any form of binding or cover than that in which it is published and without a similar condition including this condition being imposed on the subsequent purchaser.

Follow us on Amazon:

WELCOME
TO ANOTHER

CRYSTAL LAKE PUBLISHING
CREATION

Join today at www.crystallakepub.com & www.patreon.com/CLP

For Claudia and Mom, with all my love.

"All houses wherein men have lived and died are haunted houses."
Henry Wadsworth Longfellow

"If I'm going to have a past, I prefer it to be multiple choice."
The Joker

"Years ago, Matthew was the caretaker at the Poe Cottage in the Bronx and gave me a memorable tour, patiently answering my rambling questions. Now, in Poe and I, *Matthew writes the novel that only he can, bringing us into the world of a fictional Poe Cottage caretaker who takes a stunning, jolting, absurd journey of self-discovery while immersing us in Poe lore. A unique and captivating tale worthy of the legacy of Poe."*

—Matthew Pearl,
Author of *The Taking of Jemima Boone* &
The Poe Shadow

"Drawing on his years as the caretaker and head docent at the Poe Cottage in The Bronx, Matthew Mercier has crafted a wonderfully engaging and remarkably clever psychological thriller with an ingeniously Poe-ish fictional narrator who just happens to be, well, the caretaker at the Poe Cottage in The Bronx. You don't need to be a Poe fan to be caught up in this marvelous magical mystical tour, but, to be sure, the more you know about Poe and his works, the more you'll appreciate and applaud how inventively and slyly Mercier constructs his dark storytelling web."

—Mark Dawidziak,
author of *A Mystery of Mysteries*,
The Death and Life of Edgar Allan Poe

"I took joy in this book the way I take joy in the taste of harsh sour wine. I found myself smiling at the saddest moment and weeping with laughter at the darkest. Drink up Poe & I *and be annihilated."*

—Charles Baudelaire,
Author of *Flowers of Evil*

"I suppose America must have needs—and will always need— writers who enjoy the terror and murk of this life, those who stand at the prow of a storm-tossed ship and take pleasure in the sleet and rain and dark winds pummeling their own fragile human vessel of flesh and bone, so in this way, Mr. Mercier &

Edgar Poe seem perfectly matched; they are singing a similar song, and while I cannot carry the same tune, I applaud their efforts."

—Walt Whitman,
Author of *Leaves of Grass*

"I was never as enraptured with the work of the "jingle man" Poe as my fellow countryman, but I must concede that Poe & I is an object of some curiosity, and will no doubt engender strange passions in those who appreciate the darker strains of American life."

—Ralph Waldo Emerson, Essayist

"Since I no longer exist on this earthly plane and reside here in Oblivion, I could not very well not stop Mr. Mercier from scratching out his tome. I feared he would drag my name through the muck. but, to my relief, he is no Rufus Griswold. He has honored both my name and my memory. Well done, sir. I shall not send earthly messengers to sue you for libel."

—Edgar A. Poe, Revered Poet

Chapter 1
Literary Underground

I first heard about the gig at Poe's house on April Fools' Day. Does that make me a fool? Not sure. But here I am, hustling down Seventh Avenue toward my dream job.

Wanted: Caretaker for the last home of Edgar Allan Poe. Only gothic souls with a shadowy past need apply. Free room and board. No pets allowed, except black cats.

I wrote that classified ad inside my third eye. Sounds too good to be true, right? But the job is real, and so am I. So here I am, snapping at the bait, getting reeled in.

My kneecaps are burning after a full morning of pounding up and down staircases, moving rich people's sofas and tables. These moving jobs are murder on my body, but it's cash money under the table. Not a whole lot of cash, mind you, but enough to survive. I'm flexing my knuckles so my hands won't curl into claws, and I'm aching in all the usual hot spots—small of my back, shoulders, thighs, groin, brain, soul, wallet. Every car horn, every sliver of laughter, echoes inside my skull. My dogs are barking after twenty epic blocks. I've hoofed it south from a client's brownstone in Chelsea, too cheap to use the final ride on my MetroCard. I need to save those dollars for the trip home, if I still have one.

Ducking off the avenue and plunging into the rat's maze of the West Village, where I can never figure out the cramped, crosshatched pattern of streets—Bleecker and Barrow, Grove and Morton, Perry and Charles—which chase their tails and circle

1

Matthew Mercier

around to the same intersections. Right now, I'm on the corner of West 10th and West 4th—tell me how that works. I don't own a fancy smart phone with a GPS, so I step into a bodega and ask the vendor for Bedford Street.

"Round the corner," he says, waving a meaty brown finger.

I mutter a 'thank you' and start for the door, but he calls me back, reaches under the counter, grabs two paper napkins, points at my face, and taps his left cheek.

I crumple the napkin, dabbing at the corner of my mouth. Copper in my gums. I wiggle my mouth. Teeth are still intact. That's a plus. On the street, I sneak a peek in the side view mirror of some yuppie's Escalade. My left side is swelling, chipmunk style. I tap it with my finger. The ping ripples up and down my jaw. More pain.

All I want right now is to disappear, but I can't. Not today. Not yet.

Bedford Street is a shaded block of brownstones and gaslight tenements, cherry blossoms, and mimosa trees. French-style bistros and used bookstores. Sex shops with chocolate dildos and edible panties. Be nice to live here if you earned the bread.

I spit a gob of blood. *Dream on, cowboy*. This part of Gotham? Real estate porn. A fantasy. I belong in Manhattan the way a fox belongs in a hen house.

There. 86 Bedford—arched medieval door with a cast iron square of rebar framed a few inches below the pointed peak. Only entrance on the street that looks as if it might dump you into a medieval torture dungeon. I check my face again, lick and swallow the remaining blood, then lift the brass handle and push.

A heavy velvet curtain sweeps toward me, brushing my shins. Door shuts, curtain drops back into place. My eyes take half a minute to adjust to the dim light. Cool, stone-cellar air. Faint pulse of eighties music. (*Eddie Money*? *Pet Shop Boys*?) My five o'clock shadow itches, the sweat of the workday baked into my pores. I scuff my steel-toed construction boots on the welcome mat and stare down at my faded jeans, ripped in the left knee and right pocket. Not pretty, but this isn't a job interview.

I sweep the curtain back and descend four wide steps into a warm den of knotted walnut and red brick. A fireplace sprawls in the middle of the room. Curved reading lamps with green lampshades highlight a row of private booths. The bar, nicked and

Poe & I

dented, runs along the left wall. A cracked oval mirror with a gilded frame hangs above stacks of pint glasses and a glistening well of liquor. The bartender, tight round belly and a head shaped like a bullet, lifts his salt and pepper goatee at me, smiles, snatches a pint glass from the racks, and begins pulling a tap.

"Professor Peabody!" he bellows. "What's doing?"

"Afternoon, Ramses." The joint is dead. Nobody at the bar. Even the kitchen is quiet. "You give everyone the day off?"

"Had to finish up some renovations today. We open again tomorrow."

The renovations look plenty done. Ramses releases the tap, foam sloshing over the edge of the pint glass. He places it on a cocktail nap, then slides it across. "New brew. Tell me what you think."

A copy of the *Post* sits on the bar. I flip it to the horses, scanning the winners. Big Bambu, Killer Whale, Get Chipped, Rockaround Sue, and Prayer Session. Ugh. No good. I push the paper away, but it falls on the floor, butterflying into a confetti of shopping inserts and Sunday comics.

"Bad news?" Ramses asks.

I pick up the paper and place it next to the beer. "Is it that obvious?"

"You're an open book, Professor." He taps the pint. "Try it. On me."

"That's generous."

"Come on, Prof. All the college kids drink Stella and PBR. Wouldn't know a good beer if it bit them. I need your cultivated opinion."

The beer is liquid gold, swirling and settling. Stress gathers in my forehead. I pick up the pint and sip. Amber and honey. Delicious. But I don't deserve it.

"Ramses . . ."

The landline in the kitchen shrills. "Hold that thought," he says, walking into the backroom, giving me a minute to collect my confession in the pocket of my head. I turn on the stool and stare at the walls, my favorite part of this watering hole.

Across the room, suspended above the second entrance (or secret exit), is a black and white portrait of Hemingway—starched white sleeves rolled up to his elbows, fingers bent over the typewriter. English majors worship this guy. My old teachers

Matthew Mercier

creamed their pants over his dialogue, but it's boring and repetitive. And the dude next to him, sitting in profile with a caterpillar mustache hanging off his lip. I think that's Faulkner. He wrote one story I liked. *The Bear.* Not really about a bear, all about the wilderness and manhood or something. He's tough, Faulkner. I need someone to hold my hand with his stuff, and I don't hold hands much, so no more Faulkner for this Yankee.

Pick a writer or name a book from the last century, and it's likely they live on the walls in here. Old-timey black and white portraits and the occasional burst of Kodachrome color, all hanging next to first-edition book covers behind glass—pressed literary leaves. Fossils. There's Norman Mailer floating next to *The Naked and the Dead.* (Read that one on my grandfather's recommendation.) Henry Miller in his schoolboy glasses, slouched next to *Tropic of Cancer.* (My first girlfriend was into him. Sexy stuff.) Then we got James Joyce, gawking at the one-two punch of *Dubliners* and *Ulysses* (Every bootleg Irishman knows James, even if they don't read him.)

But that's it. The rest? Beats me. A strange-looking woman with an androgynous scarecrow face, a dude with electrified hair two feet high, another with thick glasses and a serious cowlick. All the writers I might have read if I'd finished college.

Ramses claims if the author is hanging on the wall, it means they drank here during the joint's heyday as a speakeasy. I call bullshit, but who cares? Close enough to the historical mark to sell pints. Here's what the tour books say: "People come to Chumley's for the slow drip of literary nostalgia, to feel like a retro outlaw, to imagine themselves consuming illegal gin and whiskey in the company of Dorothy Day and Eugene O'Neil, while Jay Gatsby and Elmer Gantry work the taps, Ella Fitzgerald croons in a haze of cigar smoke, and Zelda and F. Scott consummate their marriage at booth number seven."

It's easy to feel like a retro-outlaw with a few in you, but after you sober up, 21st century America is still waiting outside to slap you silly.

Ramses is back, holding a plate of food and coughing violently into a stained white rag, his neck the color of rotten plums. His forehead is pale, and broken capillaries crawl up his cheek in faint cobwebs. The plate is heaped with penne pasta and mushrooms, smothered in white sauce. "Here. Eat. Some starch to go with your al-kee-hall."

Poe & I

He over-pronounces the word, sells the pasta too hard. My skin prickles. The black slices of mushrooms are glistening.

"Thanks, but I don't dig on fungus."

Ramses sours his lips. "I made extra."

"Listen, I know I'm still behind from last month." I whip out my little black book of numbers. "But I got a few moving jobs coming up that should pay pretty good."

"Moving jobs? You're working for a moving company? Seriously? Minimum wage?"

"At least I'm working. Plus, I got my tax refund coming in, state and federal, so by the end of the month, I should be caught up." I tap the binder of the book. "But end of the month, I'm probably getting booted from my apartment."

The ex-fireman wipes invisible spots on the bar, clamping his bottom lip under a bridge of yellow teeth. His crow's feet multiply as he rubs his sinus, pulls out a fork from under the bar, and slides a couple of penne onto the tines.

I stare at the bar. Some bohemian has carved into the wood: *Live Forever.* What terrible advice.

Ramses chews, swallows, scratches the tattoo on his shoulder, 24 & 5. He points at my swollen cheek. "Rough weekend?"

"Dude at work."

"You owe him money, too?"

"He called my sister a whore. Listen, I took the wrong bets last week. You know I'm good for it."

"I don't, actually."

"Well, at least tell me about this job. The one at the Poe house."

He whistles, throwing his hands up. "That's going to cost you. According to your brother."

I close the black book. "Brother?"

"That's what the man called himself." Ramses gently slaps my swollen cheek.

"He looked like you. But not as handsome."

I sip the beer to steady myself. "This is good."

"Come on. Taste these mushrooms. I cooked them with garlic."

"I'm half vampire."

"Fine. Then let's go downstairs."

"Downstairs?"

Matthew Mercier

"Sub-basement. More alcohol experiments I need you to taste. Harder stuff."

"No thanks. Tell me about this so-called brother."

He snaps his fingers and leans over the bar. "I'll tell you about Poe. Downstairs."

Get up and walk out. That's what a rational person would do. But I'm no longer living in a rational world. Irrational decisions are now my jam. Irrational, self-destructive, blow-up-your-life decisions. I'm not here for beer or fancy mushroom dishes. I'm here for information. I'm here for Poe.

So, Ramses leads me down a short hallway, past the industrial kitchen and waitstaff staging area, to a dead-end corner of the building. All empty. We really are the only ones here. He taps lightly on the wall with his fist. A door in the cherry-wood paneling cracks open. He flicks on a pale light. Steps, dropping into the dark. "After you, Professor."

There's no railing. I balance myself against the brick-and-mortar foundation and move one step at a time, brushing cobwebs with my fingers. I reach the bottom, shivering in the dampness. The hum of walk-in freezers, the hiss and pump of a boiler. Ramses stands right behind me, a wheezing hulk.

"I love it down here." He pulls on a shoelace, tied off to a rickety fluorescent, his throat hacking and rattling, a fist over his mouth.

"This dampness can't be good for your cough."

"The United States Congress is not good for my cough," he spits.

Ramses is a forgotten first responder. He breathed in the toxic dust at Ground Zero and has been paying for it ever since. Lung failure. Asthma. Divorce. Every day he coughs up brown jellyfish with hot pink centers. His glassy eyes remind me of shell-shocked veterans—damaged but not broken.

He leads us across the tight, narrow room to a wooden table squeezed into the corner under a maze of copper pipes. Eight one-gallon jugs, each sealed with a crazy-straw airlock, each with a tap, arranged in a neat row.

"You need a good cellar for brewing." He draws a plastic tumbler from the first jug. "Smirnoff infused with pineapple. I'm going to call it Skull-Fuck vodka." He holds out the tumbler of clear fluid, which looks as safe to quaff as liquid nitrogen.

"Drink," he snaps. "Or no Poe."

Poe & I

I take the plastic cup. He slides a thin, crumpled envelope from his back pocket. "This is contact info for the gig. Free rent for the rest of your life."

"That's what you said on the phone. You've got to be joking." Short of camping out in Central Park or in the subways with the Mole People, free rent just doesn't exist in NYC.

"And my 'brother' gave this to you?"

"Drink."

We go down the line. Elderberry Porter. Pumpkin Ale. Chocolate Stout. With no mushroom pasta in my stomach, all the hops and rye slide straight down my burning gullet into a vacant pit where it mixes and bubbles into an acidic soup. Ramses rambles on about my 'brother,' this man who swept into the bar one afternoon and asked for me by name.

"He described you perfectly. A good kid with a lot of potential but also a bit of a fuck-up."

"Ramses, I don't have a brother."

"Maybe he's a long-lost twin."

We drink. The air tastes of blood and dirt. Ramses is saying something about God and country, and soon we're chatting as if we're old friends, as if everything is normal, which is the job of alcohol, I suppose, so therefore I don't question why he's snapping on latex gloves and grabbing my wrist, whipping out a pair of handcuffs, and locking my left hand to a low hanging steam pipe.

I yelp, dropping the tumbler.

"Got these from a cop buddy of mine. Nifty, huh?"

"Ramses! I'm going to pay you."

"Oh, you'll pay." His fingers clamp my jaw shut and he leans in, peach fuzz brushing my chin. My chest hammers as I lift my free arm into the air, but he slaps it down.

"Used to do this with my kids. Lock the brats to the radiator when they misbehaved. Worked until they got older and started fighting back. Probably why they hate me now."

His pupils are fuming yellow smoke, and my third eye is bulging, turning the whole room into a blinding whiteout.

"I like you, Jonah. You're smarter than most of the college apes who come through here. Hell, you're smarter than my own boy. But your brother is right. You are a grade-A, blue ribbon fuck-up." He squeezes my jaw until my vision softens and his face is a red blur.

Matthew Mercier

"You don't deserve Poe." He waves the envelope in front of my nose. "But your brother says I need to give this to you. That you deserve a second chance. I told him that trash like us always finds a way to screw the pooch."

"Us?"

"Son, you and I are cut from the same cloth."

Son. Maybe he needs to pretend I'm his kid. He grabs my right hand and twists it behind my back. "He told me not to hurt you, but I'm still taking payment."

"Fine. My wallet. Left pocket."

"You got ten-grand on you? I don't think so. No, I'm taking a little piggy."

It happens so quick. First, he's slipping a sharp metal ring on my finger, then pressure, sharp pain, my entire body jerks, my stomach coils, and I try to sink to my knees. My spine is a noodle as my body relays to my brain that Ramses has done the unthinkable, but then he's showing me a wrinkled pink stub resting in his latex palm, and it still doesn't register until I swing my hand around in front of me.

My pinkie is gone. A pinhole squirting blood. Now I scream, but he shoves a rag in my throat, dumps burning alcohol on my nub, and wraps it in gauze. The guy prepped for this. He prepped, prepared, and premediated, using Poe as bait.

Then, and I can hardly believe it, the old Peabody luck kicks in. A little late, but that's par for the course for a Peabody.

The ceiling trembles. Flurries of dust and drywall sprinkle into my hair, eyes, and nostrils. Ramses, his first responder instincts sharp as a tack, leaps away from me and pounds up the stairs. I hear the door bang open, his deep muffled voice bellowing in the main room.

My head pounds. I slap my swollen cheek with my own bloody hand, so I don't pass out. There on the floor, at my feet, is the hot tip envelope. I reach down, squeeze it between my middle and pointer, smearing blood over the seal, and hold it up to the dim light. A clipping of some kind.

Thudding footsteps. I stuff the bloody envelope into my pants pocket. Whatever happened upstairs has wiped the alcohol dream off the fireman's face. He lumbers over, checks my hand, wraps it tighter, then unlocks me. I rub my wrist, clutch my wound, and back away, crushing plastic tumblers under my boots.

Poe & I

"Don't show your face again until you have my money. I have eyes on you. You skip town, I'll know."

He's scanning the floor, patting his pockets. With my good hand, I slip out the stained envelope and wave it at him. He smirks.

"Go north, young man. Get the job."

I grab the roll of gauze, stuffing it in my pants pocket.

"Get the job? How can I promise that?"

"Just tell them I sent you. The man who was all used up."

"What?"

"Get out of here before I take another finger!"

Dizzy, foggy with pain, I leap up the stairs two by two and run straight into a dust cloud. The secret entrance is propped open with a brick, a brick that seems to have come from the collapsed chimney in the center of the pub, a gaping hole in the shape of an unfinished jigsaw puzzle.

I stumble through the mess and out the secret entrance, into the cobblestone street of Pamela Court. My bandage is dripping blood on the cobblestones. A white kid is gawking at me through his shaggy Brooklyn beard.

"Fuck happened in there? Hey, you're bleeding!"

I brush the swollen balloon of my cheek with my bandaged stump. "Story of my life, kid. Where's the nearest hospital?"

He points the way, and I shuffle down the alley, muttering, "My name is Jonah Peabody and everything will be fine. My name is Jonah Peabody, and everything will be fine."

This homemade rosary or prayer is something I've developed for moments of pain, moments of unreality, and since my life has been a series of unreal moments, it always saves me from utter despair.

What just happened is small potatoes, trust me.

So, mumbling my devotions to an unknown God, I shuffle and stumble my way to St. Vincent's, whose ER surgeons ask only for the finger, which I then realize I've left behind. Do we need to call the police? No, I say. No police and no finger. This is my fault, an avoidable accident—which is essentially true.

Five hours and ten stitches later, I'm sitting at my kitchen table with a bottle of painkillers, reading the want ad—the real one—from the envelope.

Matthew Mercier

Bronx Historical Society seeks adventurous, well-balanced, studious, outgoing, and ruggedly independent individual for position of onsite Head Docent and Live-in Caretaker at Poe Cottage. Ideal candidate must work weekends and special events; have full knowledge of Edgar Allan Poe, his life, and works; small gardening and Spanish language skills a plus. A small monthly stipend is awarded. If interested, contact Cynthia McMullen at cym@bhs.com

I will say this about my fake brother: The man knows me. He knows this ad will be gothic catnip, knows I'm Poe's number one fan, and that I won't be able to resist the chance to live in the master's house. It makes sense—in my world—that when you hit rock bottom of the rabbit hole, Poe's house is the second chance you're given.

And, if the pattern holds, from here on out, it's only going to get weirder.

Chapter 2

Poe Boy

My life is a Poe story.

Sad but true. However, sadness is the sugar in Edgar's DNA, so we're a match made in melancholic heaven. All the ravens and murder and tell-tale organs are fun, but sadness—pure, uncut sadness—is the bedrock of Poe's world. Sadness and, of course, death, which I affectionally call the Big D.

Poe and I both knew death from an early age, since we both lost our mothers far too soon.

A mother's early exit is a raw deal either way you slice it, but I'll admit the Poet's wound cuts deeper. Edgar's old man—failed actor, alcoholic—deserted the family, leaving Poe, at three years old, to sit by the bedside of Eliza Poe as she (and I'm quoting now), " . . . a renowned and beloved stage actress, coughed dollops of blood into a handkerchief, her cheekbones glowing that deadly shade of crimson which colored the faces of the poor and destitute in early America."

I get choked up thinking about Eddie crying into the bed sheets, wailing for Momma, but consider this: If she'd lived, he might not have written all those creepy stories we know and love.

So. A cosmic tradeoff. Worth the price? Wrong question. We don't get to make queries of the universe. I mean, ask all you want, but nobody is going to answer, am I right? We're all alone down here, I think. What I do know is that I'd be a different man if I hadn't lost my own mother straight out of the gate. Lost her while she was still living.

That loss began one Halloween night, in the long ago.

Matthew Mercier

I was eight or nine, tossing and turning in the sweaty sheets of my bed, pulling myself out of a nightmare—a giant snake slithering its leathery body up my thigh, biting off the nub of my penis, worming its way through my pelvic bone and coiling in the cliff dwelling of my stomach, under the dripping acid and masticated gobs of chocolate and gumdrops, the whole mess squeezing and contracting, boiling with sugar.

I rolled onto my back, moaning. Exposed beams cut low over my twin mattress. My window framed the dimpled cheese of the moon. Then my door creaked open.

Mother stood at the foot of my bed, face dark, the soft glow of the hallway humming behind her. She stepped forward gently, as if testing the floorboards, and passed the window, her cotton nightgown glowing a deep-sea blue in the moonlight, oil-dark hair fanning across her shoulders in long, silky tentacles that tickled my cheeks as she bent over.

"Honey?" she whispered. "What's wrong? You were screaming."

A moonbeam lit up her collarbone, highlighting the dirt-brown mole halfway between her shoulder and neck. Every year that mole grew bigger. I always wanted to touch it, see if it swallowed my finger.

"Need some water," I croaked.

She sat on the bed, stroking my damp forehead. A thread of my pumpkin-orange hair caught in her wedding band, and when she withdrew, the pinch of it being yanked from the follicle snapped me into focus. Mother ran her fingers down my cheek, along the slope of my arm, across my chest, and rested them on my stomach. She spotted the plastic shopping bag of candy hanging from the chair at my desk. She plucked out a gumdrop and held it in front of me, the twig of her elbow pressing into my thigh.

"You ate Halloween treats before bed." Her clover green eyes sparkled as she plucked the candy in her mouth and chewed. "I told you. Eating sugar this late will give you nightmares. Was it the snake again?"

"Yes."

"Why don't you ever listen to me, Jonah?"

She kissed me on the forehead, and that kiss—warm, soft, electric—is how she gifted me a third eye. I'm sure of it. Those clammy lips transferred the gift of second sight from her to me. But it also scrambled my memory for the rest of the evening.

Poe & I

Mother, rubbing a hand on my chest, comforting me. Or was she trying to pin me down? I asked for a drink of water again, but she just grinned. Or was it a scowl?

The old man—smelling of sawdust and beer—banged into the room and grabbed my mother by the shoulders, dragged her from the room as she clawed at the doorjamb, screaming. The fevered, twisted muscles of her face—anger or fear? I forced myself out of bed, the cool hardness of the oak floors under my toes, and scooted to the doorway in time to spy Mother's nightdress ripping, snagging on the banister, the bruised milk of her deformed hip shining, her skeletal arms whipping at the bulk of my father.

I didn't follow them downstairs as the heat of their battle roared. I caught a glimpse of their bodies in the kitchen, of Mother's wild hair spreading across the tiled floor as Father pinned her with his barrel-chested frame. Ice water pumped into my lungs as I made a beeline for my sister's room, where I always went during the fights.

Her door was open, waiting for me. Andromeda, my protector, her bulky, tomboy shadow filling the crack. "Come here, Jonah."

I fell into the folds of her sweatshirt as she closed the door and rubbed the back of my neck, kissing the part in my greasy hair. The darkness of her room smelled of baked bread and soiled laundry. There on her desk, wrapped in crinkled aluminon foil, was a fresh loaf of apple cake, given to her as a Halloween treat (or handout) by our neighbor, Mrs. Jones, who lived three miles down the road and knew we didn't always get dinner.

"Are you hungry, bro? Have some."

"I have a stomachache. Mom's in trouble. Again."

Andromeda shook her shaggy mane of uncombed hair. "She's just confused."

"What do you mean?"

Andromeda always claimed to know more than I did about our parents. And yes, that was her name. Andromeda. Andy, for short. Mother and Father had a fetish for celestial and biblical names. Jonah and Andromeda, the space orphans.

"She came into my room," I whined, "acting all weird and then Dad . . ."

"Don't cry, Jonah. Don't you dare cry."

"But it's scary."

"Life is scary."

13

Matthew Mercier

Muffled shouts, banging and screaming. Andy clicked on the desk lamp. Her cheeks quivered. "This is going to get worse before it gets better."

Sophisticated talk for a grade-schooler, but she'd stolen that line from our father—it was the mantra of the Peabody clan. Everything got worse before "it" got better, but "it" only got better after "it" had ripped out a chunk of your soul.

So, before it got worse that night, we decided to run away.

Or rather, Andy decided we'd run away. I just followed orders and stuffed duffel bags of clothes while she drew a map on a legal pad, showing the route we'd take through the woods and the cemetery behind our house to reach the main road, where we could hitchhike to the supermarket and get food before skipping town.

"We need camping supplies," she said. "They're in the attic."

God, I didn't want to go, but Andy snatched my hand and dragged my little boy body up those stairs, her long, knotted hair bunched over the right side of her face, the slope of her nose and chin a frozen mask, trying to hold back tears.

The attic greeted us with uneven boards, rusty nails, mold, mushrooms growing under the leaky roof, and, for some reason, a bed, along with a rug and a lamp and boxes of old toys. The camping supplies lay in a heap, and we sorted tents and sleeping bags, pots, stoves, lighters, boots, socks, and wool hats as we sat on the circular rug, my sister's thick, ropy arms draped around my bony shoulders.

"Don't cry, Jonah." She found a rusty hatchet and pointed the blade at me. "We can do this."

Could we? We'd just gone trick or treating, and it was now past midnight. November in upstate New York, the temps dropping into the low thirties. Leaves on the ground. Men hunting in the woods with crossbows and guns. Did she think we'd get very far? Yes, she said, and when I saw how serious she was, my fear doubled. What would we do for money? We'd steal or beg. We'd go to a church. Religious people were supposed to help you. What about the cold? We'd head south. To Virginia or Alabama or Florida.

She had it all planned out, and I would have given anything to view the alternate timeline of our childhood in which we escaped that house of pain on Halloween night, but soon the bellowing beast that called itself Father pounded up the stairs and blocked the doorway, a giant X of arms and legs.

Poe & I

Andy unfolded herself from the floor and stood to her full height as Father barged in. He glanced at the bags, at the tent, at the map. "What the hell is all this?"

Andy said, "We're blowing this joint, pops."

Mother's wail rose from below, and our old man's eyes, planted deep in his skull, glistened and glowed in the dark. He wanted to cry, too. He was a little boy who needed his own mother, and that mother was not coming to his rescue either.

Then, he backed out of the doorway.

Andy saw what Father was going to do half-a-second before he did it, and she grabbed her little camping axe and leapt forward as the attic door swung shut. As smart as she was, she hadn't considered the deadbolt on the outside of the attic door, or that Father would even think of shutting us in.

She screamed—a high-pitched pre-pubescent shriek—as the door swung shut, then fell at it with the axe; but it's not like the movies, and it's harder than you might think to chop a hole in a solid oak panel. All she got, after five minutes, was a few woodchips. I tugged at the elastic band of her sweatpants, asking her to stop. She spun round, sweaty and pasty, the axe hovering over me.

Eventually, she slinked back to the rug and collapsed. We sat there in the moonbeams, which streamed through the skylight, our only window. For half a minute, Andy thought we might escape through here—climb up, pop out the screen, and rappel down the back of the house with a rope tied off to the chimney—but we lacked rope, which I was grateful for, since we'd have broken our necks.

The moonlight calmed me down. Maybe that's why I've come to prefer the night over the day. I remember the man in the moon telling me to hold back my tears, or else he'd float down and eat me alive. Or maybe that was Andy, standing above me, her head twitching with plans and ideas.

"Look at me, Jonah."

I glanced at the floor.

"Look at me." Her cheeks, wide and smooth, pulsed with love. "We have to protect each other. From here on out, you and me, Jonah. It's just you and me."

"Okay."

"No matter what. Promise?"

Matthew Mercier

"Promise."

"Promise that we protect each other no matter what. From bullies, from strangers, from the bad guys. You got me?"

"Sure."

She took out her Swiss army knife. "Give me your hand."

She grabbed me by the wrist and sliced my pinkie. I yelped and yanked my hand back, sucking the blood. Then she nicked her own.

"Here. Wrap'um together. Our fingers. No, like this."

"We'll get diseases."

"Don't be a stupid baby."

I don't know where she learned that blood ritual, probably a movie or Stephen King novel, but we curled our pinkies together and swore we'd never hurt or harm or abandon the other, no matter what horrors lay for us down the road. We swore to stand with each other to the end, forevermore, a promise only children can make, not knowing adulthood was all about broken promises and lopped-off pinkies.

Chapter 3

System of Survival

I rub the stump of my former pinkie. A coarse, flat surface.

Ramses was kind enough to make a clean cut. No muss, no fuss. ER doc said to replace the bandages every few days and workout with a rubber massage ball, which I'm doing now, clenching and unclenching in order to let the nerves know that I'm still here. I'd often thought of this pinkie and the half-moon scar where Andy nicked me as a homemade charm to ward off bad behavior. Not that it worked, mind you, but it was mine.

And now my little piggy is gone. Typical Peabody—the wound heals, but in the end, we lose the whole finger.

I read the Poe Cottage classified over and over. It's a joke. Not funny ha-ha, but funny as in it's too good to be true, as if someone wrote the ad just for me, Jonah Peabody, outcast of the universe. Free rent in Poe's house? Only if the title "live-in caretaker" means what it says.

You work on the grounds—mow the lawn, clip the shrubs, plant trees—in exchange for a free room. In NYC, that means no roommate hunt, no first or last month nonsense, no security deposit. It doesn't get any better. Or weirder. Poe Cottage—the unicorn of Big Apple real estate.

But did Poe live in The Bronx? Apparently so.

When most people think Poe history, they conjure Philly and Baltimore, but for the last three years of his life, Poe brought his young wife, Virginia (dude married his cousin, which is hot) and her mother, Maria Clemm, to the Bronx village of Fordham, where he hoped the clean country air might suck the tuberculosis from his bride's lungs. Sadly, she croaked, and after her death, Poe (I'm quoting again) *"grew that famous caterpillar mustache and transformed into the dread icon we know and love: broke, lonely, melancholy, and desperate."*

Brother Poe, my kindred spirit. I see you.

No self-pity here, just stating facts: I'm desperate, broke, lonely, and a teeny bit depressed—in other words, a perfect roommate for you, Edgar, although I'm not sure what intern decided the caretaker needed to be "well-balanced." A well-balanced person takes one look at this advert and says, "Poe? The Bronx? No thonx!"

However, bad decisions have defined me, so I cold-call Cynthia McMullen to set up a meeting.

"Poe Cottage?" A thick Bronx accent drawls over the phone. "Young man, we haven't run the ad yet. How did you hear about it?"

"Word of mouth."

"Whose mouth exactly?"

"The man who was all used up."

A long silence.

"Ma'am?"

"The man who was all used up. I see."

"I'm aware that's the title of a Poe story, ma'am."

"Very good. Not many people would know that. Your name is Peabody?"

"Jonah. Jonah Peabody."

"I guess you're worth a look. Next week. Wednesday. One o'clock."

"Perfect." I rub my bruised cheek. Seven days is enough time for this beauty mark to fade. "You won't regret it."

"But visit the cottage first. Make sure you want the job."

"Why wouldn't I want the job?"

"Visit the cottage. Here's the number. Bradford Macon is our man underground."

"Underground?"

"Visit the cottage, Mr. Peabody."

My first view of the South Bronx is from the number four train.

It digs through Manhattan's underbelly, shooting out of the

Poe & I

ground at 161st into a blood-orange sunset and slides behind The House that Ruth Built. A snapshot view of navy-blue nosebleeds and the field covered in a flapping tarp. We jerk to a stop. Intercom crackles. Doors snap open. Passengers file on and off. I've been told most white people never make it past Yankee Stadium and a good number of palefaces did drop out at 125th—an undeclared border. The last of them now exit. The rubber lips of the doors bang shut and the conductor blares, "Nextstoponesixtyninth." I draw in a breath and repeat my own stop, "Kingsbridge Road."

I'm the only white dude in the car now—the skin tones around me mixing like crazy. Chestnut and café latte, baked apple, and smoked hickory. I'm hoping folks can see the Irish in me, raw milk skin and ginger black hair. I sit in a two-person seat at the end of the car, rubbing my kneecaps and playing with the zipper on my windbreaker. We roll past tenement after tenement, perched on the edges of stone cliffs that drop off into abandoned lots of auto garages encased in birdcages of hurricane fence and barbwire. Neon corporate logos and bodegas flash by. The Cross Bronx Expressway rears up, a congested hell of red brake lights and tractor-trailers, thousands of souls frozen in mid-commute.

Kingsbridge Road is a cluster of businesses—pawnshop, flower stalls, Spanish diners, pet supply, flower and hardware, a dollar general, two banks, a noodle joint, D&D and Burger King, a Korean fruit stand, a fish market, beauty parlor, cell phones, a single-counter diner called Vicki's Café, and finally your classic, garden-variety bodega. In front of the bodega is a gray-bearded man in a dirty white skullcap, hawking a card table of cotton tube socks. Opposite him, a guy sits on a portable fold-out stool above a blanket of bootleg DVDs. I glance at his selection, and he holds one up. "Five dollars, man."

"Actually," I say, "can you tell me how to get to the Grand Concourse?"

"Concourse?" He tosses a thumb uphill, over his shoulder, where Kingsbridge dips into a dingy underpass. Two feeder streets branch off on either side of the underpass and run up a slight grade to a flowing, steady stream of buses and cars.

"And Poe Cottage?"

"Say what now?"

"Poe Park. Is that up here?"

"Hell are you asking me?"

Matthew Mercier

"Edgar Allan Poe. His old home."

The guy shrugs, done with my stupid questions. The sock merchant, who's been watching, moves out from behind his table and strolls up to me, his thin robes swishing. He's wearing a brown sweater, with holes in the elbows, and his beard hangs off his chin at least half a foot.

"Can I help you, my brother?"

"I'm looking for Poe Park."

He frowns. "The park?"

"Yes."

A scowl, followed by a dismissive wave of the hand. "Top of the hill." He shuffles back to his table.

Is Poe's name poison around here? Why the gruff attitude? I say good night and soldier up the hill. The Concourse is four hissing lanes of north and south traffic, and there, diagonally across the urban chaos, sits the cottage.

A farmhouse with a peaked roof. Flaking clapboards, wooden shingles, brick chimney, paned glass—all hemmed in by a spiky arrowhead fence and planted under a spidery oak tree, with a stumpy lawn spread underneath. The spring evening is damp and misty with a tang of salt in the air, carried over from Long Island Sound, which is somewhere out there beyond the brick line of tenements, their rooftops wrapped in tendrils of fog.

All that's missing is a lighthouse to warn off wayward ships.

My pulse skips. *Turn around. Turn around and don't look back, you fool. You're always digging holes for yourself, and this will be the deepest. The Bronx doesn't like you already. You're an outsider, a country mouse. Leave. Get back on the first bus headed upstate.*

But my pinkie nub tingles and the monkey on my back—a ten-thousand-dollar gorilla of debt—hoots and screeches, swinging between my shoulder blades. *Free rent,* it hoots, *free rent, free rent, free rent! If you don't take this job, you'll be pumping gas or flipping burgers and missing a few more fingers.*

The specter of Ramses gets me hustling across the Concourse before my brain can figure out what I've done. Poe's back lawn is a landfill—plastic shopping bags, advertising inserts, Styrofoam mugs and soda cans, fast food wrappers and newspapers. It all tumbles on the breeze, catching on the bars of the fence or collecting at the base of the spider oak, in the shallow well of its

Poe & I

exposed roots. A basement window is carved into the cottage's foundation, and a soft yellow light is spilling out, blinking as the shadow of a body moves around in the bowels of Poe's basement. Another body shambles up behind me on the corner. An older man with a pronounced limp, a faux-ivory cane tapping the pavement. Baggy cargo jeans and tobacco brown hoodie. He smells of fast food and nicotine, poking his chin in my direction. "What do you need?"

I step aside to let him pass. "I'm good, champ."

"Got Newport, Camels."

"All set, thanks."

"Change your mind, I'm here."

He winks, shuffles down the hill, past the rear of the cottage and across the street to a bodega on the opposite corner, a building trussed up like a circus tent—piss yellow walls, awning framed in blinking red and blue light bulbs. Huddled under its canopy are five or six people with sunken cheeks, coat-hanger collarbones, and clothing that hangs off their limbs like wet dishtowels.

I know what I'm looking at. Bloodshot eyes, cracked skin, and the ghost of track marks dotting their forearms—we've got tweakers upstate. My guy limps forward and mixes with the junkies. Some splinter off from the group and shamble across a traffic island, where they vanish into another gray mass of men and women lingering under the tenements, eyes peering out from under their ragged baseball caps—all squirming, itching, scratching, twitching, bending, and quivering with the hunger.

At least thirty bodies hover in the oily shadows. Now, the sock dealer's dismissal makes sense. When a white boy in this neck of the Bronx asks for Poe Park, he's asking for directions to this underground marketplace.

I take out my phone and dial. A tired voice answers, "Poe Cottage."

"Is this Bradford Macon?"

"Museum is closed."

"It's Jonah Peabody. We talked."

"Oh shit. Where are you?"

"Out back."

"You didn't confirm, man."

"I'm confirming now."

"Come down the side. Across from the Indian market."

Matthew Mercier

I follow the fence downhill, behind the cottage, to a padlocked rear gate. Here, Kingsbridge exits the underpass and curves south, running parallel to the park. From behind, the cottage appears much bigger. A shed is built onto the eastern face, expanding its footprint.

A man steps out of the shed in carpenter's work pants and construction boots. "Peabody?"

"Yes. Bradford Macon? The man underground?"

"Did Cynthia call me that?"

"She did."

"Funny lady." Dark brownish skin, golden eyes, calloused palms, and a shiny bald head glinting in the dark. He scuffs his feet on the pavement and rattles a circle of keys as he fiddles with the rusty padlock. "Did the guy on the corner offer you something?"

"Just cigarettes."

"He's a pest." He swings open the gate and chuckles. "You look scared. Junkies frighten you?"

"I've seen worse."

"Oh really?"

"We got tweakers where I grew up."

"Where's that? Kansas?"

"Upstate. Catskills."

"You a redneck?"

"White trash."

"Okay then." He makes a theatrical sweeping gesture with his right arm.

"Welcome to the Poe House."

He locks us in and twirls the keys on his finger, whistling. I glance up at the spider oak, telephone lines crisscrossing the limbs.

"You ever climb that?" I ask.

Bradford picks up a soda can and tosses it into a garbage pail. "Why would I do that?"

"It's there."

"Black people don't climb trees. Strange fruit. You feel me?"

A security lamp planted in the front lawn casts the front porch of the cottage in a tangerine haze. A rat wiggles across our path and burrows under a shrub in the garden.

"Lots of those around," Bradford mumbles, as if talking about a common plant.

Inside, the shed has a flagstone floor and is lit by glaring

Poe & I

fluorescents. Rusty rakes and shovels hang on the walls. Terracotta pots are stacked next to lumpy bags of peat moss. My guide points out the apartment entrance, a red door at the bottom of concrete steps.

"The apartment is in the basement?"

"What did you think underground meant?" Bradford snaps. "You having second thoughts already?"

"No. Not at all."

"Shame. The basement scares off most people."

He leads me across the shed to a wooden staircase. The splintered railing wobbles when I touch it.

"You got any carpentry skills?" he asks. "That needs to be fixed."

"Is carpentry a job requirement?"

"Just for you, college boy."

He unlocks an invisible, handle-less door in the wall. "Wait here." He melts into the shadows.

At the foot of the stairs sits a heaping pyramid of plastic flowerpots and purple bags of potting soil and fishmeal. One of the flowerpots trembles, rolling off the pile as a rat bolts out.

My gut seizes. I brace myself in the doorframe as the rat scurries under the stairs, sniffing for an exit in the concrete wall. It scrambles under the tools, over a box of trash bags, and dives into the concrete steps leading to the apartment.

Bradford's voice reverberates from inside the kitchen. "What's the problem out there?"

"Rat!"

"Big one?"

"Huge."

"Those suckers are supernatural."

"It went into the apartment."

"No, it didn't. I'll explain later. If you still want the job. Come on in."

I push open the door, inching forward. My vision sharpens. Tight walls, low ceilings, wooden floors, the drafty maw of a fireplace.

"Easy does it. Expensive stuff all around."

More focus gives me a cast iron stove, table, chairs, and the horizontal of a mantelpiece, on which sits a pair of candles plugged into the wall.

Matthew Mercier

"Click those on. The switch is beneath your elbow."

I finger the dirty white cord of the candle until my thumb runs over the ridged oval dial. Light reveals a dining table draped with a pearl-colored cloth, place settings for three, copper mugs and knives, chipped plates, and a hurricane lamp.

Bradford unhooks a fat velvet rope that divides us from the gift shop, a series of shelves sunk into the wall outside the exhibit and protected by double doors. He hooks the rope to a wooden cube which is bolted onto a tripod. A faded index card pressed between two pieces of glass bears the words, *Poe Box.*

"For donations." He taps the cube. "Most people give two or three beans at the start of the tour."

"How many tours have you given?"

He swells his chest. "Enough to tell you that you're standing in the last home of one of the most original American writers of all time, a writer who—"

He stops.

"You don't need the whole tourist speech, do you?"

"Well, I do need to learn it."

"Only if you get the job. I'll skip it for now. Let's see how much you know instead." He points down. "Watch yourself."

The step into the parlor is a foot high, and the first thing I spot in the gloom is a bronze bust of Poe himself in the far corner.

"Poe's parlor," Bradford says. "This room gets the most sunlight. I sit up here when the apartment is too depressing."

"Depressing?"

He looks at me and then at Poe, throwing his hands in the air. "You do know who lived here, right?"

The parlor has another fireplace, another mantle, and more faux candle lights. A long bench runs under a rear window, and next to this hangs a mirror. On the other side of the bench is a folding desk and a hanging bookcase. In the middle of the parlor, a rocking chair and a tiny round table with paw feet.

"You know what this style is called?" Bradford taps the animal feet with his toe.

"I don't remember."

"School yourself. Cynthia will want you to know this stuff."

Two windows look onto the front porch. Hanging between them, a large black-and-white photograph of the cottage. "This is a shot of the house before they moved it. Used to be across the

24

Poe & I

street." He points out the front window to a row of tenements on Kingsbridge. "Two horses. Hitched it up on a flatbed, hauled it over."

"Cool," I say.

"Dope, right? That was after Eddie died."

"Eddie?"

Excitement flickers over his face as he taps the base of the bronze Poe, with the wild hair, drooping mustache, and sourpuss mouth. "Live here long enough and you get to call him Eddie. Now, pay attention. We only have three pieces in the house that are original. Two are here in the parlor. That rocking chair and mirror. Third piece is Virginia's bed."

We enter a narrow hallway off the parlor, where a square box of a room lies behind a half-door. There is only a tiny four-post bed and a nightstand. "This bed is where Virginia Poe died of TB . . . "

"At the age of twenty-five," I finish. "She was Poe's cousin."

"Basic Poe history."

"Is she here too? Virginia?"

He scratches his cheek. "You believe in ghosts?"

"Depends on the day."

"Personally, I always throw in a few ghost stories, give the people what they want. Officially, there are no ghosts."

"Officially?"

"Officially. Unofficially, I like to think Poe is here." He grins sideways at me. "And Virginia, too."

"For real?"

"Listen, in the seventies this place had no fence. You imagine that? The burning Bronx of the seventies. People say a junkie couple once broke into the greenhouse and hid there for days. They were escaping The Junkie Purge, a time when South Bronx gang members went medieval on all the tweakers. Killed a bunch, forced others to withdraw cold turkey. Lots of blood spilled."

"Jesus."

"A haunted house for a haunted block. The Bronx holds a shit ton of horror in its history. I'm writing a book about it."

"Sounds deep."

"Fuck you."

"I mean it."

"Okay. Sure."

Matthew Mercier

We back away from Virginia's room into a sliver of hallway, where three more portraits of Poe are hanging. An oil painting of Edgar in his youth with mutton chop sideburns, minus the mustache. A watercolor at age thirty-seven, still no mustache but neatly parted hair. And finally, the famous "Ultima Thule" daguerreotype taken in Providence sometime after Virginia's death and a year away from his own drunken demise on the streets of Baltimore. A kerchief is wrapped tightly around his throat, the iconic mustache drooping slightly. His left pupil is drifting upward toward his pale forehead, while the other stares ahead. It looks as if he hasn't slept in days and might never sleep again.

From the hallway, we climb up a tight, steep, curving staircase into a suffocating attic, where the gables cut in so low we need to bow our heads. Two smaller rooms up here, one with clippings from Poe's work and a larger one with a few rows of metal folding chairs and a television that plays a twenty-minute video on a loop. A pair of eyebrow windows face the park, allowing for a bit of natural light. The chimney rises through the floor and hanging on it is another version of the Poet, muskrat hair wilder, eyes crazier. Bradford takes a seat in one of the chairs, groaning.

"So, is that it?" I say, regretting my words instantly.

Bradford snorts. "Is that it? This is all Poe had at the end of his life. That's not enough?"

"I just thought . . . "

"And I bet you didn't think a black dude would be giving you a tour."

"I had no expectations about that."

"Everyone's got expectations. You think I'm nuts working here, don't you?"

"No. I want to work here."

"Yes, but as a black man, you think I'm nuts, right?"

"Why would you be nuts?"

"Sometimes I stay out late. When I come home, I need to let myself into the park at night. What do you think that looks like? I take a chance every time I leave this house. I've had to work overtime so the local pigs don't shoot me. It's stressful. And here I am talking about Poe, a racist Southerner. If you read *The Narrative of Arthur Gordon Pym* and *The Gold-Bug* you can see it. The way he writes about black folks is shameful. So, I get a lot of shit for liking him. People think I'm betraying my heritage. I mean, I get it, but I don't get it. Huey Newton liked Vincent Price."

Poe & I

He's veering all over the place now, and I can hardly keep up. "Who's Huey Newton?"

He sighs. "You sure you want to work here?"

"Absolutely."

"Are you a loner?"

"Hell yes. Plus, I'm weird."

Bradford slaps his knee. "Ha! That's right. When you live with Poe, you've just won the lotto of weirdness!"

"Never going to get any weirder."

"Exactly!"

"So why are you leaving?" I ask.

"I'm not," he sniffs.

"Come again?"

He leans back in the chair. "You on any medication, Peabody?"

"Medication?"

"Prozac. Zoloft. Whippets. Valium. Heroin."

"I take sleeping pills."

"We can't have a junkie docent. Or a drinker. You drink?"

"I'm just here for the free rent."

"Oh, in that case!" He fakes a laugh, stands, and leads me back down into the parlor and through the shed to the red apartment door. "Now, what you see in here is not for public knowledge. Don't be blogging about this. The only reason I'm showing you is that Cynthia told me to. Up to me? I'd keep my privacy, but for some reason you're a golden boy and you haven't even been interviewed yet."

I don't know why he's making a stink about the apartment. It's nothing to blog home about. First, the kitchen. Checkerboard floor tiles, algae green walls, off-white cabinets, flimsy card table, and dilapidated chairs. Then a sink, stove, fridge, boiler, and hot water heater—all inches from each other.

"Where's that rat?" I ask.

"He's hiding. They got their own network." He taps the wall with his fist. "I find any holes I just stuff them with steel wool."

"So, they *can* get through?"

"Rats can chew through concrete."

I swallow my fear, and we move into the main living room, which is directly under Poe's parlor.

A tiny alcove in the corner contains a wall of books and a file cabinet. The window that I'd seen from the street is propped open

Matthew Mercier

with a brick. There's a mouse-eaten loveseat with an ivy print cover pushed against the far wall with a large bulky safe on wheels right next to it. The safe reads *Poe Society*.

"What's in that?"

"Need to know basis. Employees only. Poe experts only. You must be an expert, right? What are Fortunato's last words?"

"For the Love of God, Montresor."

"What beast does the narrator in *The Sphinx* see?"

"A moth."

"A death's-head moth. What is the means of Hop-Frog's revenge?"

"He makes the king and his court dress up as monkeys before roping them all together so he can hang them from a chandelier and burn them alive."

"Orangutangs, but okay smarty pants." He sits at a cluttered desk and flips open a laptop. "What do all those stories have in common?"

"Death."

"What else?"

I consider all the great Poe themes. Revenge. Lost love. Murder. The grotesque.

"They were all written," Bradford types, "here in the cottage. You're welcome. Grab yourself a collected tales. Up there."

He's got books stored on the exposed crossbeam of the basement. Among the volumes of Poe and James Baldwin and Octavia Butler are strange titles like *Cries of Abandonment* by Rat Billings and *Maniacs in the Fourth Dimension* by Kilgore Trout. I repeat this last one aloud.

"That's a classic." Bradford pulls down the Trout book, hands it to me, then continues typing. "All about insanity. Poe would have loved it. Guy travels to the Fourth Dimension where all the diseases are kept. Tries to find a cure for madness and bring it back to our world but then goes mad himself."

"Wild. I have an interest in madness."

"I bet. All white people are crazy."

I ignore that and look for a copyright page or a publisher, but there's only a stamp on the inside front cover:

Washburn Library

Poe & I

"What are you typing?" I ask.

"First impressions."

"Of me?"

"No, of your momma. Cynthia's going to ask."

"And what's your impression?"

He rubs his chin, cricking his shoulders. "Not sure you're right for this job."

"Why?"

"Just a feeling."

"That's specific."

He eye-fucks me hard. "Okay. I think you're a liar. I saw your resume, college boy."

My plumbing runs hot and cold. "I sent that to Cynthia."

"And she sent it to me. What? You didn't think she'd share it? Why do you want this job, man?"

Good question. I can imagine myself sleeping here in this basement. Cozy. Secret. Mysterious. It reminds me of all the forts I built as a boy—the ones out in the woods I used to escape my family. Here in The Bronx, I could hide from the world while living in the middle of it. I could stay in one place, put down roots, pay off Ramses, keep my fingers and save money, reinvent myself (again). I figure caretakers don't get much vacation time, but I'm done with travel, done trying to escape life. I want to *build* a life. Never mind all the unanswered questions. (Is the cottage safe? Do people bother you at night?). Never mind the rats or the heroin zombies or the lack of natural light.

"I want the job," I say, "in order to find my sister."

He cocks his head, stumped.

"She's missing. I think she's here in the city."

"And you need the job at Poe Cottage for that?"

"It's a big town. I need time to find her."

"She a junkie?"

"I hope not."

He types. "Lost sibling. Possibly drug addicted."

"That's speculation. I don't need Ms. McMullen to know that."

"Too late. Interview is over. First one, anyway. Let's go."

He walks me back to the shed. Stepping out of the silent basement shocks my ears—bus brakes, police sirens, babies wailing, radios rapping. Underground, in Poe's basement, we'd literally been insulated. Now, the world sounds a decibel too high.

29

Matthew Mercier

Bradford slings the chain off the back gate and whips it open. "You didn't answer me before," I say. "Why're you leaving?"

He slaps me hard on the back. "Who said I am?"

"If the job's not open, why interview?"

"Good question. Ask Cynthia. I sure as hell will."

Great. He's being squeezed out, and I'm a pawn. We step through the gate and glance up at the corner, where the cigarette man with the cane is standing. Bradford shakes his head. "That bastard doesn't quit."

"Who is he?"

"He thinks he's a big deal. Like you."

"You don't know me, Bradford."

"I know enough, Jonah Peabody."

He slams the gate shut, then snaps the padlock.

"Thanks for the tour!"

He tosses me a wave over his shoulder.

Well. Damn. What have I walked into? As I pass Mr. Newport, he leans in again, the sales pitch bubbling from his throat. "Got everything, buddy. What do you need?"

I hold up my bare right hand, flashing my nub. "Any spare fingers?"

"Oh! How'd you do that?"

"Slicing deli meat."

I turn around and take another look at the cottage, at Bradford's shadow moving past the basement window, and wonder if I really have it in me to live here. But Andromeda would take this job in a tell-tale heartbeat, and that's who I'm doing this for. That's who I really need.

My sister. Dead or alive.

Chapter 4
The Necro Family

The grating shunk of the deadbolt woke me. I lay on the bed, wrapped in a musty comforter. Andy was a fetus on the circular rug. The door opened a sliver, father's bulk filling the crack.

He needs to let us out, my foggy brain said. We have school on Monday.

The floorboards whined. Andy stirred. The old man stepped over her and bent down to pick me up, his mountain of muscle lifting me from the bed and resting me in the valley of his shoulder and neck. His collar reeked of whiskey. Beneath us, Andy rolled onto her back. Her eyes fluttered open, registered us, and then she leapt to her feet, grabbed the hatchet (which must have been under her pillow), and braced herself in the doorway.

"Andromeda," Father's voice was soft and silky. "Put that down."

The matted nest of my sister's hair bounced as she bent her knees, spring-loaded, the hatchet brandished across her chest. Give her a winged horse and she was a Valkyrie, ready to sail into Valhalla.

"Andy. Put the hatchet down. Please. I'm sorry."

My sister told me, years later, how she had imagined the blade cleaving the old man's face in two, spilling eyeballs and brain matter onto the floorboards, and how the old man had kept talking and used me, slumped in his arms, as a bargaining chip.

"Andy. I'm holding your brother. Come downstairs, I made you breakfast."

Hunger kicked in. Reason prevailed. She lowered the hatchet

31

but carried it with her into the kitchen, a dingy and cramped room with a buckling tile floor and cabinets held closed with rubber bands stretched across their knobs. Andy placed the hatchet on her lap as we pulled up to our round oak table and a glorious breakfast. Blueberry pancakes smothered in butter and maple syrup. Golden potato wedges. Scrambled eggs mixed with cheese. Frosted chocolate Pop-Tarts. We never had Pop-Tarts. We'd woken up in Willy Wonka's candy factory, our kitchen transformed into a joyful place that granted wishes—for a price.

We knew that breakfast was a bribe. Forgive and forget, those Pop-Tarts pleaded. Don't report your father to the authorities, Mrs. Butterworth scolded, wagging her glass finger. You'll only cause trouble for the family.

The con worked for as long as it took to stuff ourselves, and then, as our stomachs gurgled with grease and fat, my sister corralled the elephant in the room, her mouth crammed with blueberries. "Where's Mom?"

My father's ruddy face heaved. He quaffed a whole glass of orange juice, coating his mustache with curls of rind, and told us a story. Our mother, he said, was in love with another man. This man had surprised Father last night by driving right up to the house, ready to spirit Mother away. (He used that word. Spirit. I imagined a ghostly hawk gripping Mother by the shoulders with its talons and lifting her off into a blood red sunset.) He said Mother loved Andy and I, but she loved this strange man even more.

"So, this guy shows up last night and says he wants to see your mother. Believe me, I almost killed him, but I don't like the idea of prison. And your mother, she wanted to go with him, but she didn't want to leave without saying goodbye, so that's why she came into your room last night, Jonah."

He rambled on, a river of words spilling from his mouth, spilling over me. We wanted our mother, and Father was spinning a tale.

"She didn't come into my room," Andy snapped. "She didn't say goodbye to me. And why is her car still here?"

The old man glanced out the window at Mother's beloved Subaru hatchback. He pecked at his eggs and coughed. "Ack. I used too much pepper. The car. Right, they took his car. Told you. He drove here." His speech was slurred, the orange juice spiked with an adult beverage.

"Who is he?" Andy barked. "This man? I'll kill him for you."

Poe & I

"I'm sure you'd try, Andromeda. But he's not worth it. He's nobody. And they're long gone."

"Where? I'll hunt them down."

"North. Up by the Canadian border."

"That's fucking unbelievable."

"Watch your mouth, young lady."

"Why didn't she tell us this? Why didn't you tell us together?"

"Told you, he surprised me."

The story spun on, and the excuses piled up. You could sniff the shit being smothered across our pancakes, mixing with the coppery maple syrup into a rich brown soup, until all that sweet food turned sour in our mouths. Andy pointed out that Father's story didn't explain why he needed to lock us in the attic, but the old man had a plot twist for this, too.

"She wanted to steal you away, but I wouldn't let her."

"You said she wanted to say goodbye to us," Andy spat.

Father rubbed his forehead, the storm building in his fists. "She was always threatening to take you away."

"That's not true."

"Andy," I whined. "Stop."

"Yes, Andy." Father hissed. "Stop."

"No. I . . . "

Father slammed his fist on the table and ranted about alimony, affairs, and divorce. The end of love. "No more from either of you, or I'll crack your skulls. I'd appreciate a little time to process the fact that my marriage is over."

Done. We started clearing the table and left the beast alone. Later, huddled in Andy's room, my sister explained. "He got lost in his own story. She's dead. He killed Mother."

I believed her, but only because I was afraid of Father. When you're a kid, even if you can sniff out the lies, there is little you can do, especially if you live in an isolated farmhouse with an old man low on information and short on patience, so you latch onto your older and wiser siblings.

I trusted Andromeda with my life.

Father killed Mother. End of story.

Growing up without a mother leaves every kid rudderless, but each kid is rudderless in their own special way. Poe turned to poetry. Andy and I turned to stone. Then we crumbled. Then we built ourselves up again, pebble by pebble. That's how trauma rolls.

Matthew Mercier

It splits you into a million little pieces that you spend the rest of your life picking up. Don't be fooled—the pieces never peter out. Forgive me, I'm not a poet, and that might be a cliché, but we don't need new words for grief. Death and dead mothers. It's all been said. Words will fail, and so will the people who speak those words. I knew that much after hearing my father talk and talk and talk. Words? Meh. Farts in the wind.

Ah yes, my first bit of poetry. I used that immature metaphor throughout grade school for anything I didn't enjoy or that I felt was useless, which was a hell of a lot. Math class? A fart in the wind. Sports? Hurricane sized farts. Black beans? The metaphor made literal. And my father? One big tragic fart of a man, wafting in and out of my life, stinking up the joint at random moments and then drifting away, embarrassed at his own stench.

As the days and weeks rolled by without Mother, he turned into a ghost. (Ghost fart, old fart—same tribe.) He drank. He gambled. He stayed out late and left early in the morning. As we grew into latchkey kids, he'd go missing for whole days at a time on "business trips." These always arrived in the middle of the week. Tuesday and Wednesday or Wednesday and Thursday. No variation. Andy had kept track all summer on a Star Wars calendar, marking Dad's away games with a giant X. The two-week, two-day pattern stayed consistent. We figured he was driving down to a casino to gamble away our college tuition and was probably too wasted to drive home, so my sister learned how to cook to keep us fed. She despised cooking and housekeeping, but with Mother gone, we had to learn how to look after ourselves, so I grew skilled in the art of mac and cheese and avocado toast, but Andy took the brunt of the labor. She told me if people discovered that our sole parental unit was too wrapped up in his own grief to take care of two little human beings, she and I would be separated. Forever.

"And that," she cupped my face in her warm hands, freckles hopping off her nose, "would be the end of me, Jonah. You and me, kid. Till death do us part. Got it?"

"I got it, Andy."

But I "got it" just to make her happy. I had no idea how much anger was building inside her. I asked how she knew we'd be separated, and she said it happened to the Monroe kids down the street. After their mother died, the old man started drinking and

Poe & I

gambling before a social worker found out and the kids got carted off to a foster home.

Andy knew these adult words. Social worker. Foster home. Drinking. Death. Well, we both knew death. That was the family business, you see.

The funeral parlor was the old man's inheritance. "The last word in death for your loved ones' last ride." (Andy's tag line, not Father's.) Bodies and coffins, wakes and burials, cemeteries and hearses. Grandfather Peabody handed it down to the old liar, and now the old liar was grooming us to take over. Fat chance, I thought, but Andy again schooled me and said if the business went down in flames, our family would crumble, and so, like it or not, as we got older, we'd have to apprentice ourselves to the business of death.

I hated the idea of my life revolving around dead bodies the way Andy hated her life revolving around cooking and cleaning, but she knew the death business would save us both from the gutter. It helped that Peabody & Sons Funeral Parlor was near the school bus route, so we could often join Father at work after classes let out. (The parlor was, I kid you not, on a dead-end road of hemlock trees.) The old man refused to get (or couldn't afford) a babysitter for us, his weirdo death kids. I have a fuzzy memory of one pale, yuppified girl trying to look after us, but Andy scared her away by walking around the house naked in a bedsheet and complaining about all the ghosts. My sister didn't need another girl looking after me—*that* was her job, not being a housemaid.

The afterschool work sessions also provided the much-needed illusion of the Peabody clan as a happy family—in case New York state was watching.

After a month or two without Mother, we assumed the worst. Her absence during Christmas, with no cards or maple syrup sent from the Canadian border, appeared to seal the deal. But she was alive. I saw her triangular face in all the stiff, pale women who passed over Father's embalming table. The blank cavities for eyes. The puffy blue lips. The bulging foreheads, as if the skulls wanted to pop out. Mother lay inside all of them. I don't know if Father was breaking any laws by letting us gawk at the new arrivals, but I can tell you that it made us aware of Death as a weekly visitor. It stirred our imagination. If I stared long enough, the women's bodies would rise off the table, fish belly skin glistening, and they'd

Matthew Mercier

shuffle over to me, bend, and whisper in my ear, "We love you, Jonah. Mother will be back. We promise."

Their breath reeked of polluted creek water—muddy and metallic. Screams clawed up my throat but never made it past my lips. Father or an employee was never far away. I wanted to be brave, so I'd stare at my father's back while he worked on the bodies, sucking out blood and painting scalps, pumping those meat puppets full of chemicals that turned dead skin the shade of cotton candy. Once, he was short on staff and Andy got to help dress a body, to pull the pants onto an old man who was as twisted and wrinkled as a dried parsnip. When she grabbed the stiff ankles, I thought her thumbs might sink into the soft parts, sending up spouts of gore and gas. Father often broke the law in this quiet way, with grade schoolers handling the dead, but Andy never flinched when he asked for her help. She was my model for how to act.

After a while, we started seeing death as nothing more than dried-up bone and formaldehyde. We grew numb to the parade of homicides and heart attacks, of drunk driving accidents and fatal raccoon bites. We made lists of the ways our clients checked out: drowning, cancer, (ten different flavors), flowerpot (dropped on the head), telephone poles, woodchipper, bear attack, tapeworms, poison mushrooms, and broken hearts. I remember the body of a young woman whose boyfriend had stabbed her in the chest but not before she'd managed to shoot his dick off. Andy helped to prepare both those bodies. She described for me the gouges and stitches and soft holes in the flesh, but she also mused on the way this young couple's story ended.

"Love gone wrong. Happens all the time. That was Father and Mother's story."

Oh, but then we had the babies, the children—that's where Father drew the line. Andy and I were never allowed to view the little ones. Bad enough we heard the wails of the mothers when they came to view their infants. On those days, my father actively prayed. Kneeled in his office and asked the Lord to please give him the strength to deal with the indifference of Death and whoever it took. *It.* That was how I pictured Death: a giant, indifferent, *It.*

The kids at school soon figured out what our old man did for a living, so it wasn't long before the nicknames started. The Undertakers. The Creeps. The Death Brothers. Yes, they called Andy my brother. Andy the Amazon. Andrea the Giant. The girls

Poe & I

said she looked like a boy, with her broad shoulders and intimidating height. Andy would lash out once or twice at the boys who yanked her pigtails or slapped at her growing breasts. Her punch was sloppy but vicious, and it earned her a few trips to the principal's office, where another classic lie was told: "These bullies are just looking for attention, Andy. Ignore them."

Easier said than done. Soon enough, Jason Cooper, our sworn enemy, discovered a new word to use against us, and he gifted it to me during gym class—leaned over with a dodgeball in his hands and said, "I heard your father is a necrophile, Peabody!"

"A necro . . . what?"

"You are, too." Jason grinned. "And your creepy sister. I saw a movie about it."

He bounced the ball off my head. "Necro! Necro! Jonah is a necro!"

This was before the internet, so I had to wait until I got home to plug the word into the CPU of my sister's brain. Andromeda was a galaxy of knowledge who educated me on the names of bugs, plants, books, vampires, werewolves, and the finer points of corpse care. On that day, I think it was in February—Mother had been gone three months by then—Father happened to be away on one of his gambling trips. When I got to the parlor, Andy and Vince—the parlor's main employee—were unloading Mrs. Potter, a retired kindergarten teacher who'd slipped in the shower and cracked her skull. She was only sixty-eight.

Vince was a burly Korean war vet with a handlebar mustache, kind heart, and shattered blue eyes. I came up behind him and peeked into the van at Mrs. Potter's lumpy form. Our body van was a Cadillac ambulance hearse straight out of Ghostbusters, with the white body and fire-red wingtips.

"What's doing, kiddo?" Vince said. "Watch yourself. Mrs. Potter never said no to second helpings. Jesus, she's a load. How's school?"

"Pretty stupid. I got called a bad name today. What's a necrophile?"

Understand that Vince had been shot at by snipers, had friends die in his arms, but my question nearly made him drop Mrs. Potter. He looked at Andy, who steadied the other side of the gurney.

"I'll let your sister field that one," Vince coughed, wheeling Mrs. Potter toward the freight elevator, which lowered the dead into my father's laboratory. Andy helped him lift the gurney's

37

wheels over the gap, hit the button, and sent Vince below ground, then spun to face me, her oily bangs flopping over her eyes like a grunge rocker.

"Where did you hear that word?"

"Jason called us necros. He said Dad is a necro-file?"

"Don't let him hear you say that."

"Is he though?"

"Jonah!"

"What does it mean?"

In a whispered hush, she told me, and I just about vomited. That night, we had spaghetti for dinner, a writhing pile of guts. The definition of a necro gave me nightmares for weeks. Father's bodies visited me at night, cold goose flesh rubbing against my crotch. Decaying faces brushing my cheeks, dripping with mucus. Rotting lips brushing my earlobe.

Even worse, Jason incorporated the word into a new nickname, The Necro Brothers, so we had to listen to it throughout the school day as his cabal of bootlickers jeered and taunted us all year, right up until Jason's own mother died.

She overdosed on sleeping pills. Nobody knew if it was an accident or not. We felt bad for Jason, even though he was an asshole, and I wanted to tell him we knew what he was feeling, thought we might bond over the shared loss of our mothers; but then I learned, our father, of all people, had landed the funeral job.

Peabody & Sons was the most reasonably priced, but holy hell. The day she came by I made a point to not be at the parlor, but Andy saw the body. ("She was pretty. Pretty, but sad. I bet Jason pushed her over the edge.") All of this just gave Jason more fuel.

"You goddamn necros. Fucking necrophile weirdos. You and your creep show family messed with my mother. You're going to fucking pay."

A week after we put his mother in the ground, I ran into him in the boys' bathroom, his face red and streaked with tears. I should have ignored him, but this idiot goodness rose up inside me and I told him it was okay to cry and how lucky he was that he even knew his mother was dead, since for all I knew mine was fucking a Canadian lumberjack.

He swarmed my body, grabbed me by the throat, slammed me against the grimy tile of the bathroom wall, and pressed the knob of his knee into my groin. "I'm not crying, you pussy. You tell

Poe & I

anyone I was crying, and I will end you. Fucking perverted necro. Don't you ever say anything about my mother."

Lesson learned. From that moment on, my number one rule for death was this: no talking, no words, no eulogies, no "sorry for your loss," nonsense. My ideal farewell is a lot of wailing and screaming and shrieking, people ripping their hair out and beating the grounds with sticks. That's how you communicate loss.

Andy and I often imagined what we might say at our mother's funeral if given a chance. We'd brainstorm that winter while playing in the graveyard behind our house. More evidence the cosmos had a sense of humor. Why else would the universe give us this cemetery as a playground? When the land of the living failed us, we'd play hide and seek among the tombstones, making ourselves laugh with fake eulogies for Mother.

"She drowned in a sea of maple syrup while being mauled by a grizzly bear."

"She was a good lady, but not good enough."

"She never wanted to be a mother, and we didn't want to be born."

"She left us behind, but she's never left us. We think about her all the time."

The dead made us creative. Sounds sick, but there's nothing like the threat of mortal annihilation to make you live stronger, dream bigger, create more stories. I told Andromeda I wanted to be buried in that graveyard, but she said there was no more room, which I didn't understand until she explained coffins and plots and the whole business of buying your slice of earth before you expired.

"Maybe Mom is buried here," I said. "Illegally. Maybe this is where Dad dumped her."

Andy wiped snow off the marble grave of Rosy Zigmund (1920–1982), picked a dead stick off the frozen ground, and slammed it against Rosy, scattering splinters over the fresh snow. "Mom's alive, kid."

"But you said Dad killed her."

"I changed my mind." Her breath fogged the twenty-degree afternoon, which made it look as if she puffed on a cigar. Her grungy hair pushed out from under her wool hat and over her ears. She no longer believed in haircuts, saying she wanted to grow powerful Celtic hair like Morgana from the Arthurian legends. "If Dad killed her, he'd have been arrested by now. Unless the police

Matthew Mercier

really suck at their jobs. Which is possible, I guess. But Dad's no murderer, and she's not in Canada, either."

"How do you know?" I stomped my feet to stay warm.

"I've been checking the mail. Dad told us she'd be sending money. Nothing ever comes."

"Maybe he's got a separate P.O. box."

I must have seen the P.O. box thing in a crime movie. The criminal mastermind or cheating spouse always gets a P.O. box in a different town to avoid detection. Already my sister and I were developing our taste for true crime and horror movies. You could learn a lot from watching and reading all that wonderful garbage.

"You'd think she'd try to get in touch with us," Andy said. "Christmas was huge. Why didn't she at least send us a card?"

"She doesn't love us."

"Maybe. Or maybe she's not dead. Maybe it's something worse."

"Worse than death?"

The scariest cliché in the world. A fate worse than death. Let's see: paralyzed from the neck down. Getting your eyeball scooped out with a spoon. Leprosy. Acid eating your face. Leeches sucking on your penis. (Jason once threatened me with that.) Live burial.

We'd known from the start Father was a liar, but he didn't count on his spawn being stubborn detectives. So, we started paying more attention. The "business trips" were the obvious red flag. He never seemed happy when he came back, and sometimes we'd have to lock ourselves in Andy's room while he drank. We'd listen to the smashing of glass, the zombified drag of his feet, the bellows for us to come out and man up. He'd drift away, and we'd hear him downstairs shouting threats at his ghosts. Maybe he was shouting at Mother.

At the breakfast table, he'd apologize with that weepy regret all drunks have the morning after, and then he'd take us out for miniature golf or ice cream or an R-rated movie. We'd all play pretend and hop on the rusty, but popular, carnival ride known as Vicious Cycle—a pinwheel of teacups powered by lies, whose whips and dips were designed to make you forget all the nasty words from the night before, so you'd get dizzy and stumble away and forget everything until the following month.

Father also grew weirder and wider. After lifting all those coffins and bodies and eating all that beer and bread, he put on

Poe & I

both muscle and fat, so he rolled through the tight hallways of our home, a barrel of a man with a bird's nest beard. And then his wardrobe. He took to wrapping himself in moldy smoking jackets the color of his tobacco and read volumes of poetry by the fire, as if he suddenly fancied himself a man of letters and had to look the part. On other days, he paired his enormous prescription glasses with striped shirts and suspenders, a ringleader at the circus.

He collected old antique bottles, polishing them endlessly in his workshop, and harvested wild mushrooms out in the forest, but we never ate them, just let them dry all over the house. Fans of white oysters. A shelf full of morels (which he could have sold for good money, but never mind). Newspapers and books blocked the doorways, their pages marked up with pink highlighter. He locked half the rooms in the house, forbidding us to enter, and taped garbage bags over the windows, which he said helped insulate the house. He built coffee tables out of coffins, and our garage morphed into a museum for animal skulls, fungi, car parts, and the occasional don't-ask-don't-tell item of unknown origin, pickled in a mason jar. That winter he chopped wood endlessly, as if we lived in Norway, as if spring wasn't on the horizon.

Somehow, throughout all of this, he remembered his role as a father and kept us alive, but Andy (again) kept the social workers at bay. She forced him out the door for parent-teacher conferences. She kept reminding me to get good grades, to wear long sleeved shirts to hide the peanut-butter-and-jelly bruises on our arms, from when Dad got too grabby. (If anyone asked, we'd wrestled too hard.) She prayed nobody would figure out that we each wore the same three outfits to school all year. (No crime in that, we did our own laundry, but still, the busybodies will busy themselves.) We kept up the appearance of a regular, motherless family.

By late March (four months with Mother gone) Father's business trips grew more obnoxious, and my sister's otherworldly and mature intelligence kicked into high gear; she'd learned how to get at problems indirectly, and so, one afternoon, a day after Father had returned from one of his trips and was sleeping off a six-pack, she seized our moment.

We were helping Vince with a body. Tragic tale—a teenage boy, Roland Drager, had been riding his bike across the local canal on a flimsy wooden footbridge with no handrails when his pant leg

Matthew Mercier

got stuck in his gears and he fell, bike and all, into the water, where the steel Huffy dragged him into a creek swollen with spring runoff.

"Vince?" Andy's voice lilted as we loaded tiny Roland onto the freight elevator.

"What was the worst part about the war?"

My guts heaved. You didn't talk about the war with Vince. Everyone knew that.

The vet slammed the doors of the elevator shut pummeling the down button with his thumb.

"I'm doing a school report," Andy continued, "and we have to interview a veteran."

Vince gazed at the panel of buttons. "School report?"

No lie. It was for Mrs. Leonard's history class. Vince stared at the slimy walls of the basement as it scrolled past the rusty gate. We hit bottom. Our spines jolted.

"Yes. I need to give a presentation. You're the only veteran I know."

Vince rattled the gate on its track, and we rolled the Drager boy into the prep room. "Worst part was losing my buddies."

"That must have been hard," she drawled.

She was imitating Father. This was how our old man spoke to grieving parents, the empathic tone needed to calm the living.

Vince unstrapped Drager. "Get his feet, space girl."

Space girl. His new pet name for Andromeda. He said she was from Mars. They lifted Drager onto the dressing table.

"He's light as a pillow," Andy quipped.

"That's what happens when you die young," Vince wheezed. "Death is stupid. Look at this poor kid." He flipped the sheet down to reveal that Drager's face was littered with freckles, just like Andy's. "Only got to fourth grade. Kid didn't know what hit him. Didn't get to smoke weed or kiss girls."

Andy nodded. "I read about survivor's guilt, Vince. Do you have that?"

Jesus, did this really happen? Did my sister really say that? She must have. Andy could be blunt when she needed to be, but this was too much. I thought Vince was going to pop her. He didn't have a problem with hitting girls, since that's why his wife had left him. Too much hitting and shouting. The way Vince coiled his body and stepped back reminded me of the old man getting ready to blow his top. He pulled his mane of brown locks into a ponytail, and

Poe & I

when he brought his hands back down, I was ready to jump in and block his punch, but all he did was speak the truth. "You're a weird little shit, space girl."

"Well, look who's raising me."

Brilliant comeback. Vince snorted, pulling out his Camels. "True enough. Your pops, he's a strange one. The rotten crab apple don't fall far from the tree."

"I'm not rotten."

"No, of course not. You're all sugar."

"Dad got in late last night, didn't he?"

"Yup. He's paying me time and a half for this job."

"Let's go outside," she said. "You can't smoke in here."

"I know, kid."

"I have guilt, too, Vince. Jonah and me. We both have it."

We did? Vince looked as puzzled as I felt. Where was this going? We strode upstairs and stood around the body van.

"What do you two have to feel guilty about?"

Andromeda stared at the ground. "For outliving our mother."

If the veteran flinched, we didn't see it. But in my memory, he turned sideways, so he didn't have to look Andy in the eye.

"Jonah and I have written eulogies for her. You know, for when Dad finally gets around to telling us the truth about her death."

Vince looked trapped, a tiger in a cage. He paced, opened his mouth, shut it, opened it again, and finally said, "I thought she ran off with some Canuck."

Andy lowered her voice. "Vince, when Father goes on these business trips, does he visit her grave?"

"Or does he have a P.O. box?" I squeaked.

"What?" Vince puffed.

"We saw it in a movie. If you want to hide something, you get a P.O. box."

The veteran hooked his thumbs into his belt loops, trying to look calm, but a blue vein now split his forehead in two. "Kids, your father is a busy man and he . . . I think he's gambling. Honestly."

"I'm sure that's true, Vince," Andy said, "but we'd like to know what else."

Vince dragged, puffed, turned in circles, disbelieving the size of the balls on this middle-school Columbo. "Your father pays me well, Andy."

"Vince, is our mother dead?"

43

Matthew Mercier

They stared each other down, two old souls waiting for the other to blink.

"Vince, we want to follow him. Next time he leaves on one of these so-called business trips I want you to drive us."

Vince threw his stub on the ground. "He'd fire me, space girl."

"We need to know, Vince. Please. We're begging you."

"Honestly, I don't know where he goes. Upstate. I don't know. And I'm not sure I want to know."

My sister gave me a live wire stare as she spoke. "We do."

I took the cue. "Please. Vince."

He opened the door of the van and shut it again. "Space girl, I'm telling you to drop it."

"Why?"

"Drop it."

"Just tell us if she's alive."

Vince never spilled the beans, but he also didn't show up for work the next day, called in sick, said he was hungover, which might as well have been a confession.

So, we didn't need to have a funeral for Mother after all, not yet, but we'd need a whole new vocabulary for what came next.

Chapter 5

Golden Boy

The mothership of the Bronx Historical Society is at the tail end of the D express train, in a cute enclave called Norwood. Chestnut-shaded sidewalks, neat little duplexes, a clean city park— compared to Kingsbridge it's a pampered suburb.

The office itself is a square red brick building squeezed between a chiropractor and a dentist. I pop a painkiller and rub my pinkie nub for good luck, stroll around the block to gather my nerves, then hop onto the tiny porch, supported by twin Roman columns. An ashtray, overflowing with stubs, sits on the wide stone railing. Venetian blinds crowd the windows. I press the intercom. Nothing. Step off the porch, double-check the address, and catch the flicker of somebody on the second floor. The buzzer crackles. "Jonah Peabody?"

"That's me."

The locks hum softly. The wicker doormat in the vestibule reads *Bronx Historical: Just the Facts*. The second door opens to a warm carpeted hallway. Directly in front of me, a staircase climbs to a second-floor landing. Beneath the stairs, the hallway leads to the shiny glimmer of a kitchen. Each window is covered with cream-colored blinds.

Laughter, paper rustling, low conversations, a telephone ringing. Slip off my jacket, hang it on a coat rack, smooth my slacks, straighten my tie. That's how serious I am. I broke out a tie.

Movement, top of the stairs. My heart jumps. A young woman. My age, late thirties, clutching a manila folder to her chest. Tatts of roses and ravens painting her forearms. Nose stud. Black leather boots. A burgundy leather skirt. Pig tails.

Matthew Mercier

"Jonah Peabody?"

"In the flesh."

"Oh shucks." She slaps the railing with her folder. "I was hoping you were the second coming of Auguste Dupin." Her green eyes glow behind Ben Franklin spectacles.

"Are you a good detective?"

"What's the case?"

"Good answer." She lowers her voice. "Murder. Theft. Extortion. Desecration of a corpse. You name it, we got it here at The Bronx Historical Society." She holds out a hand. "I'm Lizzie Borden."

"For real?"

"No jokes please. I've heard them all." When I reach the landing, she extends a hand but quickly recoils. "Oh. Did you hurt yourself?"

It's only been a few weeks. My brain is still telling me I have a pinkie. I hold up the nub. "Frostbite. I used to live in Alaska."

"Okay, Jack London."

She walks us into the rear of the building, through a carpeted hallway of ivy wallpaper and landscape paintings, vistas of The Bronx in various periods, from a pastoral paradise of apple orchards to eagle-eye views of the Grand Concourse and Woodlawn Cemetery. We reach a wine-red door at the end of the hall, where she raps gently. "Cynthia? The fresh meat is here." She looks me up and down. "He fits the mold. Skinny. Skittish. White as a ghost. Missing an appendage."

A voice, light and smooth, responds. "Come in, Lizzie."

My first view of Cynthia McMullen is the top of her head— silvery black hair, a pencil-thin part down the middle, flattened and pulled back around her ears like a steel helmet. She's bent over her wooden desk, its face tattooed with swirling hurricane knots, and she grips a Holmes-style magnifying glass, scanning an old paper, crisp and brown, as if it's been dropped in water and dried.

"Have a seat." Lizzie pulls over a brass-studded leather chair. "You'll make her nervous."

I sit, my heart pounding. The office reeks of newspaper print. A ceiling fan spins overhead. A water cooler sits perpendicular to the desk. Above this are framed shots of Poe and a retro poster for absinthe. In the ad, a busty redhead in a spaghetti string blouse sits in profile with a raised champagne glass of the green stuff.

Poe & I

Under her butt, letters reading something fruity in French. Poe, trapped in his own portrait with greasy bangs plastered over his forehead, stares at the alcohol, his pupils wide, lusting for a drink.

"Can I have some water?" I ask.

"I don't know," Lizzie replies. "Can you?"

A seventh-grade comeback. I grin, playing along, stand, make my way to the cooler, then draw two quick shots that sting my forehead. Back in the chair, the skin of my forearms sticks to the creaking leather and the hard, uneven cushions press into my lower back, as if the chair wants to spit me out. A jolt ricochets through my belly and rings the rope of my spine. Interview nerves. *True!—Nervous—very, very dreadfully nervous.* I'm ready to quote Poe endlessly.

As if reading my mind, Lizzie hands me a pen and paper. "Please fill this out while you're waiting. Good luck, Dupin." She winks and slips out of the office. I stare at the questionnaire.

1 Who killed Madame L? Who killed Maria Roget?
2 Summarize Poe's late work, *Eureka.*
3 Fill in the blanks. "I lived _____ in a world of _____."
4 Where is The Domain of Arnheim?
5 How old was Virginia when Poe married her?
6 What happened to Virginia Poe's remains?
7 Name the stories Poe wrote at the cottage. Name the poems.
8 List four theories of how Poe died.
9 Are you a Poe hero or villain?
10 Can you be trusted to handle valuable artifacts? Why or why not?

I do my best. Numbers one, five, and seven are easy, but the rest are for the superfans. For nine, I write, "A Poe detective." For ten, "Define valuable."

The plaques and framed diplomas hanging on the wall remind me that I don't belong in this scholar's office, not with my blue-collar bohemian resume. Ramses knew that, and he sent me here anyway. First rule of gaming is to know when you're being gamed. Let's be real. This interview? All a puppet show. They've probably met a dozen candidates before me. Hell, the job is probably already filled by some ivory tower prince with a PhD. I know about fake quotas, and you can bet the house I'm a working-class token.

Matthew Mercier

"One more minute," Cynthia drawls, still examining her oh-so-important document. "You don't mind waiting, do you?"

"Actually," I clear my throat, "I do."

"Well," she lifts her head, "at least you're—"

She cuts herself off. I run a hand through my ginger mop-top, then glance over my shoulder. When I turn back, she's wiped the surprise off her face and is extending a bony hand over the desk, her skin the color of raw cream.

"Cynthia McMullen, director of the Society."

"Jonah Peabody, Poe's number one fan."

She purses her lips, leans back in her chair, and jabs a finger at a color photo that bookends the absinthe woman—a tough-looking goateed white guy with glasses, standing behind five younger black and Hispanic students, all under an apartment awning.

"The oral history crew," she says, "led by Lloyd Mason at Fordham. See where they're standing?"

The photo means nothing to me. It could be any building.

"That is the famous 1520 Sedgwick Avenue." She taps her pointy librarian glasses, which magnify her dark blue eyes, rosy complexion, and poker face grin. "Mr. Peabody, for the daily double, can you tell me the historical significance of 1520 Sedgwick Avenue?"

My mind freezes. The painkiller is a fog machine, and this particular piece of trivia is beyond my ken. So help me Satan, I almost say, "Where Malcolm X was assassinated." Instead, I mumble, "Sounds familiar."

"Oh, Mr. Peabody," she shakes her head. "How old are you? Generation X? Y? Not Z, I hope. Is there even a Z yet? What are we calling the kids now? Doesn't matter. I know what happened at 1520. Of course, I also work here so I have an inside track. But if you are going to live in The Bronx, the history of 1520 is the kind of knowledge I will expect you to have. In addition, of course, to all things Poe."

"I'm his number one fan."

"Join the club." She raps the desk with her fist. "1520 Sedgwick. No bells?"

"I'm blanking."

"A shame. I'll give you some time to ponder that gap in your ignorance. I'll take that." She motions for the quiz, looking it over.

48

Poe & I

"Well, gaps might be an understatement. You've barely answered half of these. But we'll address that later. You've already met Lizzie, our resident archivist. Hope she wasn't too rude. I think all the filing, duplicating, recording, revision, and re-filing get her a bit cranky."

She pushes her document gently aside, whips open the manila folder, and slaps my resume onto the desk as if presenting dramatic evidence.

"So, the man that was all used up. You said that's who referred you?"

"Ramses. Yes."

"Ramses?"

"The man who referred me. That's his name."

"I see. Did Moses write you a recommendation letter on papyrus?"

Funny. She's funny. "He suggested I might be a good fit."

"Why? Because you're heavily in debt?"

My stomach drops into my groin.

She rubs her thumb and forefinger together. "We've done our background check, Mr. Peabody. Did you think we wouldn't find out you're deep in the hole?"

I squirm as she slashes at my resume with a pen.

"So, you imagine you're a good fit for Poe Cottage because you gamble?"

"I love Poe's work. I was born for this job."

"Ah yes. The destiny argument."

"I mean it."

"I'm sure you do, Mr. Peabody, but let me just say, a good many people feel the same way. Poe is my destiny, my soul mate. Look, I get it. Edgar Allan Poe? He just does something to people. It starts when you're a teenager. You read those stories about murder and death and live burials, and for the rest of your life you can't sleep. You start wearing all black, listening to heavy metal, and swearing allegiance to pagan gods just to scare all the kids in your school."

"You're describing my childhood."

"Naturally. His critics called him the poet of unripe boys and unsound men. But you still love him in your old age?"

"Oh yes."

"I'm not surprised. You look quite unsound. So. You can

imagine. Given the chance to live in Poe's house? People go a little crazy. They get passionate. They forget themselves. And they'll say and do most anything." She clicks her tongue. "Until they find out the house isn't in Park Slope."

"I'm not that unsound."

"Uh-huh. Sure. Okay." She picks up the sheet of paper that summarizes my so-called professional life and reads. "Jonah Winston Peabody. Great name. Don't suppose you're related to *the* Peabody family?"

"As in the Peabody museum? Distant cousins. Once removed. Maybe twice."

"Once removed? Maybe twice? Fancy that. What are the chances? Doesn't matter. No bearing on Jonah Peabody. Who I must say," she snaps the resume with a finger, "is an impressive young man."

"Thank you."

"Impressive according to this piece of paper. Which you composed."

I cross my legs, rubbing my third eye.

"And, according to this impressive paper, you've held a number of jobs over the last . . . five years."

"Yes, ma'am."

"Five years, three different states, two countries, five jobs." She ticks them off with one hand. "Packed fish in Alaska. Ferryboat crew member in Seattle. Ran a youth hostel in New Mexico. Shot kangaroo in Australia. My God, what a nomadic existence. If I may ask, are you running from something?"

"An ordinary life."

"Ah! Sharp wit! We're looking for that. But no, here's the answer. You majored in comparative literature. My God, you're basically unemployable."

"If college were job training."

"Wise words. What was your underground—excuse me—your undergrad thesis?"

"What else? Poe."

"Oh, I see. Is that why you flopped our quiz?"

"It's been a few years. I'm not proud of my underground work. Undergrad."

She laughed. "Oh, I can empathize. Thank you for being honest. What's the title?"

Poe & I

"Of what?"

"Your forgotten thesis."

"I'm too embarrassed."

"Young man, you're not allowed to walk in here and tell me you did an undergraduate thesis on Poe, the Society's gravy train, and withhold the glorious title from us."

"I buried it alive."

"Mr. Peabody." She leans over the desk. "We all buried our undergraduate work. Mine will never see the light of day." She raps a glittery fingernail against a marble paperweight. "The title. Now."

I swallow a humble grin. "Dead Women and Divine Mothers: The Feminine Influence on Poe's Work."

"Lovely." She blinks, rolling her tongue inside her left cheek. "Well-trodden ground."

"That's why I buried it."

"I'll tell you mine. Are you ready? You can't top this. Happy Endings: Erotic Sublimation in Grimms' Fairy Tales."

"Pretentious."

"Isn't it? Literary theory is the death of literature. I don't know why I was so enamored with it. Never touch the stuff now. That's probably why I'm here at this lonely outpost instead of teaching at Columbia. Not that I want to live in that ivory tower. No sir. The minute literature or history becomes too academic it's dead. Wouldn't you agree?"

"Ivory tower. Corrupts everything."

She wrinkles her nose. "Mr. Peabody, why do you love Poe so much?"

"He's the man."

"Profound. Please elaborate." She stands and walks to the corner of the desk, straightening her ash-gray business suit. "Pretend you're in school again." She drops her voice an octave. "That's an interesting point, Mr. Peabody. Can you please tell the class what you mean when you say Poe was the man?"

"Well, he wrote about our nightmares."

She crosses her arms.

"And we love to be scared. As a culture we just love it. And he was the first. Poe was the first to scare us. He's really the father of the entire horror genre."

She lifts her chin to the ceiling. "That's it?"

"I'm made for this job, ma'am. I live and breathe Poe."

Matthew Mercier

She steps away from the desk. "Mr. Peabody, you need to understand that living and breathing in the cottage is not all fun and games. You've seen the basement. The lack of light. The isolation. You'd have no problem living there? How would you handle it if someone broke in?"

"Has that ever happened?"

"As far I know? Never. It's well protected. Alarm system. Gates. Security lights. But there's a first time for everything."

"Bradford seemed comfortable there."

"He's fantastic. A grad student at Fordham. Brilliant mind. I'll be sorry to lose him."

"He didn't seem to know he was leaving."

She flicks her wrist, pushing my comment away. "So, in addition to your love of Poe, what else makes you qualified?"

I wanted to rip off my shirt and let her feast on the tattoos burned across my shoulder blades, but even my bad judgment has its limits. Besides, I have something even better—the right answer.

"I'm qualified," I say, "because my life is a Poe story."

She scans my resume.

"Good luck finding clues there."

She glances up, not smiling.

"My grandfather was a funeral director. He was a caretaker, too, you might say. A caretaker of bodies. So, it's in my blood. Death, I mean. Isn't that Poe's great subject? My grandfather wasn't a great guy. We think he murdered my grandmother, but we don't know for sure. She disappeared. Grandad claimed she wandered off, but I'm pretty sure he killed her. We always played at trying to find Grandma's body in the walls. Or getting Grandad to confess. Make him tear up the floorboards. Admit the deed."

Cynthia's face turns to stone, and I pile it on.

"My father inherited the funeral business. We drove around in his little body van, picking up dead people and dressing them up to look nice before putting them in the ground. Sometimes he took his work home with him. My childhood was very Addams Family. I won't get into the gory details. It might scare you. So, you see, Director McMullen, I'm not only qualified for this job . . . " I bare my fangs. "I'm perfect."

The woman perks her eyebrows, taking a breath. "Family, or lack thereof, is a burden we all carry, Mr. Peabody. Poe carried it

Poe & I

all his life. I've carried it myself. I'm sorry to hear of your dark family history, and while it certainly may inform your potential duties at the cottage, I'm not sure it makes you qualified."

"I can empathize with Poe. Isn't that what you need?"

"I need you to defend him."

"Defend?"

"Poe's life always needs defending." She's moving into the fast lane now, away from my crazy talk and into some of her own. "He died without an estate, without someone to look after his papers, and when that happens your enemies can rewrite history. That bastard Griswold dragged Poe's name through the gutter for years, and now, despite all the scholarship, the general populace still thinks of him as this dark, drunken maniac who slept with his mother-in-law and killed cats. And you"—she points—"will have to debunk all this. Debunk and defend in Poe's name, despite the unsavory parts of his character. Can you do that?"

"Yes, ma'am."

"Think so? He was an unsound person, on many levels, and if you're going to live in the man's house, you're going to attract a lot of enemies. People who want to tear him down. Believe me. They're out there." She cracks her knuckles. "But that's just one of the things the Society will ask of you, Mr. Peabody. Follow me." She herds me into the rear of the office, a historical junkyard.

A stone wheel is propped in the corner. Next to this, a long musket rifle, the kind you see in Civil War paintings. On the right wall, a pegboard with faded documents in plastic Ziplocs. Stacks of ancient books, with broken spines and yellowed pages. A banquet table covered in a dusty sheet of plastic and crammed with arrowheads, combs, teeth, and clumps of metal that look like chunks of dried lava. Boxes upon boxes stacked on top of each other to the ceiling. Bowed shelves crammed with medals and trophies. A wall of framed Ivy League degrees. (All degrees look Ivy to me.) Then comes the Poe Paraphernalia. Stuffed ravens. A medium-sized church bell. A signed Vincent Price poster for the Roger Corman production of *The Pit and the Pendulum*. There is even a stuffed gorilla, hairy arms frozen above its head, an open razor blade in its left paw. And deep in the back corner, positioned on a pair of sawhorses, is a wide, chestnut coffin, the lid open, waiting for a body.

Cynthia points to the stuffed ape. "Name the story."

"*Murders in the Rue Morgue.*"

Matthew Mercier

"Too easy." She opens a drawer and lifts out the key from an old typewriter—the letter X.

"Name the story."

"X marks the spot?"

"Very funny. Nobody ever gets this one. *X-ing a Paragrab.*"

"I'm sorry. Paragraph?"

"Paragrab. Paragrab. *X-ing a Paragrab.* A comic story. Written at the cottage. It's hilarious. Did you know fifty percent of Poe's material was humorous?"

"No."

"Of course not. Name the story." She points to a death's-head moth, pinned to a square of cork on the wall.

"*The Sphinx.*"

"And this one?" She points to the puppet of a jester, slouched in boneless depression at the feet of the stuffed ape.

"That's either *Hop-Frog* or *The Cask of Amontillado.*"

"Clever boy. But it is Hop-Frog. Julie Taymor gave it to me after her all-puppet production."

I walk deeper into the junk, making a beeline for the coffin. I know coffins—wood, wicker, wool, chipboard—but this beast is different. The underside of the domed lid is a network of levers and springs and bolts.

"Know what that is?"

She thinks that's she's stumped me, but I say, "A security coffin."

"Bravo. Designed by Guy Carrell. To prevent?"

"Premature burial."

"Correct." She taps the lid and pushes me gently on the shoulder. "Try it out."

"What?"

"Get in the coffin, Mr. Peabody."

"Ma'am?"

"Are you hard of hearing?"

"No, ma'am. But—"

"Son of a funeral director. Get. In. The coffin."

She drags over a footstool. I bend my head, sniffing the inside. Velvety mothballs. Varnished wood. Silk fabric. Familiar smells of oblivion. I step onto the stool.

"That's it, Pugsley Addams. In you go." She places a hand on the small of my back. "Sit slowly, or you'll tumble the whole thing over."

Poe & I

I squat on my haunches, grip the sides, and lower myself in. My neck settles into the stiff headrest, my legs bending at the knees just slightly so I can fit.

"It's a little short."

"Guess we'll need to saw your feet off."

I give a fake laugh. She returns a fake grin. A pinwheel of heat explodes in my heart, and the center of my forehead itches. The silk lining is a strawberry pattern, while the latches and springs are rusty.

Cynthia taps the large bolt in the center. "Panic button," she's lowering the lid.

"Hold on tight."

"Wait. Seriously?"

"Just a few seconds."

Okay. Game over. I've met my match. The lid is closing, and I yank my fingers before they get squished. It clicks shut.

Darkness. Instant and total. The world falls out from underneath me. My head pulls backward, dizzy and light. Light. Need light. My phone. My phone is in my pocket. Fuck. I try to shift onto my side, but I can barely move. My elbows knock against the coffin walls. My breath comes in short bursts. A disc of hot, white lava spins in the air above me. The lever won't budge. My back arches, and my lungs burp out a yelp. I hit the lever with the side of my fist. One, two, three. It pops. The lid springs open.

Cynthia stands there, peaceful as a Buddha. The white disc spins above her head. "Well done." She extends a hand to help me out. My head is jelly, my legs a pair of noodles. Less than thirty seconds and I'd snapped.

"This coffin and everything you see here has been collected by friends, employees of the Society, and board members. Everything is a piece of The Bronx or Poe. Nobody cares about him or this borough as much as we do. Devotion. Obsession. That's our bread and butter, Mr. Peabody. But do you know what's missing?"

I shake my head, bullshit all dried up.

"Have you heard about Virginia's bones?"

"No."

"Poe's tumor?"

"A little too specialized."

"Too specialized," she nods. "Well, Lizzie can brief you on those. They're both projects of hers. But either the tumor or the bones would make valuable additions to our collection.

55

Matthew Mercier

Although to be historically honest, they both belong in Baltimore, so if you recovered them, it would be good for diplomatic relations."

We return to the front office, where Lizzie is scribbling notes on a legal pad. "Did he get in the coffin?"

"Oh yes," Cynthia smiles.

"Excellent. Now he's part of the club."

Cynthia points to the Sedgwick Avenue photo. "How about it, Mr. Peabody? 1520 Sedgwick? Too specialized?"

"I'm stumped."

"Do you listen to hip-hop?" Lizzie asks.

"Used to. Old school. Run-D.M.C. Public Enemy."

"Well, 1520 Sedgwick was pivotal. It's where Clive Campbell, otherwise known as DJ Kool Herc, gave a house party and started spinning records. Hip-hop was born at 1520."

"Oh. Neat."

"I'm glad we filled in that gap," Cynthia spits. "Lizzie will show you out."

"Thank you, ma'am. I appreciate the opportunity."

She nods, sighs, drops behind her desk, and returns to her mysterious brown letter as Lizzie ushers me into the hallway. "How did it go?"

"Oh, I aced it. She's probably shredding my resume as we speak."

"Don't be so hard on yourself, Dupin."

"Jonah. Please."

"Oh, you're no fun. I wasn't kidding. We do need more detectives around here."

"To uncover Virginia's bones?"

"Did she get into that already? I suppose all you prospective Poe boys need to hear about that. Sure, the bones and the tumor are important, but I'm on the case. That's why she hired me. I'm a collector, curator, archivist, treasure hunter, and detective."

"I bet there are plenty of unsolved cases around here."

"You must be psychic."

"No," I take a breath, "but I have a third eye."

She whirls on the bottom step, apple cheeks bursting. "I haven't heard anyone use that phrase in a long time. A third eye. Wow."

56

Poe & I

"Do you have one, too?"

"Off the record?"

"Absolutely."

"Right here." She taps her forehead. "I knew as soon as I read your resume you and I would have a connection. My third eye told me you'd have a third eye. Who gave it to you?"

"My mother."

"Is she still alive?"

"No."

"My condolences. But that's how it works. They pass on their powers early, and when they die, you inherit the whole shebang. My father gave me mine. And I think Poe must have possessed one as well."

Somewhere, a Poe scholar's head is exploding. I pull my jacket off the rack, the bottle of painkillers rattling in the pocket.

"Are those pills for your wound?"

"Yes."

"Sorry. I'm nosy." She stands in the doorway, one hand on the knob. My jacket is a warm blanket that I wrap around my heart. If she asks how I lost the finger, I might tell her the truth.

"I have to say, you seem familiar, Jonah. Have we met before?"

"Not in this life."

"That's probably it. A past life. Crows of the same murder."

"What?"

"A murder of crows. You know. A pride of lions. A murder of crows. You and I probably flew together in the spirit world. I know, we only deal in ravens here, but people confuse the two all the time. Crows live in Poe Park, but everyone calls them ravens. It bugs me."

"The park. That reminds me. Can I ask you something about Bradford? He didn't seem ready to leave. Kept implying the job wasn't open. Is he being fired?"

"Oh no. He's wonderful."

"Then why is he leaving?"

The tension in her shoulders ripples up into her face. "Not my business."

"It's somebody's business. Cynthia must know."

"He's not being fired. I know that. Maybe he wants to get out of that basement. The cottage is very isolated. You've seen it."

"He's a grad student at Fordham. Seems like a perfect gig."

Matthew Mercier

"I'm unclear what's happening." She opens the door and steps outside. "But I hope we get to work together."

"You think I've got a shot?"

"Sure. But just bear in mind, Dupin. This job? If you do get it?" She squeezes my shoulder. "It ain't for lightweights."

Chapter 6

Resurrection and Return

The emotional vivisection of poor Vince continued all spring.

Andy kept needling him with all types of questions, nothing about Mother directly. "Vince," she'd say, "what do you think happens to children that grow up without a mother?" or "Vince, did your mother's love make you a better man?"

Vince would either give one-word answers or just walk away. He wasn't about to crack for a Harriet the Spy wannabe. Once, when he came by the house to pick up the Ghostbusters hearse, Andy waved from the porch and said, "How's your mother, Vince?"

"I have to put her in a nursing home, space girl."

"I'm sorry to hear that. At least she's still alive."

"That she is." He rapped the hood of the hearse.

"But death takes no holidays," Andy sighs. "I hear it's going to be a busy weekend at the parlor."

"Space girl, you are one weird chick."

"So you've told me, Vince. That is my cross to bear."

The parade of bodies that weekend ran the gamut. Two cancer victims (a fifty-year-old biddy and a six-year-old innocent), three car wrecks (all drunk driving), and a double murder-slash-suicide, with the slash being literal. A father waited until his family was asleep, then taped all the windows in their house shut and turned on the gas stove before slicing his wrists in the tub.

Andy showed me the obituary for this final case and explained asphyxiation to me. She collected the obits and news clippings for all our clients. Detailed accident reports from the car wrecks,

59

Matthew Mercier

memorials for our elderly neighbors who survived the Nazis—a catalog of strangers' stories.

If Mother's story hadn't been such a fill-in-the-blank narrative, I doubt Andy would have developed this habit. Around the same time, she swore allegiance to the color black—shirt, pants, earrings, boots, lipstick. Typical middle school rebellion, but she also claimed to be in perpetual mourning.

"Until Mother returns to us," she said, "I will forever be the woman in black."

Pretty sure she lifted that from a Hammer Horror movie, but that was my sister. Dramatic about Death with a capital double-D. During one of our afterschool walks in the graveyard, she told me, "I'm going to pry Mother's story out of Father if it kills me."

"What if he gets angry?"

"That's the point," she groaned, gazing up into the sky as a light rain fell. "Don't be a baby, Jonah."

"I'm not a baby."

"You've been acting like one. Don't you want to know what happened to Mom?"

No. Yes. Maybe. The answers could not be good. Robins and sparrows hopped about in the misty drizzle, yanking at spring earthworms. The velvety green moss beds glowed as if lit from below by gamma radiation. To get out of the dripping wet, I stepped under the awning of a mausoleum with the family name *Hoover* carved into the marbled archway. In front of the mausoleum, Andy studied the tombstone of Peter Hoover, a local banker and favorite son who, according to local scuttlebutt, was supposed to be in the mausoleum with his Father and Mother, but, since he'd also held down a side gig as a child murderer, they'd planted him outside.

Andy's face was half-hidden under the hood of a dirty black windbreaker, a five-fingered discount from the Goodwill. The rain pummeled the air in white sheets, and she stood above Peter Hoover as if hypnotized by the old devil; only when I called to her did she join me under the concrete awning.

The wind tore through the graveyard, ripping a dead limb off a nearby oak, which crashed and snapped across the face of an alabaster angel. We huddled together for warmth, her teeth clacking, hair sticking to her cheeks. She pulled me into her and wrapped our pinkies together.

Poe & I

"I'll protect you, Jonah. But you need to protect me, too. By not being a baby. It's time to grow up. No more Peter Pan bullshit. You got it?"

"Okay."

She let go of me and pressed her face to the thick glass doors of the mausoleum. "It's hilarious how much money these rich Hoovers spent to just be forgotten."

Wisdom beyond her years. She knew the wealthy spent a fortune on these elaborate homes for their bodies, and that it was all a joke. Call my sister the original old soul. Mother's absence only seemed to make her older. But she also seemed unstoppable. Take this, for example: She was only in seventh grade but was writing a fantasy novel which, she claimed, would allow her to make enough money to skip high school. Where did she learn to dream so big? If our family had been as rich as the Hoovers, Andy might have attended a special school for artists up in Vermont or the Berkshires. Money decides a lot in this life but not your moral compass.

Peter Hoover had all that money and decided to diddle children, so maybe gobs of dough just made you a pervert.

We hung with the Hoovers until the clouds parted, revealing a sliver of blue April sky. The sun warmed our skin, but the chill soaked our bones, so we went back inside and made quesadillas, dripping with cheese and avocado. Then we sat in the living room, and I read while Andy drew.

"Wouldn't this be great," she muttered, sketching on her pad.

"What's that?"

"Just the two of us, kid. We don't need anyone. Just you and me." She flipped the pad over to show a sketch of her as Batgirl and me as Robin the Boy Wonder, our superhero cowls frozen in slow motion.

I laughed. It would be great. But scary, too. Scary great. We'd been reading a lot of fairy tales lately, and the worst villains weren't the witches and goblins—it was the parents. The mothers and fathers. Always plotting to kill their kids or abandon them in the woods.

She stood from the couch and walked behind me, then stroked my cheeks with her palms. "Just you and me, kid. Just you and me." She bent and kissed my ear.

Maybe I acted the baby, sometimes, so she would baby me. "I love you, Andy."

Matthew Mercier

She leaned into my neck, the warm flow of tears dampening my collarbone.

"Look," she said, flipping through her pad to a sketch of Mother, which she'd copied from an old photo. Mother as a young stranger—smooth white skin, curly black hair, day glow cheeks. "When you draw someone, you capture their soul and when you capture souls you can keep people alive. You can resurrect them. I'm going to bring Mother back to life."

And a few weeks later, at the dinner table, she performed her first act of resurrection, although in hindsight maybe it was just good timing.

Over a plate of microwaved chicken pot pie, and with a child's blunt emotional logic, she said to Father, "Mom's not dead. Is she?"

The old man swallowed a mouthful of peas and carrots, then sipped his Makers. He glanced at me first, then Andy. "Who told you that?"

"Nobody. Just a hunch."

Father swallowed, rubbing his mustache. "Don't lie to me, Andromeda. Vince told me you were asking questions." Gray circles pulled Father's eyes down onto his cheeks. "You are just as sharp as your mother was in her youth. But this idea that you're the smartest person in the room might get you hurt someday. I . . . "

"Just tell us the fucking truth."

He rose in his seat, knees banging the table, and slapped Andy hard enough that she crashed to the floor. Father stood, rubbing his knuckles as if ready to finish her off, but I leapt from my seat, grabbed my steak knife, jumped between them, and screamed, "Don't touch her!"

Father's chin trembled. "Language. Watch your language."

His chest rose and fell with measured rage. Usually, the regret took twenty-fours to seep into his bloodstream and reach his heart, but that night it arrived immediately. He reached for Andy, but she scuttled away, pinning her back against the doorjamb.

"I was going to tell you both," Father said. "But it's been so hard, and I didn't know how to explain it. It's so complicated and so . . . I just couldn't tell you."

The mask of my father's face wrinkled. He sat back down at the table and rattled the ice cubes in his rocks glass. "She's coming home in a few weeks."

Andy covered her mouth as if she might puke.

62

Poe & I

"She's coming home, but she won't be the same."

Funny how he thought sameness might be an issue. I didn't have enough memories locked in my storage vault to gauge if Mother had changed or not.

"She'll be here at the end of May." Father got up from the table and dumped his dishes in the sink. "Please clean the house before she arrives." He grabbed the bottle of Makers and retreated to his mancave.

Andy rose, hair falling over her face. "Clean the house. I'll clean your clock."

"I'll help you, Andy."

"It's not our job to clean the house. We're not his servants." She placed a hand on my wrist and took the knife, guiding me back to the table. "But you did good, Jonah. I thought you might stab him."

I doubt I would have been able to stab my own father, but I let her think it was possible. Better to be thought of as a tough guy than a baby.

The weekend of the so-called return, Andy tried to negotiate a ride along with Father, but that proved hopeless, and the night before the promised delivery, we barely slept, our bodies jacked with anticipation. On Saturday morning, Father rose before dawn to grind coffee and warm the pickup. The house pulsed as if holding its breath. The ceiling in each room swelled and expanded, the hallways stretched into infinity. I felt a heightened curiosity, as if Father had gone out to get us a new puppy. Odd, to say that, but I can't say I felt love. Only need. Mother was our mother. We needed a mother. She needed to be here at home.

Or so we thought.

That afternoon, the diesel puttering of Father's truck reached our ears long before he entered the driveway. We watched from Andy's bedroom as he pulled in, ridiculously slow. Somebody in the passenger seat, a stiff gray twig. Father shut off the engine and spoke to the twig. It nodded. He got out and went around to open the passenger door. The twig was dressed in a knit cap, dirty white pants, and a droopy, pink sweater. Her nose and cheeks were blistered red with acne.

"Is that her?" I asked.

My sister curled the faded lace of the curtains around her fingers, until I thought she might tear it. The idea of Father

Matthew Mercier

bringing home a strange woman and calling her "Mother" hadn't occurred to us.

This woman glanced up and zeroed in on Andy. She stared right at my sister, not me. And that's when I knew without a doubt it was Mother.

The facial similarities between her and Andy were obvious—narrow cheekbones, pale Irish skin, hooded green eyes. In that moment of return, I'm quite sure mother and daughter saw in each other a version of themselves—Mother saw her lost youth, and Andy her future.

"Not if I can help it," Andy said.

"What?"

"You just asked me something, Jonah. What did you say?"

"I asked if it was her."

"Of course it is."

We jumped at the door creaking open downstairs. I strode to the landing. A pair of skinny shadows ran up the carpet. The door shut. Father called.

"Andy? Jonah?"

They stood waiting for us, holding hands, a teenage couple on prom night, Father beaming, Mother placid and calm, eyes bright. I'd never seen Father so happy, as if he might crack open. Mother took off her cap. Her black hair was stubby and short. Father let go of her hand and draped his arm around her shoulders, whispering something to her. To this day I'm convinced he said, "These are your children. Their names are Jonah and Andromeda."

Whatever he whispered, it triggered something in her brain, since that was the moment she grinned, bent at the waist, and extended her skeletal arms.

"My babies," she hissed through yellow teeth. "My sweet babies."

We had nobody on our side giving us instructions, whispering, "This is your Mother. Go embrace her." She sounded hollow, robotic, performing what was expected of a mother.

"Come here, my little ones. Come here."

My father's pleading face shouted at us. Andy went first, stepping onto the carpeted hallway as if expecting to be shot in the head. The old man jerked his chin at me, so I quickly followed, focusing on the nickel-sized holes in the back of Andy's hand-me-down sweater. Mother's arms seemed to grow wider, rapidly

Poe & I

growing tree limbs that snagged us. We got pulled into a crushing hug, one giant lump, the bones of her arms cutting into my shoulder. She smelled of mothballs and nicotine.

Believe me when I say that I wanted to love this skeleton of a woman. I'd lived inside her belly, I was her blood, but when she gripped me and kissed me, all I could think about was that Halloween night she left, after visiting me in my bedroom.

Mother was sick. I must have known that. I was convinced she'd pick me up, crumple me into a ball, and stuff me back inside her womb, where her body would remix my cells and reform me, until she produced a different child, one she wanted.

She took our hands, me on one side and Andy on the other, and Father guided her around the house as if giving her a tour. We stopped in the living room. "This," he said, "is where Jonah was born."

I jolted as Father kept narrating.

"We didn't have time to get to the hospital, but thankfully, Jonah, you were her second child, and you slid right out. Second babies are like bullets. That's what you were, Jonah. A bullet. Shooting out of her onto the floor. Right, Mother?"

She rubbed the back of my neck. "My boy," she whispered. "My precious little boy."

The word "boy" landed on my head with the solidity of a brick. Mother had only just arrived home and already I wanted her gone.

Chapter 7

A Watcher From Afar

After that train wreck of an interview with the Society, I feel delicious, sweet, light as a feather.

That resume of mine is pretty wild, right? Anyone with half a nose can smell the baloney. I always expect to be called out for it, but what I didn't expect was for the Bronx Historical Society to hurl baloney back at me. Cynthia clearly recognizes me. Lizzie, too, but at least she admitted it. Both are hiding behind masks, but hey, so am I. We're a bunch of liars. No biggie. A lie for a lie makes the whole world honest, right?

Fake it till you make it. Cheating, posing, fronting—only way to survive in this life, or the next. If Wall Street guys can have their fake money, and politicians and terrorists their fake wars based on fake evidence and fake Gods, I don't see why I can't have my fake reference letters, my fake work history, my fake life on paper. Does it really matter if I've never *officially* written a thesis on Poe? If I've never traveled above the Arctic Circle? Never hunted kangaroos? Never had the writer Wally Lamb as my high school writing teacher? Or, best of all, that I've never been dumb enough to pay thirty thousand dollars a year for a college "education"?

No. It doesn't matter. You know why? I believe in my fake job history, in my stories. I need to believe in them. If I believe, so do employers. When employers believe, they hire me, see what a great worker—a great person—I can be, and poof, they forget about the resume.

There's a thesis statement. *"The resume, as a text, represents*

66

Poe & I

history. History is written by the victors. Be the victor of your life and rewrite your resume."

Poe would dig that. He puffed his own plumage, tried to make a name for himself using his grandfather's heroics in the Revolutionary War. (Why wasn't that on the quiz?) Except it never worked for him. Historically, my puffing has won people over, but not Cynthia. She didn't buy one word, and neither did Lizzie Borden. Good for them. Game on.

The euphoria of my liar's high lasts roughly fifteen minutes. The moment I turn my back on Lizzie Borden and leave that office, my ghosts sink their phantom claws into my shoulders. Here comes the storm.

When I get back to Astoria, my Greek landlord says he's kicking me to the curb, threatening to haul me into court for rent past due, but since I never graced the clown with my John Hancock before moving into the basement firetrap he dares to call a one-bedroom studio—and since he's never bothered to fix the heat or the leaky pipe above my bed—I tell Mr. Papadopoulos Baklava that if he tries to collect so much as one red cent I'll call the fire marshal and report his illegal sardine can.

Basement rentals are a lie agreed upon in NYC, so it's a pretty empty threat on my part, but he's bigger than me and could break my legs by breathing on them, and since I've already lost a finger, I tell him, fine, I'm moving out.

I give away most of my belongings and I stuff everything else—clothes, letters, books, photos, laptop, gun, sleeping bag—into my trusty backpack and one duffel. When I go upstairs to return the key and get my deposit, the landlord, a puffy pink button of a man, opens the door in an irritated huff, and says, "Your brother was just here."

My gut gurgles.

The Greek glances over my shoulder, then muscles onto the stoop. "He was just there. Standing across the street." He points to an identical row of duplexes with their zebra striped carports and narrow driveways. "Goofy smile on his face. Looks like you."

I take the bait, glancing over my shoulder. This is how ghosts enter your life: when you start looking for them. I turn back and say, "I don't have a twin brother, Stavros."

The Greek pulls at his belt buckle. "I yell at him. Think it you. I said you should be packing. Then he walk across the street and I

67

Matthew Mercier

see it not really you. Nose and cheeks is different. He dressed all fancy. A fruitcake. Said he was looking for his brother, Jonah Peabody."

"What did you tell him?"

"I tell him you are down in the basement getting stuff together and that you were sure taking your sweet time."

"What else?"

"He ask where you move to and I said I don't know, let me see some ID. He say he wasn't here to help you move out, but move in. I tell him if he going to talk like that he can fuck off. So he did. Fruitcake."

That's the Greek's favorite slur. Fruitcake. It's his G-rated shorthand for homosexuals and blacks. "How long ago was this?"

"Ten. Fifteen minutes."

"And you didn't think to come get me?"

"Hey, I don't get into family stuff. Where do you move to?"

"The Bronx."

"Bronx." He snorts. "They will call you white boy."

He over-pronounces this last phrase, with his lips pursed around the words in exaggerated contempt. The only white boy I need to worry about is the one pretending to be my brother. I hand the Greek his keys and say farewell.

It's wild not having an address. Makes me invisible to my creditors but not my ghosts. They follow me anywhere. Stavros isn't lying about my "brother." Why would he? This brother is obviously the same person who visited Ramses. The fireman must be the middleman. I gave my address to Cynthia, Cynthia told Ramses, or Ramses told my brother, or maybe my brother is a private dick who Ramses hired to make sure I don't leave New York. The possibilities are endless. I rub my pinkie nub to try and ward off the goose flesh. When I'm out on the street, in public view, I catch glimpses of a tall, shimmering figure in the corner of my vision or reflected in a storefront; then I blink, and he's gone.

I'm being watched. Nothing new for a Peabody. It's the same feeling I had growing up—somebody out there in woods, spying on me and Andromeda.

Say her name. Resurrect Andromeda. My sweet sister.

My plan for being homeless is to crash with a co-worker in Brooklyn, who told me he'd be gone for the month of May and needed a cat sitter, but that falls through, so I bunk down in a youth

Poe & I

hostel on the Upper West Side. Thankfully, my job with the moving company keeps me flush and out of the soup kitchens. I try to save money, but I'm no squirrel, and a body needs to eat, see movies and play a few races. I win some, lose some. Not saying how much, but I come out on top.

Still, my desperation is growing more desperate. No way I can swing New York if I don't nab Poe, and for a while it looks bleak, one more fuck up to add to my long list. What a shame. I haven't felt this excited about a job—a paycheck—in forever. That gives me reason enough to hope. Nobody at the moving company knows about Poe, until the head prick finds me on break reading *The Purloined Letter*.

"What are you reading, loser?"

I don't bother to look up. It's the asshole I've tussled with before. "Detective story. One of the first ever written."

"Sounds gay."

This loudmouth butterball lives on Staten Island—a life sentence in his mother's basement. Not sure what I've done to get on his shit list.

"You don't read?" I ask.

"I'd rather be fucking your mother."

"So, you're into necrophilia?"

It's high school all over again. This shit never ends for some people. I put down the Poe and place my amputated right hand on the table, which gets the requisite reaction.

"Jesus, you're a freak."

"I'm part of a religious cult. We cut off a limb to bring us closer to God."

He backs away.

"Come on, Benny. They don't have cults on Staten Island? You want to be part of the club, you have to lose something." I rub my pinkie nub, bandage free now, a blackish plateau of stiches and bone. I take out the muscle ball and begin squeezing. "I'm working my way up to an arm or leg."

Acting weird always warded off my bullies in grade school. I mean, I got picked on for being weird, but if I made myself too weird, untouchable weird—leprosy weird—if I told people I worshiped the devil, the idiots wouldn't touch me. So too with Benny. I've broken his brain. He's just my plaything. He won't throw down with me. The boss told us one more fight and we're

Matthew Mercier

both gone, and I know the momma's boy can't afford to lose the job, so he's all talk. But with my missing pinkie, all the lifting and lugging of boxes is a tiny bit harder, and I'm moving slower, so of course the boss notices, and soon I get canned.

Now, it's Poe or nothing. The upshot? More time to read. I spend hours in the New York Public Library (with the real homeless) and memorize a handful of the master's poems, including, so help me Satan, *The Raven*. I burn all eighteen stanzas of this "classic" into my cortex, but Lenore can stay lost as far as I'm concerned. I read most of the stories, especially the ones he wrote at the cottage—*The Cask of Amontillado, Hop-Frog, X-ing a Paragrab, The Domain of Arnheim*—but Poe's vocab gives me a migraine. Honestly, when he isn't murdering old men or cats or burying people alive, Edgar is pretty boring.

All this reading makes me think about applying to college again. People say you need a college degree to survive, and it may be true, but I always take one look at tuition rates and the job market, and it all just feels like a giant pyramid scheme. I've survived on a cocktail of charm, bullshit, and luck, and all three kick into hyper-drive when I find a temp gig as a stagehand at a multi-media installation of Dante's *The Divine Comedy*, although, honestly, it's just the *Inferno* part, with *Purgatorio* and *Paradiso* tacked on at the end as a psychedelic light show. The company stages it in a warehouse in DUMBO and makes the audience walk through the performance. Papier mâché flames, naked angels swinging through the air on wires. Collapsing walls. You know. *Art*.

The gig pays well, but when it comes time for the after parties, I'm not invited. When I ask about this, one of the set designers, a blond-haired trust-fund transplant from California who smells my dirty, white trash roots a mile away, lays it out for me.

"Jonah, bro, we'd really like to invite you to this party, but, you know, it's really for the actors and the artists, and really, I mean, you're a nice guy, a hard worker, dependable, but you're a true watcher from afar."

"A who?"

"A watcher from afar. You know. On the outside. Looking in. I think that's where you operate best."

See? Even among outsiders, I'm an outsider, which means the pretend outsiders are just that. Pretenders. Phonies. But that's New York, a place where high school rejects create cliques of rejects who

Poe & I

then reject other rejects—an infinite empire of walled-off nerds. Why on earth did Andromeda ever want to move here? What did she see in this place? She said if she ever escaped our little town, this would be her first stop, but she's too good for the rotten Big Apple.

So that night I quit Dante's Pretentious Inferno and never look back. I walk right out in the middle of a lighting cue, wearing my new nickname with a badge of pride.

Watcher from afar. Fits me like a glove.

A few months later in July, with barely five hundred beans to my name, I'm ready to fall off the end of the earth when the Society hands me my destiny. It's Lizzie who calls with the congrats.

"I'm sorry it took so long," she says, "but we had to give Bradford enough time to move out."

"Was I the only candidate for the job?"

"No. There was . . . I don't want to explain over the phone, Dupin. Come back up to The Bronx for some pre-Poe paperwork."

Once I'm back inside Cynthia's historical junkyard of an office, it appears less cluttered, and the whole building is emptier. Lizzie is behind the big desk now (Cynthia's on vacation) and gives me W-2s and release forms that promise I won't sue the Society if I slip and fall in the House of Usher. "It's nice seeing you again, Dupin. I'm glad you'll be joining us."

"Thank you, Watson. It feels good to be on the case."

"The game is afoot! Now, do you have any questions?"

"Yes, actually."

A drill burrows into my forehead. The office ripples. Waves of orange and black climb the walls, tracing the seams of the ceiling. A photo on the bookcase glows, and Lizzie's fingertips drip blood onto the desk. She rubs her chin, streaking it pale brown. The nub of my pinkie is squirming with maggots, laying eggs in what remains of my finger. My mouth dries out. Bile burns my throat.

"When I first walked into this office," I say, "Cynthia recognized me. You did too. Is there anyone on staff who could be my very own William Wilson?"

Lizzie sits behind the desk, deflated. The air conditioner hums.

"When you're done with that paperwork," she says, "we'll go downstairs, and I'll show you something."

The first floors are cold and barren. Lizzie narrates a tale of budget cuts and lackluster fundraising to explain the lack of staff.

Matthew Mercier

"When you came by in the spring, it was slightly busier, but since then we've had to let a few people go. A lot of non-profits are hurting right now, and we're no different. Personally, I think we need to change our business model. We rely too much on the swells."

"Who?"

"The moneybags. Rich donors."

We're in a lower back room, in what appears to have once been a library, but its shelves are bookless. Dust bunnies clutter the corners, and the air reeks of Lysol.

Lizzie points to a photo on the wall. "And here is one of those moneybags."

The photo is a group shot on a lawn, with the ocean in the background.

"Fundraiser on City Island. These are board members. See the one on the far right? In the back row. He hates being photographed. Bit of a vampire. I'm surprised we even got this photo taken, but it was a bit of a sneak attack. The photo, I mean. It was Cynthia's doing."

The man in question is wearing a wide-brimmed straw hat that covers his face—scarecrow cheekbones, tufts of red hair. It's me if you squint, and before I ask the obvious, Lizzie volunteers it.

"His name is Arthur Quinn."

I nod, my heart galloping. "He's following me."

"I'm sorry?"

"He came to my place in Queens. Earlier this summer. When I was moving out."

Maggots drop from my hand. Lizzie glances at the photo, then at me.

"Who is he?" I ask.

"Quinn? A bored, rich man filling up his life with Poe. He's got a few original manuscripts, couple of letters, and lots of other junk. I was going to archive his collection as well, but it's too much. He says he wants to see the Bronx Historical Society thrive, but every year during the fundraising, he holds us over a barrel and makes demands before he writes a check. You'll meet him, eventually. Most likely he'll surprise you at the cottage. Like I said, he's a hermit. A vampire. Now, are you ready—?"

"Did you give him my address?"

Lizzie taps a pen on her thigh.

Poe & I

"Did he see my resume? My address is on the resume."

"He may have."

"My landlord said the man claimed to be my brother. That he looked like me."

Lizzie squints at the photo. "Is the fact you have a doppelganger a deal breaker, Jonah? Do you want me to tell Cynthia you're no longer interested?"

"No."

"Good. We'll just add Quinn to the pile of mysteries around here."

The front door opens, and a frumpy old man wanders in, sweating under a starched cotton shirt. He's surprised to see us but gives a small wave. I recognize him from the photograph. Another board member.

Lizzie waves back. "Afternoon, Lloyd."

The old timer nods. "Lizzie. Can we talk?"

"In a moment. I'm just inducting our latest member, Jonah Peabody."

"Oh, I see. How are you?"

He peers up at me, blinks, and I'm sure he sees Quinn, the way Cynthia did, but he covers it up quickly. "I'm Professor Lloyd Mason."

"Professor Mason is one of my mentors," Lizzie says. "He teaches at Fordham."

"You'll be working here in the office, Mr. Peabody?"

"At Poe Cottage."

"Ah. What happened to Bradford?"

"He's leaving us," Lizzie says. "I'll fill you in later, Professor."

Mason wrinkles his lips, and before he can ask more questions, we leave him and trot back upstairs. Lizzie is now talking loud and assertive, which tells me this is for Mason's benefit more than mine. She wants him to overhear our conversation.

"Your job, Mr. Peabody, is integral to the health of the society. The Bronx needs to be educated and proud of what they have in Edgar Allan Poe. Baltimore and Philly get a lot of attention. The Bronx doesn't. That has to change. Your job is to make Poe and The Bronx alive for people."

She rants a bit about Poe and legacies and history that needs to be written by the people who live it. She sounds a bit crazy. Not crazy-crazy, but scholar-crazy. During my cameo appearance in

73

college, I met a few Shakespeare professors like this—grizzled coots whose unpublished books on *Macbeth* or *Othello* were the only thing preventing the destruction of the Western canon. Lizzie makes the caretaker gig sound as if it's life or death.

"So," I say, "give tours, take care of the garden, make sure nobody burns the place down, and find Virginia's bones?"

I mean this last bit as a joke, but she nods.

"Recovering Sissy's remains would be a real coup. Did I mention you get a new laptop?"

She produces a light, slivery MacBook Air, the latest model. "That part of the budget wasn't slashed, but we'll take it back if your employment is terminated." She extends her hand, the fingers still dripping blood. "Congratulations. Welcome aboard."

"Thank you." I brush off the last of the maggots and shake. "So, no more Poe quizzes?"

"Do you want another?"

"Maybe later."

"You'll be getting quizzed soon enough. I'll be coming by for a tour. But I will need your bank account."

"Sorry?"

"Direct deposit. Your stipend. You do want to get paid?"

"Of course. Thank you. You won't regret this."

She looks at my bare arm. "No regrets."

In the summer heat, I've unconsciously rolled up my sleeves. These words are burned into my right forearm, overlapping old scars.

"You'll need long-sleeved shirts during the tours."

"Even in summer?"

"Yes. Unless you want the schoolkids asking you about those scars. Self-inflicted?"

I stare at the ground, rolling my neck. "I'll wear long sleeves."

She pulls her shirt sleeve up, showing me a few beauty marks of her own, puckered lips and half-smiles. "No shame. Just a pragmatic piece of advice."

A knock at the door. She rolls her sleeve back down. Mason pushes his way in without waiting for a response. "Where's Cynthia?"

"Vacation," Lizzie says. "I'll be with you in a minute, Lloyd."

The old man clucks his tongue and glances at me again. I'm sure he's on the verge of asking me if I have a brother, when his

Poe & I

tongue reverses course. "So, Bradford is no longer with us. That's a shame. You've got big shoes to fill, Mr. Peabody."

"Sounds like it."

"I'm just going to walk Jonah out. Then we can talk, Lloyd."

Lizzie ushers me downstairs and out to the street, where she goes on about how Mason owns some Poe artifacts he wants to sell to the Society, how he's another well-off man whom the Society relies on a bit too much, but he's a good teacher and a great scholar.

"He seems anxious."

"He's got his reasons."

"Such as?"

Her face is pinched. The pen is still in her hand, tapping away now at her palm.

"Listen, Jonah." No more nicknames. No more jokes. "Can I be honest with you?"

"Have you been dishonest so far?"

She doesn't talk again until we're two blocks from the office. "You just walked into a hot mess. The Society is in a tough spot right now. Budget is tight. Cynthia is under a lot of pressure from the board, so I need to know if you're on my side."

"Is Arthur Quinn on your side?"

She shakes her head.

"Then I'm on your side."

She grins and touches my arm, my scars. "Good. Then stay tuned, Dupin."

My arm is tingling, a firework ready to explode. We say goodbye and I swim down the flaming streets, sparks flying off my heels, trees melting into puddles of green, fat pink tongues draping out of first-floor windows. These visions used to freak me out when I was younger, but now, in my old age, I handle the trips just fine. Hell, I try to enjoy it. I know my triggers—heat, stress, anger, love, and fear.

Ah, Quinn my brother, cousin, double—whoever the hell you want to call yourself. Cynthia and Lizzie know who you are, so they must know exactly what they're getting into with me, Jonah Peabody, and they're hiring me anyway. Are they afraid? We'll find out. Right now, the job is mine, and I'm one step closer to you Andromeda, my dear sister.

I'm ready for The Bronx, for Poe's basement, the perfect home for a watcher from afar.

Chapter 8

Blank Period

Mother was broken.

We didn't have a name for the brokenness. No internet search engines existed, where I could easily type in, "Why is Mother sad all the time?" or "What does it mean when somebody stares at the wall all day?" and be delivered half-a-dozen Reddit chains with the so-called answers. No, this was the digital stone age of the '80s, so we had nothing but Encyclopedia Britannica and the library. Information. Moved. Slowly.

I'd come out of my bedroom and find Mother standing in the hallway, her skinny body drowning in baggy sweatshirt and jeans, skeleton face and sunken eyes staring at me as if from the bottom of a deep well.

"Are you looking for something, Jonah?"

"What do you mean, Mom? No."

She shook her head. "You're not telling me the truth. As always, my son. As always you are a liar."

This type of accusation would send me into a tailspin of sadness and confusion. She didn't trust me, so I started to distrust myself. Was I doing something wrong? The old man couldn't give me answers. All he said was that if we prayed hard enough Mother's illness might evaporate, burn itself out.

Right. Prayer. You see Father's problem. Maybe it's because Mom wasn't dead, not yet a corpse he could dress up. He didn't know how to handle the living. Or maybe he loved too hard. Love makes you blind and stupid. My sister and I were no different. We wanted a mother to love, and we needed a mother to love us, but

Poe & I

upon finally getting Mother we didn't know *how* to love her. Andromeda prayed for the illness, but that was just a front. She didn't believe in God; she was just trying to please Dad.

"She's ill, Jonah. Give her time. You think it's easy being a part of this family? What we really need is a little patience."

More divine wisdom from the Andromeda galaxy. All we needed was a little patience. Turned out she was quoting a Guns N' Roses song—Axl Rose as poetic oracle—but that bit about our family was spot on. It was not easy being a Peabody.

Andy had sniffed out the root of Mother's unhappiness: us. The Peabody clan. Father, the house, the kitchen, the silence of the woods—all of it.

But, as time rolled on, I was convinced it wasn't us—it was me. I made her unhappy. Her baby boy.

Come at me with your Freud, but listen, as a kid your needs are simple, and you wear your heart on your sleeve. When a boy says, "I love you, Mom," and the Mom in question just nods blankly and walks off, you have no choice but to think, *What have I done wrong?*" She never once said, "*I love you, Jonah.*" She did smile at me, but it was only that same crooked smile, as if she were keeping a joke sealed behind her lips. Her teeth had started to crowd in the lower jaw, square stones leaning against each other, ready to fall out with each forced grin.

Mother had returned in late spring, so our summer vacation was right around the corner. Freedom and sunshine, the months when regular families spend more time together, take vacations, have barbecues, swim in ponds and all that *Leave it to Beaver* shit. But us? We had to train Mother to be, I don't know, human? Normal? She tried answering phones at the funeral parlor, but it was clear after a day that too many conversations with too many strangers—all about death—was not suitable, so she spent most of her time around the house. As the days grew longer, she took more walks in the garden, planted a few marigolds in the shade of the porch, clipped some hedges. Father ran with that and bought her a spade and gloves, but then she dug up the same marigolds and moved them to a different spot, where they withered and died. She planted shady stuff in the sun and sunny stuff in the shade. She forgot to water. She dug holes with the spade and didn't fill them in.

We did have a few outings as a family, drove to a local apple

Matthew Mercier

orchard and picked Honeycrisps, toured a dairy farm across the river from where I first witnessed the jagged line of the Catskills, but I remember thinking, *We live inside those mountains, and people on this side of the river live above the mountains. Maybe their lives aren't so moldy. Maybe their lives are better.*"

We tried going to the movies when the local drive-in had a retro '70s night and showed that weird Disney flick *The Black Hole*, but we had to leave early because it was too scary for Mother. She lay huddled in the passenger seat, wrapped in her blanket, whimpering each time that giant red robot with the helicopter blades appeared.

We did have dinners together, and Mother started making simple meals again, but Andromeda was the one who showed her how to fry an egg or make toast. Mother knew so little about domestic chores, and she seemed to resent it more than Andy did. She'd shout at the brooms, at the dishwasher, at the stove and the spice rack, and when I offered to help, she'd scream at me. Father eventually took over the cooking duties, since he was home more, the "business trips" having ended. We didn't expect Mother to cook, but she tried anyway. One night she made a meatloaf, but the kitchen's bloody counters looked as if she'd slaughtered a steer, and she stuffed the meat with a hodgepodge of mushrooms, spinach, eggshells, and paper towels. She spiced it with turmeric and a gallon of salt. We ate it politely, along with the salad she soaked in blue cheese.

She was trying, but she was broken, in both heart and mind.

So, I spent a lot of time in the woods, playing with the neighbors' kids, who were older than me; a sister and brother, Chad and Stacy Crawford. Their father helped them build a fort in a moss-covered glade that lay between two giant oaks. They allowed me to use it, too, since I'd helped nail the planks and staple tar shingles to the roof. They were the coolest and kindest kids I knew. They'd lost their mother to cancer, and they knew mine was sick, so we shared that story. We played a lot that summer. Hide and seek among the trees, collecting frogs, testing slingshots, spotting birds—it was the closest I came to happiness, and Stacy was easily my first crush.

But not my first kiss. Chad was careful about that. He liked me, but I think he knew the Peabodys had been stamped with disease and didn't want it mixing with his own blood, so he never allowed us to

Poe & I

be alone. Still, being out in those woods away from our unhappy house healed me just a bit and helped to temper my jealousy.

Yes, jealousy.

You see, Mother spent a lot of time with Andromeda. She was always in my sister's room, the two of them laughing softly. She read Andy's fantasy novel, which my sister was now illustrating, and Mother would hang these drawings on the wall. Andy was on a big dragon kick, and so all around the house were sketches of Smaug and Kalessin and other famous winged serpents. Mother never shut up about it and spoke as if dragons existed, as if Andy had invented them. Mother read each chapter, and Andy always blushed and stared at me over the dinner table as Mother bragged about her brilliant daughter. Afterward, my sister and I would often have a post-dinner detox, in which Andy reassured me that Mother loved me, too.

"She just doesn't know how to express it," my sister lied. "It's up here." She tapped her head. "Something's loose. It's not your fault, Jonah."

My bear of a big sister wrapped me in her hugs, lay with me in her bed, wiped away my tears. Sometimes we fell asleep together. She was my rock that summer, my insurance against total despair.

"Does she talk about me?" I asked once. "When you two are together, does she ever talk about me?"

Instead of answering, Andy suggested I show Mother the fort the Crawfords and I had built. "I think she'd love it. That's creative."

My gut told me it was a bad idea, but I had nobody else to give me advice. Dad just offered Hallmark proclamations. "She's better now. Love conquers all. We have to be here for her."

"But, Dad, what if I'm making her sick?"

"Jonah, don't be stupid."

Silly boy, look away. Everything is fine here. Sweep that sickness under the carpet.

One hot, humid afternoon in July, I found Mother sitting on the porch in a rocking chair, sipping lemonade and wearing a wide straw hat. The spade lay at her feet and her forearms glowed red with sunburn. I thought she was sleeping, but as I stepped onto our wrap-around porch, she opened her eyes and gave me that crooked grin.

My balls shrank and sunk into my pelvis as she leaned forward. "Darling? Do you want something?"

Matthew Mercier

"I was just wondering," I said. "I've been building a fort out in the woods all summer with some other kids, and it's really cool, and we go there to play, and I was wondering if you want to see it?"

She sucked in a breath, and it took her a full minute of silence before coming back at me with some nervous questions. Would there be bugs? Snakes? Poison Ivy? Mud? I said I knew where all the poison ivy was, and that we could wear boots for the mud. As for the snakes, only little ones. Garters. Nothing to worry about.

"I'd really like you to see it, Mom."

She picked up her lemonade, sipped, lifted the hat, and brushed her bangs off her forehead. "Okay." She stood, pulling on some muck boots. "Lead the way."

Like a fool, I was excited.

We needed to walk through the graveyard to get to the woods. This slowed her down. She stopped and read the names. Peter Rohor. Mary Clatterskill. Norman and Marie Bateman. "This couple died on the same day," she mused. "What do you think? A car crash? Lightning?"

She claimed to know a few people under the ground and marveled at the wealthy mausoleums, staring into the crypts, and lingering in the shade of the weeping willows. The day was sticky, and the air buzzed with insects. I don't know why we didn't just remain there among the tombstones, where she seemed most comfortable. I would have been happy with that, too. But I was also a single-minded child, and I needed her to pay attention to me, not the dead. So, I urged her to keep walking, and we soon reached the opposite end of the graveyard and arrived at the creek.

Calling it a creek sounds silly—it was a runty, brown finger of water that usually ran dry in the summer, but we'd had rain the night before, and so on that day it was bubbling over mossy rocks and muddy weeds.

"Do we have to cross that, Jonah?"

"Yes. But it's easy." I laughed and hopped over in one quick leap. Nothing to it. For her adult stride, it would be simple. But she clutched her shirt collar and remained rooted on the opposite bank. She glanced up and down the creek as if it were the Mississippi. Maybe she just needed help. So, I hopped right back.

"Jonah!"

"What?"

"Don't do that!"

Poe & I

"What? This?" I bent my knees and hopped again Now, she screamed, and a bolt of white lightning shot down my spine. When I hopped back, she slapped me across the face. I staggered into the creek, dunking one sneaker into the water. The mud sucked at it as Mother towered over me. My cheek stung, and she glanced over my shoulder, into the woods.

"I'm not going in there. You can't make me."

"Mom, I just want to—"

She slapped me again. "Don't say that. Wicked child."

Tears, hot and burning, running over my cheeks. "Say what? What did I?"

"Mother! Do not call me that! I am not your mother!"

She turned and swiftly retreated to the graveyard, shoulders pumping. A cloud slipped over the sun. I shivered and lifted my foot from the creek as the world fell away. Then I ran all the way to the fort, which I had to myself. I sat in the dirt corner and wept as birds chirped in the doorway, as the sun reappeared, as the earth kept spinning.

I took out my Swiss army knife, flipping the big blade up, down, up, down. I brushed the dull edge lightly across my forearm, across the new fuzz of hair I'd grown that summer. Hair was sprouting in all the dark crevices of my body, and it scared me. I slipped the blade under each fingernail, brushed it over every knuckle, and pressed the tip into the center of my palm, drawing blood.

Soon, the buzzing, drowsy heat had me nodding off, and I woke in the gray haze of dusk to my name being called. Andromeda appeared at the door of the fort, swept down next to me, dabbing my wounds with her shirt, and whispering false promises in my ear, as we hiked back to the house in warm darkness. Father came into my room and tended to my wounds, but he was on autopilot and asked, "What did you do to upset your mother?"

If I'd been a little older, I'd have strangled him. Instead, I spat, "She's not my mother."

I thought he'd slap me, but he just shook his head. "Please, Jonah. We need to keep her on an even keel."

I didn't know who I was anymore; I shared that at least with Mother. We were strangers to each other and strangers to ourselves. I don't think it's a mistake that, after the creek incident, Mother started sleepwalking, maybe trying to find her old self.

81

Matthew Mercier

Father attached sleigh bells to the bedroom door—a bulky constellation of metal balls that either woke her up or alerted him that she was trying to escape. Sometimes, the tinkling bells filtered into my dreams, followed by the floorboards creaking and father's haggard whispering, "Come back to bed, Pamela." This played out at least twice a week. Sometimes the bells failed, and I'd get up to go to the bathroom and find her swishing up and down the hallway, her dirty yellow nightgown hanging off her bones. I'd wait to see if she'd wake up or hit the wall and start marching in place like a toy solider, but more often she'd just turn around and shuffle back toward me. Then I'd wake Father.

One night, I found her standing at the top of the stairs, a hand on the railing, mumbling and staring off into the dark pit of the house. I peed, washed my hands, and when I came back out, she was still there. I stepped closer. She didn't turn around.

"Mom? Are you awake?"

Stupid question, but I wanted to give her the chance to respond. I'd heard you weren't supposed to wake a sleepwalker, but it never made sense to me. Why was it so dangerous? Would the person crumple to dust?

Mother's sour milk complexion glowed underneath her nightdress. She smelled of baby powder. I tugged on the hem of her gown. "Come back to bed."

Her black hair had grown in quickly, and it was fanned out—a Medusa of rich dark locks, the same way it looked that Halloween night she left. And then my forehead—my third eye—burned with a vision from that night.

I was in bed. Mother sat by my side, scolding me for eating Halloween candy, smiling that crooked smile. And then the whole room—the whole vision—tilted, pitched forward, and I was sitting up in bed. Mother was holding something in her right hand, holding it below the bedframe, trying to hide it from view.

A knife.

I snapped out of the vision, as if I was the one sleepwalking. Mother was still at the top of the stairs, breathing ragged, muttering. I placed a hand on the small of her back. The residue of the vision—the truth of it—hovered in my third eye.

"I am not your mother. You are not my child. The universe made a mistake. And so, therefore, I'm going to correct that mistake."

Poe & I

I placed a hand on the small of her back and pushed gently.

"Jonah!"

Andy, in her doorway. I let my hand drop and turned to face my better half, her sooty hair mussed.

"What are you doing?"

"I was trying to wake her up."

"That's not what it looked like."

Andromeda placed herself one step below Mother and began speaking softly. This got Mother to turn around, and Andy led her back to our parents' bedroom. Father's voice, Mother moaning, and then Andy was back in the hallway, dragging me into her sanctuary.

"I was trying to wake her up," I repeated.

"Jonah, don't."

"Andy, she tried to kill me."

My sister closed her door and put a finger to her lips.

"The night she left. Halloween. She had a knife. I remember it."

"Don't lie, Jonah."

"She was trying to kill me. She hates me."

Even though it was a warm humid evening, we both chattered, as if we lived in an igloo.

"No," Andy lied. "No, baby. She wasn't trying to hurt you."

"Stop calling me baby."

I don't blame Andy for lying. I know it was her job to protect me, to shield me from death, especially my own, but she was wrong. We had to protect ourselves from Mother.

I forget how long we argued, but I refused to leave my sister's bedroom that night, proving her point that I was still a baby. I pouted and sat at her drawing desk, clicked on the small light, and started flipping through her sketchbooks. In addition to dragons, she'd been obsessed with little people. Pixies. Brownies. Wood trolls. Leprechauns. Creatures that lived in Nature. But then I flipped to the image of a gaunt, frail woman in a nightgown. Gray circles for eyes, bony wrists, a heap of hair filled with dirt and spiders.

"Why did you draw Mother this way?"

Andy considered her own sketch. "Why do you think it's her?"

"Same body type. Same face. Same hair."

Andy reached for a book on the shelf. An illustrated edition of

Matthew Mercier

Edgar Allan Poe. She opened to *The Fall of the House of Usher* and showed me the drawing of a thin woman, barefoot and dressed in a tattered nightgown. The woman stood in a darkened house and pointed at two men who cowered in high-back chairs, covering their faces in terror.

"That's Madeline Usher," she said. "I was just trying to copy this style."

Andromeda read the Poe story to me that night. I didn't understand the language, but I sure as hell understood Madeline crawling out of her tomb to accuse her brother Roderick of burying her alive.

My sister was a prophet, a seer. Our mother was Madeline Usher. Buried alive in her own mind. Unable to get oxygen.

Andy could no longer comfort me with lies. Mother had been trying to kill me that Halloween night. And she would try again. I knew it. My third eye had shown me the truth. I reminded Andy of our promise in the attic. I told her I'd be on my guard, ready to defend myself, ready, if need be, to burn the house of Peabody to the ground.

Chapter 9

Brother Poe, Brother Peabody

Let's talk geography.

Poe Cottage is not in the South Bronx, but South is the only point on the compass when people hear The Bronx. The Bronx is burning folks, the Bronx is burning. Well, Poe missed getting singed by the fires of the '70s by a few blocks. All those landlords torching units for the insurance money stopped flicking their lighters just south of Fordham Road, and Poe Cottage sits right above Fordham.

Now, since the South Bronx is no longer burning, it's gentrifying. Folks want to call it SoBo, or even worse, "The Piano District." (Leave the Steinways in Astoria, please, unless you want to make pianos here.) Business types say the name "South Bronx" carries too much stigma. *Oh, you think?* Well, good luck changing it. You'll need a Whole Foods next to Yankee Stadium before you can get that issue on a ballot, whitey.

Listen to me. A country mouse throwing shade before he even moves in, but I'm already feeling that swell of borough pride.

Up north, above Fordham Road, I can't get over the difference in the sky—bigger and bluer than Manhattan, with no towers cutting up your view. It's not Montana or Alaska, but after seeing those horizons, I can appreciate a good sky. And let me tell you, the North Bronx owns it in spades. Sure, on the ground it's clogged and chaotic, but I expected that. I didn't expect big sky.

I did expect to stand out—a white guy walking down Kingsbridge sweating under a fifty-pound backpack and duffel bag, like one of those dopy rich kids kicking around the European

Matthew Mercier

countryside after college. My calves buckle under the weight, and I keep switching the duffel from hand to hand. Bradford razzes me the minute I walk in.

"Christ, gingerbread. It looks like you just got out of Rikers. Is that all you got?"

"Ayup. Hope you're leaving some furniture behind."

With the place emptied out, the blood-red basement walls look even redder, as if they've just been freshly soaked. The bareness makes it feel industrial, not homey. Bradford, thankfully, is leaving five hand-me-downs—a kitchen table, a giant oval rug covering the floor, an armoire, a two-person loveseat, and right next to this, crammed in the corner, is the Acme safe that reads, *Poe Society*, which I point to and say, "Okay, what's inside?"

"Oh, you entitled now, gingerbread?"

I place my duffel gently on the rug. "Gingerbread?"

He grins and swipes at a sprig of pumpkin hair dangling over my ear. "You're a gingerbread boy."

"Very creative. What's in the safe?"

"You sure you want to know?"

"It's part of the job, right?"

"How did you get this job anyway?"

"Charm. Experience."

"My ass. Cynthia's a tough nut. She don't crack easy. How much did you slip in the envelope?"

"I promised to find Virginia's bones."

"Wait. For real?"

"You know about the bones, right?"

"'Course I do. She asked me to find them, too. But I'm no Indiana Jones. That's a fool's errand for a mediocre white man."

"What's in the safe?"

From the crossbeam library, he pulls down an ivy-green volume of Poe, illustrated by a guy named Fritz Eichenberg, and shoves it into my hands. "Combination is on the inside cover." He lowers himself onto his haunches and twirls the safe's dial. The locks click. The door swings open, and a daddy longlegs scurries out. "Here we go. Guest logbooks. Extra set of keys. Security codes for the front door."

"Wait," I bend down. "That's it? You made it sound—"

"I didn't make it sound like anything. You dreamed up some voodoo, Lovecraft magic. Unless you count this." He hands me a red folder: *Virginia Poe & Other Matters*.

Poe & I

"Our friend Lizzie Borden compiled all this. Everything you need to know about that bullshit treasure hunt for Virginia's bones. Personally? I think the bones are lost to time, if they were ever real. But Virginia Poe is the least of your worries."

"That's what Lizzie implied."

"The archivist implied correctly."

"What's her story?"

"I don't know Lizzie at all. She's studying at Fordham, too."

I flip through the dossier. Documents about Virginia's bones and Poe's tumor. A statement on the recent discovery of correspondence between Alexander Dumas and Poe. A list of the various theories about Poe's death (hydrophobia, rabies from a cat bite, election day cooping). A notice about the digitization of the Society's archives. A budget marked up in red sharpie. Detailed plans for a Poe Cottage renovation.

"The Society's been struggling financially," Bradford said. "Cynthia watched the Poe house in Baltimore get defunded, and she's afraid the same is going to happen up here and . . . "

He's squatting in front of the safe, staring up at the folder, at my hands, at my ghost pinkie, which is on full display.

"Land shark," I say. "Got me when I was sleeping."

He rises with a groan. "I do not want to know."

I hold up the blueprints of something called *The Eureka Dome.* "What the hell is Eureka?"

Eureka, Bradford explains, is Poe's masterpiece. Forget *The Raven* and screw *The Black Cat.* Minor stuff compared to *Eureka.*

Poe scratched out his magnum opus up here in The Bronx, with his life hanging at the end of a tattered rope. Virginia's death had sent him over the edge. More than ever, he needed to believe in God, the afterlife, the soul, and so he wrote this gonzo essay proposing that the universe originated from one blazing, exploding point and that it would end the same way.

Sound familiar? That's right. With the perfect combo of spiritual longing, half-baked cosmology, and full-throttle imagination, Poe described the Big Bang theory, pre-dating that French priest.

But of course, his ideas got mocked as the work of a crackpot amateur (which they were) even though he wanted the work to be judged as a poem (which it never was). He toured and lectured and did all that academic stuff (without being an academic), tried to find a respectable audience for this ultimate mash-up of faith and

Matthew Mercier

science, but he failed, hard, and it's been tossed in the dustbin of his "lesser works," except by fans and scholars and Poe caretakers.

"Now, I'm not sure I understand *Eureka*," Bradford says, "but I do understand it could only have been written by a man who did not get a traditional education. Poe got booted from West Point and UVA and didn't buy into religion or democracy or transcendentalism or any of the traditions of early America. This left him isolated, but it also left him free to tumble down the rabbit hole, which can lead to a whole lot of crazy but also a whole lot of genius. I mean, trying to imagine the origins of the universe and the mind of God? That takes an ego the size of Jupiter. When I shatter the hodgepodge piñata of my own education, I imagine—someday—dreaming up something like *Eureka*. Okay, let's go upstairs. Few more things."

He first demonstrates the security system in the shed, which screams and calls the cops if anyone busts into the museum or the greenhouse. "People think the cottage is a trove of valuable antiques, but it's not."

Outside, he rubs a hand over the tar shingle roof of the greenhouse extension, which is blooming with concentric circles of moss. "A green roof," he chuckles. "Just not the Norwegian kind. Can't say the greenhouse is really a greenhouse without a skylight, but you'd just be asking for someone to throw a rock."

"What about the gardens out front?"

"The city helps with those." He gestures to the middle of the park, where a pair of women are working out of a green pick-up with trash pickers and rakes.

I remind him of the story he tossed off about the junkie who broke into the greenhouse and overdosed. He laughs, rapping the clapboard with his fist. "A junkie? Shit, I guess I was just trying to scare you away. That's more of an urban legend. Sounds good though, don't it?"

"So, it's not haunted?"

"Do you want it to be haunted?"

"What the hell kind of answer is that?"

All around us the Bronx is honking and squeaking and booming. "It's the answer I'm giving you. You wanted this gig, right? You lied and cheated to get it, so."

"Cheated? Bradford, I told you. I have no idea what's going on behind the scenes here. Lizzie said the society is . . . "

Poe & I

"What are they paying you?"

The question catches me off guard, but I confess the amount, and he leans back and laughs. "That's what I thought! They're cutting the salary in half, and you're an independent contractor, right? That's why I'm getting the boot. I asked for a raise, and they're cutting the budget. Unbelievable."

His anger makes a lot more sense now. Squeezed out of a plumb gig and replaced with a scab.

I pride myself on being a connoisseur of anger, the different grades and vintages, and Bradford's is plenty rich in aromatic odors of resentment and confusion— but he's also giving off vibes of fear and worry. At the front gate, he pops the padlock in one swift move and we're out in the park, in the bright, warm glow of the sun, where the humidity coats everyone in a sticky film and the asphalt is a furnace. Kids scoot up and down the plastic slides of the playground. A grizzled, stooped old timer scrapes shaved ice from a cart. Teenagers zip past on their skateboards and flow into a circular blacktop, with an alabaster gazebo in the center.

We stop in front of a park bench, where two kids are slouched, a girl and a boy, decked out in tinted glasses, black shorts, Doc Martens, and, for some reason, long black overcoats draped over their shoulders, exposing forearms that are chestnut brown. Their nose studs and earrings glint in the sun.

The boy claps his hands once, raises a clenched fist in the air, and yells, "Poe Presente!" while the girl smiles, teeth sharp. "Hey, Bradford."

Bradford bumps knuckles with both kids. "What's doing, youngins? Enjoying your last month of summertime freedom?"

"You know it," the boy says.

"Grades are good this year?"

"Hells yes," the girl shouts. "The Garcias are no joke."

"Good to hear."

The boy slides the purple tinted glasses down his nose, pupils bright. "This the new vampire?"

I unconsciously rub my throat. "Vampire?"

"The new man underground. The Poe Phantom."

"My brother loves giving the caretakers nicknames," the girl says. "But you are the new guy, right?"

"In the flesh."

The boy spreads his arms over the bench. "Welcome to the jungle, kid."

Matthew Mercier

His overcoat drops between the slats of the bench, scraping the ground, and now I see that it's not a coat—it's a velvet cape. They're both wearing capes. The girl's lipstick is purple. The boy's eyebrows are pierced. Goth kids in the Bronx. Go figure. Teenagers flying their freak flag have a special place in my heart. It's not easy being so bold when everyone wants to conform, and I imagine being a goth in the Bronx might be double the trouble it is anywhere else, but these two don't seem to give a rat's ass, so I like them already; but then I step right in it.

"Aren't you both hot?" I ask. "Wearing all that black?"

"You my old man?" the boy snorts. "Don't be sweating how I dress."

"He's right though," the girl laughs. "It's steamy out here. Let's go hang out in a cool, dark basement."

I throw a glance back at the cottage as Bradford slaps me on the shoulder. "Oscar and Carla, meet Jonah Peabody. My replacement."

"No replacing you, dude." Carla snaps a wad of gum.

"Why you are leaving, man?" Oscar pouts his lips. "I still don't get it."

"Not my choice, son. The administration wanted a regime change, so here he is."

Oscar rises off the bench, his cape fluttering. He's got a little belly poking over his buckle, but he's tall, with a broad chest, and he tilts his body toward me, our shoulders brushing. "Bradford tell you about our privileges?"

"Privileges?"

"Poe's Basement," Oscar says, "is our basement."

"We love it down there," Carla chirps.

"You two work for the Society?" I ask.

"Unofficially. Off the books." Oscar thumps his chest. "We look after Poe, too."

"How so?"

"This is our park. We've always got eyes on him. There's a larger group called The Ravens, but we're the underground faction. Nocturnal. Punk rock. You feel me?"

"Nocturnal?"

Carla stands, shaking out her curly hair, tinged red. "We're the Puerto Rican Vampire Club."

"And nobody bothers you?"

Poe & I

Carla mummers, "We only dress like this on Sundays. Keep unholy the Sabbath, you know?"

"Sundays in the park with Poe." Bradford snorts and glances between us as if we're supposed to react. "That's Steven Sondheim. He's a . . . never mind."

Oscar laughs. "Don't let this one fool you. He tries to act street, but he's a real nerd."

"Those aren't mutually exclusive, Oscar."

"See what I mean?" The kid winks at Bradford. "Mr. PhD."

Behind us, a jangle of keys announces a woman in regulation park department duds—tight khakis, olive-green shirt with two breast pockets, and a riot of braids stuffed under a hat. She holds a ragged broom and a folding dustpan.

"Park's closing," she snaps. "Everybody out."

Oscar rolls his head. "Watch out for this one, Jonah. She's married to Jesus."

"Demon child, I will pray for you."

"Can't save my soul, sister. It's promised to Satan."

The park lady clucks her tongue. "Wickedness. Both of you dressing up like clowns. You best avoid these children," she says to me. "Else they drag you to hell."

"I'm already headed there, ma'am."

The siblings howl, bending over at the waist. Bradford introduces the woman as Achebe. She knows I live in the basement, too. Works in the park three days a week and at the hair salon on Saturdays.

"We all look after each other here," she tells me. "Even the sinners. Your name is Jonah? That's nice. Your momma was a good Christian, I bet. Everyone is bathed in His blood. You believe that, right?"

I don't want to offend her, so I just agree with her dime store Jesus talk. Bradford winks at me from over her shoulder and begins guiding us out of the park. "We're going now, Achebe."

Oscar and Carla swoop past the park lady and give her the finger as she slams the gate shut.

"Stupid old timey bitch," Carla mutters.

"She's just saying her piece," Bradford says. "Why you getting all worked up?"

"She's a Republican," Carla hisses. "An immigrant from Nigeria who's a Republican. You believe that shit? Voted for Bush twice."

"God bless America."

Matthew Mercier

Carla groans, rolling her eyes. "She's always going on about abortion or how the races shouldn't marry."

"Wait until she finds out you've got Irish blood."

"Oh, she knows!" Carla fluffs her bouncy, red curls. "It makes her head explode."

We cross the Concourse, and Bradford finally holds up the keys. "Okay, this is where I get off, Jonah. You ready?"

"Born to it."

"This job is harder than you think."

"I believe you, Bradford. But I'm ready."

"Okay, gingerbread. You look after Poe." He places the keys in my palm, then puts a hand over mine. "It's a special place. And next time I come by, I want to hear about this sister of yours. She sounds special, too."

"She was. She is. Special, I mean." I slip the keys into my shirt pocket. "Please visit anytime, Bradford."

"Oh, I will." He reaches out a hand and we shake, four fingers to five.

Carla and Oscar mug my mutilation but don't ask questions.

"And you two," Bradford smiles at the vampires. "Behave yourselves. Stay out of trouble. Make sure he doesn't burn Poe down."

"Consider the torch passed," Oscar says. "Oops. No pun intended."

Carla smiles at me. "Come on, Mr. Caretaker. Let's chow."

We say good-bye to Bradford, and the siblings unhook their capes (not great to go the full goth outside the park, they explain) and walk me back up Kingsbridge to the Empire Diner, a time warp '50s joint resting in the shadow of the 4 train on the corner of Kingsbridge and Jerome. We gorge ourselves on open-faced turkey sandwiches and split pea soup, buttered corn, and garlic-mashed potatoes, with rice pudding and cappuccino for dessert. In the air-conditioned hush of the diner, the vampire act starts to fade, and the real kids start rising to the surface. Friendly, talkative, curious.

They'll be juniors in high school and are trying to plan their next move. They admit they don't really know how to "do college." They could probably go to a CUNY or a SUNY, but they'll need to save up. Nobody in their family finished high school, so college hasn't even been on the radar. They ask me where I went to school.

I swallow. These two seem loyal to the caretaker—not Cynthia,

Poe & I

not the Society—and I want to be honest with somebody. After a while, storytelling gives you a headache.

"I don't have a college degree."

Oscar whistles. "That is mad white. Bradford is mega-qualified. PhD. Masters. You telling us you have no degree, and you just waltz right in and take his job? Man, this game is rigged."

"Ricky Thurston had a degree and was going for a second!" Carla says.

"Ricky Thurston?" I repeat the name. "He's a former caretaker?"

The siblings give each other a not-so-secret glance and go silent, shoveling food in their mouths. Oscar is the first to speak, but he's rubbing knuckles over his lips and looking out the window at the traffic on Kingsbridge. "Ricky came to a bad end."

"Bad? What happened?"

"That's the million-dollar question, isn't it?" Oscar waves his butter knife in the air, watching the number 4 train rattling above. "But we're not going there. Not yet. You're still fresh off the boat, son."

"Just tell him," Carla says.

Oscar shakes his head, and won't look at me, until Carla blurts it out. "Ricky died in Poe's basement. Heart attack."

"Nah, nah. That was no heart attack," Oscar fidgets and waggles a finger at her. "Ricky was . . . " He lowers his voice. "Ricky was straight up murdered."

"That's what Lizzie thinks."

"Lizzie is right," Oscar hisses.

"Bro, Ricky was diabetic, plus he drank, smoked."

"You saying he deserved it?"

"'Course not. Just saying. How was it murder? He was alone in the basement."

"Don't know. Just a feeling."

"Feelings aren't facts."

Now Oscar turns his fury back on me. My lack of higher education crawls under his skin, and he's prattling on and asking me why the hell I'm here at Poe Cottage if I didn't go to school, and what could I possibly hope to accomplish by coming to The Bronx if I'm not a Poe scholar.

I drum the table with my stump, which quiets his tongue for the moment, but then, blunt as a hammer, he asks, "How'd you lose that?"

93

Matthew Mercier

"Alligator in the sewer."

He smirks. "Gangster. So. Why are you here, Mr. Jonah 'I don't need a college degree' Peabody?"

"I'm here to find my sister."

Carla holds a lump of sausage in her mouth. "She a missing person?"

"Maybe." I sip my coffee. "Or she might be dead. It's a long story."

Oscar cracks his knuckles then glances at a wristwatch he doesn't have. "We got time. Indulge us."

I thought a bleak nugget of my family history would kill the conversation, but then again, why not sprinkle some clues? If they listen, and then tell everyone Jonah Peabody is here to find his sister, I might get to Andy faster.

"Okay, but then you tell me about Virginia's bones."

"Didn't Bradford give you the skinny on that?"

"Sure. But I want to hear how much you know."

"Oh, so you're testing us?" Oscar leans his head back, chin bunched to the ceiling. "Fine. We're ready to go."

"I have no doubt."

"So, what happened to your sister, Jonah?"

His question stings my heart, and I suppose if I'm going to be Poe's caretaker than I need to get used to both lies and confession, but how do I tell the truth when I'm so unsure of it myself? How do I say, 'She was kidnapped by my fake brother? By this man Quinn.'

"I think I'll just start," I say, "by telling you a little about her."

Chapter 10

Poe Family

Once it was clear Mother was Madeline Usher, I entered my Poe phase.

Granted, I was already an unripe teenager chemically destined for bad choices, so a nihilistic attitude felt organic and locally sourced, but after a year of living with Mother, it was clear her sickness was here to stay, so I had to buckle in and cope, which also meant I ended up breaking my promise to Andromeda.

I could not protect her.

I mean, if the woman who birthed us could end up with a warped mind, then how could my sister and I shield ourselves from a psychic roll of the dice? If we survived childhood, our DNA would be lurking just around the corner. This knowledge, plus hormones plus middle school equaled a white-hot anger that sprouted in my cortex and never stopped growing.

And it wasn't just about Mother anymore. It was about our life, our upbringing, my growing awareness of what I called "existentialist economics."

Kids like me and Andy? We usually appear on the five o'clock news for selling crystal meth the same week most kids are starting college. We're the ones you see walking the sidewalks of your hometown when you come home for the holidays, the ones who never got out, economic leftovers of what you might have been. You give us those sidelong glances when you pass us and think, "Damn, I went to high school with that dude, and he's still here? How pathetic."

But it's not pathetic. It's people. It's life. Americans prefer the

Matthew Mercier

fantasy that everyone gets a fair shot, but we can't handle the truth that some people always get left behind. The propaganda starts in middle school. *Go out and live the American Dream. You can do what you want.* Do I need to state the obvious here? It's a white lie, even for white people. Sure, some of us might get out, but all the rest? Good luck. The universe (and the government, and the church, and the cops, and the DMV) is just bound to take a dump on some people. Poe knew that. Andromeda knew that. I think that's why we loved Poe so much. He didn't lie to us. We were Poe's people. The lonely, the forgotten, the discarded.

Still, I bought into the shiny happy people nonsense like everyone else, even as our teachers and guidance counselors—all those goddamn professionals—faked their way through all that "guiding" and "counseling." By sophomore year of high school, I could read between the lines. Whatever bromides these clowns heaved at us, what I really heard was: "These poor kids. They're going to end up as addicts. Townie burnouts. Guests of the state at the local prison."

That prison is on the outskirts of our Catskill hamlet. It's visible from Main Street—a true town hall, with a pinwheel maze of barbed wire spinning out from the turrets and battlements. Father dubbed it "The Castle," and it's where a good number of my high school classmates—black, brown, and cracker—would end up. For us it was either the castle, or the nuthouse, or laboring at the cement factory, or running a Stewart's gas station—those were the slots on the roulette wheel designated for us, the Peabodys and our people.

Again, none of the adults said this aloud, but you could hear it in their sighs when we even mentioned the idea of college. They knew it would take a miracle for us to make it out. A state university, maybe, or a trade school. Not a bad fate, either of those, but when the herd is gunning for Harvard, they make trade schools sound like a horror show of sawdust and lead poisoning.

Once I figured out the fix was in, high school felt like the beginning of the end. Having Mother at home only made it worse. I regretted her return. Andy not so much.

"I'm glad to know she's alive," my sister said. "We're lucky to have her with us."

"She might as well be dead," I muttered.

"Don't say that. She's our mother. It's not her fault she got sick."

Poe & I

"Maybe so. But she's not my mother anymore. She's somebody else."

This wedge between my sister and I grew thicker as we rolled into high school. Mother's weirdness stabilized, but she remained the same, a blank slate of robotic emotion. True madness is boring. They don't tell you that in the movies; but madness is just a routine. The mundane routine from hell. Pills, sleep, more pills, food, TV, sleep, wake up, pills—day in and out. To break the routine invited chaos, or so Father seemed to think.

As Andy and I started to branch out and make new friends, it became clear we could never invite these friends home. Routine for Mother meant no new faces. She might freak out. So we only saw these friends at school or in the woods if they lived nearby. Andy started hanging with a gangly girl named Clarissa, who lived in the trailer park beyond the graveyard. Her mother was a heroin addict, its own sickness, so she and Andy found lots to talk about. Clarissa had a butterfly tattoo on her hip, but I only ever saw one half of it. The second wing remained hidden under the waistline of her Daisy Duke shorts.

She and Andy would sit out in the graveyard smoking weed, laughing, and bitching about their families. I was the only boy allowed to join them during their secret meetings.

"You got a good sister here," Clarissa would say to me. "One day I'm going to steal her away."

I believed her. Hell, I wanted to steal Andy away. I wanted her all for myself. I didn't want anything to change between us, but high school was a churning black cloud of change whose advance I could not stop. I wanted to drop out so badly, but Andy said, "Without high school, we're going nowhere, Jonah."

That's how she was still pitching it. 'You and me, kid. We're a team.' But who's kidding who? Andy was in a class all her own. She was saving money for college. She was going places. And listen to this: She'd actually started checking out books from the library about mental illness.

"We should learn about what Mom has," she lectured. "It's in our blood."

That's the brilliant mind we're talking about here. She could transform trauma into a teachable moment, without the teacher. She knew Mother's demons might be coming for us, but my hormones drowned out the warnings. Even worse, Jason, the

97

Matthew Mercier

eternal bully, piled on the mythology. "Jonah's mom was in the loony bin for killing a baby! I heard she eats her own shit!" I don't know how the asshole found out, but we weren't the only ones tagged with the stigma. Marcy D'Angelo's father ended up in the hospital after Marcy's mother died. (Driven mad by grief?) And Stacy Cunningham's older sister had been committed after she stabbed her boyfriend. (I remember that trial, and I remember thinking, 'That woman is not insane. Her boyfriend was an abusive asshole.') So, *The Necro Peabodys* soon became *The Crazy Necro Peabodys*.

But you know what? I leaned into it. Accepted my fate. I went the full punk rock Poe. Long leather jackets, Doc Martens, feathered mullet, tattoo ink painted on all my naughty bits. Between classes, I started hanging with metal heads, the ones who smelled of bong water and unwashed hair. We smoked American Spirits under the football bleachers and railed against the system, one rebellious cliché after another. Membership in this faction of the high school food chain earned me name recognition with Mike Murray, the grunge king, who, one lunch hour, as I was heading for my usual table with Andy, waved me over.

"Peabody! You're into Sabbath, right?"

"Hells yes."

"We're sneaking into a concert on Friday. You down?"

Mike wore all black and grew his sandy blond hair way past his shoulders—the '80s glam rock look, which earned him a few quiet snickers about how he might be gay, but he lifted at the gym and was built like a linebacker, so the preppies didn't bother with him. If Mike liked you, he became your protector.

I stared across at Andy, who sat at a table with her sketchpad. Jason and his followers hawked spitballs at her. She'd flipped up her hood, so the spitballs bounced off and collected under her chair like paper hailstones. My sister had also leaned into the goth look, more than me—black lipstick, skull necklaces and pentagrams, all-black T-shirts. Our school had a few goths, but Jason decreed that Andy was the gothiest, the weirdest.

On that day, as I joined Mike's clique, Andy glanced up at me, and when she saw me sitting with the other grunge heads, the look on her round face told me she knew this day had been coming, that our drifting apart had been pre-ordained. She went back to sketching in her pad, the lonely lady of the cafeteria, and we

Poe & I

became strangers at school. I wasn't worried. She had Clarissa, and I had Mike, who introduced me to his crowd, people whose names I can't even remember now, but I so badly wanted to be a part of a group that I gave up my sibling. Old story.

Mike thought it was killer that my father was in the business of death and that Mother had been shelved in the nuthouse.

"Just for a little while," I told him.

"What did she do?"

"What do you mean?"

"How did she crack?"

"I just don't think she likes being my mom."

I said that to be funny, sarcastic, to show how much I didn't care, but reflecting on that horrible nugget, I can now taste the rotten caramel of truth. (*I am not your mother, Jonah.*) But we're in the hinterlands of hindsight. Back then, I was being phony. When Mike asked about the funeral business, I pretended to know all about crime scenes and the dressing of corpses, when it was my brilliant sister who held all that knowledge.

"Andrea the giant isn't as cool as you, Jonah," Mike said. "Why does your sister read so much?"

"She's a nerd."

Another clichéd betrayal. I mocked her to save myself. Teenagers are the worst offenders of stale mythology. For the better part of the year, I watched Andy from a distance as she continued to grow in height, but also gentleness making her a target—she wouldn't fight back. You could toss soda cans at her head, throw punches at her shoulder, and she'd just move away. If the weather was nice, she'd eat out in the woods behind the school with Clarissa, who often got into fistfights on Andy's behalf. The inevitable rumors spread about the two of them, but everyone knew Clarissa was going to marry Ronny, her older boyfriend, who'd already dropped out and had a full-time job as a mechanic. Andy eventually started avoiding the cafeteria entirely, so I never saw her unless it was in the hallway between classes. Meanwhile, Mike got me girls. He smoked me out. He threw parties in his basement, and I lost my virginity to a skinny punk girl on his couch. We watched horror movies and cut ourselves. We drank whiskey and broke into cars.

Andromeda kept reading weird books and sketching dragons, devils, warrior women riding dragons and devils. She got attention

Matthew Mercier

from a saintly art teacher, who told Andy she could easily get into a school in New York with her talent. Father seemed to love this idea, but Mother hated it. "Andromeda can't leave us," she kept saying, over and over, so eventually Father also came to hate the idea. Art school was too expensive. How would she live in Manhattan? No, it was ridiculous.

That's the year Andy started wearing smoking jackets to school, after she'd found an old black and white picture of a woman wearing a suit. The kids had gotten used to her all-black Satan outfit, but the smoking jacket—with its wobbly shoulder pads, felt elbow patches, and mothball stench—was new material. Jason screamed, "You smell like my grandmother!" He and the crew ripped out the foam shoulder pads and tossed them like frisbees, but Andy didn't stop wearing the outfits. Each time the bullies destroyed one, she'd go down to the Salvation Army and get a plaid hunting jacket or something equally masculine. She and Clarissa began skipping classes together, and Andy's grades slipped, even though she did work, just not the work our teachers wanted.

Like the rambling paper she turned into English class on *The Lord of The Rings*, her favorite book. The teacher, Mr. Sullivan, couldn't deny the paper had the smack of genius, but since the paper was supposed to be on *The Scarlett Letter*, Andy failed. The guidance counselors didn't know how to guide her when she thought for herself.

Andy's breaking point came one rainy afternoon in the spring, when it was pouring outside and all of us were crammed in the cafeteria, a screaming echo chamber. Jason had somehow gotten hold of a broom and was using it to swipe kids on the head. Andy walked into the lunchroom that day wearing a plaid flannel shirt, but the rain had soaked through it, so her breasts sagged underneath, revealing the outline of her bra. Jason zeroed right in, and because he was a teenage boy and a bully, his eyes went straight to Andy's boobs. I could see what was happening before it happened. In my faulty memory, I try to be a hero, to get between my sister and Jason, but I don't trust my memory, and neither should you. Jason stood, raised the broom, and brought it down hard on my sister's chest.

A large chunk of the cafeteria went quiet. Jason froze, holding the broom in place, as if surprised at what he'd done.

Andy grabbed the broom, ripped it away, flipped it over, and smacked Jason upside the head. He staggered backward, tripped

Poe & I

over his ankles, and crashed to the floor. And then Andy was on top of him, those tomboy hands of hers going for his throat, and all that rage and hurt that I thought she didn't have rose bubbling up into her pink face, her body a tightly wound spring that now unloaded itself on Jason's wriggling form.

She might have killed him. It wasn't even close. Kids screamed as Andy bellowed and shrieked. It took three male teachers to pull her off.

Father was called in for a meeting. Andy was suspended for a few weeks and labeled "mental." Jason was not suspended, which is how it goes. The school talked of getting Andy a therapist, but Father waved that off. For once, he knew what to say. "She's not crazy. She's being bullied, and that bullying is driving her crazy. You all need to protect her."

But that was a joke. The teachers couldn't protect anyone. When Andy started skipping whole weeks of classes, Father looked the other way. She started working at the parlor, so he benefited from her playing hooky. There was talk of homeschooling, but Andy was already doing that for herself. (Her bedroom overflowed with overdue library books.) She promised Father she would graduate, as she still wanted to go to art school.

We all had to fool ourselves to survive.

Oddly enough, our crazy family—our house of pain—is also what protected her.

Mother was Andy's shield against the world.

Mother, too, had started wearing men's jackets and mismatched clothing. She and Andy went shopping together at the thrift stores and brought home fur coats, rainbow stoles, shit-kicking work boots. They ate out. They gardened. They developed this routine on weekends, one that comforted Mother, and so Father encouraged it. But when they drove into town, they were radioactive—a mother and daughter whom people feared, loathed.

I was afraid, too. I figured it was too late to get back into my sister's good graces, that she'd throttle me as well. I didn't know how to answer her, in those rare moments when the Peabody family all gathered at the dinner table, and she'd ask, "Why don't you like me anymore, Jonah?" Mother would repeat the question, with a hint of threat. "Yes, Jonah. Why don't you like your sister? What's happening to you?"

Defensive and full of my own hurt, I'd hurl the questions right back at them.

Matthew Mercier

"What's happening to you? Why are you both so weird?"

The absurdity of teenagers. What you gain in pubic hair, you lose in self-awareness. Andy and I kept drifting apart until Mother—again—brought us together.

It was the summer between sophomore and junior year. Dad was at work. He and Andy had calling hours at the parlor that night, so they'd be home later. Mother had gone to the grocery store by herself, which was now part of the routine. She was driving again, a huge step toward independence.

So, I was home by myself when she rolled into the driveway. The Subaru was packed with bags of groceries. When I asked her why she'd bought so much, she just said, "It's my job to provide."

Sugar, meat, fruit, vegetables, pancake mix, frozen meals, beer, whiskey—it was absurd, the excess, and I laughed. Mother, for the first time, laughed with me, and we set about making dinner together, which, if you want historical markers, was the first and last time we ever did that. Not that Mother was anything less than her usual self—her mind skipped to various subjects, none of them connected, and I had to make sure she didn't burn the pork chops, mushrooms, creamed cabbage, and apple cobbler.

"What the hell is all this?" Andy mumbled when she and Father sat to a full table of food. Father, too, didn't seem to trust the meal, and he picked and prodded at his plate until Mother took off her jacket.

She hadn't removed it the whole time we'd been cooking. Now she shrugged it off and dropped it on the floor. Andy picked it up but looked at the sleeves and asked, "Mom, did you spill something on yourself?"

A series of black streaks ran in and out of the folds, blending with the dark blue material. Father got up from the table.

"Andromeda, give me the jacket."

Red dots on Mother's shirt. Her neck. Her cheek. Up and down the left side of her body. Andy sat next to Mother, who smiled and sliced into her pork chop.

"Mom, did you hurt yourself?"

"Hmmm?"

Andy brushed Mother's cheek, scraping one of the dots with her fingernail. Mother leaned away, annoyed, as my sister said the words that changed our family forever. "It's blood, but I don't think it's hers."

Chapter 11

First Night

I tell the Puerto Rican vampires enough to satiate their thirst. Andromeda, my sister, was a goth. An artist. A rock in the stormy ocean of childhood, but we drifted apart, and now I'm afraid the distance is too great.

I stop short of Mother's return home, stained with blood. Save that for later, if I end up trusting these two. I spread my open palms over the table. "We good? Or do you want more?"

Oscar is flicking his earring. "Who names their kid Andromeda?"

"My parents were odd people."

"It's a pretty name," Carla says. "Better than being named after a Muppet."

Oscar raps her on the shoulder with his fist and leans across his empty lunch plate at me, the short order chef barking orders in the background. "Did your sister go to college, Jonah? Because she seems a lot more qualified than you."

The kid doesn't know how right he is. "Poe Cottage would have been my sister's dream job."

"Not many women have been caretakers," Carla says. "Too isolated."

With my side of the storytelling fulfilled, Carla unspools the tale of Virginia Poe's bones and her untimely resurrection.

A Poe super fan by the name of William Gill—Eddie's first biographer and a man who tried to refute the slanders of Rufus Griswold—claimed to have rescued Virginia's bones from the Fordham Dutch Reformed Church, where she was first buried. The

Matthew Mercier

church was marked for demolition, including the adjoining cemetery. Gill claimed to be walking by just as they were digging up Virginia's grave.

Seriously. In the pre-DNA days, Gill looked at a shovel of remains and said, "That's Virginia Poe." Even nuttier, he claims to have taken the bones and stored them in an apple box under his bed for three years, until he was able to bring them to Baltimore to rest at Poe's side. Legend says not all the bones made it to Baltimore. After all, this was Annabel Lee herself, so who knows how many sickos paid Gill for a femur or rib. Some of those sickos might live here in The Bronx.

I imagine Gill thought he was being respectful by clinging to a box of yellow shards—after thirty years, how much could be left? —but hanging on to bones and bodies after their due date with the afterlife is just asking for karmic kickback.

"That story sounds a bit . . . apocryphal," I say.

"Maybe," Carla replies, "but the pervert had somebody's bones under his bed, so either way the spirits have got to be pissed off."

"You believe in spirits?"

"For sure. You?"

"I grew up in a haunted house. Corpses. Ghosts. The whole package."

"Us too. Spirits, not corpses. We live with our grandmother. She's a bruja and herbalist. I want to hear more about your haunted house."

"Maybe later."

Oscar slaps the table. "That's right. Time for you to get to work, Jonah. Let's see if you can fill Bradford's shoes."

Shade being thrown. Perfectly legit. But I volley with a pointed question. "So, what happened in the greenhouse? Bradford told me its haunted by a junkie who overdosed."

"Not an overdose. Forced withdrawal. Just as bad."

"So, the story is true?"

"Maybe. But don't worry about that. Poe's basement has enough stories."

And that's it from the vampire bodequas. They cut me off faster than a bartender on St. Patrick's Day, and we part ways outside the diner in the dusk of a late summer evening. The sodium streetlights make my gringo skin glow in the dark. I pass a flashy check-cashing joint with huge block letters in fire engine red, a hefty bruiser

Poe & I

sitting on a stool behind bullet-proof glass waiting to take my money and five percent. This is followed by a liquor store, an Off-Track Betting site, and finally a chapel of the Holy Redeemer Whatever.

This trifecta of tricky real estate is a conspiracy against the poor—money, booze, gambling, redemption. Wash, rinse, repeat. It's the same upstate. And when in Rome.

I buy a forty of Corona and pop into the OTB, place five dollars on Bamboo and Get Chipped, and five more on some newcomer named Beauty. Results flash across an ancient Zenith TV bolted to the wall. An old timer is slumped in the corner, clutching his tickets, scratching his neck. I leave before we can make friends and cross the Concourse with my beer, skipping religion and redemption. I once toyed with the idea of entering a Buddhist monastery, since it offered everything I wanted—peace, forgiveness, family—but I'm too earthy for a life of denial, and my brain is too noisy.

Poe's basement will have to do. For now.

On the corner of the Concourse is the cigarette hustler, who leans in as I pass. "Newports, Camels. What you need?"

"I'm good."

"You the new guy?"

I stop. He nods at the cottage. "For Poe."

"That's me."

"Welcome to the neighborhood, boss."

"Thank you."

"Bradford gone?"

"Yes. He left."

"Shame. You need anything let me know."

"I will."

I hustle down Kingsbridge, fumbling for my keys, forgetting which one fits the rear padlock. When I swing open the gate, I glance up at the corner. Mr. Newport is silhouetted under the streetlights, leaning on his cane, staring down at me.

Lock the gate and duck into my underground living room, cold and gray. Keep the lights off and perch beneath the window. The dealer stands with one hand on the fence, staring at the cottage, but with his other hand he tugs at the zipper on his pants, leans his head back, and pisses in Poe's park.

No sense in yelling. I let the man finish his business and start unpacking.

105

Matthew Mercier

Hang my clothes, stack my books, roll my socks, stock the kitchen with a little tea and granola bars. Been a while since I made house. I'll need pots and pans, soap and shampoo, ironing board and shirts.

The last item I remove from the duffel bag is wrapped in a Foxwoods sweatshirt. Unfurl it gently, and here is a little bit of the old Peabody homestead—a precious cache of handwritten letters and a Saturday night special. They fit perfectly in the bottom rack of the safe. I shut the door, spinning the dial.

The Society-issued laptop is brand new. Can't imagine it's cheap to hand these out to your employees, especially if you are on the financial ropes. I log on to the Wi-Fi. (Network: Raven101. Password: LiveBurial) and check my email. There, at the top, is a bright new message, with the subject line, *Welcome to Poe Cottage*. It has a historical society address, so I click, figuring it's from Cynthia.

Greetings Jonah Peabody,

Welcome to Poe Cottage. Or should I say, "Welcome to Oblivion." I hope you'll be with us for quite some time. Enjoy the following videos and know that you are, indeed, not alone.

Sincerely,

Grip

My heart jumps. This is a test.

"Grip" is a backhanded Poe reference. Grip was Charles Dickens's pet raven. He wrote the bird into his novel, *Barnaby Rudge*. Poe reviewed *Barnaby Rudge* as a mixed bag, not worthy of Dickens's talents. Soon after, Poe composed *The Raven*. Question is, did Poe steal the raven? Does anyone care? Fuck if I know. The takeaway is that Dickens's raven was often called Grip the Clever, Grip the Wicked, Grip the Knowing.

Scan the video for a virus, then click. Fuzzy electronic snow; cut to a static shot of the cottage from behind the front gate. There I am with my backpack, Bradford letting me in. Cut to a shot of Bradford and me leaving the cottage, then a long shot of me and Bradford and the vampire siblings all talking in the park. It's taken from behind the gazebo. Achebe walks over and tells us to leave. Cut.

I sit back on the loveseat. I don't remember anyone with a video camera pointed in our direction. I know some cellphones have a video feature now, but not this level of quality. It must be my "brother."

Poe & I

So, I write back.

Dear Grip,

Only cowards film people anonymously. Why don't you show yourself right now? I'll step onto the porch. Take your best shot . . . with a camera.

Not smart, provoking a troll, but it's better than twiddling my thumbs. I take my tea, exit through the shed, and walk round onto the front porch. The park is all locked up. Mr. Newport is gone. The Concourse is bustling with teenagers enjoying the last month of summer. I sit on the stoop and glance up at the sky. No stars. I miss stars. I think about Andromeda, how over the moon she'd be about my living in Poe's house. It's too poetic that a Peabody would end up here in Poe's basement. If she hadn't been my sister, if we hadn't come through the fire together, this job would not be possible.

Tears come fast now, blurring my vision. Run my hand across my face, gaze up and down the fence, my gated community of one. No Grip. Nothing. I wipe my face, go back inside, wait ten minutes, and check my email.

Dear Jonah,

Your tears are fake. What a phony. I can see I'll have to prove this to everyone.

Grip

Great. The asshole is playing games. I unlock the safe and retrieve my gun. Wait. Listen. Silence, pressing down on my head, curling my ears. I've camped in the wilderness, and I can tell you the forest is never truly quiet, day or night, but The Bronx—my city park— is still. No birds, no breeze. Only the ground rumbles, but I quickly realize it's the D train, far below.

As the evening wears on, my hearing grows sharper. The hum of the orange security lamps, the traffic light shunting from red to green to yellow to red again, and somewhere above me, the soft tinkling of wind chimes. My bones are brittle, wafer thin, and my chest hair is greasy. The air of the basement is a cornucopia of raw sewage, dried semen, burning cinders, rotten fruit.

To distract myself, I pull down Poe's collected works and start reading *Landor's Cottage,* an idealized portrait of the cottage itself. No plot—just static, boring, detailed prose that sits on the page and stares back at you. Beautiful, precise, and dull as dirt. Grains of sand slip under the jelly of my eyes.

Matthew Mercier

When I look up from reading, Mother is hunched in the doorway.

Stringy gray locks falling over her eyes, yellow nightgown burned full of holes. She's barefoot with cracked skin rimming her toes and purple spots dotting her legs. In her right hand, she grips the knife she carried into my bedroom that Halloween night.

"You're early," I say, body frozen on the loveseat. "Stay right there, Mother."

She sways side to side, humming, arching the small of her back to stare up at the ceiling, the curtain of hair falling back around her nostrils and red cracked lips.

My sleeping pills are still in the duffel. (I haven't told you about the pills yet, but Mother is why I take them.) My body is lead. "Stay there, Mother. Mother, don't. Please."

Her head snaps down; she growls, then descends onto her belly and begins creeping across the floor, knife out front, sniffing.

She's on me before I can move, her skeletal frame slithering up between my legs, the tip of the knife brushing the inside of my thigh. My entire body convulses, as if I'm having a seizure, and her slimy thumb pushes between my lips, trying to force open the brick wall of my clamped teeth.

"*Let me in,*" she croaks. "*Let. Me. In.*"

Warm foam gushes from her mouth, soaking my collarbone in saliva. She straddles me, and the knife is poised above my heart. With her left hand clamped around my chin, she pushes the blade slowly into my chest, an icicle of white-hot electricity, sinking it to the hilt.

The pain forces my mouth open, and she's able to slip her thumb inside.

She screams in triumph, a banshee wail that shatters my teacup on top of the Poe safe. Shards sprinkle across my head, landing inside my ear. Her thumb is growing longer, skinnier, a snake winding its way across my tongue, down my gullet. Her form is shrinking to a ribbon, ready to slip inside. My arms move through an invisible web of molasses as I reach for the knife and slowly extract it, a string of barb wire plucking and popping in the meat of my chest.

As I pull out the knife, Mother slips down my throat. I gag, but don't swallow, throw the knife down, and stumble into the bathroom, sticking a finger down my throat, retching the tail end

Poe & I

of her back up. I squeeze her between two fists, but she's slimy and wriggling, an eel coated in slime.

She slips through one fist, then the second, and when she drops into my throat, I moan, gasping for air, my chest burning.

My head swims and my stomach heaves. "Just like old times, Ma. Just like old times."

The doorbell rings.

A tourist? Now? Who? My head is a fog, Mother clouding my logic. I stumble out of the bathroom, unlock the safe, take out my gun. Upstairs the front door bangs open, and the whole cottage shudders as somebody enters the museum.

I walk out into the shed, to the bottom of the museum steps. Breathe. Listen.

"Grip?" I shout, with a throat full of Mother phlegm. "Show your face, coward."

Silence. I pull over an empty five-gallon bucket, turn it over, and sit, waiting for the museum door to open. Ridiculous. What am I going to do? Shoot somebody on my first night?

Twenty, thirty minutes go by. My head grows heavy. How long can I stay out here? All night if I have to. My job is to protect the museum. No, first job is to protect myself, but . . . if Mother is going to show up before the sun goes down . . . I stick a finger down my throat, trying to throw her back up, but I'm dry. She's deep inside. I lean my head against the stone wall, gun between my knees. Breathe. My name is Jonah Peabody, and everything will be fine.

The cottage shudders as the front door slams. I leap up, shaking the sleep from my eyes. The shed is empty. I'm still here. No Mother. How long was I out? I scoot over to the shed peephole, hoping to catch a glimpse of my intruder, but there is nobody on the front walk. The gate is locked.

I take the basement steps one at a time. My unpacked duffel rests in the middle of the floor. Out come the sleeping pills. These are my best shot now. I bend over the toilet one more time, attempt to puke Mother out, but nothing. I draw a cloudy glass of Bronx water from the tap, pop a pill, and then with the gun by my side, settle onto the loveseat and wait for blissful oblivion.

Matthew Mercier

Gray daylight. Limbs stiff. Gun between the cushions.

I open the window. Sparrows and squirrels skittering past the screen. On the corner, a small crowd waiting for the bus. All systems normal. In the bathroom, cold water splashed over my face, then I retch into the toilet, expunging the night's demons. I feel my chest for holes. Mother is gone, for now.

A baseball hat pressed over my uncombed mop top, I take a breath and climb the steps into the shed, glance out the peephole, and crack open the door.

At my feet sits a tiny cream-colored vase of purple flowers.

The flowers are tiny feather dusters—u-shaped petals bunched together on the stem, four to a rung. A gray envelope is tucked underneath the vase. It reads:

Poe House Caretaker.

I pick up the vase. Dust shoots into my nostrils. Coughing, snorting, dropping the vase. It shatters on the flagstones. Pressing a finger to my nose, blowing a snot rocket into the shrubs, wiping my upper lip, grabbing the envelope, and falling back into the shed. In the kitchen, hacking and spiting into the sink, digging into the supply cabinet for a box of latex gloves. My brain swells with *stupid, stupid, stupid*.

Once it's clear I'm not having a heart attack, I pull on the gloves, tie a napkin around my face, grab a steak knife, sit at the table, and slice open the envelope.

A note card falls out. Typed symbols.

t o*;;(? S;48(
WW

I stare at them for a good long while then stick the note cards in my collected tales and take the ship's ladder up into the museum. Bronze Poe glowers at me.

"Quite a night, Edgar." I pull open the curtains.

There's a man at the front gate, snapping photos. He grabs the padlock and shakes it, staring at the cottage as if it's broken his heart. My first tourist. But it's not time yet. He'll need to come back. I unlock the porch door and swing it open hard.

Another envelope falls to my feet.

Same cream-colored paper as the first. I pull my sleeve out to cover my fingers and pick it up, heart galloping. The shutterbug tourist shouts at me above the traffic.

"Sir? Are you open?"

Poe & I

I suck in my gut and stroll to the end of the porch. "We'll be open in two hours."

He wrinkles his Poindexter glasses, looks me up and down, then points to his upper lip. "You have something. Here."

I flinch, dabbing at my face. White powder. From the flowers. Crap. Just once in my life I want to start a job off on the right foot. Guess Poe's not the winner. Back away, run into the museum, slam the delicate 19th century door.

Downstairs, the mirror shows me white powder smeared on my upper lip. Jesus. As if I'm snorting lines. I wipe away the evidence, rub my skin raw, go back to the shed, and collect the shards of the vase, picking up the flowers. No trace of powder on the petals. I drop the flowers in a coffee cup, fill it with tap water, and set it on the window ledge in my parlor. I wash my face a second time, then slice the seal of the second envelope.

UOW885t8^;
;6M8;+(8$5Y

It's too much. I can't play these games on my first day. My third eye grows puffy with heat. I place the second note card in my book with the first, then punish myself with a Marine Corps shower— thirty seconds, arctic cold.

Getting dressed, I play it conservative. Jeans, whitened sneakers, and a tight-fitting navy-blue dress shirt. Respectable. For me. Before I open the gate, I patrol the exterior of the cottage. No more flowers or letters, just bags of dog shit and a new plague of scattered newspapers.

On Valentine, the drug marketplace is in full tilt boogie, a cluster of zombies bottlenecked beneath the Mormon church, twisted handshakes between dealer and fiend. No sign of Mr. Newport.

I grab a watery cup of coffee across the street and then, at ten o'clock, I unlock the gates, open the windows, snap in the screens, drag a metal folding chair onto the front porch, and take out Poe's Complete Tales, trying to look normal. I decide to give *Landor's Cottage* another shot, but it's just as dull in the daytime. Listen to this passage.

"As regards vegetation, as well as in respect to everything else, the scene softened and sloped to the south. To the north—on the craggy precipice—a few paces from the verge—up sprang the magnificent trunks of numerous hickories, black walnuts and

Matthew Mercier

*chestnuts, interspersed with occasional oak; and the strong
lateral branches thrown out by the walnuts especially, spread far
over the edge of the cliff. Proceeding southwardly . . . "*

I gaze over the porch railing, due south—the sloping south—
and read the passage again. After a minute, I think, 'Okay, Eddie.
I know what you were trying to do. Replicate a lost time, detail for
detail.' From this porch in the 19th century, you could see the
shimmer of Long Island Sound. The park was an apple orchard.
The Bronx River, a gurgling crystal vein. Now, if you glance south,
all you see are gray tenements and the clusterfuck circus of
Fordham Center.

If visitors ask about *Landor's Cottage* I'll tell them it's not a
story. It's a sketch. A painting. Poe was trying to preserve his home
and the landscape with language, as if he knew all those rivers and
apple orchards would be paved over, so he wanted to describe
everything. Literary preservation. How's that for analysis? Who
needs an English class?

Lizzie at the front gate, hair in pigtails, and the shutterbug
walking up behind her. Both are carrying backpacks. Lizzie's face
is sharp, green eyes drilling into me.

"Poe Junior. You have your first guest."

The shutterbug purses his lips. "Parlez-vous français?"

"Uh, sorry. No."

"C'est dommage. Je suis un Baudelaire érudite."

I look at Lizzie. "You speak French?"

"You're on your own, Junior."

Great. The French love Poe, but parley vooing wasn't in the job
description. The man looks around the cottage, disappointment
melting his face, as if to say, "This is it, you ugly American? I flew
across an ocean to see this dumpy, little home?"

"How'd you sleep?" Lizzie asks. "Let me guess. Not well."

"Correct."

"First night is always rough."

"Did you—?"

"Don't talk to me. Give this man a tour. He might not
understand everything, but I want to hear you."

Poe's life crumples in my mouth. Screwed up dates, misquoted
poetry. All the material I'd read that summer vanishes like SAT
words, and every time I mess up, Lizzie corrects me with a snap of
the fingers and a click of the tongue.

Poe & I

Nope, sorry pal, Poe was not born in Richmond. That honor belongs to Boston. He went to live in Richmond with his benefactors John and Fanny Allan.

Have to stop you again, Jonah. Poe did not get discharged from West Point by showing up naked to drills. That's a myth. One of many.

Are you crazy? Poe didn't vote Democrat! He was a Whig, if he had any politics at all. Remember, he was raised in the South.

Her brain is so crammed with Poe factoids she can barely get one out of her mouth before the next one crashes into it. She challenges everything I say with leading questions. Do you really feel that Poe is a great writer, given his penchant for operatic purple prose? Don't you think there are better poets from the period? Don't you feel that his popularity is really what keeps his work alive and not so much the quality of it?

After I fail to remember the name of Poe's cat (Catterina, for the record), she sighs. "Do you know anything about Poe's blank period?" She's rubbing the balled end of her left pigtail.

"Blank period?"

"Poe went missing for a few years. Completely vanishes from the biographical record." She arches an eyebrow. "I think he was spying for France."

"Really?"

"Yes. We have letters and correspondence. That's what Cynthia was looking at when you came in for your interview. A letter from Alexander Dumas. Even if it's not true, there's enough evidence to spark the imagination."

"If he spied for the French, wouldn't the biographies cover it?"

"It's all there. Read between the lines. So, look, obviously your docent rap sucks. Don't worry. I won't tell Cynthia you flunked. Not yet."

I'm standing behind the velvet rope, inside the parlor exhibit, with my back to the window, trying to conjure a snappy comeback, when she glances over my shoulder and says, "What's that guy doing?"

I turn, see nothing. "Who?"

"He went behind the house. He had a cane."

I unhook the rope and stalk out to the porch in time to meet Mr. Newport as he limps around the flowerbeds. A patchwork of

Matthew Mercier

scars and stitches mar his left cheek, which the darkness had concealed. The other cheek is smooth and tight.

"Yo! Can I get a tour?"

"Just started one, chief."

"Three dollars, right? Let's see if you're as good as Bradford." He sports ragged jeans and a baggy sweatshirt that falls past his waist. He takes off his baseball cap—a shaved head the color of a bruised peach—and slips a fiver in the donation box. "Keep the change. I support the cause."

In the parlor, Lizzie and the frog say nothing but look at me as if I've made the wrong choice by inviting Newport inside.

"We're going upstairs," Lizzie says. "To watch the video. But Jonah . . ."

"Upstairs?" Newport frowns. "That might be trouble for my leg."

"I have to cue up the video for these two," I say. "Hang tight, pal. I'll be right back."

Lizzie beckons me into the hallway as Frenchie creaks his way up the staircase. "We have a problem," she says, pointing to the wall.

The "Ultima Thule" portrait is gone. In its place, a dull head of a nail pokes through the crumbling plaster.

And where the portrait should be hanging is a single word, faintly written.

Oblivion

That's it. I'm sunk. Eighty-sixed. Canned. Booted. Less than twenty-four hours into my new job, and I've been burgled and vandalized.

"What happened?" she asks.

"I . . . somebody was here last night."

"Somebody broke into the cottage?"

"Yes. I think so. I mean, yes. I noticed the motion sensor going crazy on the porch, but . . ."

"Why didn't you call the police?"

"They seemed to let themselves in. As if they had a key." The events of the evening play over and over in my head, and the emails are blaring loudly. You are not alone. You are being watched. Your tears are fake.

"I'm sorry, Lizzie."

"You've gone pale."

114

Poe & I

"I'm fine," I lie, even as the room tilts, side to side, the deck of a ship.

"I'll start the video upstairs. You stay here."

Mr. Newport is standing at the front window, texting.

"So, you're a Poe fan?" I ask.

He concentrates on his phone.

"I'm Jonah."

"Like the Bible," Newport says, looking up. "My name's Alabama."

"Like the state."

"Like me."

"Alabama. You got it."

"So, where Bradford at now?"

"I don't know."

He snaps his phone shut. "He just moved out?"

"Moved out and moved on. You knew him? Do you live nearby?"

Alabama sighs, as if admitting guilt. "Most of my life."

I roll into my Poe talk, but he keeps sneaking glances out the window. "You waiting on a friend?"

He shakes his head and glances around the parlor. "This old stuff worth anything?"

"Not a dime. All reproduction."

"You mean fake?"

"Yes."

We make small talk, and soon enough, the ceiling creaks, and Lizzie and the frog descend, entering the parlor.

"Maybe I'll check out that video now," Alabama says.

"What about the stairs?"

"I'll take it slow."

Then, the universe gives me one of those moments when everything happens at the same time.

The front doorbell rings. Alabama's cell phone blares loudly—some familiar hip-hop tune—as he takes the stairs, favoring his right leg. I run up to rewind the video, leaving him there, then go back down. Lizzie and Frenchie are in the gift shop, the front doorbell shrieking.

I'm hot, dizzy, my throat parched. On the porch is the blistered face of a disheveled woman, dressed in a stained windbreaker and sweatpants.

Matthew Mercier

"Dónde está? Dónde está?"

"Ma'am, slow down. I can't."

She glares inside the cottage. "Dónde está?"

Lizzie says, "She's looking for somebody."

"Old man, shit face," the woman hisses. "You seen him?"

"Older man?"

"Yes, papi! Dude with a cane!"

Lizzie jerks her eyebrows at me. Your call, not mine. She turns back to the gift shop.

Maybe Alabama stiffed her. Maybe she's a jilted girlfriend or a needy customer, or a long-lost sister. I don't know and don't care. But I do know I'm no snitch. Bet on that. So calmly—and with sincere regret—I tell her, yes, I've seen a man with a cane.

"Headed east. Over the Concourse. Toward St. James Park."

The woman bolts off the porch and through the gate. Her urgent shuffling, the desperate look in her eye, makes me wonder if I've done the right thing.

Frenchie, who's watched the whole display, holds up a facsimile of *The Raven*.

"How much?"

"Five dollars."

Lizzie wanders back into the parlor as Frenchie pays, shakes my hand, and says in broken English, "Good night, thanks for it," before scooting off without another word.

"You know," I say to Lizzie, "we could stand to have these exhibits translated. Spanish, at the very least."

"I've been telling Cynthia that for years. Did anything happen last night? You really don't look good."

"I . . . got some flowers."

"Flowers?"

"And I think I inhaled something."

"There's a walk-in clinic down the block on Bainbridge. Go see a doctor named Rosen. He should be able to help you. Listen, I'll be here tomorrow with Lloyd Mason and Cynthia. They both want to hear your rap."

"Fine. I'll be on my game."

"You're a work in progress, that's for sure."

Alabama wanders into the parlor, as Lizzie leaves out the front gate.

"What she tell you?" he asks.

Poe & I

"Who? Lizzie?"

"No, that crazy ass ugly."

Deaf and dumb, I shake my head.

"That wrinkled little woman! Uglies always want me on pay day! First of the month, I get my money, and right away the uglies are sniffing 'round looking for a handout."

"Your money?"

He taps his right leg. "Disability. Vets pay."

"Iraq?"

"Yup."

"You just return?"

"Nah, buddy. Not the sequel. Part one." He taps the ripped and damaged flesh of his left cheek. "That's where I got my Two-Face mask. Gots to get myself up to the VA today. Catch a bus before that woman comes back." He peers out the curtains. "What you say to her?"

"That I saw you headed to St. James."

He chuckles. "My man."

"You're welcome."

"You got a pretty good job here. Wish I could get one like it."

"It's not as easy as it looks."

"I bet. Be seeing you round." We shake hands and he limps out the front gate, cane clicking on the pavement.

I deadbolt the door and let out a breath, unlock the money box, and count the day's take. A whopping thirteen dollars.

I snap off lights and shut the windows. Despite my third-stringer performance, I tell myself I held it together, that I calmed down enough to keep my third eye under control, and that tomorrow will be better. Tomorrow my tour will be sharper, more informative. Tomorrow I'll make twenty-six dollars. And I'll meet more people from the neighborhood, build my ambassadorship. If this job goes well, who knows where it will take me? A genuine reference on the resume—something that isn't fiction—might really turn the page.

I get swept up in this tide of good feeling until I return to the basement, and there is Mother on the loveseat, hyperventilating and rubbing her bare arms. She reeks of bile and vomit, and her teeth clack so loudly I'm sure her jaw will snap off. Her belly is distended, and her skin appears rubbed raw with the gray ash of a firepit.

My own chest heaves with a decade's worth of pent-up tears. I

Matthew Mercier

hate seeing her this way, and I want to give her peace, I truly do, but then she looks at me with that horrible childlike need, and all I want are my sleeping pills so I can say good night.

I grab my sleeping bag and pad, but she slinks off the loveseat and grabs my arm, an icy hot grip, her fingers burning my wrist. She screams my name and digs her fingernails into my veins, but I'm able to drag her to the door of the apartment and then, when I reach the stairs of the shed, her fingers loosen, and I slip free.

Up the stairs two by two and into the shed, I turn, and there she stands at the bottom of the steps, unwilling—or unable—to come any further, her gray hands rubbing the doorframe, staring up at me through her tangled mop of hair. She falls to her knees and begins to weep, uttering my name over and over.

Jonah, stay with me. Jonah, Please. Stay with me, Jonah.

This is the worst it's ever been. Over the years, we've developed a pattern. She tries to climb inside; I fight her off. Sometimes she wins, and I have to vomit her out later, but I've never seen her this obsessed, this desperate. Something about Poe's house has turned up the volume.

"I'm sorry, Mother. I'm going to sleep upstairs with Poe. I can't tonight. I'm sorry."

I retreat to the parlor and bed down beneath the bronze bust, her wails invading my dreams, until the pill scrubs me clean.

Chapter 12

Last Night

"It's blood," Andy said, "but I don't think it's hers."

Mother lifted a finger and rubbed the dark spots on her cheek, chewing her pork chop with her mouth open, smacking her lips.

Father glanced out at the Subaru, stood, and left the kitchen. Andy rubbed Mother's hand, but Mother batted her away, even as Andy whispered soothing nonsense. We ate in horrible silence, until the old man came back inside and pulled his chair close to Mother.

"Pamela?"

At the sound of her first name, Mother's neck twitched. Father rubbed his mustache and took his wife's hand. "Pamela. You have to tell me what happened."

She patted the inside of his arm, smiled, hummed. Silly boy. Don't worry about it.

That casual gesture sent Father pacing around the house, whimpering, a stressed-out dog. "It's going to be okay. We're going to be okay." Whatever fiction he was telling himself would soon be obscured by fact—cold, hard, irrefutable, public fact. Mother was guilty. But of what? Did Father keep pushing for a confession? I don't think so. Did my sister offer to wash the blood off Mother's face? Or did Father ask my sister to wash Mother's face? Did Andromeda then refuse? I think he may have asked me, and I refused.

That's a more believable version since I wanted Mother to get caught, both for her sake and mine.

Did Andromeda get Mother to strip off her clothes? Did Father

119

Matthew Mercier

then do a load of laundry? Did Mother take a shower? All I know for sure is that Mother began wailing, a high-pitched keening that split me down the middle and shattered all remaining hope we held out for being a normal family. The cosmic terrors of Cthulhu can't compare to my father's shuffling mummers or Mother's primal cries. Maybe she realized what she'd done and knew her brief time with us was, effectively, over.

Detectives showed up in the morning. Here's what they pieced together.

Mother had been shopping at our local supermarket, which was built up against a creek, the whole store crammed into a triangle of woods and pavement. She'd parked at the edge of the lot, almost behind the building, where the trucks turned in to make their deliveries, the creek gurgling right below. Given the load of groceries she bought, Mother was asked if she wanted assistance getting to her car. She declined the offer, and I often wonder what might have happened if those minimum-wage bag boys had insisted on helping, but instead they sent her out to the car alone, where she began dropping avocados and grapefruit on the pavement.

A woman pulled into the spot next to her, saw Mother struggling, and approached from behind to see if she could help. She placed a hand on Mother's shoulder. Mother, startled, grabbed a tire iron from the trunk and cracked the stranger over the head. The poor lady fell against her own car, staggered, and dropped onto the brown slope of earth that lay between the parking lot and the creek. Mother stood over the slope for a moment, staring at the woman, threw the tire iron back in the trunk, finished loading up, and drove home.

It took far too long for the woman's body to be discovered on that slope. She'd fallen just out of view and bled to death from her head wound. A delivery person eventually spotted her, and security cameras told the rest of the story in addition to capturing the Subaru's plates.

The detectives found the tire iron in our house. Father had removed it from the car. I don't remember if he volunteered the murder weapon or not, but I think, with all that puttering around the night before, he'd been weighing his options. Turn his wife in? Or try to cover it all up? The detectives interviewed my father, who told them Mother had come home last night and acted as if nothing

Poe & I

was wrong, which was the truth. But that truth set nobody free, and the detectives then interviewed Mother, who sat on the couch, a wrinkled sprout of a woman, withering under the questions put to her. The detectives were kind and calm, unlike the brash TV cops pop culture was obsessed with. Even the perp walk to the squad car was quiet, although Mother did shake and tremble and cry softly as they put the handcuffs on her.

The social contract dictates that I should have been screaming "Don't take my mommy!' and bawling my eyes out. Whatever tears came that cold morning, came from knowing that if I didn't cry, it would look strange. So, I turned down my mouth and did my best sad face. And I was sad, just not the right type of sad. I was sad for my family, sad for Father, sad for Andy, who was standing next to me on the porch, her eyes steely but her chin bunched into a cauliflower. She wasn't going to fake tears. Or spill real ones.

Mother's trial lasted a hot minute, open and shut with the insanity plea. Off she went to a hospital, one for bad crazies. Now, the Crazy Peabodys were legally crazy.

At school, Andy and I were shunned outright, and since our status had been low to begin with, it was like being kicked out of a bottomless well. We drifted in an aimless orbit. Andy's only friend, Clarissa, stayed loyal but also got pregnant and dropped out to have the baby. On my end, Chad and Stacy avoided me in the woods, and Mike Murray kept me at a healthy distance, although perverse curiosity about the crime made for a few weird conversations. Most kids were now truly afraid of us.

Can't say I blamed them. Andy and I skipped school on a regular basis. Andy's art teacher kept pushing the idea of Pratt down in the city, but even her enthusiasm dimmed, although she pretended not to give up. The woman had a savior complex and wanted to protect Andy and me from our future, which seemed to have turned pitch black. Counselors told us we were not murderers—but I didn't buy it. We may as well have bludgeoned that woman ourselves, the whole Peabody family.

Because we knew. My father knew.

He knew Mother was dangerous. He knew since the first Halloween night when she'd tried to slice me up in my own bed. And, if he knew she was dangerous, if he knew her brain was rotten, if he knew and thought one little stint in the loony bin would heal that rot and scab it over with a rainbow ribbon, if he

Matthew Mercier

knew all that and still brought her back into the waking world, then we were responsible and deserved everything that followed.

Once it was discovered that Mother had been in the loony bin before, the family of the victim sued us, but when they couldn't prove any previous violent behavior, the case was thrown out. In my imagination, I testified against Mother. Yes, your honor. She tried to murder me. She needs to be taken off the streets.

After Mother was shipped off, the victim's family moved away. Andy asked Father if we could move away, but Father said that was impossible financially. He couldn't just start a funeral parlor in the next town over or in another state. No, we had to stay. We were trapped. Game over.

I cried now on a regular basis. Andy kept calling me a baby and said I needed to toughen up, but it all seemed so hopeless. The bullying turned brutal. Jason and his crew now had a lifetime of material. They once cornered me out behind the bleachers and burned a cigarette in my back. When Father tried to get Jason arrested, nobody would listen to the old man, as if Mother's crime had wiped away our right to be safe. And once the bullies got driver's licenses, their territory expanded.

A red pickup began driving past our house at night, and more than a few times we found it idling in the pull-off across the street as we headed to school in the morning. And then we'd see it parked outside the school or in the grocery store parking lot or trailing behind us as we rode out to collect a body. Finally, a crew of boys followed Andy home in broad daylight, and one stood in the bed of the pickup and threatened her with a crowbar, but Andy just went inside and got Father's shotgun, which she only knew how to hold, not shoot; but the punks didn't know that.

"We'll be back, you skanky bitch! We're going to kill you and your creepy brother!"

"You fuckers are such clichés!" Andy shouted, which confused them.

Then came the death threats. The answering machines both at the parlor and at home filled up with such ditties as "We're going to rid the world of your diseased blood." "You necro fuckers have fucked your last dead body." "We're going to firebomb you, corpse lovers."

The tires on the Ghostbusters hearse got slashed on the regular. Business at the parlor dropped off, although it would

Poe & I

eventually go back up. Death, as Father often said, was great job security. We asked about switching schools, begged and pleaded. We feared for our safety, and the admin people listened with a sympathetic ear, but nothing was done.

Andy continued to skip school. She filled up her days with drawing and writing and working at the parlor. She could barely tolerate the old man, but she understood, as always, that the family business was keeping us afloat, so she and Father had brokered a rough peace. He didn't force her to go to school every day, and she learned the ins and outs of coffins and burials. She was biding her time, she told me, waiting until she was old enough to escape.

When I got home, I'd find her alone in the house, with the day's sketches littered on her bed. She still drew her precious monsters and dragons, but one afternoon I walked in and found her sketching a man—double chin, reddened cheeks, worried forehead, eyes closed.

"A regular human," I said, "that's new."

She lifted her charcoal pencil off the pad, considering her work. "His name was John Monaco." She picked up her purple pencil and colored the tip of his nose.

"Alcoholic. Died from cirrhosis of the liver."

"Monaco?" I'd seen that name in the obituaries and among our invoices. "You drew a body? A client?"

She shrugged, sketching the wispy contrails of John Monaco's receding hairline.

(Or, receded. His growing days were over.)

"Is that legal?"

She gave John a few liver spots on his cheek. "I was alone with him this afternoon, so I made a quick sketch and committed the rest to memory. No biggie. I think I'm going to write a book about the dead. Pictures of the bodies and stories to go with them."

"Does Dad know?"

She nodded. "He was there. Son of a bitch actually encouraged it."

So, Andy started collecting faces. Gray-haired elders who'd lived through the Great Depression. Strung-out tweakers in their twenties who'd barely gotten started.

Young women murdered by their boyfriends. Women murdered by their husbands. Husbands murdered by their wives, who'd taken up arms in order to prevent their own murders. Drunk

Matthew Mercier

driving accidents. Drunk hunting accidents. Drunk drownings. Drunk cocaine overdoses. Heart attacks. Cancer. A bear mauling. Lung infections. Bad luck.

And, as promised, she also wrote stories to accompany the bodies, giving everyone happy endings with fantastical detail. Sometimes, she told me that she'd fallen in love with the body of a young man or woman, the way the Prince fell for a comatose Snow White.

"Gross," I shuddered. "You fall in love?"

"I don't kiss them, stupid. I just draw them. I love them from a distance."

"It's still nasty."

"No. It's a celebration."

This project took her further away from school. What use did she have for history or science? She was doing what she wanted. Why change that? Mrs. Carol, the art lady, always asked about Andy, and of course the admin officials asked, too, since legally they needed her to return to school, pronto. Plus, it was junior year, when everyone's sphincters were wrapped tight trying to impress colleges with their fabulous grades.

"I'll go when I feel like it," Andy said. "And I'll graduate. But only so they leave me alone."

Andromeda chose when to be visible or invisible. (News flash: She preferred invisible, on her own terms.) School, she told me, during one of our walks in the graveyard, was too much of a wild card. She couldn't control the environment. School would drive her crazy and now that medical crazy was on the table—now that either of us could inherit mother's illness—we had to avoid stressful environments.

"Stress is what drove Mother over the edge," she explained. "I'm convinced of it. And if I have to be at that school more than necessary, I'll be pushed over the edge. I might just . . . if Jason comes near me again . . . "

I finished the dark thought for her. "You'll murder him."

She rubbed my back. "And a few of the teachers as well."

The isolation of our new life had brought us back together, returned us to the same wavelength, and allowed us to finish each other's sentences. We resumed our walks in the graveyard.

"It's you and me against the world, bro. Everyone in authority is watching us closely."

Poe & I

"The principles," I said.

"Guidance counselors. Teachers."

"All the people."

"Who didn't give a shit before."

"Now they're just waiting for us to snap."

"Precisely." Andy lingered in the shadow of the Hoover mausoleum and leaned on the precarious tombstone of Richard Hoover, the child murderer, whose marker leaned at a forty-five-degree angle. She spat on the stone, pressed her boot over his name, and pushed. The stone shifted, then I kicked it too, and Richard the pervert toppled into a bed of Kentucky bluegrass, where as far as I know he still lies, overgrown and forgotten.

"You know, Jonah, when Mother was living with us, she told me a lot of stories about herself. You know she wanted to be an artist?"

"Well, I wanted a Mother."

"Stop it."

"We didn't have one anyway."

"I know you got the short end of the stick, bro."

"What other big secrets did she reveal?"

"That someday a man would come and try and steal me away. That he would look at my face and . . . and see her face."

My heart jumped. "Dad? Are you talking about Dad?"

"Have you noticed how he looks at me?"

"Jesus. Andy."

"You know I lock my door at night?"

"We should call somebody."

"It's under control. If he touches me, it will be a good excuse to fight back. You'll be my witness."

She was not exaggerating. If the worrywarts and busybodies wanted to worry, they didn't need to look at us—look at Father, you morons. But no. Andy and I were the ticking time bombs, with Andy being their primary concern. They claimed she was already showing early signs of a breakdown.

The first so-called "sign" was that her schoolwork went completely off the rails.

What's the saying? For each and every action, there is an equal and opposite reaction.

Well, for every class assignment, Andy performed an equal and opposite reassignment. If Miss Levanto, our history teacher, asked us to write a paper on the American Revolution, Andy would write

Matthew Mercier

one on the French Revolution, which she said was far more interesting, plus there was a musical about it. In art class, if asked to draw a still life, she'd insert trolls or fairies peeking out from behind the apples and pears.

But my favorite was her reactionary reassignments for English class. She still refused to read *The Scarlett Letter* and instead wrote how Clive Barker's *The Hellbound Heart* was just as religious as Hawthorne, since both stories believed in an afterlife and devils. She enjoyed *Macbeth* but wrote a paper defending the witches ("They're not evil. They're just telling Macbeth what he wants to hear.") She did write a paper on *The Catcher in the Rye* but titled it *Why I Hate Catcher in the Rye*. ("Holden is an entitled little rich boy who should have killed himself and spared us two hundred pages of self-pity.")

She barely passed most of her classes, for simply not doing the work she was asked to do, and when she did do extra work, nobody gave her extra credit, although the English teacher, Mr. Sullivan, admitted to my father that Andy was some kind of a genius—case in point when they discussed Edgar Allan Poe.

Andy turned in a paper about how our Mother was Madeline Usher and how Poe's bleak vision of the universe was more comforting to her than Catholicism since it was far more honest. Mr. Sullivan told Father he was torn between recommending Andy to a special school for the gifted or to a shrink.

To make matters worse, Andy stopped shaving her armpits and plucking her mustache. She let her black hair grow knotted and curly. She started wearing suit jackets again and dealt pot on the side to make money. A lot of pot. Our clueless guidance counselor didn't know about the drugs and was more concerned with Andy wearing men's clothes, so my sister kept dressing like a boy to distract from the weed.

As high school marched on, we marched backward and accepted our fate as townies, eccentric shut-ins with no hope of escaping the Catskills. We rode with Vince to collect bodies. Andy worked on her book of the dead, I decorated my arms with tiny smiles and Xs, and Mother faded into the background—until one sunny day in April, when I came home to find Andy sitting on the porch, soaking up the spring sunlight.

She wore black jean shorts, construction boots, and a ripped flannel shirt. Her freckled collarbone was burned pink, and her

Poe & I

frizzy hair was bunched in an unruly ponytail. Her arms and shoulders had grown thick with muscle from all the coffin lifting, and her white, meaty legs could easily kick down a door. Her weight was what mean girls teased her about, but for me, it's what made her so pretty. And, God help me, with her sloped nose and shadowed eyes, she did look like Mother.

"Hey, bro!" She bounced one leg over a scabby knee. "You're just in time." She whipped out a driver's license.

"You passed?" I shouted.

"The only test worth taking! Let's go for a ride." She held up the keys to the Ghostbusters hearse.

"I have a science project."

"You got all weekend. Come on. We need to get out of this house."

True that. So, we piled into the hearse, its dashboard covered in soda cans, invoices, and old cigarette boxes. The engine coughed and hacked as my sister slowly backed us out of the driveway and onto the country road, cruising through silent, green woods. When we passed our neighbors' houses, I slunk down in my shotgun seat, afraid to be seen, but the Ghostbusters hearse would be recognized anywhere, so I gave that up and turned on the radio, blasting Guns N' Roses, AC/DC, and Twisted Sister. Andromeda turned onto a mountain road and began driving us into the sun. I leaned back on the cracked leather seat. The warm light made me drowsy, and the world curved away beneath us as we drove higher and higher. The homes up here—weekend spots for city folk—started to get bigger, fancier, richer.

"If they keep building like this, we're going to lose our nice, dark mountain," she mumbled.

We reached a lookout point, and she pulled over. From up here, we could see the grim chessboard of the graveyard, Chad and Stacy's humble box of a house, the trailer park and the power lines, the Hudson River, the lumps of the Taconic hills on the Massachusetts border. Our world, I thought, was so small.

"I can't believe Dad never drove us up here," I said.

"He did. Once. You were little. It was Mom's idea."

Andy leaned over the steering wheel, and my heart skipped. There was a spot of blood at the corner of her mouth.

She caught me staring. "Lipstick," she said. "Thought I'd try it out. Wasn't for me. The color, I mean. I'm sticking with black."

Matthew Mercier

"You bought lipstick?"

"Hell no. I got it in Mom's room. Dad still hasn't emptied it out."

I stepped from the hearse and sat on the hood, trying to imprint the view on my memory. For some reason, I thought I'd never see it again. Andy sat next to me, took out her license, and kept running her thumb over it. For the picture, she'd let her hair down and fluffed it up around her ears, bulging her eyes.

"This," she tapped the license, "means freedom."

Next year, she'd be a so-called senior. She'd already been held back once and was now limping across the finish line, just to get that damn diploma, but she was saving up money and making plans.

"So, you're leaving?"

She put freedom in her pocket. "Not yet, buddy. My work here isn't done yet." She scratched the back of my neck. "First, I'm going to go visit Mom. You want to come with me?"

"No."

"She can't hurt you in there."

The minute she said this, she looked as though she wanted to swallow her tongue.

"How do you mean?"

"She's probably all drugged up."

"No, I mean, why tell me that she can't hurt me?"

Andy shook her head and kept rubbing my neck.

"Sis, that Halloween night. When she came into my room."

"Told you, Jonah. I think you were dreaming that."

Protecting me. Even now. I rolled up my sleeves, my arms a constellation of scars. Her eyes grew wet. "You need to stop that, baby."

"Stop calling me baby. It feels good."

She grabbed me by the wrists. "Sex feels good. This"— she kissed my scars and rubbed them—"is just the devil talking."

"You don't believe in the devil."

"Sure, I do. Please stop cutting. For me."

"I'll try."

"Listen," she said. "There's something else." She hopped off the hood and strode to the edge of the lookout. "Those kids in the red pickup."

She trailed off, finding a cloud to look at instead of finishing her thought, then wiggled her pinkie. "Remember our promise."

Poe & I

I held up my pinkie and roped it around hers, our old scars kissing.

"Promise me if somebody hurts either of us," she said, "the other will take revenge."

"Revenge?"

"Swear it, Jonah."

My pinkie pulled against hers, ready to snap like a wishbone. "If someone hurts you, Andy, I'll take revenge."

"If someone hurts you, Jonah, I'll take revenge."

"I love you, sis."

"I love you, bro."

"So," I said. "The red pickup?"

She rolled her tongue and tapped the hood. "I'll show you. Back home."

We took a circular route back to the homestead since Andy wanted to buy art supplies in town. Between school, working at the parlor, and drawing, her whole life was now dead bodies and artwork and escape. She was saving up for a car. She was looking into art schools. She was determined to get out.

Then, we drove past the parlor. The parking lot was full. Calling hours. Nothing strange about that, except there was the red pickup, dented and rusty, standing out among all the polished black and brown sedans.

On the steps of the parlor stood a group of five men and one woman. The woman held the hand of a young boy. As we drove by, they glanced up, and Andy swore under her breath, pressed gently on the gas pedal, and quickly drove us to the dead end, a circle of hemlock and white pine. As she swung the hearse in a wide arc, she said, "Don't make eye contact. I thought they'd be inside. Shit, shit."

"Andy, who?"

"Be quiet."

On our second pass, I tried to make out details, but the only thing I noticed was that the young boy had red hair, and the adults glared at us.

"This was a mistake. Shit, shit. Okay. We're okay. Shit."

Back in the safety of her bedroom, Andy flipped to her latest drawing, the body who'd just been delivered to the parlor. Young. Square jaw, fresh blond hair, sharp cheekbones, pinched nose. Andy's chin crunched into that familiar cauliflower shape, which meant she was holding back tears.

Matthew Mercier

"This is the son. The oldest son."

"The son of who?"

"The woman." She now broke down and wept. Understand, this never happened. My sister was made of steel. She never cried, so to see her weep over a stranger's death was unreal. "The woman that mom killed. This is her son. The one who drove the pickup."

"Wait. That's who the wake is for? Right now?"

Andy nodded.

Let that sink in. The kid in the pickup, who stalked us, was the son of the woman that our mother had killed. And now he was dead. Now his body was in our funeral parlor.

"He shot himself," Andy said. "Dad had to stitch his head back together. He . . . " She cut herself off and gripped my chin. "Jonah, if I go down the same road as Mother, you have to promise me." She grabbed both sides of my face. "If I crack up and lose it and go mental, I want you to shoot me."

I wanted to say, 'You're acting pretty mental right now,' but then she let me go and picked up her drawing.

"Vince and I got a call, and we went to get the body. And right away I noticed the red truck in the driveway. When we went inside his whole family was there. The father and his siblings, his little brother. We're horrible people, Jonah. We're a horrible family. It's our fault. Mother. She is our fault. If we'd kept her off the streets, if we . . . "

I withheld my darkest impulse to speak the truth: Mother had tried to kill me, so if you'd listened to me, your baby brother, none of this would have happened.

It was no mistake that we had the son's body. The family had sent him to us on purpose, sent him to Peabody & Sons Funeral Home so that we could see the wreckage of Mother's crime. Their family wanted to see our family bleed. They wanted us to never sleep again. They wanted to send a message.

Your debts are racking up. They're unpaid. And the bill will come due.

Chapter 13

The Poet

When I wake up, Poe is sitting at His desk, head in His hands, groaning.

I'm leaning against His bronze likeness. I'm groggy, short of breath, deep underwater. When I stand, I'm swimming to the surface. My head keeps floating up, up, up. I steady myself on the bust. It's dark outside. The fake candlesticks throw up pointed arrows of yellow onto the ceiling. I shift my footing and the boards creak.

Poe turns, sees me, stands, and floats across the parlor, speaking in a Southern accent.

Who are you, and why do you haunt me?

My mouth is cotton. I rub my third eye. Cold. I feel my head, throat, glands. No Mother. All systems normal, except my pulse. It's galloping. Maybe I'm dehydrated.

Right. That's what I need. Just a drink of water. Some food.

Poe flickers in the half-light. He's wearing a frock coat, muddy pants, ratty kerchief, and knee-high knickerbockers. His greasy, black hair is bobbing over His eyes, and the iconic mustache is bristling under His nose. He drifts through the velvet rope into the middle of the parlor and stops by the catgut rocking chair, inches from me. We stare at each other, a pair of dumb animals.

I will ask you again, spirit. What do you want?

It takes me a second or two to find my tongue, then I stammer, "What do *I* want?"

Spirits often leave behind unfinished business.

Matthew Mercier

"Do I look like a spirit?"

You are a nightmare built from memory. A dream within a dream.

My chest and head are wet, clammy. "Mr. Poe, I—"

You call me by name?

"Well, you're famous, sir."

Naturally.

"But you're also," I clear my throat, "dead."

This goes as well as you might expect. Try telling a fish he's swimming in water. Poe's laughter bounces off the plaster. He tells me what a fool I am, how tricky I must think myself, although I can see His cockiness wavering each time He glances around the bare cottage or stares outside at the alien world of cars and streetlights. Then we crash into the hurdle of His memory—it's Swiss cheese. He knows His name, and that He's famous, but little else. And since I've gorged myself on Poe biographies for months, I know more about His life than He does.

"You died, sir. In Baltimore. You were on your way back from Richmond, Virginia."

Virginia, He moans, looking toward the bedroom.

"Do you remember your wife, Sissy?"

Sissy . . .

"Your cousin. She . . . "

Died in this house, and on this bed at the age of twenty-five from tuberculosis. How do I know this?

He knows this because those are the exact words I use during the tours. The bastard is plagiarizing me.

Poe rubs His head, nervous and jittery, a person with Alzheimer's knowing they should remember something. He floats into the hallway and stares at the sketch of Himself walking across High Bridge, at the excerpt from the *Southern Literary Messenger*.

"That magazine," I say. "You helped increase the circulation. You wrote critical essays and reviews."

I vaguely recall that.

"Does the name Longfellow ring a bell?"

Longfellow?

"John and Fanny Allan? Sarah Helen Whitman?"

He shakes His head.

"What about *The Raven*? It's your most famous poem."

Concerning the family Corvidae?

Poe & I

I recite the opening stanza, painful as it is, and stop at the first "Nevermore."

Did I compose that jingle?

"It was very popular in its day."

Well, I see nothing in it.

"That's what Emerson said."

Who?

"A frog from Boston."

You speak very oddly, spirit.

"My name," I say, "is Jonah Peabody." And everything will be fine. "Look, Mr. Poe. If I were dead, could I do this?"

I take out my Swiss Army knife, flip open the longest blade, and roll up my left sleeve. My forearm is layered with scar tissue, tapeworms writhing under the skin trying to push through. A souvenir from the bad old days.

Poe's face contorts, and He backs away. *You are a demon.*

"Watch me." It's difficult holding the knife with four fingers, but I'm able to press the tip of the blade into a soft spot on my left forearm, until it blossoms with a pinhead of plasma. The blood trickles into my arm hair. Poe wrinkles his brow and covers his mouth.

Stop that, He barks.

"Now you."

I will not.

"Just take the knife. Go ahead and try."

I place it on the windowsill. He stares at it for a blank moment, then scissors a pale thumb and pointer through the red handle. He tries again, and again, before holding up His hand and staring through His fingers. He then dips a thumb into the soup of His wrist and drags it up His forearm, rippling the surface. He pulls the thumb out at the shoulder joint, a tiny and disgusted *Oh* escaping his lips. He drags fingers through His hair, and every single strand falls back into its original place. He tries to yank one out. A sprinkling green vapor trail floats off His knuckles with each jerk.

Resurrected, He hisses. *Resurrected against my will.*

His moans shake the walls. I can only imagine what it's like when your old self comes crashing into the watery brain of your resurrected self. I want to give Him a hug or say something comforting, but I've never been good at that with the living, never mind the dead, so I keep my distance.

133

Matthew Mercier

Virginia, He moans. *Why is she not here with me?*

I think, *Because the afterlife is a big fucking lie,* but how do you tell a spirit there's no heaven? You can't.

"Edgar, I don't know the answer to that. But I'm looking for somebody, too."

There we go. That's what we need. Solidarity.

You have lost somebody to oblivion?

Oblivion. That word. The stolen portrait. The writing on the wall. "Oh, yes. Lots of people. Yes. Oblivion twenty-four seven. My . . . own mother. For starters."

Your mother?

"Yes. But I still see her all the time. She's . . . downstairs . . . right now.

Downstairs? This house has no basement. Is that a metaphor? You said your mother is no longer with us.

"Yes. No. That's the point."

You still have not explained your presence here.

"I give tours," I say. "I give tours of your afterlife, Edgar."

No, He says, *that is not the reason.*

"Sure it is. That's my job."

No, there is another reason.

He floats toward me. I drop into the kitchen, bumping the hurricane lamp off the table with my hip. It shatters in the fireplace, startling The Poet.

He hovers in the doorway, taking in the fireplace, the broom, the stove, the table and chairs, then floats down and tries to touch each and every object.

This place, He whispers, *I remember this place.*

He must see Maria Clemm in her bonnet, cooking dandelions for food, or Virginia, pale and sickly, seated at the table, coughing into a napkin. Whatever the trigger, He collapses onto to His knees and wails, green tears streaming into the cracks of His face.

Now I backtrack into the parlor, leaving Him to his grief. It's only a few hours till sunrise. The choice is between upstairs or downstairs. Poe or Mother. I'm sure she's still down there waiting for me. Until I can find a way to control her, I'll take my chances up here. At least with Poe I don't need a sleeping pill. I curl up in my bag and wait.

The kitchen goes quiet after ten minutes of laments. Poe floats

Poe & I

back in, cheeks stained with phosphorescent ribbons. The tears have eaten into His ectoplasmic skin.

My memory, He says, *is slowly returning. Everything is flooding back in an unmitigated, unbearable, and ungodly torrent of images. And I can only conclude that you are the cause, Mr. Jonah Peabody.*

I stand and wrap myself in the sleeping bag, using it as a force field.

"I'm not going to accept blame for that," I say, rehearsing some lines my therapist taught me, "but I acknowledge that you're in pain Mr. Poe, and I see you."

Stop talking in riddles, He bellows.

"That's not a riddle. It's the truth."

Well then, if you favor truth-telling, enlighten me yet again as to why you are making a residence of my home. What is your purpose for being here?

"I'm here to find my sister."

He floats right up to me, so that His nose brushes mine. His fingers reach up and brush the lid of my third eye.

Liar, He hisses.

"I'm here to find my sister. Her name . . . "

Liar, He repeats. *That is what you tell others, but you cannot hide the truth from me, Jonah Peabody. Your mind is as transparent as glass and just as fragile. Do not force me to break it. If you will not speak the truth, then we shall remain locked here in spiritual combat until the truth reveals itself.*

I should have known that the man who pioneered the unreliable narrator in His own stories would be able to sniff me out without blinking. Fair enough.

"Well," I said, "I guess we'll just have to sit here and wait to see what happens."

Poe smirks and pulls away His finger, tugging a strand of green along with it, until He's sitting at his desk again, the string glistening between us.

So be it, He says. *I have all night to transcribe your thoughts.*

I try to wipe the string away, but it's useless. Every time I break it in half, it just keeps reforming. So, I huddle in my bag as Poe does his mind-meld trick or whatever the hell it is, and soon enough I'm drifting off, dreaming within my dreams.

Matthew Mercier

I wake up at nine in a sheer panic, late for work, but then I remember: Sunday. Tours don't start until one o'clock.

The cottage is full of sunlight. No Poe. Bus brakes and car horns float through the screen windows. I stand, collect my sleeping bag, and slowly make my way back downstairs. No Mother either, which tracks. Historically, she only shows up a night, so I guess Poe operates on the same principle. I shower, make coffee, scramble some eggs, and carry my breakfast up to the porch to sit on the front steps.

A few bites in, as my puppies adjust to the daylight, I realize something is off.

The porch. There's twine looped from post to post, the white thread blending with the flaking off-white paint. I put down my coffee and step into the garden for a closer look. Glistening lumps strung together on the twine, like popcorn tinsel.

The lumps are teeth. It's a string of human teeth. Up and down the porch.

A deranged dentist saved every rotten tooth he ever pulled, stored them in a sock drawer, and then, on a whim, decided the perfect place to hang them would be Poe Cottage, in the middle of the night. Might as well be thumbs or pinkies hanging here. I drop the twine, shuddering, and glance around the park, but The Bronx is going about its Sunday, nothing unusual.

I reach for the twine, ready to yank it off the post, then stop. No. Let Cynthia see it first. Let's see how she reacts.

I go to the shed, grab my trash picker, and begin stabbing newspapers and Styrofoam until the boss breezes down the front walk at eleven, wrapped in an ankle-length sand-colored jacket, hair teased out and bouncing on her shoulders. Underneath the coat, she wears a take-no-prisoners business suit that looks more Wall Street than Historical Society. Tapered gravel-colored slacks, starched cream-cotton shirt, and a gleaming suit coat straight off the rack at Bloomingdales. She gives me the once over. I'm wearing jeans and a T-shirt.

"I can't collect trash in my nice clothes," I say.

"Please go change, Mr. Peabody. If you're done."

"Is this trash ever done?"

Poe & I

"Ah yes, it's truly a Sisyphean task."

Before I can ask what that means, she glances at the porch and goes as pale as the clapboards. She climbs the front steps and walks the length of the creaking porch with the business coat flapping around her. She bends over the railing and lifts the twine with one finger.

"We had a visitor last night," I say.

She inspects the shutters, the windows, the rotting rain gutter. The cottage needs a facelift badly. "No other vandalism," she sighs. "That's a plus."

"Should we call the police?"

"Just help me remove this."

"Somebody leaves a necklace of incisors and molars hanging out to dry, and you don't want to report it?"

"Would you like to explain all this, Jonah?"

Point, Cynthia. We cut it down, and she dumps the mess in a plastic bag, brings it inside, and places it on a sideboard in the gift shop.

So, she had a sincere reaction, but points off for the follow through—she's acting way too casual, as if this stuff happens all the time at Poe Cottage. And hey, maybe it does. So, I tell her about the portrait.

In the hallway, she stares at the blank wall where Poe's suicidal mug should be hanging. "Oblivion," she mutters.

Hail Satan. She sees the words, too. "I don't know how the thief had time to write that."

"They didn't. It was already there. Left by a former caretaker."

"Why did they? . . . "

She cuts me off, berates me for losing the portrait, and I promise to ban all backpacks from the cottage, to not ever let people wander the halls by themselves. In the back of the parlor, from a cabinet above the telephone, she takes out a placard: *This exhibit has been temporarily removed.* She hangs it on the nail. It covers Oblivion perfectly, as if the card has been cut for just this reason.

"So, Jonah. Any other confessions?"

The codes. The flowers. Mother. Poe Himself. "No."

"Good. Let's get to work. We've got a high maintenance guest coming today."

I dust and sweep while Cynthia polishes the teapots and

137

Matthew Mercier

silverware. Our prima donna guest, she explains, is Lizzie's mentor, the older man I met at the office. Mr. Lloyd Mason, professor of history and a Longfellow scholar at Fordham University. A refugee from the sixties, who'd been one of the leaders during the student takeover of Columbia's campus. He makes his living, she tells me, at writing esoteric histories on eccentric topics—the Weather Underground, porn, Jackson Pollack, the Grand Guignol theatre—and he doesn't write in a predictable or linear fashion. He pushes the bounds of objectivity and structure, angering most of his contemporaries. His book on Pollack mimicked the master's style, zigzagging all over the canvas, dipping in, dipping out, giving an erratic picture of an erratic man. His tome on the American porn industry bordered on exploitation itself, with salacious and titillating descriptions of starlet's bodies and men's plumbing.

"And in his latest book," Cynthia huffs, "he claims to have unearthed new evidence regarding Poe's missing years."

"The blank period? When he was spying for the French?"

"Where did you hear that?"

"Lizzie told me about it."

"Ah yes. She's Lloyd's little disciple." She polishes Poe's bronze mustache. "Lloyd's a talented man, no doubt about it, but he's a pain in my ass. He's on our board. Can you believe that? A Longfellow scholar on the board of Poe Cottage? He thinks that entitles him to access whenever he wants, but since he's a bigwig with lots of connections, it's best to play ball. He's got the keys to the park but not to the cottage itself. I won *that* battle."

"He has the keys to the front gate?"

"Yes." She reads my mind. "He's got nothing to do with those teeth. Not his style."

"Maybe it was Grip the Raven."

"Get serious, Mr. Peabody. They'll be here at one o'clock on the nose, if I know Lloyd. Punctual little snot." She places a hand on my shoulder. "I didn't just say that."

"No, ma'am."

"Good. Now go get dressed."

On my way through the gift shop, I snag the bag of teeth. She doesn't notice. Downstairs, I hide them in the safe, placing them on top of my bag of letters.

Poe & I

Sure enough, at one o'clock sharp, Lizzie and Lloyd appear at the gate.

"Lloyd will try to give the tour." Cynthia snaps off her gloves. "Don't let him."

"No way."

Even from the porch, Lizzie is magnetic. Vulcan eyebrows, nose stud, pigtails. She wears a brown leather skirt and knee-high boots. Lloyd Mason steps forward and bellows, "Jonah! Nice to see you again. How are you settling in?"

"Just fine," I say. He's projecting far more confidence than our first meeting.

"Consider yourself lucky, young man. You've scored one of the best jobs in the city." He nods at Cynthia. "And how is the Queen of the Bronx treating you? Watch out for her. She can be a regular Simon Legree."

"Oh gee, Lloyd," Cynthia wedges the doorstop under the front entrance. "That's not offensive."

"Bah! Don't give me that PC crap! How's the book coming?" The scholar winks at me. "Did Cynthia tell you she's writing a book?" He lowers his voice. "She's been toiling on it a very long time."

"I'm keeping the door closed until the first draft is done. Good books take time. You know that better than anyone, Lloyd."

"I do indeed, my dear. I do indeed. But when it's finished, it's going to be a masterpiece, I just know it. Pulitzer Prize. National Book Award."

"You're very generous."

"Well, I've been through the process. Going through it now as a matter of fact."

He glances at Lizzie, then at me. "Son, did you know Poe was a spy?"

Cynthia kicks the door open, rolling her eyes at the ground.

"I'm familiar with the blank period," I say "Quite a mystery. You've picked a tricky subject."

The man's eyes twinkle with fairy dust. "It is tricky. Nobody's ever taken it on."

Cynthia curls her fingers on the railing. "Because it's a bunk theory."

"Don't be bitter in front of your new employee, Cynthia."

"Just trying to save you time, Lloyd."

139

Matthew Mercier

"Come now. I scooped you fair and square. That's part of the game."

"Scooped?" I ask.

Lloyd dumps his hands into his pockets and rocks back on his heels. Cynthia needlessly kicks the doorstop. Both wait for the other to fill in the gap, but Mason jumps right over it.

"Mr. Peabody, you have some big shoes to fill here at the cottage. Bradford Macon was a great docent."

"Well, it's my first weekend. Go easy on me."

Lizzie trots up the steps, whipping out a small, dark notebook from her backpack. I try to get a peek inside, but she zips it shut as Mason and Cynthia walk on ahead. "Go easy?" she whispers. "Not likely. You better step it up, Junior."

"Hey, I'm on fire today. Your little head games won't get to me."

"Head games?"

"The teeth? Pretty gruesome stuff. Whose are they?"

"What teeth?"

"Right."

She flicks a hand at me and slinks past, twisting her legs around the tightly packed space of the kitchen and stepping sideways into the parlor, where everyone has more breathing room.

"We should let Jonah show you his stuff," Cynthia says.

Three pairs of eyes, all on me. Lloyd the scholar, difficult to impress, especially if he liked Bradford. Cynthia, already unimpressed. And Lizzie, whose expectations are low enough. This tour is nothing but a test. All three want to see me fail. Well, this is what I signed up for, so, man up.

I close my eyes, all three of them, and when I open, the bust of Poe is glowing, its bronze pupils pulsing yellow.

Sweat prickles my neck. Mason puckers his lips and strokes his mustache, waiting for me to start. The Poet's eyes glow hotter.

"Why don't we begin on the porch?" I clear my throat, turn my back on Poe, and lead my audience outside, where I ask them to gaze at the cityscape and to imagine, in the distance, just a few miles to the sloping south, the glimmering sliver of Long Island Sound, the rolling green hills dropping into the ocean.

"Imagine," I say, "apple orchards, dairy farms, fields of

Poe & I

wildflowers, brooks and streams —the vista as it would have been from Poe's front porch in the 19th century. All this abundant oxygen and sunlight would, Poe imagined, cure the diseased lungs of his young wife, Virginia. All the fresh air would slip down through her nose and scare out the blood and mucus clogging her lungs, flush the canals, cleanse the plasma."

Mason blinks. "Cynthia, aren't those your words?"

The boss is beaming. "I'm impressed, Lloyd. You've read my work. Nice job, Mr. Peabody."

"Thank you." I made a point of memorizing that passage last week.

I lead the group into the kitchen. Here, on this cast-iron stove, Virginia's mother Mrs. Clemm—Muddy—prepared the family's meager meals with dandelions rooted from the garden.

"Dandelions," Lizzie repeats. "That always sounds apocryphal."

"That's how poor they were," I insist.

Cynthia tag-teams. "Oh, the dandelions are well-recorded."

"Okay. Score one for Poe Junior."

So, I nail the kitchen, but when I step into the parlor, it's a repeat performance of Saturday, with screwed-up-dates and timelines. Doesn't help that The Poet's bronze pupils are a pair of burning stars, His lips twisting in a sneer.

Lloyd's eyes linger on the bust, too, but he's reading the gold metal plate with the artist's name, so he misses the puff of breath escaping Poe's mouth. He reaches into his jacket, sneaks out a flask, and throws back a nip. Cynthia stomps her foot. "Lloyd! Please!"

"Just a little snack, my dear. Relax."

"This is my house, sir! You will respect the rules. I don't care how many books you've published."

"It's actually Poe's house, and I doubt he'd mind." Mason slips the flask back into his jacket. The glow in Poe's eyes now spreads to His face. The mustache ruffles. My heart is a lead ball. My palms itch. I slip underneath the velvet rope into the parlor exhibit— docent's privilege—and charge through my rap, on fire with facts and dates, ticking them off, but giving no context, no substance, no depth. I'm lost, afraid to stop and ask for directions. Cynthia gives me the slow-motion pat down—a single palm bouncing in the air—so I take questions from the group.

"Did he write while he was drunk?" Lizzie asks.

Matthew Mercier

I almost say, 'Why don't you turn around and ask him yourself?' as Poe's lips blow smoke rings, but Cynthia cuts me off. "We don't deny the drinking, but we do think it's over-emphasized."

Lloyd jumps in. "See, that's where I've always disagreed with you, Cynthia. How can we say he wasn't a drinker?"

"I'm not saying that at all. But the Griswold memoir exaggerated the drinking and it forever stuck in people's heads. You can't drink all the time and write brilliant prose."

"Sure you can," Lloyd pats his flask. "But Poe was out of control at the end of his life."

"He injected cocaine, right?" Lizzie asks.

"God no," Cynthia says. "Did the internet tell you that? Laudanum, certainly. But everyone used laudanum."

My head grows hot as a sickly green cloud drifts from the bust. I moan, rubbing my forehead. My third eye is still cold, which makes me sweat even more. Lizzie flicks the air, as if batting a fly, and Lloyd slaps his neck. I lead the group to Virginia's bedroom. Lizzie leans over the half-doorway. "Cousins," she drawls. "Did they consummate their marriage, Jonah?"

Sweat drips into my eardrum. I press a fist tightly against my mouth as Poe's green cloud drifts over the bed. "Silly question."

"Agreed. That's quite irrelevant," Cynthia says. "As far as history is concerned, their bedroom is nobody's business."

Lloyd clears his throat. "Again, I must disagree, Cynthia. I think the question is entirely relevant. We need to imagine the emotional life of historical figures. The parts not always recorded."

"A man who's a virgin," Lizzie says, looking at me, "behaves differently than one who's not. It's an important detail." Beads of sweat pepper her forehead. "I think I'll step outside. Need some air."

She takes out a handkerchief and covers her mouth. I follow her to the porch, where she sinks onto the front steps, coughing. "What's going on in there, Poe Junior?"

"How do you mean?"

She taps her forehead. "Remember. I've got a third eye, too. And right now, my needle is in the red."

I swallow. To confess or not to confess?

"I felt it yesterday, too," she says. "Did you sleep any better last night?"

Poe & I

"No."

"I'm worried about you, Jonah."

The earth moves, but it's just the D train, a screech floating up through the sidewalk grills.

"Well," I say, "Grip is concerned, too."

Now there is the reaction I'm waiting for. Her eyes pop with fear.

"Is that Quinn's nickname?" I ask. "Did he send those videos?"

She shakes her head, nods at Cynthia who appears in the window, and says loudly, "Your docent rap is a lot better, Jonah. Still needs focus." She digs in her knapsack for her notebook and scribbles, *We'll talk about Grip later.*

Okay. Game on. "I can help," I whisper. "I can help with your Grip problem."

Back in the parlor, Lloyd and Cynthia argue in the shadow of Edgar. His pupils are still glowing. Neither genius notices a thing.

"My dear, are you okay?" Lloyd moves toward Lizzie with grandfatherly arms.

"I'm fine. It's a bit stuffy in here."

"Maybe we should go. Jonah, you look a bit pale yourself."

"I didn't sleep well last night. Still getting used to the cottage."

Lizzie glances at the bust. Her face betrays nothing but discomfort. Lloyd takes her by the elbow, and they move to the front door. She flicks one more look my way, and then Cynthia walks the dynamic duo out to the gate. I stay in the parlor, watching Poe vomit green ribbons.

When the boss bustles back in, she's frazzled and flushed. "Well, that wasn't too much of a train wreck. You seemed a little distracted there at the end."

"Everything is fine. My name is Jonah Peabody."

"What?"

"Sorry. I'm a little tired."

"Okkaaay. Nice job quoting my work. That really got Lloyd's goat."

"Happy to help."

"Now, I'm going to try and enjoy what's left of my Sunday."

She walks into the gift shop, and for a moment I think she's going to forget, but then she places a hand on the empty sideboard, turns, and says, "Where are the teeth?"

To which I say, "What teeth?"

143

Matthew Mercier

She crosses her arms, features twisting into a mask of bemusement—wrinkled forehead, cocked eyebrow, faint smile.

"It's not the first time I've found teeth here. A dentist used to own this house, long after Poe died. He painted a raven on the Concourse side to draw in clients, told everyone *The Raven* was written here, along with *Berenice* neither of which is true. So, every now and then some joker leaves teeth. Fake ones, usually. This is more of the same, I imagine."

"I imagine," I say. "The cottage does something to people."

"Indeed."

"Poe draws all types of devotional madness. Nothing unusual in that."

"Nothing at all. The grave in Baltimore has the Poe Toaster."

"And we've got . . . a Poe Dentist?"

"Doesn't quite have the same ring."

"No."

We step onto the porch, the traffic of the Concourse droning over her closing comments. "Compost the teeth, Jonah. Please."

"Yes, ma'am. One more question."

"Of course."

"The caretaker who wrote Oblivion. What was his name?"

She rubs her chin with a finger. "Ricky Thurston."

The name Carla and Oscar mentioned. "Did he go mad?"

She speaks to the steps. "Ricky was a bad hire. Plain and simple."

"What happened?"

"He died."

"Where?"

She points to the circular window of my kitchen. "Downstairs. In the basement. Heart attack."

"You didn't think to tell me that?"

"Would it really have made a difference, Mr. Peabody? The cottage is, as you said, your destiny."

Touché. Speak truth, boss.

For the rest of the afternoon, I dive into a marathon binge of docentry—four straight hours of Poe. My listeners include a gaggle of hyper-caffeinated kids from upstate passing through on their way to Comic-Con, a lonely old grandmother who traveled all morning from Staten Island, and a slew of foreign tourists—Australian, British, a sprinkling of German. I answer questions,

Poe & I

recite poems (from books, not memory), make jokes, and botch the facts again and again. When I speak in front of the bust, a wet bubble clogs my throat, but Poe stays quiet, and I make it to five o'clock, ghost free.

After I lock the gate, I sit in the coolness of the kitchen, munching on a bag of plantain chips and sipping a can of Tecate. I wish Andy had been here to see my first weekend. I wish she'd been here to see Poe. She would appreciate Him calling me out on my bullshit.

He knows, Andy. He knows you're just one part of the puzzle.

I try to channel my sister, since she'd know what to do with the strange flowers and the weird codes that I got yesterday. I pick up the notecards and place them next to the vase of purple buds, trying to grok the meaning.

to*;;(? S;48(

WW

UOW885t8^;

;6M8;+(8\$5Y

I breathe in, out, in, out. My name is Jonah Peabody, and everything is going to be fine. My chest rattles. I'll head to the walk in-clinic later, see if they have any mid-week blue light specials for people without insurance. I pick up the notecards, ready to file them away, when it hits me. How could I not see it? And I call myself a Poe fan?

I grab my collected works and flip open to *The Gold-bug*—Poe's famous adventure story with its hunt for Captain Kidd's buried treasure on a remote southern island. It's also, sadly, got an embarrassing portrayal of Jupiter, the black assistant, a horrible caricature who speaks in a minstrel dialect and acts like a clown, but the centerpiece of the story, the whole reason for its existence, is what the hunters use to track down the treasure: a cipher.

My cipher isn't an exact copy, but there are a number of shared symbols. I quickly write down the ones in Poe's story and what they mean.

5 =a
t =d
tt=o
8=e
3=g
4=h

Matthew Mercier

6=i
* =n
(=r
; = t

I'm trembling with excitement. I need to get out of this basement. I grab a notebook, set the security alarm, and boogie up Kingsbridge to Vicky's Diner, where I plop myself on a stool and order a Cubano sandwich with a side of chicken soup. Pure heaven to eat after forty-eight hours of stress. I dip the sandwich in the yellow broth to get the bread good and soggy, then chomp down on pickles and mustard and pork. I jot in my notebook between bites, translating the cipher, my hand shaking. Vicki, the owner, is a short pistol of a Greek woman with a steely blonde perm, shuttling up and down the counter, delivering coffee, silverware, the occasional one-liner. She raps my notebook with her pencil.

"What is this? Library? You eat. Don't read."

"Sorry. I'll be done soon."

The po-po come in and stand at the register, ordering burgers to go, radios squawking on their blue-blood hips. The Mexican chef at the skillet is a dervish of golden potatoes, sunny-side eggs, and grilled cheese. His television, a black and white shoebox balanced on the edge of a shelf between stacks of plates and loaves of white bread, is tuned to a fútbol match, Peru vs. Spain. The whole joint reeks of grease and burnt toast.

Halfway through my meal, after a few bulky men rise from their stools, I notice Alabama, sitting further down the counter, in front of the skillet.

"Mr. Edgar Allan Poe," he smiles. "What's doin'?"

I smile back. "Day's over."

"How's biz? Saw you giving those tours."

"That's what I do." And then, with a mouthful of meat and bread, I ask, "Hey, you happen to see anyone messing around the cottage last night? Or early this morning?"

He snaps to attention. "You need eyes and ears?"

"Did you see somebody?"

"Wasn't looking last night. I cut out early. Somebody fucking with you?"

I don't know how to explain the string of teeth, so I just tell him about the stolen portrait.

Poe & I

"Who you think done it?"

"Not sure."

Alabama swivels on the stool, the mask of scar tissue and burned flesh catching the glare of the fluorescents, turning it a hot pink. "I'll keep my eyes open, man."

"I'd appreciate it."

"Maybe you could kick me a few beans if I bring you intel?"

"If I'm paying you, how do I know it would be good intel?"

"Fuck off. You can trust me. I did it for my nephew, so I'll do it for you."

"Nephew?"

Alabama sips his coffee. "Bradford didn't tell you?"

Vicki snaps a check under my water glass. I shake my head.

"Not surprised. He's ashamed of his uncle. I'm the black sheep of the family."

I don't bother hiding the surprise I feel. "You want me to relay a message?"

"I'll make peace with him when the time is right. What are you scribbling there? Looks like Morse code."

I laugh, close the notebook, and tap it. "Somebody's fucking with me."

Slipping a ten under the water glass, I hustle on out of there before Uncle Alabama can ask any more questions. Over the Concourse and down the hill, the notebook a hot iron pressed against my chest, I'm ready to spend the rest of the evening in Poe's parlor puzzling out Grip's message, but as I approach the back gate, I find the lumpy shape of my past waiting for me.

"Professor!" Ramses swings his bruiser body around, as if ready to embrace me. "Am I too late to get a tour?"

Chapter 14

The Woman in the Box

The son's name was Brad McKittrick. It must be said. It must be remembered. Even if I don't want to remember it.

The day of the funeral, Andy and I were told to stay away from the parlor. We obeyed, although I wish we hadn't. I wish we'd gone and paid our respects. Walked up to the family and apologized. But Father said the McKittrick clan didn't want to see us, so he suffered through it alone. After the funeral, he went on a three-day bender, hibernating in his man cave with a bottle of bourbon and his Remington. I thought for sure we were about to be orphans, but he emerged later as if all was just fine, nothing to see here.

This is what Peabodys do; we stuff the darkness into our lower depths, where it simmers in our stomachs for months, years, decades, the pressure building and building until it finally explodes in a gooey mess. It's how we arrived here at Brad's funeral. We suppressed and ignored the darker side of Mother's behavior until she exploded. If we'd acknowledged the darkness in Mother, nobody else would be dead. It was that simple. Now she was locked away in the loony bin (I refused to call it a hospital), but for me, she might as well have been dead, so I tried to forget her.

Impossible since our house had turned into her mausoleum.

Every room was a memorial. I could walk from the den to the library to the kitchen and get an analog slide show of her youth—photos of Mother as a child, teenager, college student, young wife. There was a shot of her in Father's study, cradling me as a newborn, with Andy staring over her shoulder. They all looked so happy to see me, but I didn't trust it. Where did this beautiful

148

Poe & I

family go? Why did Mother insist I wasn't her son? Maybe that baby in the picture was me, but maybe afterward I'd been switched out for a changeling. Maybe I was a fake son, a demon, replaced in the night by trolls and who had yet to discover his true destiny as a monster. Which meant another Jonah Peabody—the real Jonah Peabody, my twin—was out there in the world, living my real life.

See? Too much time alone and your thoughts begin to eat their own tails. *I'm not real. I'm a double of a double. My true self is out there, not in here.* Crazy talk, right?

Except it's not. Let me explain.

Andy and Father visited Mother at the loony bin once a week. Andy tried to go by herself, but even though she'd graduated high school she was still a minor, so they needed to visit together. During these visits, I'd often snoop around the house, searching for evidence of my former self—instead, I found Mother's self in Father's man cave. He forgot to lock it up one afternoon after he'd gone to work, so I slipped inside, hot with adventure, and went straight for his closet, where I knew he kept his liquor, his gun, and his painkillers. It was in here that I found a box labeled, PAMELA.

It held slide shows of her artwork. (She idealized Blake.) Photo albums of her street photography. (New York. Madrid. Central America.) Lots of charcoal drawings, mostly of women draped over couches and chairs. It was an impossible archive. Impossible since I didn't recognize the mother in the box as part of our family, even as I tried to reassemble her. Why did Father hide all this? Why didn't we share this as a family? How many parents have boxes of their true selves locked away? And what's the price of losing that self? Does it always have to be madness?

I didn't dare ask the old man these questions. Instead, that night, I confessed to Andy what I had found.

"I've seen that stuff," she said. "Where do you think I got my inspiration to be an artist?"

My heart rippled, as if someone was blowing on it. "Does everyone in this family keep secrets from me?"

"Relax. Dad doesn't know that I've seen it either. Did you notice those drawings of women?"

"They were all women."

The implication was not lost on me. My hormonal combustion engine pumped out visions of Mother inside those drawings,

Matthew Mercier

walking and talking with those women, living another life beyond the one she ended up with.

"So, Father inherits the funeral parlor," I said.

"And Mother," Andy says, "decides to marry him."

"Rather than admit she loves women."

"And Father hides that part of her in a box."

"Then she cracks."

"Quite a story."

"How does it end?"

True or not, this narrative my sister and I cooked up saved me, again, from absolute despair. Mother didn't hate me. She just didn't recognize me as part of the life she had planned for herself. She didn't get to finish living her life before she lost her marbles—but Andy could live hers, and so Mother was living vicariously through her artistic daughter.

Too much pop psych, I know, but in the absence of any decent health insurance that might offer real psych and real insights, my imagination filled in the blanks.

My imagination also constructed a picture of the loony bin, and when Andy and Father arrived home, I was tempted to ask detailed questions, but I'd take one look at their faces—gray, haggard—and just ask, "How is she?"

Father's answer was always a variation on, "That place is horrible. We need to get her out of there."

Horrible? No, cracking a stranger's skull open with a tire iron was horrible.

(Father was referring to the sanitary conditions, but I couldn't care less back then.)

My sister placed a hand over mine. "She wants to see you, Jonah."

I considered it for a hot minute. But now that I was building an alternateMother—a woman who took walks in the woods with me and taught me about Blake and showed me how to take a great photo—I didn't want the real thing. I wanted the woman in the box, but since I couldn't have that mother, I tried not to think about her and focused on finishing high school.

I put my head down and got decent grades. I had friends but only during the school day. It was still impossible to get somebody to come home with me to the haunted house of Peabody. Folks probably thought they'd get sick if they stepped inside. I got a few

Poe & I

invites to play D&D, but these were across town, and it was hard to get rides, so I mostly had to come home or head to the parlor, where I'd answer the phone, get socialized, and reluctantly begin learning the funeral business from the old man. The time spent with him among the caskets confirmed what I always knew about Father—he emptied himself for the grieving public, which is why he had nothing left for us.

A sample of the script he used when talking to the bereaved: "Mr. and Mrs. Caron, my deepest sympathies for your loss. We're going to ensure your son gets the best treatment here." Or "Mr. Yezzi, tell me, what did you love most about your mother? I see, she sounded like quite a woman. Do you have photos from her time as an army nurse?" Or "Yes, Mr. Olsen, I know. When the young are taken from us, it's as if somebody has ripped out the last pages of a novel."

You hear that? He was a poet of grief. He listened. He gave advice. And then listened some more. He didn't push the expensive coffins. He advocated for cremation, which meant less profit, but his main concern was the families. I watched him handle the most delicate of deaths with grace and charm. I heard him recite prayers and poetry, make jokes, and—get this—laugh. The man laughed. He sounded happy.

It was performance art. An act. For the sake of the business.

He was convincing in the role. His sparkling personality was on tap for anyone who might use the services of Peabody & Sons, but not for his kids. Working with him wasn't that much different than living with him—blunt, cold, detail-driven, anal. The only time he ever loosened up was when Andy sketched one of her drawings, which she added to her secret book of the dead. Maybe her skill reminded him of what he'd lost with Mother. He'd stare at her sketchbook and marvel at the way she embellished the corpses.

An old rich man who died alone and whose family wanted nothing but his house and money—she drew him as a saintly Robin Hood. A young boy who drowned at the lake and who loved animals—Andy drew him as a cat. A young woman from school who'd taken a shotgun to her mouth—Andy simply restored her face, based on photos the family provided.

She never asked permission to draw the bodies, so she was afraid to show the results, but I think she may have tracked down

Matthew Mercier

the family of the shotgun girl and mailed the drawing anonymously. She told me drawing the bodies was a way to resurrect them. She meant this metaphorically, of course, but over her desk, she hung two pictures of the souls she wanted most to revive—Mother and Brad McKittrick. She didn't want to forget Mother's role in Brad's suicide, so she needed these faces staring down at her every day. And, while Mother wasn't dead, Andy wanted to kill the diseased version of Mother and bring back the woman in the box.

Eventually her black magic succeeded but not in the way she intended.

That summer, after escaping the prison of high school, I reconnected with Mike Murray through the funeral parlor. One of our old buddies, Thomas O'Neil, had overdosed on coke. I'd met Tom at the Black Sabbath concert. He'd been my dungeon master a few times, and we'd shared a few joints in Mike's basement. He was an enormous kid who never should have been near sugar or diet soda, let alone drugs.

"Is this one of your friends, Jonah?" Father asked as we stood in front of the humbling pasty white hill of Thomas's corpse.

"Yes. He was a nice guy," I said. "Always treated me well."

"Well, maybe you can talk to the family. We'll have to custom order a casket."

Thomas didn't have a family. His parents, both addicts, had cycled in and out of rehab and left Thomas to raise his two younger siblings in the trailer park. Those kids would be headed to foster homes now, so hearing their story made me keenly aware my story, while bad, was not the only nightmare.

It was Mike Murray who was stepping up and handling the funeral stuff. He'd raised a little money for the coffin and got folks to donate pictures of Thomas for the memorial.

"But you know what would really be special?" he said to me. "Can your sister draw a picture of him? She does that, right?"

"Sure," I said. "But how did you know?"

"Some weirdo dude who showed up at one of my parties. He's a smarty-pants sophomore. Said your sister drew his brother, Brad, after he offed himself."

I swallowed. "What's this kid's name?"

"I forget. Like I said. He's weird. Drives a red pickup."

"McKittrick?"

"That's it."

Poe & I

I didn't tell Andy about this, just submitted the drawing request. She turned in a faithful sketch of Thomas, but wiped out his acne, erased his double chin, and had him cradling a Stratocaster over his Buddha belly. (Thomas had ambitions of playing in a band.) This is the one drawing I saw her give away. She rolled it up, tied it with a blue ribbon, and handed it to Mike at the wake. The tough guy unfurled it and wept.

"It's amazing," he said. "Andy, I'm sorry I treated you like shit at school."

"You never did," Andy whispered. "It was other people. Not you."

"But I never said anything nice either."

Death turns everyone into a weeping sentimental sap, but that's how it works. Atone for your sins in the face of mortality. Thomas's funeral did a number on me and Andy. He died without family or future, got wiped out without leaving a mark on this earth. No thank you. We needed to step up our game.

Andromeda started applying to art schools. I figured I'd work a year or two for Dad while trying to get into the local community college, make up for lost time. We'd never felt the heat and urgency of life as much as we did that year.

But then, resurrection.

Andy and Father came home from their weekly visit with Mother. I'd made cheeseburgers and sweet potato fries with an avocado salad on the side. I'd just finished an application for Three Rivers Vocational School and was feeling good, but the minute the dynamic duo came walking in with sour faces, that mood got snuffed out. They both pulled up their chairs and sat down to eat without comment. I tasted the bitter tang of an argument in the air. They must have been shouting at each other the whole car ride home. One word from me might trigger their tongues, but I had no problem waiting for them to speak.

Finally, Andy blurted, "Mom has cancer."

Father picked up his knife and cut his burger in half.

"She's dying, Jonah. She's remembering her past life in bits and pieces. It comes and goes. But lately,"—she looked at Father but spoke to me—"she's remembering you."

"Is she still on about how I'm not her son?" I asked. "That I was switched at birth?"

Andy stared at her food. My father's red face quivered.

Matthew Mercier

"Tell him," Andy said. "Or I will."

Father sipped his whiskey, chewing his dead cow. "Your mother," he said, "would like to see you, Jonah."

Right. I wanted to see Mother the way Rodrick wanted to see Madeline Usher climb out of her grave. Except, Father was lying. His tell was a twitching cheek, as if his own face muscles found his lies revolting, and his left side was fluttering wildly, like his tongue wanted out.

"That's not the whole story," Andy said. "Tell him."

I chugged my beer. "Told you both I'm not going near that prison."

My father froze, and Andy said, "Prison?"

"She's a criminal and deserves to be locked up."

"Jonah, Mom isn't in a prison. She's in a psych ward."

Oh dear. Wait. I know this must be confusing for you, since it sure as hell is confusing for me. Am I remembering my own story correctly? Did Andromeda just tell me the truth? Or did I say "prison" to try and rewrite my own history? Is my brain refusing to be a co-conspirator?

"Prison," I said. "She's in prison. She's not crazy. She knows exactly what she's done. You've both fallen for her act, but I know the truth. I was there. Halloween night. Neither of you saw the knife, but I did."

See? I was confused even then. What's wrong with me? Maybe it's that I'm now poisoned, here in the present, in Poe Cottage, and that poison is infecting how I see the past. Or maybe I'm just delusional. Most likely it's a little of both, a heady cocktail of lies and truth, shaken and mixed so violently I can no longer separate them.

"Jonah," Father says, "I would like you to visit your mother because . . . she's very confused. She thinks . . . she actually thinks that you've already visited her."

I put down my utensils.

Father's cracked face was a jigsaw puzzle of divots and pockmarks and ruddy rosacea. "You haven't visited her . . . have you, Jonah?"

I snorted a laugh, but he was sincere, talking to me as if I was a client about to bury their loved ones six feet under. I turned to Andy. "Who? Who is this visitor?"

"The last McKittrick boy," she said. "He's a little older now, and he looks an awful lot like you."

Chapter 15

Invisible Hands

Ramses is not interested in the museum. He wants to see the basement, but since he and I have a lousy history with basements, and since I have the keys and I'm calling the shots, I insist on taking him through the museum first.

The fireman is faintly amused at my fear masquerading as authority, but he plays along, pretending to be interested in Poe's history, his barrel-chested bullet of a body stomping over the planks of the cottage as gently as a Clydesdale. I guide him through the kitchen and into the parlor, late afternoon sunlight giving me a false sense of security as Ramses invades the space with wisecracks and disrespect. He slaps the bronze cheek of the Poe bust and runs a finger over the Poet's mustache.

"Be careful," I say. "You might wake him up."

Ramses snorts and throws up his palms. "Ooo . . . scary."

"It's only my first weekend. You know I haven't been paid yet."

"Oh, I know that, Professor. Believe me. I got eyes on you."

"Your buddy Grip?"

"What?"

"My brother, Grip. Quinn. Whatever he calls himself. I've already heard from him."

"I don't know anything about that. Far as I'm concerned, you and your brother got to work shit out for yourselves. He's fucking creepy, by the way. And cheap. But all these rich guys are cheap. Nope. I just want my money. And for that,"—he swings around and points a pinkie in my face—"you need to stay healthy."

"On that we can agree."

Matthew Mercier

Across from Virginia's bedroom, he flips the latch on the basement door, swings it open, and peers down the ship's ladder.

"This the bachelor pad?"

"Home sweet home."

"After you," he says, and we descend.

It's roughly seven thirty. Time for Mother to appear. The back of my neck is tingling, my third eye drilling a hole in my forehead, but she's not here. Maybe Ramses has scared her off. The fireman surveys the four red walls, rubs a hand over the cross beam, the Poe Society safe, inspects the bathroom and kitchen, and then delivers his final verdict: "This place is filthy. And unsafe. I count about five code violations. Where's your fire exit?"

"Through the kitchen. You going to report me?"

He snorts and draws up his shoulders, rolls his neck, not meeting my gaze as a full body shiver runs through him. "That your only window?" He points to the filthy screen and the spider oak beyond the sill. "Quite the view."

"It suits me. I'm part vampire."

"You and your brother. Pair of weirdos."

It then hits me that this macho man is shaken, even scared to be down here in Poe's basement, and so, riding this instinct, I walk over to the safe, bend down, and take out the bag of teeth. "Want to see what my brother left me?"

I hold up the tooth necklace, a pair of them glinting with silver fillings. Ramses wrinkles his lips and shakes his head. For a man who enjoys cutting off body parts, he appears seasick with disgust, cheeks bloated, as I wave the necklace back and forth.

"You are one strange duck, Professor. You and . . . " He stops, squints, and drills me with a look of sheer confusion. "What the fuck is up with your eyes?"

"My eyes?"

"They're green."

Mother. Inside me? How? No, she's behind me, passing through me, a cold glove sliding over my heart, trying to settle inside me the old-fashioned way, the way she thinks ghosts are supposed to, a method she's tried before, but it's never worked. What mother can fit neatly inside her own son? Mortals and ghosts are not Russian nesting dolls, and I will not shrink for her. I will not.

"Get out," I croak.

Poe & I

"Don't worry. I'm leaving pal."

"No. Ramses. I.."

To my surprise, Mother obeys, but she's holding the knife, and its slicing through my chest, a whistling paper cut running across my ribs. I lean on the safe and drop the teeth on the floor. Ramses moves to catch me, but I back away.

"Don't touch me."

Plopping onto the loveseat with Ramses towering over me, I try to slow my breathing, but the panic is crowding in. The fireman is going to hurt me again, I'm sure of it, but when I look into his eyes, he backs off, scared off by my freaky behavior.

Mother is on the ground behind us, holding the necklace and counting the teeth, sliding them across the string like an abacus. She's able to hold them between her fingers; they don't slip through.

My brain cracks, a pair of tectonic plates splitting apart, and I howl hysterically at the mad logic running through my head—of course she can touch them.

They're her teeth.

Tears, giggles, and laughter so violent I can barely stand.

Ramses is backing up into the kitchen. "You seem to be dealing with a lot, Professor. But don't . . . don't you run out on me."

I lurch toward him, slap his shoulder, and walk him out to the back gate, with the sticky, Bronx summer night in full swing. "Oh, don't you worry buddy. She won't let me."

"She?"

I take a breath and do my best Anthony Perkins. "Mother," I burp. "She isn't exactly herself today."

Slam the gate in his dumb face and retreat to my hovel, my kingdom of pain, where I pop a sleeping pill and crawl into bed early.

I wake up later that night, alone. No Mother. My notebook with the unfinished cipher is next to me on the loveseat.

All the adrenaline has drained out of me, and my mind is sharp, clear. I grab my sleeping bag and the notebook, walk upstairs, and sit in Poe's parlor, my palms sweating. I look down at the cipher.

Donttr__ __her

Why is this now so easy? No special skills necessary. Just add a few letters.

Don't trust her

As for the second half of the equation, a bit harder. Here's what I have so far.

    ____ ____ u__u__e__ea__e__t ti__etore__a__

The lines are running together like they do in The Gold-Bug. My brother, Quinn, doesn't want me to be confused. He wants me to get the message, but he's still playing around, mixing up Poe's cipher and some modern vernacular. Look at the first line again.

UOW885t8^;

'U' like texting. 'U' means 'you.'

You ____e__e.a__e__t

Now that last half of the sentence, it's all Poe's symbols, right? The lowercase 't' stands for 'd.' The '8' is an 'e.' The semi-colon is a 't.' Spell that out.

You de__t

Okay, now separate and fill in the blanks. First word is 'you.' And the last? Debt. Only word that fits. Okay, first and last words. 'You' and 'debt'. Now the 'O' makes sense. Read it aloud. "You O debt." And the rest? Well, there's an 'a' in there, right before 'debt.' Assume that's by itself. Right. So now we got.

You O a debt.

And the second line is this.

ti__etore__a__ into
ti__e to re__a__

Time. To Repay.

Don't Trust Her. You O a Debt. Time to repay.

My chest quivers. My hands itch. The powder I inhaled that morning is still clinging to my nostril hairs. My fingertips are tingling, and the whorls of all ten digits are spinning. I stand, dizzy. My shoulders are anvils. And then, in the center of my right palm, a black dot appears and begins to spin, drilling into the meat and bone. I scream, clutching my wrist as the dot spins out a black ribbon that shoots up my arm, snaking parallel to my veins, looping around my elbow, climbing my shoulder, burrowing into my ear, and funneling into my brain.

Poe & I

I wake up with Poe's voice in my head.

I flip off my sleeping bag and wipe the crust from my eyes. It's dark out. Three in the morning. The witching hour. What day is it? Sunday. No, Monday morning. I gave the tours yesterday. Poe is across the room, cursing, sobbing, lamenting the limbo He's stuck in. I sit up. My arm burns. Dead skin is flaking off my palm. The black dot is still there, in the center of my palm, and the black line running up my arm, undulating, as if it's trying to hypnotize me. My notebook is open to the cipher.

Don't Trust Her. You O a Debt. Time to repay.

My name is Jonah Peabody, and everything will be fine.

Poe's moans are shaking the plaster walls. The poet is at the back window, palm on the glass, staring outside. He turns, His face a wavering puddle of green rage.

You are a vile human specimen, Jonah Peabody.

"I've been called worse."

You massacred my life story these past few days, and you expect me to stand by and listen without comment?

"Massacre? Hey, I'm no Rufus Griswold, pal. What did I get wrong?"

My dear Sissy. You said I deserted her, in her time of sickness!

"Oh, that. I'm just going by the script they gave me." (But folks, Poe did visit Fanny Osgood while Virginia was ill. Look it up.)

Stop speaking, He hisses. *It is torture, listening to you drag my life story though the mud. And to think I will have to endure this for as long as I am trapped in these walls.*

Oh, why have I returned? This is hell on earth.

"That's a bit dramatic."

He steps away from the window, and there's movement in the greenhouse beyond. At first, I think it's a streetlight, refracting and zigzagging through the glass, but then I make out an orb—two or three—drifting, circling each other.

My mouth is dry. I touch my forehead. Cold and hard.

Listen, Poe says.

I hold my breath. There. Coughing. Soft and delicate. Somebody is out there on the street, but no, the sidewalks are empty. The coughing continues. The lights in the greenhouse are bright yellow. Poe floats through the velvet rope, His cheeks again streaked with ectoplasmic tears.

You will help me, Jonah Peabody. You will bring her back to me.

Matthew Mercier

"Who? Bring who back?"

My cutting scars are crawling under my skin, worms pushing to get out.

Reunite us. Bring my Sissy back to me.

"Virginia? I'm not sure I can do that."

You must, Poe gargles, *or else I will end you.*

I hold up my blackened arm. "I think somebody beat you to it."

Poe floats as close as he can, backing me up against His own bronze bust. *Hold out your palm.*

I obey, and He sinks a finger into the black dot. The rush is unlike anything I've ever felt in my life, a ripple of spicy, hot pain. The black line crackles, and my skin breaks open, but there's no blood.

Fascinating, Poe says, withdrawing his finger. *I appear to have powers here I could only imagine in my waking life.*

From my crouch, I whisper, "I'll help you find Sissy."

His sallow cheeks stretch into an impossibly wide grin. *Of course you will. But do not think me ungenerous Jonah Peabody. I will help you in return.*

"How?"

I will help you find your mother. Pamela.

Hearing her name on His lips pulls me out of the burning river.

Do not look so disturbed. I know what you know, Jonah Peabody. I came upon her name, buried in your head.

"My head?"

I've been digging in there. While you sleep.

"No. I told you. I'm looking for my sister."

Poe cocks His head. *Why do you persist in this fiction?*

I swallow. Poe has my number. No way to hide my lies from the man. "My sister is easier to explain."

Fair enough, although I remain puzzled as to why you continue to obfuscate the matter.

"If you keep digging, you'll find the answer."

Very well. Then if you hunt for my Virginia, we will find your Mother.

"I need time," I blubber.

I believe you have very little left of that, Mr. Peabody.

Those words slip into my bloodstream. "I'm sick, aren't I?"

Poe rubs His mustache and nods.

"Quinn poisoned me. The dust in those flowers."

Poe & I

I regret to say that is a distinct possibility.
 The heat in my skull is expanding, spreading in tickling threads across my forehead. Poe's voice is trailing off. A white veil slips down over my eyes. My chest is rattling, and I'm coughing, heaving, lying down, and embracing the darkness.

I wake up drenched in sunbeams, bronze Poe leering above me.
 I stand, groggy, pick up my notebook, and glance outside. Sky blue, drugs on the corner, trash smothering Poe's lawn. I stumble down into my kitchen. I make coffee, then grab the trash picker and go around to the greenhouse and peer through the one grimy window. Broken glass. Terracotta pots. An unused space, greenhouse only in name. No glowing orbs. No Virginia.
 The black dot on my right palm is still there, same hand as the missing pinkie. My name is Jonah Peabody, and everything will be fine. Panic makes poison work faster, right? I have a feeling I'd be dead already if Grip (Quinn) wanted me to be. No, he's doing this Poe style. He wants me around for a while, and he'll want me to know it was him who did the poisoning.
 Doesn't mean I can't hunt him down first.
 I find Mason's office hours listed on Fordham's website. My first instinct is to pop in unannounced, but ambushing the professor turns out to be an impossible mission since, like me, he works in a gated community. The Fordham campus is locked up tight. To get past security you need an appointment, chaperone, and swipe card. So, I call him directly, with the pretense that I'd like to ask him more about his book, and he says that he'd be happy to talk after giving one of his Poe lectures.
 "I think Bradford was planning on coming. He can be your guide."
 The former caretaker is rightly pissed when I call and ask to tag along. "First you take my job, and now I have to babysit you?"
 "Why didn't you tell me about Ricky Thurston?"
 "Who?"
 "The caretaker who died in the basement."
 A long pause. "Somebody fucking died?"
 "Oh, we need to talk, Bradford."
 He shows up that weekend, hangs out during my tours, and

Matthew Mercier

critiques the halting way I speak, how I stare at the floor to gather my thoughts, and how I mispronounce "sep-ul-cur." I guess I'm saying sep-ul-*chair*.

Between guests, he quizzes me relentlessly. "Who translated Poe into French?"

"Charles Baudelaire."

"Name a cousin. Besides Virginia."

"Neilson. Or Rosalie. Rosalie was mentally ill."

"Who was Poe's childhood sweetheart?"

"Elmira Shelton. Or Sarah Elmira Royster. Shelton was her married name."

"Which major Hollywood star is working on a script about Poe's life?"

"How am I supposed to know that?"

"It's your job."

"Tom Cruise."

"Wrong. Sylvester Stallone."

"You're kidding."

"No. Sly wrote a rough draft back in '79. Apparently, it's Rocky's dream project."

Downstairs, he teases me about my lack of furniture in the apartment, even though I've found a coffee table, bookcases, a few skillets for the kitchen, drapes for the window—all right down the block at the Our Lady of Guilty Sinners thrift shop. I know why he's poking fun. The furnishings make the basement habitable. It shows I'm not leaving.

"You're holding up pretty good, ginger, but wait until winter. When you're all snowbound up in here? It takes a strong individual, son."

"I'm used to living on my own."

"Get any crazies yet?"

"Define crazy."

"People been asking about ghosts?"

"Oh sure," I smile. "And I've been hearing stuff at night."

"For real? Don't play."

"I'm not. Wouldn't you like it if I flamed out? You might be reinstated."

He shakes his head. "Not happening. Cynthia seems to want you for some reason. And besides, it was rough living here." He looks off to the side. "You really hearing things at night?"

162

Poe & I

Trust is won with honesty, so I bare my soul and say, "Yes and . . . I'm seeing things."

Bradford rubs a thumb over his lips, nodding.

"But I'm weird like that. Been seeing things my whole life."

"I bet. I wonder if Ricky Thurston saw things?"

"I know as much as you do."

"So, he died? Here?"

"According to Cynthia."

"Damn. She hid that from me, too."

This bout of honesty leads to a weekly habit of chowing at Vicki's after the tours. Turns out we have a lot to talk about. History, horror movies, science-fiction novels—lots of shared interests. These nerdy bull sessions make him stick around longer than he needs to. I figure he doesn't have folks in his inner circle who want to gush about Tolkien and LeGuin, Earthseed and Middle Earth, Earthsea and Water Sharing. We grok each other, and eventually, as we get closer to the visit with Mason, I get a piece of the real Bradford, when he references his graduate work at Fordham.

"What's your thesis?" I ask.

"My thesis is that white people are crazy."

"Come on."

"You want to hear this or not, flyboy?"

"Of course I do. But—"

"Then shut up and listen." He stuffs a wedge of potato in his mouth. "White people have made a horror show of America. Underlying everything in our past is a current of deep, deep horror. All the slavery and genocide and torture they laid on the Native Americans and black folk? It's still there, bubbling under the surface like something out of Lovecraft. Hell, it's worse than Lovecraft 'cause it's real. And it touches every one of us, this horror. The original sin in our drinking water. That's what true horror is. Unstoppable and ever-present. Biblical. Cosmic. Not all this teenage tits and ass shit you see Hollywood making. You ever read Moby Dick?"

"Parts of it."

"Liar. Well, Melville knew the real color of horror, of insanity. Can you guess? He's got a whole chapter on it."

"I missed that one."

"Of course you did. Chapter forty-two. The Whiteness of the

163

Matthew Mercier

Whale. Melville lists everything bad about whiteness. Albino men, whiteouts in a storm, ghosts, the KKK. Well, that last one is mine, but you get the idea."

"Sounds awesome."

"And I'm not writing it in the typical academic language either. I'm doing it narrative style. Like a story. The American Horror Story. So, Mason is the perfect guy to advise me."

"Does he know anything about Ricky Thurston?"

Bradford bites into his cheeseburger, the grease dripping onto the counter. "He might. But listen, since I'm doing you this favor, afterward, you and I need to get square with the truth."

"Truth?"

"About your fake resume."

I nibble on my sweet potato fries.

Bradford holds up a palm. "You swear to me everything on that paper is true?

Packing fish in Alaska? Shooting kangaroos in Australia?"

"Scout's honor." I stare into the dregs of my coffee, hold up my own palm, the black dot fleshy and bulging. "Want to shake on it?"

"Not until you get that checked out."

The day of our Fordham visit, he shows up at Poe's rear gate dressed to kill in a flashy gray suit and tie. We cross over Kingsbridge to Valentine. The marketplace is low-key. One of the dealers, a mope with a ratty wife beater and long silver athletic shorts, slides out of his doorway as we approach. We give him the cold shoulder, but he stares at us as if we've broken some law of nature by walking together. I guess we do look funny—a black man the size of a tight end and a lily-white ginger toothpick.

As we trot down 194th across Webster Avenue and enter the fenced-in Fordham campus, my pulse jumps. I'm allergic to college. Dorm rooms, with their cheap, scratchy rugs and bland five-and-dime furniture, make my skin itch. Cafeteria food gives me the runs. Textbooks, a hernia. And I always feel the urge to punch anyone wearing a tweed jacket. Brushing up against oversexed intellectuals fills me with a hot desire to wreak holy vengeance on the perfectly trimmed lawns and polished study halls. I want to grab co-eds by the throat and re-educate them by screaming, "*You know this is all a game, right? A giant hoop that*

Poe & I

society is forcing you to jump through for thirty thousand dollars a year at a variable interest rate!"

Sure enough, my forearms begin to crawl with the old panicky itch as we enter the heart of the mothership—a lecture hall with stadium seating and high ceilings.

"Why are you twitching?" Bradford asks.

"Just a little cold."

We huddle in the nosebleed seats, where the recessed lights have burned out, but since we don't have to take notes, we just sit and listen to Mason pontificating in pressed slacks, a polka-dot bow tie, and, yes, a tweed jacket. Every time he opens his mouth, I think the handlebar mustache will peel off his face like Velcro and take flight, dive-bombing us. I chuckle at the rows of students scribbling in their notebooks, trying to keep up with Mason as he discusses the Ludwig article, that scathing obituary written by Rufus Griswold that destroyed Poe's reputation (the parts he'd left untouched himself) and gave us, Mason argued, the fabled icon we love today. A gloomy, doomed, romantic Poe who wore all black and took long walks in graveyards and committed the crimes he wrote about. A pop-culture idea of the man, rather than the man himself.

"Poe is ubiquitous," Mason drones, twirling his wrist and pacing across the waxy half-moon at the bottom of the hall, "and he will be with us until the end of time. But that does not change the fact that Poe remains, in the symphony of literature, a very minor chord." He clears his throat. "A side effect of having, as your most prominent spokespeople, Vincent Price and Roger Corman."

Laughter. I writhe in my seat, rub my knuckles, and then raise my hand to speak.

"Professor Mason, are you implying something is wrong with the Vincent Price movies?"

Mason slips his hands into his pockets and squints up. I can't tell if he knows it's me. "I hope I'm implying nothing. Let me speak directly. Those films are crap."

Bradford pats my knee. "Easy, killer. What gives?"

"He's being a snob."

"Sure. But cool it before I drag your ass out of here."

Mason clears his throat. "Moving on. Let's talk about Poe's time in France as a double agent."

Lloyd Mason's office reminds me of Cynthia's—cluttered with

Matthew Mercier

historical junk that needs decoding. A bookcase filled with bricks. A signed album cover from a hip-hop group. A smoky black and white photo of FDR waving to the crowds on the Grand Concourse and another of Poe Park with a mass of people swarmed around the alabaster gazebo.

"What's that all about?" I ask. "The crowd circling the gazebo."

Mason admires the photo as if he took it himself. "Bandstand."

"Sorry?"

"That's a bandstand. Not a gazebo. And it's a meeting for Jewish statehood. Incredible, right? Lot of history in that small park. I was raised on the Grand Concourse. Right down the street. The Emerald Chain, they called it. Modeled after the Champs-Elysees."

He waxed on about his "lost Bronx." (A lot of white people, it turns out, have versions of the "lost Bronx.") He talks about the Paradise movie theater and soda fountains and watching Yankee games for free on the subway platform before they built the Great White Wall. He goes on for a good five minutes before noticing our polite smiles.

"Pardon me," he snorts. "Fake nostalgia is an occupational hazard of being a historian." He slaps his desk. "Would either of you like a drink?" He opens a drawer, slips out a bottle of brandy, rocks glasses, and a flask. We both pass. It's one o'clock. "You know, Jonah, by coming to Fordham today, you're following in Poe's historical footsteps."

"Am I?"

Mason smiles. "Bradford, what have you been teaching this young man?"

"It's his first month, Lloyd."

"No excuses!" Mason snaps. "Poe used to stroll over here and chat with the Jesuit fathers. Except it was called St. John's College at the time."

Bradford chimes in with a Poe quote. "The Jesuit Fathers were highly cultivated gentlemen and scholars . . . "

Mason lifts a palm in the air. " . . . they smoked, drank, played cards like gentlemen . . . "

I rap the desk and finish. " . . . and never said a word about religion."

"Very good, Mr. Peabody. You've done your homework."

"That's part of the video we show at the cottage. It's stuck in my head."

Poe & I

"Of course. Well, let's get to it, shall we? You wanted to ask me some questions about Poe."

"Who's Grip?"

The tenured troll reduces his smile to a flat line. He pours himself a plug of brandy, no ice. "Grip the raven?"

I nod and pull out the notecards with the cipher from my pocket. "These arrived the night before my first tours at the house."

Mason folds his hands, steeples his thumbs, and digs them under his chin. "I see."

"You have keys to the park."

"As do all board members."

"I found these wedged in my front door. Along with some poison flowers. Wolfsbane, I think. From what I could find on the Internet."

"Lloyd," Bradford says, "I didn't know about this."

"Can I see those?" Mason gestures for the cards.

I rub the cards between my fingers and hand them over.

The professor hops from his chair and strolls to a paned window that overlooks the campus. He stands in the sunlight and brings the cards close to his face. He opens a file cabinet, takes out a ragged piece of paper, holds it next to the notes, then shakes his head, and puts the paper away without showing it to us.

"It would be his style to do something like this. Leave mysterious notes."

"Whose style?"

"Arthur Quinn."

I swallow. "My double."

"You've met him?"

"His picture is up on the wall at the Society. A group shot."

"Oh, that's right. The two of you do look alike. It's remarkable. But you don't know him?"

"No."

"Well, that's odd." Mason sits. "I got the impression you were old friends. You do know, Mr. Peabody, that Arthur Quinn wanted you for the job?"

I've heard about moments like this. When the air leaves the room. You get a piece of news so abrupt it sucks away your oxygen.

Bradford glares at me, his body coiled. "Quinn is the old president of the Society, right Lloyd? The weird one?"

Matthew Mercier

Mason nods, sipping from his flask. "Weird is an understatement."

I roll my knuckles. "So, he recommended me?"

"He strongly recommended you," Mason says. "I guess your resume impressed him."

Bradford snickers. I ignore this. My vision telescopes. Mason sits at the end of a long, dark tunnel.

"Cynthia fought him on the decision. She simply could not figure out why Quinn wanted you to be the top candidate. After all, you had a lot of competition."

"Including me," Bradford snaps.

"Quinn has that much sway?" I ask.

"So goes Quinn, so goes the board."

Now, both men poke and prod me. How did I know Quinn? What made me so special? Had I really not had contact with him before?

"Maybe he liked what he saw on my resume," I say. "Maybe he saw that I was as qualified as anyone."

"When I say he strongly advocated for you," the professor clears his throat, "I mean that he insisted."

"Insisted?"

"You are a little Myna bird, aren't you? Yes, he insisted. To the point of questioning Cynthia's competence."

Bradford says, "You mean he railroaded her?"

"I'm not calling it that," Mason said. "But you know how boards work on these nonprofits, Jonah."

"I don't, actually."

"It's all very political. People throw their weight around, make threats of reprisals and such. Quinn has a reputation for this sort of stuff. He's put up a stink before. But that's what boards are, right? A bunch of bored, rich people making a stink."

"You're on the board."

"True, but I'm hardly rich."

"And Quinn is?"

"Very wealthy. I think he was in finance during the eighties. Made a fortune. Hedge funds, stocks. Now he's ensconced in his mansion. Lives off dividends. Has a huge art collection. A lot of Poe relics. He fancies himself a Poe expert."

"Don't we all."

"He throws a big fundraiser for the Society every year. *The* fundraiser, actually. They couldn't survive without it. A

Poe & I

masquerade ball and auction. It's quite the party. So yes, Quinn's got the dough-re-mi to get whatever he wants. Does a lot of good with it, too. He underwrites the oral history project here at Fordham. Did you know that, Bradford?"

Bradford shakes his head. He looks as shell-shocked as me.

"It's one of the major projects here in the history department." Mason nips from his flask again.

"Did somebody interview Ricky Thurston?" I ask. "The caretaker before Bradford?"

Here Mason pretends to think, but I know what this type of performance looks like. A fake furrow of the forehead, stroking of the chin. All that's missing is the cartoon lightbulb dinging above him when he finally vomits the answer.

"Ricky Thurston. The name sounds familiar. I think . . . you know, I think Lizzie Borden conducted that interview."

"I'd like to hear it."

"Well, it's in the archive somewhere. You'll need Bradford here to help you with that. But what are you looking for?"

"Just curious about other caretakers' experiences. Plus, I'd like to pay homage to him. I heard he died in the basement."

"Yes. Tragic story."

"Do you know what happened?"

"Heart attack," he spits. "You know, I don't think Quinn has ever listened to a single interview? So typical of big money. He writes a check and then retreats back into his mansion. I think he enjoys the stature it gives him."

"So, Quinn told Cynthia to hire me, or else?"

Mason nodded. "Looks that way. But I guess she wouldn't tell you all that. Why would she? Boy, she's had a few rough years. Her husband died. Then her mother got ill."

"And you stole her book."

That just burps out. I can't help myself. Bradford throws up his hands.

"As I explained during our tour," Mason says, "I scooped dear Cynthia. A common phenomenon. The great game of our profession. And it's not stealing. I did my own research."

"What's your thesis?"

"Are you writing one, too?"

"In my head."

"My thesis," he snorts, "is that Poe was a sniveling, two-faced,

Matthew Mercier

double-crossing agent who betrayed the republic while, at the same time, advocating for an American literature, forcing him to lead a Jekyll and Hyde existence—not unlike a character in one of his stories."

"So, it's a smear job."

"Not at all. Completely objective."

"You said there wasn't much evidence."

"It will be a slim volume."

"I read that the Alexander Dumas letter was a fake."

"Oh, there was a false letter, but there have been new discoveries."

"Which you've made yourself, right?"

Mason steeples his fingers again, the way all snobs do when they feel trapped. He then collapses the steeple and rests his chin on the ruins of his liver-spotted digits.

"I know you feel the need to defend your boss," he says, "but you could stand to be a bit more diplomatic. As for Quinn, I have no idea why he'd bother to leave you such a note at three in the morning. He is known to be a bit eccentric. Possibly even a drug addict."

"Drug addict?"

"That's the new rumor. Heroin, I think."

"Why would you say three in the morning?"

"What?"

"You said he dropped off the notes at three in the morning. Why so specific?"

"I just tossed a number out there. I don't have time for this." Mason begins collecting papers and stuffing them in folders. "I've got a class to teach."

"Which one, Lloyd?" Bradford asks.

"Hip-Hop Culture and African American Identity."

"That's a great class."

"I didn't know white guys were allowed to teach black history," I say.

Bradford knocks me on the shoulder. "Don't be small-minded, ginger."

"It's Bronx history, Mr. Peabody. American history. And I'd ask you to sit in and enlarge your worldview, but I think it would be a little over your head. I'll be talking about 1520 Sedgwick Avenue today, which I'm told you know nothing about."

"Grandmaster Flash. DJ Kool Herc."

"Bravo."

170

Poe & I

"Where does he live?"

Mason slams one of his drawers and eye-fucks me. "Who? Grandmaster Flash?"

"Quinn."

Mason rubs his sinus. "I think he's over in Riverdale somewhere. Are you going to go knock on his door? Be my guest. I'll send you his address."

"I'd like that. Thank you. So, one more thing. If you're on the board, you voted for me, too."

"Of course," he grabs his keys. "I don't care who lives in that filthy basement. Now, if we are truly finished,"— he walks around the desk and opens the door—"get the hell out of my office."

Bradford reams my ass all the way back to the cottage. "Gone out of my way for you, put my good name on the line, and what do you do? Act all crazy!"

"That guy is dirty."

"Dirty? You think you're in a cop movie? You think Lloyd is making that shit up?"

"Did you ever meet this Quinn?"

"No. I wasn't employed long enough to get the inside baseball. Look, if you think Mason had answers, why the hell would you up and accuse the man of stealing Cynthia's book? How's that going to get us answers?"

"Us?"

"Oh, we in this together now. You best believe."

"How you figure?"

"Nobody told me about this Ricky Thurston guy. And then, eight months into my job, Cynthia tells me I'm just an interim caretaker. Surprise! Thank you for your service, but we were just waiting for the ideal white boy. No explanation. Just said my time was up."

He slaps a stop sign with the palm of his hand, the metal clang reverberating down Heroin Ally. Junkies swarm about as we cross to the Mormon church, positioned over the block like the prow of a ship. "I knew Cynthia didn't want to let me go! I knew it! I knew she was being railroaded."

"Or blackmailed by Quinn."

He adjusts his shoulder bag and fiddles with the collar of his suit. "Okay. So. Pay up."

Matthew Mercier

"Say what now?"

"Don't play dumb. One thing from your resume. We had a deal. Wait, don't tell me." He smirks. "You didn't really go to college, did you?"

A pit opens in the rubbery well of my stomach. "For one year."

"I knew it! You drop out?"

"Not like I didn't want to finish."

"And that kangaroo hunting?"

"You said one thing."

"Right. Kangaroos my ass."

We stand in the shadow of the church, on a section of sidewalk that slopes upward toward the Concourse. Bradford angles himself on the slope above me, extra tall. "How did you get this job without a college degree? Is this Quinn guy part of your family?"

"I don't have a family."

"Everyone's got some family."

"Not me," I say. "Quinn stole it."

That makes him flinch. But he's right. We're in this together now. So, I need to calm down. We walk over to Vicky's, and we're about to go in when he waves it off and suggests the Empire diner instead. I peer inside and see Alabama at the counter, scooping soup into his mouth. He doesn't see me or his nephew.

At the Empire, I lay out the ciphers and tell Bradford everything that's happened so far.

Don't trust her. You owe a debt. Time to repay.

"Why am I not surprised that you've pissed somebody off, gingerbread?"

My arm is throbbing. The snake is fat with poison as it slides up and down my arm, trying to find entry to my chest, my heart. My name is Jonah Peabody and everything will be fine.

During these first few months here in The Bronx, I've fooled myself into thinking I'd won the cottage on my own merits when I knew, deep in my heart, that Quinn—or somebody like him—lay in the shadows, turning my position with Poe, like so much of my invented life, into one more hoax.

Chapter 16

A New You

Mother was being visited by the McKittrick family. This, apparently, was part of the McKittrick-Peabody truce.

A truce is never clean or entirely peaceful. Before the truce, blood is spilled, lives are shattered, and then, after all that warfare, the parties compromise. They sit across from each other at a table and pretend to eat crow. Father had, unbeknownst to us, been feasting on crow for the better part of a year. This crow-flavored compromise is what he and Andromeda argued about on the ride home, since on this visit to the loony bin Andy discovered the McKittrick Compromise.

No, she didn't care if the visits were supervised or validated by the state of New York. What she cared about was Mother's confusion. Mother thought her son was visiting her, and I, Jonah Peabody, had never set foot in the hospital or prison or cracked corn compound where she now lived.

Had I?

Father and Andy asked me this point blank over the dinner table. No, I boasted, looking at Father. Hell no.

My cortex wrapped itself in a pretzel as Andy tried to explain how the surviving McKittrick boy, oddly enough, looked a bit similar to me.

"He's much taller and skinnier, but he's got red hair, and his face, you both have the same cheekbones and nose. It's weird. I think he's trying to look like you. I think its deliberate."

"Ridiculous," Father grumbled. "Sheer spooky coincidence."

"But why are they visiting?" I asked.

173

Matthew Mercier

"The father is on some new Christian path of forgiveness," Andy said. "He's trying to forgive her. To forgive us."

"And you think I should visit her because . . . ?"

"You're the real Jonah."

"Am I?"

This set off another round of arguing. Father thought if I started showing up now, it would just further confuse Mother, and while Andy agreed, it disturbed her that she agreed, so she disagreed with herself and said I should show up anyway.

"We need to keep Mother steady," Father retorted.

A little late for that. I wanted no part of this. Mother always told me I wasn't her baby. So, prophecy fulfilled. Jonah Peabody was dead. Long live Jonah Peabody.

But then Andy begged. "For me. Please, Jonah. She hasn't got long. She's got cancer. This might be your last chance. Visit her. For me. Just once."

And, since I would die for my sister, I said yes.

You'd think the loony bin would at least be something out of those Hammer Horror films they show on Creature Double Feature. Silent brick buildings with barred windows and gothic archways, the grounds planted with ancient weeping willows and oak trees, all perched atop a rocky cliff that plunged into the churning brown throat of the Hudson River.

Instead, we just drove south an hour to a square, gray building in the middle of a parking lot. No romance, just an Orwellian box.

In the car, Andromeda gave me a pep talk. "Remember to stay positive. Be patient. Let her talk and just listen. She is the woman that brought you into this world."

Was that a reason to be grateful? I'd heard some comedian on TV complaining about this. *"I was a free spirit, floating around in the ether, a being of pure light, and you two mortals had to fuck and bring me into this world of pain!"*

We waited in a drafty, dropped-ceiling cafeteria, which doubled for the visiting room. Long Formica banquet tables with stiff orange seats, everything plastic and smooth and rounded. No sharp edges anywhere. Other families sat at the table with us. No privacy, no hiding. Across from the cafeteria sat another square box of decrepit sofas and chairs, where patients slumped, heads either resting on their chests or watching television—no glass partitions, no chained ankles, no screaming of tortured souls.

Poe & I

(Maybe that was behind the scenes.) Just a quiet, anti-septic dullness—remember, madness equals boredom.

The orderlies appeared at the edge of the room with Mother wedged between them—a ferocious mane of black hair, an uneven gap-toothed smile, and claws for hands. She looked sixty but was only in her late thirties. Next to me, Father stiffened. Andy put a hand on my knee as I measured my breaths. As they brought her closer, I saw myself in the hooded eyes, which darted over the room, landing on us. Her tongue flicked in, out, and she twitched and scratched her left shoulder. The orderlies each held an elbow and shunted her toward us, even though she seemed capable of walking on her own. I thought she'd be wearing handcuffs, but I guess they kept her well medicated. As a result, she'd also gained a double chin and expanded waistline.

"Hi mom," Andy said.

Mother cocked her head at the greeting (You talking to me?) and the orderlies guided her to a chair, where she sat down hard, shivering inside a cement-colored sweatshirt. She'd lost a number of her teeth, and gray hair sprouted from her ears.

The orderly said, "One hour. Mrs. Peabody has another visitor later and then physical therapy."

Another visitor. The McKittrick's had muscled in on our time. How? Andy swore under her breath, but Father shrugged it off and jumped right in. "Hello, Pamela. How are you, love?"

Mother's chapped lips scrunched, and she ran her tongue over her remaining teeth. "You have to get me out of here, Peter. This place is so horrid. They don't let me draw or paint. All I can do is read, and that's boring. I hate reading."

Father's name was not Peter.

Mother's chattering mouth went on for a good ten minutes. Her gaze eventually circled round to stare at me dumbly. I sat forward. She recoiled slightly, as if I might hit her, so I leaned back. She rubbed the tabletop with her fingers, knobbed and swollen. Her chin waddled with fat, and wrinkles crawled up her neck and throat. Her face was dotted with pockmarks and craters, pink acne shaded the corner of her nostrils, and the skin encircling her eyes was pale from migraines. Finally, she parted her cracked lips, nodded at me, and croaked: "Who are you?"

Andy squeezed my knee. "Mom, this is your son."

Mother surveyed me again, then smiled. "Your name is Jonah."

Matthew Mercier

I nodded.

"Your name is Jonah Peabody, and everything will be fine."

Andy rubbed the back of my neck, as if making a wish. Mother tilted so far to the right I thought she'd tip over. Her eyes went from Andy, to me, to Father, then back to me. My heart flapped. My mouth gummed up. If she wanted to accept me, great. If not, no worries. Truly. No Hallmark bullshit here. I kept thinking of those photo albums in Father's closet, that museum of Mother's youth. She and dad on their honeymoon, hiking in Hawaii, dad with a handlebar mustache, mom with her silky black hippie hair running down to her waist. Her pregnant with me at the kitchen table, eating from a jar of pickles, juice spilling over her chin. Another with her sitting cross-legged with a guitar, Andy and I are on her lap, her wild green eyes trained on sheet music my father was holding. Images of a family that existed before my memory.

Mother blinked and repeated my name. "Jo-nuh."

"Your son," Andy repeated.

Her mouth dropped open. "But you're the old Jonah. Where is the new Jonah?"

Now, that circular conundrum might have ruined a lesser man, but I was a little older now—still immature but old enough to recognize the possibility here. The old Jonah Peabody, me, had been wiped from her memory. The McKittrick boy was the new Jonah. My head began churning. The clinical thing to say, the right thing to say, was that I was the only Jonah, but instead, I replied, "Yes. I'm the old version. I work at the funeral parlor."

Believe me, I was just as surprised as everyone else in that room at what I said.

Father said, "Don't . . . Jonah no. Don't confuse her. Don't."

"It's the truth, isn't it? I'm the old Jonah."

Father looked sick. Andy advised me to be positive, so here I was, Mr. Positivity. Mother believed I was *a* Jonah, but not *the* Jonah, so I was just playing my part. Either way, she soon branched off into other topics. She began discussing Blake, who I only knew from that box in the closet. With her wild hair and saucer-shaped eyes, she looked like a Blake painting.

This babble went on for an hour, with Mother tossing off subjects like Richard Nixon, The Black Panthers, and Jackson Pollock. Then she was scrolling through her Rolodex of imaginary ex-lovers and spooling off a profanity laden screed against marriage.

Poe & I

But she saved the best (or worst) for last.

"You're such a handsome young man, Jonah. I wish you were my son."

I hedged my bets. "I think I am your son."

"Oh no, dear. You were replaced at birth. But maybe I'll adopt you. You're a nice boy."

She placed an open palm on the table, the flesh laced with a half dozen little slits. "I don't know why I'm here. I'd like to come home with you, Jonah. Do you know how to cook? The food here is terrible. All I get here is starch and sugar and pills. That's probably why I'm so fat and have cancer."

"That's horrible, Mom. Well, I'd like to come back and talk more about Blake."

No snark. I meant that. Mission accomplished. I wasn't going to get my childhood back, not now and not ever, so maybe I could build an alternate sandbox to play around in. But the orderlies were behind her now. The other visitors were here. We had to go.

Andromeda eye-fucked the old man, who just said, "I'll meet you both at the car."

I felt that old shiver, of something good being taken away, and said good-bye to Mother, who gave a childlike wave.

Outside, Father walked briskly across the parking lot, shoulders pumping under his flannel jacket, towards a silver Chrysler. I could barely make out the driver's features as he rose into my line of sight—dark blond hair, glasses. He turned, as if on cue, to greet the lumbering beast of my father. They gave each other curt nods and a weak handshake. The stranger stood leaning over his open door. My father bowed his head and looked off to the side as he spoke. Only once during their conversation did the stranger glance over at us.

"McKittrick?" I asked.

Andy rolled a tongue in her mouth. "The father."

The Chrysler's passenger door opened, and a young boy unfolded into the air, tall and lanky. Hair spiky, face narrow as a triangle, and the whitest skin I'd ever seen. An albino worm, sickly and translucent. He shone in the sunlight and wore sunglasses.

The remaining son. He looked at Father, then at us. Andy looked away, but I looked right at him, daring him to take off his sunglasses. Now the old man was walking back to us, the light drained from his eyes.

Matthew Mercier

"We'll write a letter," I mumbled to Andy. "We need to write a letter to that kid."

Do I need to tell you that we never wrote that letter? This was the moment when Father's guilt became our guilt. When we did nothing. As we pulled out, we had to roll past the entrance and I got a better look at the son, who I guess was my twin if you squinted—red hair, skinny frame, broad shoulders. He turned to glare at us as we drove by, and even through the shield of those sunglasses, his eyes burned me with their hate.

Look at me, they said. *Look at me.*

I'd see him again a year later.

In that time, I visited Mother once a month, the cancer nibbling at her stomach, Poe's conqueror worm taking her back, inch by intestinal inch, her body a block of wood being whittled to splinters.

Andy always came with me, and Mother always called me "Old Jonah." Despite the reams of conversation, we never connected emotionally, but after each visit, I did feel a little bit of her inside me. We always avoided the McKittrick family, never building up the requisite courage.

As death approached, the prison granted her a "compassionate release" and hospice set us up in our living room, with a view—wait for it—of the graveyard. Tell me the universe isn't a giant trickster crow, cawing and laughing and shoving us around the chessboard with its beak.

When the moment arrived, Dad performed his manly stoic act, Andy wept openly, and I sat there on a stool thinking of how in the world to say goodbye to a woman I never knew, who never knew me, and who never wanted me in the first place. Andy brushed her cheek with the side of her hand while Mother moaned.

Her body started to wind down. Every human needs to see another human wind down, just so they understand—our bodies are clocks. Machines. Her chest rose and fell, with a phlegm-filled death rattle on the downbeat. That rattle filled the room. (It's filling my head now, as I relive it.) Her chest rose and fell, rose, fell, rose, fell . . . and then, fell.

Full stop. She didn't move. Nothing moved. In the room. In the hospital. On the whole planet. We all leaned forward. She was a stick on a pillow. We waited.

Poe & I

"Okay," Dad said. "I'm calling the cor—"

Her body jolted and jerked. Her eyes shot open, with a high-pitched wheezing, and Andy fell backward off her seat. My father swore and hit the ceiling. I covered my mouth and bit my lip so I wouldn't laugh.

Mother's arms shot up like a puppet, fingers loose and wiggling. She grabbed the sides of my head tightly, pulled my face closer to hers, and hissed, "I'm still here."

She kissed me in the corner of my mouth, all teeth and rubber band lips, and then fell back. Andy was on the floor, Father behind me. She gave us one, two more breaths.

Then. Gone. Thank you and goodnight.

My mouth tasted of her metallic kiss. I rubbed my head, feeling for dents.

So. She'd tried to take me out, one more time. The knife didn't work, so I'll try popping my son's head like a melon. Or maybe that was her version of "I love you."

But those last words, "I'm still here," proved to be her final prophecy.

While she was dying, Dad was a beast, but after she passed, he grew into a beast with a broken heart, a wounded animal—the most dangerous kind.

We drove her to the parlor, where Dad embalmed, polished, shaved, and dressed her. It's beyond me how you could do that with your own wife, but he was made of iron on that day. We helped move her tiny body into a fat mahogany coffin. She was light, but the starched blouse she wore bunched under my fingers, and I thought I might drop her. It felt akin to moving a delicate antique—you break it, you buy it. (Relax. It's my mother.) Then Father asked for some time alone.

The funeral brought out the family we never talked about and with good reason. Ex-cons from Western New York. Aunts on my mother's side who felt their niece had married below her station. Cousins who wanted nothing to do with us. But everyone agreed on one point: our father handled Mother's illness poorly.

"You'll notice they weren't around for her illness," Father said later. "They couldn't handle it. They abandoned her. I'm the one who saved her."

The strangest moment came when Andy and I were talking to

Matthew Mercier

our Uncle Louie, and we asked him about Mother's college life. He blinked and said, "College? She never went."

We told him about the box, about the Blake, the photos, but he shrugged. "She could have gone to college. With her smarts, she could have done anything— but she didn't."

The fuzz of that conversation stuck to our brains as we put her in the ground on that drizzly November afternoon. The McKittrick men showed up but stood off in the distance, a pair of trench coat wraiths. Only after the crowd dispersed did they approach the open grave. Again, we failed to apologize.

The family dispersed (no post-funeral meal for the Peabody clan), and Father drove us back to the parlor. He told us to wait and went inside, then popped up in the freight elevator with a coffin on the gurney.

Andy, slouched in the back seat, sat up. "That's a hemp coffin. Fuck is this?"

Hemp. The cheapest and lightest coffins we sold. We figured this was a body for tonight's calling hours, but instead Father loaded it into the Ghostbusters hearse.

"Andy, you can drive the car back to the house. Jonah, come with me."

Andromeda's eyes burned. "Wait . . . "

No discussion. Father whistled for me to get in the hearse.

It started to downpour, the rain sweeping sideways. That screwy Dylan song came on the radio, something about a one-eyed midget screaming for milk. Orange and red leaves drifted across the road as a sliver of creeping panic climbed the knots of my spine.

"Dad?"

"Hmmm?"

"Who's in the coffin?"

Father smiled. "We're keeping her, Jonah." His voice cracked. "We're taking Mother home.

Chapter 17

Ricky Thurston

There is a cat outside.

Its horny caterwauling seeps into my pill infused sleep. I keep my eyes shut. Mother is hovering over me—stale breath, musty damp clothing, and the cold triangle of the knife slipping in and out of my chest, despite my measured breathing. Give it another five minutes. She'll go away.

Your mother is not here, Jonah Peabody, says a voice with the lilt of a Southern accent.

I open my eyes. Poe is hovering above me, flecks of dust in His mustache, a gray finger buried in my chest up to the knuckle.

"Gahhh! Get off me!"

The Poet pulls out His finger, floats off my chest, and settles on the loveseat, picking up a butterflied book that rests on the cushions. It's a volume of Lovecraft.

"How did you—?" I rub my eyes, gazing at the ceiling. Green fluid is tracing across the plaster walls, a spider web of fluid, dripping onto the floor in front of the library.

It was fairly easy to descend, once I conquered my fear of passing through solids. I have been perusing your library.

He holds up Lovecraft.

This man is a horrible writer. Operatic hyperbole seems to be his stock in trade.

"He learned it from you. Wait, how are you able to hold the book?"

He stares at His hand, wiggling the fingers. *I seem to have acquired a bit more solidity.*

Matthew Mercier

"That makes no sense."

Indeed. My sense of touch is not consistent. I cannot, for example, take a hold of your heart, which I was just now attempting to do.

My chest hammers, and I massage the spot where His finger penetrated me.

Do not fear, Jonah Peabody. I have no wish to stop your heart, merely to touch it. As a scientific experiment.

"Please don't," I say. "Mother is enough to deal with."

That is actually what brought me down into your part of the abode.

I pull on a sweatshirt and rub my core to warm up. "So, you saw her?"

Oh yes. She is a terrifying apparition.

"I've carried her around my whole life, but for some reason your basement is the worst it's ever been."

My cottage does something to people.

"So I keep hearing."

On the brighter side, you did marginally better with my life story during your tours this weekend.

"Glad to hear it."

Marginally. I would sue you for libel if I could.

The cat turns up the volume. Beyond the window, it's all sunlight and traffic. Sounds of a Monday. I rumble into the kitchen for coffee. What time is it? Sleeping underground rewires your biological clock. I crack the kitchen window and startle the stray cat, who's perched outside in the bushes.

I attempted to give the feline entry, Poe says, *but the creature is scared of me.*

"It can see you?"

It would seem so.

I pull on my jeans and pop outside. The cat is now on the porch, crouched in the museum doorway. It's gray with flecks of white on its chin. It looks healthy enough, but when it turns, it shows off a milky right eye. I hold out a finger and coo, but it hisses and arches its spine, so I go across the street and buy a few cans of tuna. I peel off the lids, place the cans on the porch, and step back. The one-eyed graybeard gobbles them both in seconds. As it licks its chops, I sit on the steps and sip my coffee, giving Poe time to evaporate. The cat watches me. I rub my pinkie nub, thinking of

Poe & I

Ramses. It's been a month since his surprise visit. I have a little dough in my bank account now, but the paychecks are a trickle.

My phone buzzes. A text from Carla.

Still cool to stop by today with friends?

Shit. I forgot. It's October. Almost Halloween.

I text back. *Of course, please do.*

I stand, and the cat hisses, but not at me. Its eyeline is directed at the shed, where Poe is standing in the doorway, sweeping His transparent foot across the concrete, a swimmer testing the temperature of the water.

I cannot seem to cross this threshold, He says, *nor enter the greenhouse.*

There are people walking down the Concourse and Kingsbridge with a full view of Poe Cottage, but nobody blinks at the two strange white guys talking.

"Let's go inside, Edgar. I need to ask you some questions."

I am not in a mood to discourse with you, Jonah Peabody. Unless you have news about my dear Sissy.

"Not today. Maybe soon. Do you know anything about my mother?"

She clearly terrifies you.

"Brilliant observation. What is Quinn's real name?"

Do not give me queries to which you already have the answers.

Poe turns and coos at the cat, but it arches its spine and backs away. Poe's brow furrows and He drifts backward into the shed. Once Poe is gone, the cat's spine relaxes, and it settles into the doorway again.

The rest of the day is housekeeping. I scrub mold off the basement walls, since the docs at the local walk-in clinic said the source of the black dot on my palm might be that—mold. I'm likely inhaling all kinds of dust and fungus, but I know that's only part of it: Quinn poisoned me with the dust in those flowers.

Still, I bought an air freshener for the apartment, and I clean on the regular, plus I'm sleeping upstairs with Poe, both for the cleaner air and to avoid Mother, although when I leave the tooth necklace out it seems to distract her.

Ever since the visit with Mason (Two, three weeks ago? I'm losing track of time) when he confirmed that Quinn had gotten me this job, my mind has been a riot of nerves. I've been so

Matthew Mercier

concentrated on keeping Mother out of my body that I've barely focused on finding Quinn. Mason never got back to me with that address, and Lizzie hasn't returned my phone calls about this Ricky Thurston interview.

The cat hides in the garden when the Puerto Rican Vampire Club shows up with their friends, all dressed in leather trench coats. They whoop and vamp across the lawn. Carla, creeping up the front steps, asks me "Podemos entrar?" Her brown cheeks shine with a light rouge, lips glistening Metallica black.

"Please do," I say.

She curls her fingers in a Bela Lugosi pose. "Are you surrrrree?"

"Entra, por favor."

Tea-kettle shrieks. "Escuchan eso hermanos? Vamous a chuparles su sangre!"

Their crew is a mixed group of first-year college kids and locals who haven't left yet. The conversation inside the cottage is not so much about Poe as their own future, how they're hustling to feed their families, how they so badly want to escape. One kid, Benny, a beanpole with tats of snakes and skulls on his forearms, is joining the army. (There's a recruitment station smack in the middle of the Concourse and Fordham Road—a deceptive portal out of poverty.) Another kid, Vanessa, is hoping to study journalism at Columbia, but Carla is telling her to not go because the scholarships are a scam and she'll just be in debt afterward.

"You'll be the token brown person," she says. "It's a joke."

"Well, we can't all grow up to be brujas like you, girl."

"I'm just saying. Don't get in the hole. It's not worth it." Carla is volunteering at the Botanical Gardens after school and tells Vanessa this is the key to success. To volunteer and talk your way into jobs, but Vanessa isn't buying it. You can't get anywhere without a college degree, she says, but Carla keeps pressing her points.

Meanwhile, Oscar is going on to Benny and another young woman, Jade, a student at Monroe College, about punk music and why it's the superior protest music, but Jade is teasing him about how listening to Black Flag and the Misfits makes him whiter. Cleary Jade is madly in love with Oscar, but Oscar is too wrapped up in his fanboy pontificating to notice this. Worse, he doesn't take her teasing lightly.

"You wait and see! Me and the boys are going to release a punk Puerto Rican album, and it's going to be dope."

Poe & I

"I believe you," Jade laughs. She's the aspiring poet of the group. "I just think you need to slow down. Work on your lyrics. I can help you."

"I don't think you'd get me, girl. I'm deep."

Hilarious and beautiful. Just having their youthful energy around helps me to stave off the moldy vibes crawling across my chest, my lungs, my arm. I give them a tour, and when I get to the story of Virginia's bones, I dare to say that I'm actively looking for the remains myself. Carla and Oscar back the story up, so I don't seem too crazy. It all inspires Carla to recite poetry.

"Hace muchos, muchos años, en un reino junto al mar, vivía una doncella cuyo nombre era Annabel Lee . . . "

Jade sighs. "Ay, es muy triste aquí. No me imagino a nadie viviendo aquí."

Carla nods and winks at me.

"I'm sorry," I say. "I lost you there. Que dijiste?"

Jade stares at me. "I said it would be sad to live here."

"Oh."

"And that you look a little haunted."

"Even better."

"Jonah is Irish," Carla says. "Sad and haunted are normal for him."

I laugh for the first time in weeks.

"You've got a kitty," Carla squeals, seeing the cat frolic in the drooping Hosta plants.

She tries to pet the stray and tells me about her plans for the spring, how she wants to plant flowers here that show up in Poe's writing.

"A living version of *Landor's Cottage*," I say. "That's a good idea."

"Claro, yes. Exactly. Honeysuckle, jasmine. It was my idea, but Lizzie said she had to run it by Cynthia."

"That's great. I need to talk with Lizzie, but she doesn't pick up her phone."

"I know. She's been busy." Carla says this with a pinch in her face.

Oscar tells everyone they need to jet, as they've got a party to go to, but then at the front gate, he turns to me. "Jonah man. Got to ask you a personal question."

"Shoot."

"Be honest with me now. You tweaking?"

185

Matthew Mercier

"What?"

"Your arm, bro."

The black line running up the inside of my forearm looks like a tattoo. "Oh, my mold scar? Nah, that's just a result of being the man underground."

"Mold?" Carla sounds incredulous.

"That's what the doc said."

Now that Oscar has drawn attention to my arm, he sees my other scars. "You a cutter, Jonah?"

I scratch and twitch. "Not anymore."

He nods and lifts his shirt, showing me a slice of his hip and some faint rainbow shaped cuts. "I liked doing my legs, too."

"Past tense, right?"

"Kicked it after I found punk."

Carla tugs her brother's shirt down. "Don't be flashing that shit like you proud, bro."

"I'm not. But Jonah. For real. Are you?"

"Oscar, I'm not shooting up."

"We can't have a junkie working here. You can't be getting sick on us. Especially if you're really looking for Virginia's bones. You weren't playing back there?"

"No. Cynthia asked me to find them."

"Let us know when you find Sissy," Carla says. "She needs a proper burial. Only way to appease the spirits. You should talk to Poe. See what he knows."

This is said with a wink and a nod, and all I say is, "He's looking for her, too."

They both chuckle and, without another word, we bump fists. We're on the same team. Happy Halloween.

First things first. Call—harass—Lizzie and Bradford about this Ricky Thurston interview and Quinn's address.

Lizzie finally calls me back, apologizing for not being in touch. "I've been traveling for research."

"Oh? Poe stuff?"

"No," she says. "Quinn stuff."

"What?"

"I can't explain right now." She fiddles with papers on her end, the rustle loud and abrasive. "So, you're really playing detective?"

Poe & I

"That's what you wanted, right?"

"For sure. But that Ricky interview. It should be in the Fordham archives. And I can tell where you Quinn lives. You don't need Mason for that."

"Any leads would be greatly appreciated."

"Call me after you watch those interviews."

It occurs to me that, if she conducted the interview, she might have a copy herself, but I don't push. She wishes me well, and we say good bye.

A few days later, after corralling Bradford, we're in the archives, searching for the Thurston interview. An hour into the search, Mason staggers into the office, shirt un-tucked and hair uncombed, as if he's just woken up. "Bradley!" The professor looks right past me. "What are you doing here?"

"We didn't want to bother you, Lloyd."

"Bother me now. What do you need?"

"That old interview. Ricky Thurston?"

"Oh." Mason shifts from foot to foot "The Poe caretaker. Yes."

"Professor Mason," I say, "I know I was a jerk the last time we met, but I was a little scared. Honestly, I thought you might be Quinn."

The professor snorts. "Certainly not."

"Then prove it to me."

Mason mumbles, glancing at the computer. He works something out in his head, then takes hold of the mouse. The folds of his jacket drop open. The flask hangs inside. "Ricky Thurston. Yes, I think it's filed under Parks."

"We checked there," Bradford says.

"Dammit. Hold on." Mason runs through several files, the logic of which makes no sense. He's double-clicking and dragging through an infinite hall of icons, until he hits one labeled *Eureka*. "Here. Yes. Don't know why it's in there. Looks like somebody buried it."

"We'll need a few copies, Lloyd," says Bradford.

Sweat is beading Mason's neck as the computer whirs and hums and burns the interview onto a pair of DVDs. "You didn't get this from me, understand?"

"Thank you, Professor Mason." I shake his hand. "You won't regret this."

"I'm sure." The frumpy teacher reaches for his flask.

187

Matthew Mercier

Back in the basement, we slip the disc into my computer. The screen quivers, and an index card flashes across the lens. Date. Time. Name of subject: Ricky Thurston.

Cut to the man himself. Light skin, cropped fro, big square jaw. Bradford pauses the video so we can get a good look. Ricky has a zig-zag scar running down his left cheek. He smiles at the camera, a gap between his front teeth. He's seated in the parlor, with the bust of Poe framed over his left shoulder. Bradford hits play.

"You want I should start?" Ricky asks.

"Start whenever." Lizzy's voice, off-camera.

Thurston's voice is a gravely tenor. We listen to his life story, growing up on the Grand Concourse in the late eighties. Dance battles with rival gangs in the shadow of the bandstand, rocking and popping his young heart out, while the South Bronx crumbled and burned. He names all the right people. Afrika Bambaataa, DJ Kay Slay, and Riche "Crazy Legs" Colon. He says he ran with Young Lords in the twilight of the gang era, then tried to make it to college with aspirations to be a journalist. Finally, at the halfway mark, we get to Poe Cottage.

"I was trying to get my life on track. Figured Poe's house here would be a pretty good way to do that. Stay in the hood without paying rent. Society hired me'cause I was a local, friendly with a lot of people, good with the kids, no felonies on my record. I made a good ambassador."

"Ricky," Lizzie says, "I have to ask this because people always want to know. Is the cottage haunted?"

A loud shuffling as Thurston's chin bumps the lavalier mic on his collar. "I get that question a lot. I used to say no. But that's what you're supposed to say. Sure, I heard things at night. Seen things. There's something here, mos def."

"See?" I say, "it's not just me."

Bradford bites his knuckles.

"But folks never believe me," Ricky goes on, "even though they be the ones asking the question. I say, 'Why you asking if you don't want to know?' It's silly. So yes, I do get visits from Poe."

"And Virginia?"

"Her too! I can hear her coughing at night. Out there in the greenhouse. I think they're trying to get back together, but something is blocking them."

"Is that why you're leaving? The ghosts?"

188

Poe & I

"Oh, I don't mind them. They keep me company. No, I got health issues. My teeth. My knees. And this." He points to his left eye. "I'm getting a cataract. Harder to give the tours. Bumping into the furniture, you know?"

"Where will you go?"

"Not sure yet. Hopefully Cynthia can give me a bit more time. Mr. Quinn offered to help out, but I don't know about him." Ricky's eyes flicker off camera. "Speak of the devil. There he is."

The camera swings around, and there is Lizzie Borden, dressed all in black, nose stud flashing. The lens quickly pans to the front window and finds a gaunt figure coming through the gate.

"You invited Arthur Quinn?" Lizzie asks.

"He invited himself."

"Did he know we were doing this interview?"

"I might have mentioned it. We've been chatting a lot. He invited me up to his place for dinner. Up there in Riverdale. They say he's got quite the Poe collection."

Ricky moves across the parlor and opens the door. Low voices on the porch. The figure steps into the gift shop, backlit by sunlight, his face cloaked in shadow.

"You must be Lizzie Borden," Quinn says. "Are you going to hack me to bits?"

"Gee, I've never heard that one."

Quinn steps into the parlor, his face shadowed by a wide-brimmed hat. A pair of green eyes sparkle under the rim. He flicks a hand at the camera. "Shut that off."

The camera lens drops to the floorboards.

"No audio either."

Cut to black. Bradford immediately rewinds the video and hits pause, studying the distorted mess of Quinn's video face, then mine. "His chin is a little sharper. And those eyes are different. But damn. He could be your brother."

I rub my hands together, unsettled but not entirely surprised. "So, Ricky goes to dinner and dies soon after, right?"

"Sounds like it."

"Lizzie gave me Quinn's address. Up in Riverdale."

"What are you going to do?"

"Not sure yet."

Ricky Thurston's history has been erased, and somehow Quinn is involved. It's Andromeda, all over again. I owe them both a

Matthew Mercier

resurrection. That night, after Bradford leaves, the one-eyed cat returns for more tuna, and I'm finally able to coax it into the shed. It's a boy. I name him Dupin. I'm glad he's here. I need the spirit of detection right now, and he keeps Poe and Mother at bay, hissing whenever either gets close. Edgar insists He loves cats, and the historical record backs this up, but when Dupin sees Poe's ghostly face pushing through the ceiling or hears The Poet mumbling and ranting, my kitty friend works himself into a fever, and Poe retreats.

As for Mother, the teeth continue to distract her. She still can't follow me upstairs, but the nights are getting colder, the parlor less inviting, and I'm not counting on the teeth trick lasting forever.

I go back to the clinic, get more blood tests, and it's now confirmed: I've ingested spores, mold, a fungus of some kind. The perfect disease for a shadow dweller. The doc says if I'm not careful, the mold will slip into my lungs, so I need to get outside more. I begin sitting out in the park, in the cool November air, which is heaven on the chapped and blackened skin of my right arm. The dark line has crawled further up my shoulder. Soon it will reach my brain, I'm sure of it, but not before I reach Quinn.

Next stop, Riverdale: the fake Bronx.

It's a relief to have a mission now, to get on a bus and travel somewhere, but even the Bx9 won't take you all the way to Riverdale. It carries you down West Kingsbridge, over the river, and through the woods to Broadway, before it dumps you at 262nd, which is only halfway there. You then have to catch another bus that runs deep into the mansions of Riverdale, and even that won't take you into the maze of fortresses that the Irish and the Jews and the Russians and all manner of rich white people have built.

Quinn's house is literally a castle, with turrets and towers and sprawling extensions, a wall of ivy crawling up a brick façade. He's well insulated from the world, a gothic Hugh Hefner.

So, I can't walk right up to his door—he's fenced in too—but today I've just come with a message. I thought about playing games and writing out a cipher, but that's too much work. Traveling all the way out here is work enough. I stand in front of his gated parcel and do a few paces up and down the block, to make sure I get on whatever security cameras he's got, then I take my prepared note,

Poe & I

neatly stuffed in an envelope, and slip it through the fence. It simply reads:

Dear Mr. Quinn,

I know who you are and what you've done. Let's talk. I'm guilty, too.

Jonah Peabody

There. Ball is in your court, McKittrick.

Chapter 18

Living Death

Mother is coming to live with us, Father said. We're not putting her in the ground with the worms. She's going to live forever.

I wish this part of my story was a lie.

We'd now fulfilled a prophecy: the Family Necro. The Necro Peabodys. The Necromancers.

Father and I rode in silence. We cruised along in that clown car of a hearse, with Andy trolling behind us. I grabbed the door handle, almost flung it open to hurl myself on the rolling pavement.

At the house, Father backed into the driveway, the better to load Mother inside. Andy rolled up behind us, a stiff corpse herself, hands frozen at ten and two on her steering wheel. Father opened the rear of the hearse and unfolded the gurney. It was dark by then, a night in the lonesome October—Mother's season—with nothing but the dark woods and empty road to hide us, but Father still looked around nervously, as if someone might appear at any moment. "Help me. Both of you. Quickly."

If we refused, where did that leave us? Report him to the authorities? Bring down more trouble on our already troubled family? No way. Not now. So, Andy and I robotically walked to the rear of the hearse, automations on a clockwork timer. My sister looked ready to vomit, her cheeks swollen and pale.

"Dad," I said, "what's in the other coffin?"

I purposely said "what," not "who," giving him the benefit of the doubt.

"How do you mean?"

192

Poe & I

"The one we put in the ground?"

Father slid the hemp coffin to the rear bumper. "A bunch of sandbags."

My sister and I both exhaled. Father was a sad sack of grief, but he was no body snatcher. (Of strangers' bodies, anyway) Just a faker of funerals.

Mother and the hemp coffin were light, so the three of us easily lifted her onto the porch and wheeled her down our wide hallway to a spare room at the back of the house. Father had been clearing this room out for weeks. Two nights before he'd brought in a pair of sawhorses. I thought he was prepping for a crazy renovation, or building some bookcases, and then I remembered Mother's last words:

"I'm still here."

Had the future flashed before her eyes? Had she known this was coming?

We lifted the coffin onto the sawhorses. Andy's cheeks flushed, and she crossed her arms tightly across her chest. I put my fingers on her waist, and she stepped away from me. Father, oblivious as always, stepped toward the coffin, reaching for the leather latch. Andy grabbed his wrist.

He put a hand over hers and said calmly, "Let go of me, Andromeda."

She slapped her other hand on the coffin lid. "I'm not the one who needs to let go."

"She is my wife. Husband trumps daughter."

Father went for the latch again, but Andy pressed down tighter. Father shoved her backward. She fell and her coconut cracked the floor so loud I thought it would break open.

"Oh, Andromeda," he cooed, with that fake instant regret, "look what you made me do." He bent down to help her up, but I jumped between them.

"Don't touch her, Dad."

I didn't say this harshly with venom or spite. Just weariness. I was so, so tired of this man, who I thought had turned the corner on his grief but had only jumped deeper into the pit.

Andy sat up and leaned against the doorjamb. Father turned his back on us and opened the soft lid. I could see the tip of Mother's cotton candy nose. How long did an embalmed body last? A few weeks? A month? How long before she (it) started to rot?

193

Matthew Mercier

"Hello dear." Father placed a hand on her forehead. "Welcome home."

Andy stormed into the hallway and made a hard right into Father's bedroom. She returned with the Pamela box—the photos, the journal, the mystery mother—and pulled out a binder of slides. "You have this to remember her! What is wrong with you?"

Father glanced at the binder, indifferent. "Oh, that."

"Her thesis," Andy said. "Her photos, her—"

"It's not hers. It's who she wanted to be."

We hadn't wanted to believe our uncle, but Mother, the old man explained, had purchased a great deal of the photos and scholarly material from estate sales, bookstores, and thrift shops. Some she'd even stolen from libraries. She built a narrative around the term papers and journals. A brilliant narrative, to be sure, but still. A fiction. All invented. The truth was she came from a small town and a small-minded family who limited her, so she built a dream life for herself. As Father told it, he rescued her from that family, who saw the illness coming down the pike and disowned her.

Andy glanced at the coffin, at the box, at Father. He must have been aware of the irony. He was relating this story to a daughter who'd built the foundation of her own life on the person she thought was her mother, and that daughter was aiming to live the life her mother never could, except now that so-called life was just a dream life, a dream within a dream—according to a man whose track record with the truth was spottier than a dalmatian.

Andy clutched the binder. "No, she was a beautiful, creative soul, and you smothered her."

Much later, I would be able to research Mother's birth name and discover that most of what Father said was true. She was from another small town, a few mountains over, and from all evidence, she never left. Graduated high school, but then got married and popped us out right away. So, it seemed Father was telling the truth, but back then, it tasted of more bullshit. Andy wanted the woman in the box, not the woman in the coffin.

But what did it matter at that point? Print the legend. It made you dream bigger.

"This alternate life kept her happy," Father said. "For a while."

"Until she came into my bedroom," I spat.

"Jonah . . ."

194

Poe & I

"You know what I'm talking about, Dad."

"I don't, actually."

Andromeda picked up the box. "I'm keeping this."

Father sighed. "We have no more use for it."

"Dad," I croaked, "why didn't you tell us any of this?"

His bunched face grew red, either with embarrassment or shame. "You wouldn't have believed me."

You have to laugh. I mean, the man wasn't wrong.

So. Onward and downward. Mother stayed in her room, where Father paid daily devotions. The body (we read up on this) would only last a month, at most, and with the winter coming on there would be no way to get her in the ground without a steam shovel. Father kept the room cold, but eventually, he'd have to turn on the heat to prevent the pipes from freezing. Meanwhile, he kept the doors and windows of the room locked, as he was quite sure Andy might steal her away.

My sister pretended the old man didn't exist. She quit the parlor and ramped up her pot dealing. She was saving for a used car, bookmarking a road atlas of the places she wanted to go. Clarissa hung out with her most weekends, sometimes with a wailing baby on her hip.

Andy's book of the dead was now a hefty portfolio. She'd begun to organize them in three-ring binders, dozens of them, and started on some new stuff that I can only describe as a hybrid between Blake and Poe, gothic Gods walking through blasted fantasy landscapes. The one that caught my eye was a skinny albino with an electrified hairdo. He wore an ankle-length black coat and a puffy pink shirt with buttons open to reveal a U-shaped scar on his chest.

"Who's this?" I asked.

She told me, "I watched Re-Animator last night. Felt inspired to draw somebody who looked as if they'd just been sewn up."

"It looks like me."

"Well, you inspire me, bro."

How could I have been so blind? I was so absorbed in keeping the parlor afloat that I didn't bother to connect the dots. Vince had quit long ago, but he'd taught me how to order coffins, how to paint faces, how to soap a body and drain it of blood through the jugular. I had the dead to thank for my financial stability, but I wanted Father to sell the place. Scuttlebutt in the business was that there

Matthew Mercier

was a big company buying up little funeral homes like ours, trying to build a national chain.

Still, in that horrible autumn, the parlor, once again, saved me, since the more I worked, the more I could stay away from home which meant less time with Mother.

You see, this is when she began to haunt me.

Oh, her corpse stayed in the coffin, but Mother ghosted the property on an endless loop. I'd come home, and she'd be sitting in the living room, staring off into space or out at the cemetery, as if she knew that's where she belonged. Sometimes she perched on the roof or stood at the edge of the woods. But the worst was when she appeared in my bedroom, to recreate that infamous Halloween night, sinking the knife into my chest over and over. At least once a week she attempted to murder me.

I tried to switch out the knife for a soup spoon, but it's hard to fool your memory with the carbon copy of that memory floating nearby, so I tried sleeping in the attic, but she was in there, too, sitting in profile, reading *The Raven* to her invisible children—reading it ten, twelve, thirteen times a night. Once upon a midnight dreary, ad nauseam. Placid busts! Plutonian shores! Over and over and over.

By November, the weight of Mother's presence threatened to drag us into a vortex, and I knew we had to act; but, once again, fate intervened, which is what happens when you don't make decisions—life acts on you. Take note, friends. Life will bury you alive if you don't dig your way out first.

I returned home from the parlor one early afternoon, leaving Father to organize calling hours, to find a familiar red pickup in our driveway.

I leapt onto the porch, pushed open the front door, and called for Andy. It took her a few seconds to answer, but then her voice, soft and frail, responded. "I'm in the kitchen, Jonah. We have a visitor."

Chapter 19

Date Night

Lizzie and I are sitting in Poe's parlor on a Sunday afternoon, the weekend before Thanksgiving. I've locked the gate. Cottage is closed. We had zero guests today. Weird, not having at least one ear to chew about Poe history. Go figure. I've grown too dependent on tourists for company and conversation, so I'm thrilled Lizzie is here. I've told her about my visits to Mason's archives and Quinn's house, and now she's looking at me sideways, although I'm not sure why. Didn't she want me to be a detective?

"Yes," she says, "but I have to admit that I was performing a bit when I first met you."

She's huddled inside a brown peacoat which is clearly second-hand, its pockets and wrists frayed. Her pigtails are jutting out from under a red wool hat, and her legs are crossed, one Doc Marten bobbing in the air. "It's what I do. I perform around new people. I didn't know how serious you were about the job or that you knew what it entailed."

We're behind the rope, inside the exhibit, sitting on the bench by the back window. The sun has set, but Poe has not yet arrived. I'm hoping he'll surprise us. The wind rattles the eves, and the limbs of the spider oak out back are shaking wildly, setting off the tinkling chimes.

Lizzie turns and looks out the window. In profile, her sharp, pierced face is even sharper, prettier. "Those are some loud-ass wind chimes."

"I don't think they're up too high."

"They weren't here when Ricky was the caretaker. Hmmm.

Matthew Mercier

Well, as I said, I couldn't get a read on you, Jonah, after our first meeting. Even after our second. I didn't know if you were committed to Poe."

"And now?"

"I think you're committed to yourself. That much is obvious. So, I'm glad you were curious about Ricky Thurston's story."

"His story seems connected to your boy Quinn's."

"My boy," she scoffs. "Quinn needs to disappear, needs to just go away."

We're on the same side, we have to be. We're meeting in the middle of a mystery. "What else can you tell me about him?"

"I know he's rich," she says. "I know he lives in Riverdale and that he's been at the historical society forever. I know he and Cynthia hate each other's guts, but they've found a way to co-exist. I know he's creepy and that he's got all kinds of weird shit in his house, and in his past. Like you."

Now she looks directly at me, as if trying to commit my face to memory. "And I know he's your spitting image. If you squint. He's not your brother?"

"No."

"Do you know him?"

I swallow. "I'd have to meet face to face to be sure."

"Hell does that mean?"

"I think . . . I think he used to be somebody different. Is he addicted to heroin?"

"Cynthia may have started that rumor."

"What else do you know?"

"I know he wanted you here in the cottage. I thought it was nepotism, after Cynthia told me your resume was most likely a fake."

"It's not fake."

"Did you go to college?"

"A year."

"Well, Ricky was going to school while he worked here, so you don't really need a degree." She takes a flash drive from the pocket of her coat. "These are excerpts from a video diary that he made in the month before he died."

"A diary. Which is not in the Fordham archive?"

"Correct."

I'm about to suggest that I grab my laptop and we watch them together, but then Poe's moans echo in my ears.

Poe & I

"He's here!" I yip, without thinking. "Poe."

"Jonah, don't mess with me."

The bust is beginning to glow. "Here," I whisper. "Look."

He arrives piece by piece—legs, torso, mustache—solidifying in the doorway between the parlor and Virginia's bedroom. Face worn out, broken blood vessels running in a delta across His forehead. A circular, peanut-colored bruise sits above His left eyebrow. His fingers are knotty and scabbed, as if He's been punching a wall.

"Are you okay?" I ask Him.

"I'm fine," Lizzie says. "What am I looking at?" She stands, and Poe floats toward her, His fingernails black and rotting.

"Don't!"

"Don't what?" Lizzie asks.

Poe drifts a hand over Lizzie's head as He pivots to face her. I need to look through Him at her, His fingers hovering over her nose studs.

Why have you mutilated yourself, woman?

Lizzie swats the air, rippling Poe's body, and walks through Him. Poe twirls around, lips glistening with aqua-blue saliva.

Her sweaty hand clasps my wrist, my blackened forearm. "Jonah, your arm looks worse. And, my god, your pulse."

Coughing now, from the greenhouse. Loud and wet. Poe sweeps through us, straight to the window. My legs turn to jelly. I fall backward onto the bench. My elbow hits the window, cracks the glass. The bench sways, tips, crashes forward, and all goes black.

A moment later, Lizzie is slapping my face, hissing my name. I hear myself babbling. "Did you see Him? Did you see Poe?"

Lizzie leans me against the bench. The parlor is empty.

"Jonah, let's go downstairs. It's warmer."

I almost say, 'We can't. Mother will be down there.' Fuck, it's just like childhood. Can't bring anybody home because Mom will creep everyone out. But Lizzie is pulling me to my feet and we're walking down through the shed and into the apartment.

Mother is waiting for us, sitting on the new bed and mattress I picked up last week. The knife is by her side. Lizzie looks right at the bed and congratulates me on the purchase. Mother is scowling through a web of uncombed hair. As we enter, her green eyes are laser-focused on me and she reaches for the knife, but Lizzie now draws her attention.

Matthew Mercier

No, Mother.

"Watch this," I say to Lizzie, walking quickly over to the Poe Society safe. "I mean, look at this."

I crouch, open the safe, push aside my gun and the stack of letters, pull out the tooth necklace and hold it up. Mother, as always, stares at it the way a dog pants for a bone.

"Quinn left these for me."

Lizzie holds her stomach. "He . . . would do that. Whose are they?"

Mother's green eyes are burning pits of Medusa rage as she floats through Lizzie, grabs the necklace from my hand and drifts across the room to the table.

"What the fuck!" Lizzie screams. "Who's holding that?"

I swallow as Mother sits at the table with the necklace spread out before her. The teeth click and clack on the string. The archivist is as pale as a bride of Dracula. The teeth must appear to be counting themselves.

She plops onto the loveseat, shaking. Dupin appears from the bathroom, notices Mother, hisses, and scoots under the dust flap.

I point to the table. "You can . . . ?"

"Just the teeth." Lizzie covers her face. "God this place, this place."

For a distraction, I show her the translated ciphers above my desk. She reads the first aloud. "Don't trust her." She shakes her head, as if in wonder. "That's why you were so defensive."

"Does he mean Cynthia?"

"No way. That woman's carrying more than you can possibly imagine. Arthur Quinn likes to sow dissent. It's his specialty." She lifts her chin at me. "And this debt?

Something to do with that sister you mentioned?"

"No," I say, looking at the table. "My mother."

Lizzie covers her mouth. "Those are her teeth?"

The spirit in question looks up, knowing we are talking about her, then goes back to counting.

"It's a story. Let me put on some music. You dig Leonard Cohen?"

"Are you kidding? Cohen's the official musician of Poe Cottage. You know an angel gets their wings every time someone plays *Hallelujah*?"

Cripes. Fastest way to my heart is to tell me you enjoy Leonard

Poe & I

Cohen, patron saint of loners. On any other evening, these might have been the ingredients for a fantastic date. I call up *Everybody Knows* and amp the volume.

"Appropriate," Lizzie hoots as the molasses-soaked voice drifts into the air, singing about loaded dice and fingers crossed. She digs the heels of her boots into the fibers of my cheap rug and starts swaying back and forth. Even Mother begins to sway to Cohen's melancholy lyrics.

"Do you gamble, Peabody?"

"Sorry?"

She points under my bed. OTB tickets litter the floor, little white squares of loserdom, mixed in with the dust bunnies.

"You never play the horses?"

"Can't say I have, Junior. Do you win much?"

"I don't play much."

"Right. I'm only drunk when I drink." She plops onto the loveseat, startling a mouse from under the dust flap. Dupin bolts after it into the kitchen. "So, you're not related to Quinn?"

"Hell no."

"Is he your bookie?"

"Nice guess, but I have one of those." I wiggle my stump.

"God. Is that another story?"

"He's part of the story."

"Great. So . . . this debt. It's not monetary?"

Here we go. Do or die. Man up or wuss out. Only way she'll ever trust me is to bare my soul, right? Statute of limitations has passed on paper, but you can't write off guilt with a pink slip, and if I don't bleed out for her now, she'll probably imagine worse—that I've popped a guy, or poisoned a dog, or buried my sister in a dank hole upstate.

I lay out my history, as briefly as I can, ending with Mother's return home after her own funeral. I'm quite sure this sob story will put a damper on the evening, but instead, Lizzie swings towards me and loops a hand around my neck. "That," she whispers, "is absolutely horrifying."

For the first time in forever, my soul feels light and fluffy, until she says, through obsidian lips, "It better be true."

"It is. I swear."

"Sounds as if Quinn has a legitimate bone to pick. And I bet that's not even the whole story."

Matthew Mercier

Nothing is lost on this woman.

"There is more. Isn't there, Jonah?"

"Yes." I rub my chin. "But first. Who did you see upstairs?"

She lets out a long breath. "Our mutual third eyes . . . they must not see the same thing."

"Who did you see?"

Her eyes are moist. "This cottage," she says, "this basement. It does something to people."

"Did Ricky know that?"

"Ricky," she moans. "I can't." She drops the flash drive into my pocket. "Watch this diary of his. That's just a copy, but guard it with your life. For your eyes only." She places a hand on my forearm, on the pitch-black mold scar. "What is that?"

"Fungus infection," I say. "I've been sleeping upstairs with Poe. The air is better."

"And you can avoid being down here. With your other ghost."

Before I can answer, Mother squeezes my balls and the doorbell rings.

Might as well be a swat team crashing through the window. I yelp, Lizzie screams, Dupin yowls.

"Didn't we lock the gate?" Lizzie asks.

"Yes."

"Then who?"

The cottage door bangs open. "Quinn. It must be."

Lizzie hisses. "Why is he here? Did you set me up, Peabody? You son of a bitch."

"No, Lizzie. I swear. I didn't. I—"

"Why would he show up tonight? Of all nights!"

"I don't know."

Lizzie grabs my collar and sticks a finger in my windpipe. "If I find out you're lying, I will fucking kill you."

Footsteps creaking across the parlor. Even Mother's head is now cocked and listening. I take the flash drive, place it inside the safe, grab my gun, close the door, and spin the dial. I brandish the pistol across my chest.

"Jesus, Peabody. What the fuck are you doing?"

"Don't worry. It's not loaded." I tuck the gun in my coat pocket. "Lizzie, you have to believe me, I didn't know he'd come by tonight."

Rivulets of sweat running over my ribs. Breathe. My name is

202

Poe & I

Jonah Peabody, and everything will be fine. "You can stay down here if you want.

"Fuck that. We confront him together. Or not at all."

Okay then. We step into the shed, walk around to the stairs, then climb into the museum, ready to meet my double, my destiny.

Chapter 20

Whispers

The man sitting in the kitchen with Andy did not turn to look at me when I entered. "Is that Jonah?"

My sister sat on the opposite end of our round table; her gaze locked on the stranger in a staring contest. First one to blink died.

He wore a leather jacket. The crown of his head was a spiraling bald spot, a white dot smack in the middle of a ginger whirlpool. The freckled skin crawling up the back of his neck was a patchwork of light and dark blemishes, and flakes of it collected in his collar. Eczema, if I had to guess, or something worse.

"That's me," I said. "Jonah Peabody in the flesh."

Andy's gaze now dared to drift in my direction. *Caution,* it silently screamed.

The man sat in Father's chair, his left hand resting on the wicker placemat, his right hand below the table, resting on his knee. Andy's eyes, after warning me, went briefly to the man's lap, and it was not difficult, given her rigid body, to figure out what the stranger held down there.

I scanned the counter for a weapon, but the stranger read my mind.

"If you try to lunge for a knife or meat cleaver, Jonah, I will shoot your sister dead. Maybe you'll get to me before I can shoot you, but she will be lying on the floor in a pool of blood." He sighs. "And then my life will be ruined as well as yours. Three lives down the drain. No need for that."

Adrenaline spiked my whole body, cleaving my head down the middle.

204

Poe & I

"Why don't you walk around so we can greet each other properly?"

I did as I was told. I stepped to the opposite side of the table and put a hand on my sister's shoulder, whose face registered more sadness than fear.

The man in front of us was not a man, but a boy. His cheeks plump, ears pink, a sloped hawk nose dotted with acne, and the eyes of a lost fawn, alone in the woods. I knew this face. I knew this boy.

"Jonah," Andy croaked, "meet Richard McKittrick."

The eight-year-old at his mother's funeral. The pre-teen at his brother's funeral. The young adult outside the asylum. It felt as if I already knew him, and when he spoke, his rubbery, elastic jaw filled with hypnotic words that sounded as if they'd been said already. "The last McKittrick man standing," Richard laughed. "My father passed away last month. Leaving me an orphan. Did you know that?"

"Richard," Andy said. "we're sorr—"

"Shut your mouth." He cocked the gun. "You Peabodys. You talk too much, and when you do talk it is all just blather, sludge, nothing worth listening to. My father fell for your father's fake apologies, and that sent him to an early grave."

"What can we do for you, Richard?" I asked.

"Oh, are we on a first-name basis, Jonah?"

"What can we do for you, Mr. McKittrick?"

"Oh, I'm kidding. I feel as if I know the both of you. The purpose of my visit today is twofold, but mostly I just wanted a closer look."

"At what?"

"Your house. Your estate. Both of you. We've only seen each other from a distance our entire lives. I've especially wanted to meet you for a long time, Jonah, after talking to your mother so much, which I must say was torture."

"You visited her. In prison. I mean . . . ."

"Prison? Is that what you call the nut house?" He gave me an appraising glance. "Well, prison would have been justice served. I thought for sure she was faking the madness angle, but after seeing that dump of an asylum . . . well . . . no, she was the real deal. Which means, you, her offspring, might also lose the lottery of mental stability."

205

Matthew Mercier

Andy, hands folded neatly in her lap, said, "It would have happened by now, Richard. If that were true."

"More talk. Blah, blah, blah. Either way, the two of you need to be monitored. Lord knows you failed to monitor your mother." He looked me up and down. "My, Jonah, we do look alike. No wonder I confused our old lady."

"Our?"

"She's mine as much as yours."

I said nothing to this. I didn't think he was entirely wrong.

"And you," Richard twirled a finger at Andy, "are beginning to resemble her. I bet your father loves that. Have you reconsidered my offer, Andromeda?"

Andy snorted and looked off to the side. Richard smirked up at me. "I've asked for your sister's hand in marriage. A shotgun proposal!"

My palms rippled with cold. "I thought you didn't want to see us ever again."

"That was my father's directive after Brad's death. But I'm my own man now. I wanted to meet the family that destroyed my family."

"We're sorry."

"Please. Spare me your thoughts and prayers. I must say I'm not impressed with the Peabody homestead. It's quite sad and run down, but I suppose that's in keeping with the spirit of your family."

"You have a way with words," Andy whispered.

"Do I? Well, you're all sad and run down, in love with death. I must say, it's ironic that you are in the death business. I wonder, does it become a fetish? Do you make tables out of coffins? Do you keep totems of the dead hanging around the house? Emotionally, your father seems to be in love with mourning. He just can't seem to let go of your mother."

I made the mistake of glancing down the hall. Richard noticed. "Are you taking over the family business, Jonah?"

"For the time being."

He chuckled. "So, you won't be leaving town."

"I will. Eventually"

"Of course. And you, Andromeda?"

"I'm blowing this popsicle joint the first chance I get."

He nodded. "That's normal. Nothing is happening in this town,

Poe & I

right? I plan on leaving, too. Before I go, however, I just wanted to come by and say hello. Hello and goodbye. It seemed wrong not to since our families are joined at the hip. I've wanted to come by ever since I found my voice. Did you know I didn't speak for a long time? As a child. Did either of you know that?"

"How would we?"

"Let me tell you the story. I wasn't born mute. No, I stopped talking when I was about eight. The doctors said it was PTSD. I got a pretty nasty shock when I was young. You see, I was in the car that day. When your mother snapped."

My gut turned end over end.

"I saw my mother hit the window, blood trickling down her forehead, and I saw Ms. Peabody's skeletal face peering in at me. It stopped my heart and sealed my lips."

The young Richard, as he told this story, began to look old, withered, as if a psychic space vampire had sucked out his life force. I told myself he was lying. No way he was in the car. The timeline didn't work. Not for a man this old.

"We didn't know," Andy said.

"Why would you? Your father doesn't tell you anything, and he clearly doesn't care about anyone but himself."

"That's true," I laughed.

"See? We agree on something. So even though I've wished for your death many times, I don't blame either of you. I don't even blame your mother. It's your father who truly needs to die. He's the source of all this misery. My brother's death is on your father's shoulders, too. Speaking of which, he might be home soon, so if you're not going to accept my proposal, Andy, we should get on with the next step. Can I call you Andy?"

"You don't need the gun, Richard."

"Oh, but I do. It makes me feel safer."

Look, Richard Quinn—I mean, Richard McKittrick—had a right to be angry. One hundred percent. But I can tell you now that all those ugly words he spat at us—however justified—aged him before our eyes. When he stood, he seemed frail. "It's good you arrived when you did, Jonah. Your sister will need your help."

He glanced at Andy, her face as gray as one of her drawings, and then she stood and motioned for me to follow her to the back of the house, Richard following behind us with his gun.

Chapter 21

Face to Face

Lizzie and I stand on the stairs that lead to Poe's kitchen. The gun pulses in my jeans. Lizzie is above me, unlatching the museum door, and waving me back, insisting on going first.

"You're going to shoot somebody, you macho asshole."

"I told you it's not loaded."

"Then why bring it?"

"Trust me."

"Famous last words, Dupin."

It's too much story to explain, the gun, but I know I'm telling the truth, so I'll just have to show her. Lizzie presses a palm on the kitchen door, and it creaks open. We step quickly inside, the floorboards groaning. Impossible to sneak quietly in Poe Cottage. The stove and fireplace are dark, but a pale-yellow glow quivers over the plaster ceiling of the entrance. The candle lights are on in the parlor.

"Hello?" Lizzie calls out. "Who's there? We're closed."

No answer. The front door of the cottage is wide open. The Bronx night is bustling away, oblivious to the drama inside Poe's house. "Quinn?"

We reach the velvet rope by the donation box and unhook it.

"Jonah? Is that you?"

I step onto the porch, shut and lock the front door. "Yes, it's me. Jonah Peabody."

A beat of silence before the voice says, "*The* Jonah Peabody? Well, don't be shy. I'd like to meet you. Sounds as if you have company."

Poe & I

Lizzie's eyes are bulging with confusion. I take the lead, stepping into the parlor.

He's seated inside the exhibit, on the bench by the window. Gaunt, broad shoulders, leather pants, white shirt, black leather vest. He's also wearing my face.

No. Almost mine. The pale slivery forehead, the freckled cheeks, the plump, red lips and the spiky, cropped, red hair jutting out from a dapper newsboy hat—it could be me if you blinked—but it's not. This is Richard McKittrick.

He brightens as I enter the half-light of the parlor and stands. "At last. The famous Jonah Peabody. And I thought I recognized the authoritative voice of the equally famous Lizzie Borden."

The archivist's face is a mask of repressed hatred. "Hello Arthur."

"Young lady, I'm very disappointed in you." He scowls behind his tinted shades and leans on a silver-headed cane, which must be for show. He's not that old—if he's Richard McKittrick, it's only been a decade. But he seems withered, worn out, the way my grandfather looked at the end of his life, skinny enough that he might blow away. "Here I thought the historical society hired you, Lizzie, to catalog and organize our collections, and instead I find you digging into my own private collections."

I'm unsure of what he's referring to, but Lizzie volleys right back, her neck peppered with droplets of perspiration. "Your collection is more interesting."

Quinn cackles, and the sound is ear shattering inside the cottage. "Flattery will get you nowhere."

"So," I say, drawing his gaze to me, "you're the infamous Arthur Quinn."

He eyes me from trotter to snout. "Just Quinn will do."

Fine, Richard. I'll keep playing along. "I guess I should thank you for the job."

"Thank me? Well, I enjoyed your resume. Such creativity. But you're the one who sold Cynthia on your competence."

"So, you're president of the Society?"

"I'm more of ceremonial figure these days."

"That doesn't entitle you to just show up here at random times," Lizzie spits.

He flinches and frowns. "Cindy didn't tell you I was coming?"

"Cindy?"

209

Matthew Mercier

"He means Cynthia," Lizzie growls.

"My pet name for the director. I told her to warn you that I might stop by." The man says it with such brio and confidence that I think: Did I miss an email? But no, he's here because I left that note in his mailbox. *I know who you are.*

Quinn's shoulders are turned in and his back is hunched, as if his spine is battling with his neck and head for space. He's coiled, ready to strike. His smile is black, the gums eaten away just enough so the gaps between his teeth are blinking. Whatever he's been doing to his body for the last ten years, he's not taken care of himself.

"I'm usually a professional hermit," he says, "but I had to crawl out of my hole to see if it was true." His smooth face smiles up at me in fake wonder. "The resemblance, I mean. Between you and me, Jonah. You don't have my green eyes . . . but it's remarkable. Are we related? Who's your grandfather?"

"Peabody on my father's side. McKenzie on Mother's."

"Interesting. Have we met before?"

I want to say his real name, it's on my lips, but instead, I say, "I've paid my debts, Quinn."

"I'm sorry?"

"If you disagree, we can make another truce."

He's a good actor, looking sincerely puzzled. "A truce? Are we at war?"

The top button of his dress shirt is open, making visible the upper U of a surgeon's stitch.

"Mr. Quinn, let's stop pretending."

"Who's pretending?"

"I'm sorry for it all. For my family."

"What are you talking about, young man?"

He's not giving an inch, just shakes his head and looks at my waist. "Is that a gun in your coat pocket?"

I nod, whip it out, and point it at him.

Lizzie yelps, but Quinn does not even balk or take a step back. Instead, he pulls off his glasses and slips them in his shirt pocket.

"That's a foolish thing to do, young man. Carrying a gun around. You don't wear that in public, do you?"

"Of course not."

"Good. Because if you were African American, you'd be shot."

The rumble of the D train floats up from far below, and Quinn's

210

Poe & I

eyes glow, two cold stars burning deep inside his gaunt skull. He steps forward, reaches for my wrist, and pulls the gun to his forehead. "Do what you must, young man. I've been a bad boy."

"Arthur, please." Lizzie's hands are fluttering in the air, unsure and useless. "Jonah, don't be a fool."

"Don't worry, Ms. Borden. I think I know Mr. Peabody's game."

I open my mouth to offer a challenge, when, out of the corner of my eye, Poe's bust shivers, and The Poet's green cloud seeps into the parlor. Quinn sniffs the air as Poe floats through him, but he does not move away from my gun barrel.

"Smells like ectoplasm," Quinn says. "Cinnamon and ginger."

Poe ignores us as His body takes shape, and He sits by the back window, staring out at the shed. The wind chimes tinkle their slivery music as Quinn turns back to me.

"Ah, the chimes. I love that sound. So incongruous with the urban surroundings. Have they comforted you at night, Jonah?"

"They're wind chimes."

And now Quinn roils with hysterical laughter. I keep the gun leveled at him as he sits down inside of Poe, who, annoyed, floats out of Quinn and back down on the bench a few feet over.

"You are a funny man, Jonah Peabody. A funny man. I'm glad I stopped by."

"How did you know I was here, Quinn?" Lizzie spits.

Quinn's patronizing glance is withering. If I don't separate these two, they're going to hurt each other. "I've been impressed with your work, Ms. Borden, even as I resent the invasion of my privacy. Very industrious. I can see why Cynthia hired you. You have the drive of a journalist and the passion of a true social justice warrior. Your mother must be very proud."

"My mother?"

"Oh yes. A single woman raising a young girl in the country, all on her own out there in a Jersey farmhouse, with all that open land and woods. She must be so happy to see you thriving here in the big city."

"She doesn't live alone, Quinn."

"Oh no. She's got a boyfriend. But they are both getting on in years."

"Stop!" Lizzie shouts. "Get out of here. Right now."

"Temper, temper. So, you want me to disappear?"

"I want you to stop making threats."

Matthew Mercier

"Who's making threats? My, you are as paranoid as Jonah. Look, I clearly have come at a bad time; you are both raw and open wounds. So, I'll just leave these." He holds up a hand, pointing to the inside of his jacket. "May I?"

"Go slow," I say.

He pulls out two red envelopes with a raven emblazoned across the front and puts them on the mantle. "Invitations," he says. "To my annual Poe celebration on January 19th. But Jonah, I sincerely hope you to come visit me and see my collection before then. I'm sure you'd appreciate it. I know Lizzie does."

"Where do you live?"

At this, he scowls. "Now who's pretending, Mr. Peabody? By the way." He points at me. "What is wrong with your arm?"

The sleeve of my flannel shirt is unbuttoned and falling open. The black line of the mold scar is ragged, and now seeping yellow pus.

"I'm fine."

"Living underground can be dangerous for long term health."

"I'm fine."

"Have you inhaled a foreign agent? Mold? Cocaine?"

We all move to the porch now, and I slip the gun back into my pocket. The orange glow of the security lamps wipes away our facial differences, and Quinn is just an old man with a cane.

"If you've inhaled spores or mold, Jonah, your immune system may be compromised."

"I'll be fine."

"Your name is Jonah Peabody, and everything will be fine."

"Get out of here."

"Touchy, touchy."

"I'll get the gate for you," Lizzie says. "Don't let it hit you in the ass."

"It's fine, Ms. Borden. I have a key."

Back in the basement, I check my emails. Nothing from Cynthia about Quinn's visit. My brain boils. Lizzie calls her mother out in Jersey while my Mother is draped under the window, listening to the Bronx. The black mold inside my arm is pulsing, throbbing.

"Mom!" Lizzie cries into her phone, walking up into the shed for better reception. "Are you okay? Where's Greg? Is he with you? Okay, yes. I'm coming to see you. Tomorrow. Yes."

Poe & I

I'm breathing too fast, need to calm down. Dupin hops onto my lap and paws my chest. Lizzie finds me this way when she storms back down, and if not for the cat I think she might have chewed my head off.

"How's your mother?" I ask.

"Still alive. But." She points to the gun, resting on top of the safe. "What the hell was that? Do you think you're Rambo? Are you as crazy as he is?"

"Pick it up."

"What? No. I've never held a gun in my life."

"Just put your hand on it."

As if she's touching a hot iron, she taps the pistol with her pinkie, then finally places a hand over the barrel. "Is that . . . plastic?"

"Hard plastic. Yes."

"Okay, what the ever-living fuck?"

"There's a story behind it."

"No more stories. I'm out of here."

"What am I going to see on that flash drive?"

"Just watch it."

Outside in the park, we glance around for Quinn, but he's long gone. Even still, Lizzie lowers her voice.

"After I interviewed Ricky, I loaned him my video camera and told him to keep a diary as caretaker. I thought it might be fun, but then he met Quinn. Ricky used to be a journalist, so he was always asking questions. And for Quinn, he just got too nosy. Quinn does not like questions. As you saw, he's weird and prickly, and I just know . . . I know Quinn had something to do with Ricky's death. But I can't prove it."

At the front gate, she lowers her voice as I fiddle with the padlock.

"So, Ricky goes to dinner with Cynthia and Quinn, and then a few days later Ricky is dead. Forensics found traces of plaster on his face, which they couldn't explain. I'm convinced that Quinn was down there with him after he died. And maybe before. But the security camera showed nobody entering the house."

"We don't have cameras."

She points up into the maple trees that bookend the front entrance. In their nooks, blending with the bark, are a pair of telescoped brown cameras. "They were operating right before

Ricky's tenure. Then they cut the budget. Alarm system was enough, they said."

"So, you have a bunch of theories but no evidence. And what is this about Quinn's collection?"

"The fucker has his own museum. In that house up there in Riverdale. Some of it—most of it—was acquired through dubious means. That's what I've been researching for Cynthia. I don't know how he found out. Okay, I've got to split."

"I'll call you."

"Don't. I'll find you." She holds up Quinn's invite. "But maybe I'll see you at the ball."

Right. If I live that long.

I let her out and lock all the gates. I'm not sleepy, and I don't want to pop a pill since it's still early, so I take my laptop upstairs. Poe is lying on Virginia's bed, eyes closed, snoring, so I take a seat on the back bench and pop in the flash drive.

As Lizzie said, it's a video diary of Ricky as docent. He's sitting on the loveseat in the basement with the camera balanced on a tripod or flat surface. The first segment is him sounding off about the wacky people who visit Poe Cottage. A dude from Baltimore claiming to be an ancestor of Eddie and how the cottage belongs to him. Or the filmmaker looking to make an action film of Poe's novel *The Narrative of Arthur Gordon Pym,* and who keeps trying to get Ricky to read his screenplay.

"The guy has it handwritten in a spiral notebook," Ricky laughs. "These people, man."

Next is the Norwegian all-female punk band who slapped on mustaches and filmed a music video on the porch. After this, the various would-be scholars who want to argue about the granular detail of Poe's life. Then there is the A&E network, who shows up to film an intro segment to their *Biography* series, hosted by the old actor from *Mission Impossible,* Peter Graves. Ricky keeps barnstorming their shots, humming the MI theme song, and trying to get Graves to autograph his arm.

Then it gets serious. Ricky is in the parlor, sitting on the loveseat.

"So, I'm not alone down here. Poe and Virginia are around, but ... this place, this basement has strange vibes. I keep seeing shit,

Poe & I

and when I came back home today my furniture was all rearranged."

Ricky is flustered, self-aware, knowing exactly how he sounds. "But if you're watching this, it means I trust you. Poe is here. For sure. You can feel him inside the walls and,"— he taps his chest— "in here too. But he's not the only one down here with me."

A massive crash off camera. Ricky jumps up and rushes out of frame. Yelling from what must be the kitchen. A full minute goes by until Ricky walks back into frame, looks right into the lens and says, "My Uncle is here. This isn't for your eyes."

Cut.

Ricky on the loveseat. "Arthur Quinn came by again today. He invited me to dinner at his place over in Riverdale, but no way in hell I'm going without Lizzie or Cynthia. But Cynthia, man, she's another strange duck."

He goes on a bit of a rant about the boss lady; how she's stressed and overworked and letting "this Quinn guy run the show."

"I was doing a little digging on the society, and Quinn is pulling down a hefty salary for doing nothing. Have you looked into that, Lizzie? You might want to."

As the diary goes on, Ricky begins to get progressively worn down with work at the cottage—the loneliness, the boredom, the repeated historical questions, the long and creepy nights spent watching and listening to the angry spirit banging around above him. Poe does not make an appearance, but Ricky talks about him. The diary segments get progressively shorter as his health declines.

"Doc says something is in my lungs. Says I need to get out of the basement, but where else am I going to go? Can't give up the free rent. I bought a dehumidifier and an air freshener."

As he points to all these things, I notice that running up the inside of his forearm is the same black mark running up the inside of my forearm.

"Doc says it's only going to get worse the longer I stay down here, so I've been sleeping upstairs with Poe. And besides, down here, I keep seeing my uncle, who died in 'Nam. He visits me at night." Ricky hugs himself and shivers, as if the ghost is sitting right next to him. "I know everyone thinks I'm crazy for staying here. Too many eyes. Too many eyes and ears. But where am I going to go?"

Matthew Mercier

He looks off camera, panic scouring his face. He coughs, scratches his arm. "I'll see you this weekend Lizzie, so I'll give the camera back, but in case I don't see you, I want you to know that whatever happens to me, this was the best job I ever had, despite all the pain." Tears glisten on his cheeks. "Best job ever. All the stuff about Quinn, I'll leave it in the safe. Okay? Okay. Ricky Thurston, over and out."

Cut. That's it. End transmission.

What the fuck did I just watch? The last days of a man's life. I'll never sleep again. Maybe even the ghosts are freaked out, since both Mother and Poe keep their distance that night, my brain whirling.

The following Sunday afternoon, first weekend in December, Bradford walks in as I'm giving my last tour to an Australian couple. He sits in the parlor as we finish up, and by the way he's watching the windows and rattling the change in his pocket, I can tell he's bursting with news. He smiles at the tourists and plays nice, but the moment they leave and I lock the gate, that smile disappears. "We need to talk," he says.

I hold up the flash drive. "Yeah we do."

We watch the video diary together, and the whole time Bradford is trying to swallow his fist, his teeth working the skin of his knuckles. This is good, this is progress. Maybe we'll have a breakdown together.

"That's bad," he says. "God, that's some creepy shit. Why did I have to see that? God, god, god."

"Look," I say, "Lizzie thinks Quinn had something to do with Ricky's death. She has no evidence. But I have more questions for Mason. About Quinn. We need . . . "

Bradford slams a palm flat on the arm of the sofa and wipes his face with the cuff of his shirt. "That's just it, gingerbread. Lloyd Mason is dead."

Chapter 22

Freedom

How do I describe the mood after Richard left our house with his prize?

A shellshocked vacuum. A cold vortex of fear. Father would be home in an hour. We needed to prepare for violence. We needed to lock ourselves in our rooms, as if we were children again.

Andy wept, shaking with rage at her own perceived failure. "We should have just buried her. Why didn't we just do that?"

"Father brought this on himself," I said. "We did nothing wrong."

It didn't help when the old man walked in the front door whistling like one of the seven dwarfs. He strolled to the back of the house, found Mother's door busted open and his pickled princess gone.

He exploded into the kitchen.

"Where is she? What did you do with her?!" He stuck a finger in Andy's face. "You did this, you witch! You did it!"

I rose from the table and braced my feet in a boxing stance, prepared to weave and duck if he threw a punch. "We cut a deal with McKittrick."

Father whipped around, grabbed my collar, and breathed a hot stew of Mad Dog 20/20 into my face. "McKittrick? Which one?"

"Richard. The last son. The father is dead."

He let me go, flummoxed and inoculated by the suddenness of the news. "Dead? How?"

"Don't ask me, Dad. But the son was here. He took Mother at gunpoint. Andy did nothing."

Matthew Mercier

He didn't report the crime. (Hello? Yes, I want to report that someone has stolen the corpse of my wife which I stole from the graveyard.)

In my faulty memory, Father did storm out of the house, leap in the Ghostbuster hearse, and careen out into the Catskills to try and recover Mother's body, but even if he'd found Richard—and the McKittrick clan had moved, so we no longer knew their location—how would that conversation have ended? Not well. More bloodshed.

Father's temper eventually cooled, but now he was the eternal drunk, his only comfort being Mother's ghost.

That's how I knew her bones remained above ground. Her spirit kept trying to murder me at least once a week. Everywhere I travelled in that house—on the toilet or in the shower or in the basement—she followed me. Even when I was outside, I saw her standing in the windows, waving at me from the attic window. And I knew my cracked family members saw her, too.

It was a rare moment of solidarity. We'd sit at the table and recount our days, and part of that was always the Mother report.

"She was in the pantry trying to eat raw beets."

"She was out in the woods screaming into a dirt hole."

"She was in my bed last night."

We'd given up the ghost, but the ghost would not give up on us, and so we went on with life as if Mother's corpse hadn't just been used as a poker chip.

"Did Richard ask for anything else?" Father asked my sister.

"He wanted me to do some drawings of his own mother."

"How will you manage that?"

She held up a photo Richard had given her. Mrs. McKittrick. Blonde, blue-eyed, razor-sharp cheekbones.

"That's it? Just a few drawings?"

"Or my hand in marriage."

Richard had told Andy he was attracted to her. Andy told him that was creepy as fuck and that Richard should seek professional help. Richard said he'd be able to buy all the help he needed, as he was going to be quite wealthy due to the inheritance he received from his father. He bragged to Andy that he could support her in her artistic career, but Andy told him to kindly go to hell. He told her fine, he'd settle for taking Mother's body instead.

And if Andy didn't give him the corpse? Oh, he'd just report us

Poe & I

to the police and have Mother put in the ground the old-fashioned way. He'd been watching us closely, and it wasn't hard to figure out that Father had taken her corpse home.

"If McKittrick knew about Mom," I said, "then wouldn't he know about your drug dealing?"

That snapped her spine straight. "I'll be more careful, but I don't think he cares about that."

My ass. Richard wanted to destroy us.

Father, now incapacitated with drunk madness, became useless. I had to focus on the funerals, which kept me sane. Talking to others about their sorrow was a way for me to get outside myself. The young teenage suicides were the hardest, but they were ones I empathized with the most. The scars from my own cutting career glowed when these young men and women came through, and their methods ran the gamut—guns, pills, hanging. But no matter who I spoke with, my major piece of advice was this: "Don't let their death haunt you. Don't carry the body around forever. Metaphorically."

That went double for the folks who lost a baby. A hard truth, but it needed to be said. You can bury the body, but if you don't let the wee one go in your heart, you'll be the walking dead. Forever. You don't have to forget them, but you do need to say good-bye.

I saw a lot of parents choose zombie land, but who am I to judge? I'd probably want to be dead, too, if I buried my kid.

These heart-to-heart conversations about grief made me sincerely want to learn the funeral trade. Sure, I'd arrived here by way of inertia, but the profession was a lifeline. The only drawback was that I felt Father creeping into my head, right alongside Mother, and when I spoke about death to folks, I heard his voice overlapping mine. "Grieving is a lost art. Americans don't do it properly."

On the upside, as I took control, I had more access to the parlor's financial records and learned Father was deep in the hole. We either had to sell or declare bankruptcy, but neither was happening so long as he was alive. I kept waiting for that corporate buyout, but no offer came.

Richard, no doubt, was pleased to see us struggle. This was our punishment—death by self-destruction.

Andy and Father treated each other like hated roommates. She used the back door while he used the front. Everyone came home

219

Matthew Mercier

and went straight to their rooms. We ate dinner apart, socialized apart, lived apart. Andy was twenty-three now, which seemed to irk Father, and during his drunken binges, he'd mumble confessions to me.

"You know," he slurred, "your sister is now the age that I married your mother. When she smiles, lord, those dimples."

"Jesus, Dad. Go to sleep."

"You don't see it?"

I did see it, and it terrified me. Andy was wise to him, locking her door at night, keeping her gun loaded. Father would call her Pamela when he was drunk, and I'd have to drag him off to bed.

It all began to feel so hopeless and dangerous until the day I arrived home to find Andy making dinner. The kitchen was a flurry of boiling water, simmering soups, and roasted vegetables. Father was speechless, but Andy spoke for him.

"It's Mother's birthday," she said. "It felt right to start over."

Do you know what she cooked? Pork chops, mushrooms, salad, and bread pudding. Nearly the same meal we'd had when Mother came home the night of Mrs. McKittrick's murder.

Fuck me if I didn't trust it, but Andy had the highest highs and lowest lows, and you take love where you can get it. If Father noticed the meal was the same, he didn't say, but after we ate and pretended everything was okay, he went on a three-day bender. He locked himself in his bedroom and drowned in his gin.

On the third day, he plopped into my room, onto the soft chair next to my desk, while Mother sat on my bed, staring at her ex-husband with pity and loathing.

"Your Mother is right, Jonah."

"What do you mean?"

"She needs to go in the ground."

"Dad . . . .her body is gone."

"No!" he shouted, then lowered his voice. "No, we can find that bastard. But."

Behind him, Mother nodded, her face flickering.

"She wants to go in the ground. I failed her."

A flare went off in my brain. He began to weep, loud enough that it brought Andy to the doorway. She hung there, just out of sight, listening.

"Your mother . . . she's the only one who put up with me. The only one who could love me. Nobody else wanted me. I was so

Poe & I

alone, Jonah. I wish . . . I wish I could tell you how happy she made me. How happy we made each other. You two never saw that part of us."

One weepy, drunken, sentimental confession didn't make up for a lifetime of arid, parched nothing. When a man as inarticulate as my father is the keeper of memories, it's a disaster for memory making. You can never rely on just one human mind to hold the stories. You need multiple brains, multiple memories, even if the final story comes out imperfect.

My father was a man who could love only one person in one lifetime. Old fashioned, but better to love than not at all. Except. His love had grown so calcified it now threatened to crumble. Which is maybe why Mother now floated off the bed, whispered in her husband's ear, and then slowly stroked his shoulders, so that he whimpered with pleasure.

So help me Satan, when his eyes lit up, her eyes lit up. Andy saw this, too, and later she would tell me that yes, something happened in that moment, something was communicated. Mother worked her hand down to Father's chest.

He held out his arms, either to Mother or Andy—I couldn't tell. "Don't worry. I'm still here."

Mother, with green tears staining her cheeks, sank her fingers into Father's chest and squeezed.

Father gasped, leaning on the door jamb as Mother held tight. He turned back round to me, glassy eyed. Mother's hand gripped Father's deflated heart, and it oozed between her fingers. Then he dropped to the floor, all two-hundred pounds, dead as a doornail.

Chapter 23
Unlocked Doors

A cleaning lady discovered Lloyd Mason's body at Fordham—in his office, behind his desk, slumped between stacks of Poe and Dumas, his flask open and dribbling Kentucky rye in his lap. A classic locked door mystery—except the door was unlocked, and there was no mystery. Heart attack, doctors said, plain and simple.

"I know Lloyd was pretentious," Bradford said, "but he didn't deserve to check out early."

"Of course not."

"And it's selfish, but now my thesis is screwed. I'll get some fool who doesn't understand my work."

"That sucks."

"What do you know? Never wrote a thesis in your life."

"Easy now. You suspect foul play?"

He glares at me, dancing close to an accusation. "Mason gave us that interview with Ricky."

"You think Quinn found out?"

"You tell me. All I know for sure is this shit started happening when you showed up, Jonah. If you hadn't come to The Bronx hunting for your stupid sister."

"Don't."

"Am I wrong?"

I cover my face, ready to cry or throw a punch. "No."

"Look," Bradford says, "Mason's wake is on Friday. Come by and pay your respects. It's the least you can do."

Poe & I

That's it. I'm done fucking around.

I arrange with the local hardware store for all the locks on the cottage to be switched out. I can afford it now. The one bright spot in this black hole is that my bank account is finally swelling with unspent paychecks. Plus, I won a few big races last week. (Food, beer, and OTB tickets form the unholy trinity of my budget.) My winnings are enough to buy some answers from another person who's met Quinn.

I rub the pinkie nub against my cheek, call his cell, and get his voicemail. He sounds different.

"Ramses. I'm going to stop by Wednesday. Around three-thirty. Hope to see you."

Next, I call Cynthia. She picks up. I give her the riot act, telling her about the changed locks on the cottage and the front gate. "If you meet me at 84 Bedford Street on Wednesday around four, I'll explain. Maybe I'll give you a copy of the new keys. Sound good?"

I'll spare you the response, but let's just say I spiked her blood pressure. On Wednesday, I stuff a wad of cash in my shirt pocket and hop the D train to West 4th.

The Bedford Street entrance to Chumley's is still boarded up, so I slip around to the cobblestone alley. I imagine Ramses puttering inside, rebuilding the chimney, hanging portraits. I knock. Above me, a window slides open, and a well-greased yuppie in a gray sweater and a bob cut leans out. "Hey. Bar is closed."

"Obviously."

"Closed for good. They're not re-opening. Too much noise. We've got a neighborhood petition."

"This bar is historic."

"Got that right. Its days are numbered."

People are silly. They come here for the nightlife but want peace and quiet on weekends. Seriously, move to the country. I pound the door with my fist as the yuppie settles in for a fight. "What's your name?"

"Poe Junior."

The door shifts, a bolt sliding across wood. It swings open to reveal a hulk dressed in layers of flannel, a black wool hat pulled down to his gray eyebrows. A battered, craggy face. His belly is bigger, wider, and his facial hair is a tangled frizz, black whiskers mixing with gray sideburns.

"Long time no see, Professor."

223

Matthew Mercier

There's a reverb to his vowels, echoing in the bottleneck of the alley. "Ramses." I toss a hand yuppieward. "This guy is giving me trouble."

The fireman cranes his neck. "You the asshole started the petition?"

"No."

"Course not. Come inside, Prof."

"I'm here to talk business."

He's not listening. He barks at the yuppie, tries to sound intimidating, but that odd echoing voice of his can't raise the temperature. Then, above the collar of his shirt, I see the black necklace embedded in the pink meat of his throat. A voice box. Shit.

The bar is a gray, dusty version of its former self. Square tables crowded against the walls, upended and resting on top each other. The bricks of the chimney stacked in a neat pile by the gaping hole, wind whistling in the flue, the portraits of Hemingway and Faulkner leaning against the stools.

The door shuts behind me. "Kegs are dry," his voice crackles. "But I got some IPA from the deli. You want one?"

"I'm trying to not drink."

"Me too." He walks behind the bar, cracks open a bottle, and toasts the air. "Key word is trying."

"How's the rebuilding?"

"You just saw it. Neighbors are making it hard to get a new alcohol permit."

"You working?"

"Collecting disability and unemployment. Like a welfare mother."

In the stillness of the speakeasy, his electronic voice is louder, scratchier. He reaches under his collar and rubs his fingers across the necklace. "Makes me sound like a gay Darth Vader. All that Ground Zero confetti finally did a number on my pipes."

"I'm sorry, Ramses."

"Fuck your pity. It goes with the Korean shrapnel in my thigh." He chugs the beer. "How's Poe?"

"Profitable." He's being oddly agreeable, so best get to the point. I unfold the bills and place them on the bar.

"What's this?"

"First payment."

Poe & I

He picks it up, flicks it with his thumb, and pockets it. "Your brother paid off some of your debt. Said to leave you alone for a while."

"Did he now?" My mold scar is hissing and squirming with excitement. "Ramses, that night back in April." I waved my nub. "You'd met him already. He's the one who gave you the tip, so . . . "

The fireman drinks, stares, drinks some more.

"How did he know that I was hanging out here? How did he find me?"

The hero rolls his neck, letting out a long-ragged breath. "He had some private shamus on your ass, learned I was a part-time bookie, came in here asking if I had a Jonah Peabody on my rolls. Imagine my surprise. He tossed your last name around like you were family. Sounds like he's got a grudge."

I scratch my moldy arm, then drag my nub across the bar. "Did Quinn pay you to lock me up?"

The fireman is dangerous again, staring daggers. "You a detective now?

All these questions?" He leans over, poking under my shirt with two fingers.

I pull away. "A wire? Seriously? You watch too many cop shows."

"Hey, this shit is getting weird, and I didn't ask to be a part of it."

"Join the club."

A text buzzes. Cynthia.

"Do me a favor? Tell this story to my boss when she gets here."

"She?"

We sit in the darkness of the speakeasy, waiting for Cynthia to find us. It's warm down here, cozy. Like Poe's basement. The heat clanks in the pipes, and I shed my winter jacket. My arm is swollen black, yet I want Cynthia to see it. Ramses putters around the bar. Five minutes later, Cynthia McMullen swings through the secret entrance, ready to kill.

"Mr. Peabody. You're lucky I don't fire you here and now."

"You won't, or else you'd have eighty-sixed me months ago."

Ramses whistles. Cynthia raps the bar. "I hate to barge in, but I'd like some privacy with my employee here."

"This is my bar, lady. You want me to disappear, there's a fee."

Extortionists everywhere. I love it. "Ramses is part of the story

Matthew Mercier

now, boss. Plus, I think you two might have common ground, which is why I've brought you together."

Cynthia eye-fucks me. "First, give me the new keys."

"No. The cottage is mine now. You want access, you'll have to go through me."

"That's a bit above your pay scale."

"I changed the locks to ensure my safety."

"Your safety?"

I hold up my arm. Skin flakes off and yellow pus drips onto the bar. I dab it with a napkin. "Someone has been letting themselves in. Besides you."

The boss reaches for my arm in faux concern. "Have you been to a doctor?"

"Yes. Mold spores. Gifted to me by someone who knew that Ramses was my bookie, who knew to use Poe Cottage as a lure. After all, it's the only job I've wanted since coming to New York. It seemed too good to be true."

"I know what you're thinking, Mr. Peabody."

"Please. Show off your psychic abilities."

"That you can't trust me." She holds up her palms. "I don't blame you." She looks at Ramses, back to me, her words drifting slowly into the air. "I'll be honest, Mr. Peabody. You were not my first choice for the cottage, and I had no idea what to expect once you moved in, but it seems we're now stuck with you."

"The feeling is mutual."

"However, let's make a deal. If you leave the job, right now, I will offer you six-month's compensation and another apartment while you transition."

Ramses perks up at this. He's on the outside of the story looking in, but even he knows this sounds off.

"I thought the Society was nearly bankrupt."

"Reports of our demise have been gravely exaggerated. Besides, we have a bit of wiggle room for cases like yours. You're not the first caretaker who's checked out early."

"I'm no Ricky Thurston."

She presses a thumb under her jaw and her pointer finger over her lips, letting the name sink between the creases of her forehead. I'm tempted to say more, but I want to see her squirm.

"I take it that's a no?"

Poe & I

"Correct," I say. "Quinn just invited me to Poe's birthday party. I've got to stick around at least until then."

"Very well. You do whatever you need to at the cottage. I'm still your boss and you'll be the boss of Poe, but you need to trust me, Jonah. Understand?"

"Ma'am, you're a broken record."

"It's a track worth replaying. Your life is indeed a Poe story, Jonah."

"*William Wilson.*"

"I was thinking more *The Imp of the Perverse.*"

"Written in 1845. At the cottage. Murder by poison candle."

"Bravo. About man who can't help but self-destruct."

"Guilty as charged."

"The cottage is your destiny, isn't that what you said? Well, quite the self-fulfilling prophecy. But maybe if you stay, we can both get what we want out of this. We just need to be more careful."

What the hell is she getting at? Whose side is she on? "Oh, I understand. You need to protect him. I get it."

"Protect who?"

"Arthur Quinn. Or . . . Richard McKittrick."

She says nothing.

"Did Quinn kill Ricky Thurston? And Lloyd Mason?"

She sits back on her stool. "A tragedy," she whispers. "I just heard."

The shock and grief seem genuine. "Lizzie has theories about all this. She thinks this might not be Quinn's first rodeo."

Now the boss cocks her head. "Ah yes. Our missing archivist."

"Missing?" My bar stool is slipping.

"She hasn't been to work for a few weeks, Mr. Peabody. Word is, you were the last person to see her alive."

"She came to the cottage. We . . . I showed her."

"If she turns up dead, you're the first person the police would interview."

"She was going to see her mother. I mean . . . Quinn."

"Mr. Peabody, don't pretend to be the smartest person in the room. It's not a good look. If you want to play this game, if you want to see Lizzie Borden alive, then I suggest you do what I say from now on. Mr. Ramses, I think I will have a drink."

The fireman cocks an eyebrow.

"Whiskey on the rocks. Jameson, please." She settles in for a

Matthew Mercier

round as Ramses pours her medicine. "Bring a spare key to Lloyd Mason's wake. I suppose that's the next time I'll see you."

I swallow. Guess that's my cue to leave. "The cottage is mine, director."

"It surely is. Good-day, Mr. Peabody."

Ramses plunks a rocks glass onto the bar and pours me a plug of whiskey. "One for the road, Professor? Looks like you need it."

A lot of people cared about Lloyd Mason—students, Jesuit priests, fellow scholars, friends, and family who fly in from California and Paris. It's a love fest, a celebration of the man's life and work. I feel petty for thinking badly about the guy. I overhear Bradford gushing. "Even when he disagreed with you, Lloyd was always a gentleman. And he loved The Bronx. Truly. He knew its history inside and out. He was the only man I knew who could quote both Poe and Grandmaster Flash."

Laughter, tears, amen. Bradford is a star here, so I recede into the background, trying not to be noticed, but then Cynthia strides in, surveying the crowded room. "No Lizzie Borden yet?"

"Boss," I say, handing her a copy of the new keys, "you have to believe I'm on your side." I start scratching my arm, the oozing pus trapped under a stiff cotton shirt.

"Dear God, Jonah. Get that checked out. I don't want another caretaker dying on me."

She can't hide the panic in her eyes as she glides across the room, glad-handing people, acting the politico. Bradford, too, is catching up with old faces, so I wander back to the viewing room and kneel at Mason's casket, where he's been embalmed for our viewing pleasure. I'll never get used to this—the cotton candy wax statues we become after the morticians get their hands on us.

And then, as I'm focusing on the polished liver spots of Mason's folded hands, the earth falls out from under me. Mason's lungs catch fire, a pair of hot blue valentines glowing in the dead cavity of his chest. He's sitting up, bones snapping, jawbone clacking, worms wiggling out of his fingernails, dirt crumbling out of his graying mustache. He's pointing at me, accusing.

I stumble backwards and find Bradford talking to Lloyd's widow, Peggy. She's short and stocky, with a silver streak running through her crown. She's rubbing the inside of Bradford's arm.

Poe & I

"Lloyd just adored you, Bradley. Always spoke about his brilliant original student and his brilliant original thesis."

"I'm going to miss his counsel."

"Someone has to finish Lloyd's book. Maybe you?"

"Don't know if that's my department, Peggy."

Bradford turns to me, startled. I must look like hell on two legs. My forehead is burning, and my arm is twitching with a life of its own. For a minute, I think Bradford is rightfully going to ignore me, but he puts a hand on my shoulder. "Peggy, this is Jonah Peabody."

"Oh, another student of Lloyd's?"

"No, ma'am," I croak. "I look after Poe Cottage."

"Aren't you the caretaker, Bradley?"

"Cynthia made a regime change. Lloyd didn't say anything?"

The widow lowers her voice. "Oh, that woman. I know Lloyd was competitive—I'd be the first to say that—but she's just as bad. Even before this whole book nonsense she was nasty. Lloyd scooped her, fair and square, and, honestly, I think she deserved it. Did you hear how she tried to make peace?"

"Peace?"

"She had us over for dinner a few nights ago. Wanted to clear the air about their silly academic drama. And I don't know how, but . . . " She sniffs, beginning to cry, and Bradford puts an arm around her. "Cynthia's always spooked me. She and her counterpart. The tall, skinny one. Looks like death."

"Arthur Quinn," Bradford says, looking at me. "Don't worry, Peggy. Jonah and I are going to pay that man a visit."

Chapter 24

Escape

After Father collapsed, after the EMTs tried to resuscitate him, after the lump of his body lay there on the ground with Mother's ghost surveying the wreckage —that crooked smile on her face—after they carted his body to the morgue and my sister and I returned home to an empty house—even then I still couldn't say, "We're free."

Oh sure, we were free to sell the house, or burn it, or better yet, abandon it outright, but your ghosts can still piggyback on your tailwinds, and I knew I'd be carrying Mother and Father with me everywhere.

Father did have a life insurance policy. Not much, but we cashed it and split it.

The house wouldn't sell without repairs, and a quick survey of prices in the area told us we wouldn't get much anyway. The funeral parlor was the key. If someone bought the business, a good chunk would go toward paying off debts, but we'd still have a bit left over. Declaring bankruptcy was an option, but the best solution, much as I hated to admit it, was to buckle down and make a go of it. To run the parlor until we balanced the books.

"That could take years," Andy grumbled, her patience wafer thin.

Andy had gotten a job at the art supply shop and amassed a bit of savings, so the insurance policy added to that, but it was hardly a nest egg, and the money would run out without a revenue stream. Her drug sales had tapered off, unless she wanted to expand her empire and become a kingpin.

230

Poe & I

Over dinner, Andy showed me a road atlas, marked up with Post-Its and red Sharpie, detailing all the monuments and national parks and historical houses that she wanted to see. Guess what her first stop was going to be?

"Poe's got a house in The Bronx." She'd circled my future home. "Then I'm going to his grave in Baltimore."

Her years of dreaming were dangerously close to reality, but first we had to attend to some burials.

The horrible irony of Father's inability to let Mother go was that we couldn't bury them together—he was headed to the graveyard, but who knew where her bones might land? Father's funeral was a non-event, with most of the family refusing to show up again. ("Another funeral? What are you kids doing?") Just as well. Freedom from family is the best kind of freedom.

At Father's grave, Andromeda and I found some kind words to say. The man had brought us into the world, and we were grateful for our lives, damaged as they were. More so, we were grateful for each other, and we held hands over his plot and thanked him.

With Mother, we had to settle for symbolism. Andy had more than a few drawings of her and a necklace. We chose a spot at the edge of the property, a short hop from the cemetery. The ground was soft enough that I could dig a small hole. Mother watched us the whole time, sullen and resigned, crouched on the stone wall with her bruised knees pulled up under her chin.

When Andy and I placed the drawing and necklace in the ground, Mother hopped off the stone wall and began pacing, picking at a hangnail. Once she realized she couldn't stop the process, she blew us a kiss, turned her back, and walked off into the graveyard.

"There she goes," Andy said.

I was looking at Mother, but Andy was staring into the hole. She dipped a hand in the displaced soil. "Thank you, Mom. Thank you for the burden that you carried, thank you for your creativity, for your mind, for bringing us to life, for trying your best. You didn't get a fair shot, but who does?" She tossed dirt into the hole.

I picked up a handful and did the same.

"No. Do it again. Say something, Jonah."

I grabbed more dirt and cleared my throat. "I wish I'd known you better, Mom. I wish we had a different relationship. I wish."

"Something positive."

Matthew Mercier

I scrambled my brain, searching each hemisphere. *Thank you for being an incompetent murderer.* "Thank you for my life," I said. "Thank you for giving me a sister."

"Good," Andy said. "Now the dirt."

I tossed it in and scanned the graveyard. Nothing. Mother hadn't listened to our eulogy, even from a distance.

When locals discovered that I'd taken over the parlor, they seemed happy for me. I suppose I was now respectable, which I hated. Andy wasn't going to wait for me to sell the parlor. She began packing the old Subaru. I asked her what she was going to do with all her drawings.

"I'll take a few, but maybe you can look after them for me? Mail them when I land somewhere. Or I'll come back for them."

"You're not coming back."

She scratched her forehead. "If you sell the house, take them with you."

I resented her for leaving and didn't hide it. As the days wore on, her tone morphed from defensive to aggressive to untrusting, and I realized she was talking to me like I was Father. I reminded her of the old bastard, and I'm sure that drove her desire to escape even more. Fair enough. I steeled myself for life without her, but none of that prepared me for the day I arrived home and found the car in the driveway, all packed up, the house empty.

I figured she was at Clarissa's, so I cooked dinner for two, then watched TV and fell asleep on the couch. When I woke up at dusk, the Subaru was still in the driveway.

"Andy? You here?"

I wandered into her bedroom, still littered with keepsakes. It was a full moon that night, moondust in every corner, and after searching the rest of the house, I went back to bed and fell asleep. When I woke at sunrise, my cheeks were wet. I'd been crying in my dreams. I'd slept at an odd angle, and my back and neck didn't want to unfold. I stumbled into the hallway, calling her name, and began to shake and tremble.

I went to work, telling myself that I would call the police if she didn't show up that afternoon. I wandered the woods, drove around town, and called Clarissa, but her husband answered, so I hung up. By nightfall, I'd filed a report.

The second and third nights I didn't sleep. On the fourth,

232

Poe & I

Clarissa pulled up in a fury and got out of her car with the engine still running.

"Where is she you little shit?"

"Good question." I pointed at the car as evidence.

"She said she would take me with her!"

"I'm sorry, Clarissa. I really am. She left me, too."

"You're a liar, Peabody! You're a liar! Did you kill her, you sick motherfucker!"

How could she think that? We'd both lost a piece of ourselves, as you always do when someone you love exits your life, but the way Andy left—without a word—that loss was a chunk, a gouge, a bone-deep wound.

I had the drawings, but even that would soon be taken from me.

A week or two after Andy's escape, the circus lights of a squad car flashed across the ceiling. When I got to the porch, the detective asked, "Are you Jonah Peabody?"

"Far as I know."

"Sir, we have a warrant to search the premises for narcotics."

Well, shit.

Chapter 25

Quinn's Collection

Bradford owns a secondhand Dodge Dart that he keeps hidden in a garage on Jerome Avenue. He acts as if owning the car will ruin his street cred. I tell him to drop the tough boy act. He tells me to fuck off. Anyway, we now have a Batmobile, so it's up Kingsbridge to the Mosholu, and over the river and through the woods to Riverdale we go.

The homes up here are unreal. Mansions. Estates. Driveways. Garages. Security gates. Backyards. Trees. Swimming pools. Plenty of space to hide a body.

"Listen, Bradford," I say, drumming the dashboard, "I owe you an apology."

"Five times over, gingerbread."

"Quinn isn't my boy, but I do know him."

He clicks his tongue. "The hits just keep coming."

"Sorry, past tense. I knew him. My family knew him."

"Like in another life?"

"Might as well be." We have time, so I give Bradford the bare bones of Mother's story, no pun intended, and to his credit, the man does not throw me out of the car, even though he's got the look of somebody locked in a padded cell with Charles Manson.

"That. Is. Fucked. Up. Are you lying to me?"

"Scout's honor, man."

He's silent for a minute, before saying, "My uncle is like your mom."

"Oh?"

"After high school, he enlisted in the Army, shipped out to the

234

Poe & I

Gulf to fight Saddam. Comes back, his face is all scarred, and he's loopy in the head. He started hating on me after I got into Dartmouth, called me white. So, fuck him. I think he did some Poe-like shit in the war. Buried people alive with a bulldozer."

I guess my confession opened a wound, and Bradford feels the need to bleed out.

"He's chilled some. But."

"Right. So now he's just selling Newports on the corner."

Bradford flutters his lips. "So, he introduced himself?"

"Oh yes."

"He's still a trouble magnet. Keep your distance."

By the time we reach Quinn's house, we've agreed on a game plan. Quinn knows we're coming—we left another note in his mailbox, and then he wrote an actual email inviting us, which we both saved—so we're going to make this a friendly visit. No need to stir shit up. We've both got our phones. We won't separate, and we won't surprise Quinn with any questions that might piss him off.

We get a spot right in front of his mausoleum. On Google Earth, the pad extends back at least a few acres, with a greenhouse and patio.

"You think Lizzie is in there?" Bradford asks.

"No way. She's not on his side."

"No, idiot. I mean she found dirt on Quinn, right? So, he threatens her family and then abducts her."

"No, she's just hiding out."

Let that be the truth. The darker alternative is that she is inside Quinn's house, a black widow leading us into a trap, hoping we play the role of macho detectives riding to her rescue, only to lock us up with the rest of the bodies.

Quinn buzzes us in the front gate and meets us on the porch, all smiles. "Gentleman, welcome. Nice to finally meet you, Mr. Macon. Do I need to frisk you, Jonah?"

Bradford shoots me a look.

"No, Mr. Quinn. No need."

"Just Quinn will do."

Just Quinn. I'm jealous. He's legally erased his old family name. I've wanted to kill the name Peabody for years, but it's expensive, and, with a record, nearly impossible.

"Cool name," Bradford says. "Irish?"

Matthew Mercier

"Yes. But the name Quinn is also deeply connected to Poe," he explains, as we walk into a high-ceilinged kitchen, too big for one man. "There's a Poe biographer, Arthur Hobson Quinn. And you've seen the bust in the cottage parlor? The artist is Edmund T. Quinn."

Silly reason to rename yourself, but as a detective I now practice restraint, so I listen and observe. Richard looks even worse than when I first met him. If he's my age, that would put him in his late thirties, but while his skin looks tight—nothing saggy or loose—the grooves in his face run deep. A young man who looks old. He's taken off his winter coat and walks around the kitchen in a flimsy button-down, open at the collar. At the top of his chest is the hint of that U-shaped surgical scar.

He lifts the tea kettle off the stove, and his thin arms tremble as he pours with his back to us. Adding poison to our drinks? No. Why kill us now? Think of the cleanup. Two healthy young bodies, one skinny, one tall, for a combo of three hundred plus pounds. Where could he stuff us? And then he'd have to make the Dodge disappear. No, he won't drug us, but still, I let my tea steep a little longer while Bradford sips his with no fear.

"I can't get over this," he says, looking between Quinn and me. "You two could be brothers."

"Impossible," Quinn replies. "Mr. Peabody here is an only child."

My heart leaps. "I never said that."

Quinn tilts his head. "That's what Cynthia told me."

"I had a sister. Her name was Andromeda."

"Had?"

"She went missing. A few years back."

"I see. Well, maybe you and I should take a DNA test."

"My family kept a lot of secrets, but a secret child wasn't one of them."

"If you say so. Myself, I used to have a brother, but he died young. Took his own life."

This is spoken with absolute sincerity. He's good. My brain is overheating.

"So, gents, let's raise a glass to Lloyd Mason."

"Rest in peace," Bradford says. "He was a good man."

"Good? I suppose. He was known to steal ideas from people."

"The competition in academia can be murder." Bradford is a

Poe & I

total dope, trotting out these cheesy puns, but Quinn seems to enjoy it.

"Indeed. You know, Bradford, I have a PhD. in history. I would love to read your thesis."

"I'm not sure it's your cup of tea."

"Oh, I doubt that. Mason told me all about it. The horror of history? Of my people. White people, that is. I'm quite interested. We had dinner right before he died."

Bradford puts down his cup. "Maybe I'll gift you a copy when it's finished. All dissertations end up as museum pieces anyway."

That gets another laugh, and Quinn is worked up now, babbling on about history and the different paths that lead to conflict and tragedy and horror. We finish our tea and then walk deeper into the house. A wide staircase leads to a second floor. The ceilings rise so high I expect ravens to be roosting in the crossbeams. My arms itch. I sneeze. "Do you live here by yourself?" Bradford asks.

"Sometimes I'll have a visitor," Quinn says. "A scholar or student who wants to study my collection. I have a few guest rooms."

Our host takes out a ring of keys and begins unlocking a pair of double doors.

Hanging on the wall is a portrait of a woman. It's one of Andy's.

"My mother," Quinn says, gesturing at the drawing. "Rest her soul."

"She's beautiful," I say. No lie. Bright blue eyes. High cheekbones. Oaky blond hair.

Quinn nods. "She's doubly dead in that she died so young."

"My mother died young, too."

"It's primal, isn't it, Jonah? Losing the mother."

"I never knew mine."

Quinn looks right at me. "How did your mother pass, Jonah?"

"Cancer. Yours?"

"Murdered. By a random maniac. It's a sad story."

"I'm sorry."

He avoids my gaze, but I see the quivering lip and heaving chest. Genuine sadness. The doors swing open, and we enter a rainbow tunnel—a chain of railroad-style rooms straight out of Prospero's castle in *The Masque of Red Death,* one leading to the next through wide entryways, draped with heavy velvet curtains.

237

Matthew Mercier

Quinn clearly wants us to notice his devotion to the Poe story as he announces each color loudly.

"This is the blue room. All my paintings."

Naked women, floating chickens, foreign cites I've never been to. Next is a purple room of stuffed wolves, owls, and bears. ("From my Teddy Roosevelt period. I killed all these all myself.") A green room for the Medieval era—unicorn tapestries, goblets, Inquisition torture devices. A yellow room of Eastern artifacts such as samurai armor and Japanese pottery. If the color is a racist joke, Quinn is oblivious.

We move through it all quickly, looking but not seeing (a classic symptom of museum going) with Quinn rambling on, the most boring docent in history. The white room is, I kid you not, full of Civil War trinkets and artifacts from the Antebellum South, including a mannequin dressed in Klan robes, its cone head shining, as if freshly bleached.

"I'm a Civil War buff," Quinn says, "and your theory, Bradford, about horror underlying everything in American history—well, isn't this one of the primal tentacles?"

"It's the tentacle," Bradford mumbles, staring at the Klan robe and then looking around for an exit.

Our guide gushes about Lincoln and the number of men the president sent to die, the Native Americans he executed for treason, and how this most beloved and hallowed of presidencies was actually the most horrific.

"Lincoln himself was a monster. A gaunt, gaping, and sickly zombie who presided over so much bloodshed."

"And an American who died for our sins," Bradford says.

Quinn ignores this. "Speaking of Lincoln, here's my slavery collection."

The man either has no self-awareness or he's performing, trying to turn our stomachs. Who talks like this? We approach a Plexiglas case mounted on the wall, overstuffed with whips, thumbscrews, and leg chains. Stocks, cat-o-nine tails, paintings of slaves on the auction blocks and running through swamps.

"Why do you collect all this?" I mutter.

"I enjoy collecting history."

"Be a lot a cheaper to read a book."

"But not as much fun. I need to spend my money on something. And it all needs to be preserved. Do you know what this is?"

Poe & I

He points to a rusty metal contraption, a hollowed-out gladiator helmet.

"A slave mask," Bradford says. "For transport."

"Exactly. Note the portion that covers the mouth. Just a few air holes to breathe, so slaves wouldn't commit suicide by drinking alcohol or eating dirt."

Quinn's hands charade the air, painting the gore and pain inflicted on slaves by neck collars, whips, castration. I can barely listen. Rule number one in the docent handbook: When describing something historically horrible, it's not kosher to get off on the description. The way Quinn talks, you'd think he'd applied this mask to a slave himself. And enjoyed it.

Eventually, he leads us into the Poe room (black, naturally), and there in a cone of light, under glass, is a collection of bones, tiny slivers crisscrossed in an obscene pile.

Remains of Virginia Poe.

In 1875, the cemetery of the Fordham Dutch Reformed Church, where Virginia Poe was buried, was due for demolition. William Gillespie, Poe's first American biographer, rescued her remains and placed them in a box under his bed, with the intention of bringing them to Baltimore for burial. They never made it into the ground, as you can see.

"It's my understanding," I say, "that William Gill kept Virginia's bones under his bed for a whole year before taking them to Baltimore to be buried with Poe."

"That's half right," Quinn says. "Not all the bones made it. Gill kept a few, passed them on to his relatives. You don't just give up Annabel Lee."

"These are real?"

"Quite legitimate. See the certificate in the corner?"

Certificate. Bought and paid for, no doubt. The rest of the Poe collection continues to meld fact and fiction. The West Point cadet cape Poe gave Virginia to use as blanket while she was dying. A cutlass belonging to Poe's grandfather. Daguerreotypes and oil paintings of Poe's ladies—Sarah Helen Whitman, Francis Osgood, Elmira Shelton. Clippings from the *Southern Literary Messenger* and *Burton's Magazine*.

Matthew Mercier

Framed letters Poe wrote to John Allan, Charles Dickens, and finally a letter from Alexander Dumas, which begins with the words, *"We have received this fine gentleman, this fine American named Poe . . . "*

And then he moves us into the final room—a circular arena.

"Welcome to the Eureka Dome," Quinn says. "Or, as Poe might call it, oblivion."

A galaxy painted on the domed ceiling, infinite orbs and exploding stars. Quotes from Poe's barking mad prose poem are emblazoned on plaques. A circle of wax statues runs the perimeter.

"Eureka is Poe's masterpiece, in my opinion, and it deserves a spotlight at Poe Cottage since that's where Poe wrote it. But Cynthia didn't have the imagination to budget for one, so I built my own. We're working on a show that replicates the big bang, using actors and lightning design. It's going to be magnificent."

"A show?"

"For my annual fundraiser and masquerade ball this winter. As Poe caretakers, you're both invited."

I walk the circle of statues. All famous Bronxites. Bella Azbug. Ed Koch. Isaac Sidel. Ann Hutchinson. Colin Powell. Jonas Bronck.

Wait. Go back. Ann Hutchinson. A pioneer woman supposedly killed by Native Americans. The wax face has a sloping nose. Pinprick eyes. High forehead.

It's Mother. He cast Mother's face in wax.

Worse still, resting at the base of the pedestal is a book of illustrations. Andy's Book of the Dead.

I feel Quinn's eyes on my neck. I flip through the book. Page after page of familiar faces, clients from a decade at Peabody & Sons. Including Mother.

And then on the last page of the book, the cover is hollowed out to make room for a small, raised box. Inside the box, is my finger, my pinkie, with the moon-shaped scar.

My throat dries up. Quinn is on the opposite side of the dome, fiddling with a light switch. Bradford is gazing at a wax statue of Grandmaster Flash, posed in front of a turntable with headphones around his neck. On the base of the Flash statue, mounted behind a plexiglass square, is a vinyl record.

"That's a first pressing of *The Message*." Quinn raises the lights so that each statue is cast in a sickly yellow. "Flash's first real hit."

Poe & I

"A first pressing," Bradford whispers. "Does he even know what he's got?"

"Yes, I do," Quinn says.

"No disrespect, sir." Bradford snaps to attention. "I just didn't expect to see this here."

"Hip-hop is a part of Bronx history," Quinn smiles, "and I wanted to have it."

"So nobody else could?"

Quinn taps over to him, slightly amused. "I paid good money for it. Fair and square."

"Do you appreciate the musical significance?"

Quinn clears his throat. "It was an early prominent hip-hop song that provided social commentary."

"Do you know the lyrics?"

"Not by heart. But I believe it tells the story of young man born in the ghetto without prospects who then turns to a life of crime."

Bradford nods. "That's the Wikipedia summary, but sure."

"It'd be disingenuous if I didn't know a little about the song. As poetry it is amateur, but as protest, it's ideal. And as I said, it was Grandmaster Flash's first real hit. Flash was a genius."

"Except Flash didn't write it."

Quinn looks up at the statue.

"The lyrics," Bradford says, "are attributed to Ed 'Duke Bootee' Fletcher and Melle Mel of the Furious Five. Flash just jumped on the bandwagon. Made it popular."

"Are you sure?"

"Pretty sure."

"Well," Quinn huffs, "this white boy stands corrected."

We're so far down the rabbit hole that I think it can't get any weirder, until we notice Grandmaster's face.

Bumpy nose, thin lips, a milky white eye, and a zig-zag scar on the left cheek.

Most people won't know the difference. Just another famous black man from the Bronx.

But that's Ricky Thurston's face. No doubt.

Bradford sucks in a breath. The dome, I suddenly notice, seems to be a dead end.

No exits.

"Is this a true likeness?" I ask.

241

"Close enough." Quinn smiles. "Flash wasn't around to model."

"And what about that Book of the Dead? On Ann Hutchinson's pedestal?"

"Oh, that. A strange antiquity I picked up in a thrift store. Somewhere upstate."

Accusations lodge in my throat. I swallow them. My third eye blazes. I look up at Ann Hutchinson's face again. It's Mother's face. I'm sure of it. And Grandmaster Flash is Ricky. Bradford can see it, too. Ann is swaying side to side on her pedestal. Flash is flicking his finger across the record. Jonas Bronck is muttering the Bronx motto. *"Yield not to evil. Yield not to evil."*

"I need some air," Bradford croaks.

"Why don't we take a tour of Arnheim?" Quinn says. "My gardens are out back. They're in hibernation, but . . . "

"Arnheim?"

"Oh yes. I've got one of those, too."

"We should go," I say.

"Very well. We can save Arnheim for another evening."

I expect an iron door to slam, locking us in, but Quinn simply leads us back to the kitchen. My brain is overstuffed. You can never see a museum all in one trip. The past is too much, frozen in time.

Quinn walks us to the car without his jacket. The scar on his chest is rippled with goosebumps. I can't help but gawk.

"Heart surgery," Quinn pats me on the back. "Didn't your mother teach you not to stare, Jonah?"

"She wasn't around much."

Bradford's Dart has an orange parking ticket under the wiper.

"Oh, pity," Quinn says. "You do need a residential permit to park here. I should have told you to pull into the driveway."

Bradford removes the ticket. "I'd like to study more of your collection, Mr. Quinn. Maybe I could be one of your visiting scholars?"

"Now that's an idea," Quinn says. "You could correct the flaws in my exhibits."

"I'll be in touch."

"Oh, just stop by anytime. You know where to find me."

Poe & I

The car ride home is hysterical with conversation—two amateur detectives spit balling ideas and theories.

"Was he your guy?" Bradford asks. "Was that Richard?"

"Yes. That was a drawing of his mother. And the maniac who killed her—" I lean on the dashboard, head between my legs. "That was my mother. And that was Ricky's face, right? On the Flash statue?"

Bradford's voice is shaking. "Damn straight. I'm glad you were there. I thought I was seeing things."

"And my sister. That was her book of drawings."

The snake inside my arm is writhing. My chest is a furnace. I open the window, even though it's freezing outside. We're at a stoplight underneath the elevated nine train. It rumbles and clatters above us, the segmented shadows flickering across the windshield.

"Well, at least we know Quinn's weakness," I say.

"We do?"

"Money. Destroy that collection, and you'd really get his goat. Steal Virginia's bones, and he'd probably explode. Maybe we'll just get him voted off the board. Not sexy, but it's legal. Shut him out. Negate his influence."

"Peggy Mason is talking about the same thing, ginger. I think they're going to try and do it at the next meeting. But Lloyd Mason was spot on. That guy's a straight up tweaker."

"You think?"

"You see how skinny he was? Roll up those sleeves, I bet you find track marks. That guy reeks of junk. Maybe we'll catch him buying his medicine."

"Guy like that doesn't buy on the street."

"Good point. So, we build a case."

"Slowly. And then we bust him."

"Or find a way to bankrupt the fucker."

"Or force a confession," I say.

It's too much, and we know how ridiculous it all sounds. We're outmatched. All we can do is keep moving forward and hope that somewhere Lizzie is doing the same.

When Bradford drops me off at the cottage, he asks, "You going to be okay by yourself, Jonah? You look pale."

"I'll be fine," I say. "Everything will be fine."

Liar, liar, brain on fire.

Chapter 26

Guilty

The cops found less than two grams of weed in Andy's room, enough for a misdemeanor, a gift package that included a fine of five-hundred beans and three months in the clink. Small potatoes you might say, but jail is jail, folks, a blotch on your record, and I'm not going to bore you with the details since prison—my stretch of time, anyway—was thankfully as boring as madness.

While I was a guest of the state, I had to call Vince out of retirement to look after the parlor, but even still, when I got out, the business was comatose, the house ransacked, and Andy's hatchback stolen, along with her all her precious belongings.

And it gets better. The cops questioned me about Father's death and Andy's sudden disappearance, a pair of cases in which, it turns out, I was now a prime suspect. Take one guess who called in the anonymous tip. *Keep an eye on that Peabody boy. He knows something.*

Richard (who I'm certain had broken out of his chrysalis and was now Quinn) still had eyes on me and just wanted to make my life miserable, but neither my old man's demise nor my sister's vanishing had anything do with my poor life choices, and the pigs seemed bored with me after a few sessions. When the state finally declined to press charges, everyone left me alone.

So only the drug charge stuck, along with the rumors. Jonah, the sister killer. Jonah, the corpse fucker. Jonah, the perverted necromancer. That was Richard McKittrick's true intent: Soil my reputation and the rest will follow.

If before my shitty little town looked at me sideways, now it

Poe & I

ignored me completely. I was truly alone for the first time in my life and somehow avoided going the full Ed Gein by dating a few locals and getting a few buddies, a lot of them older like Vince. (Old souls attract old friends.) I got a job driving a truck for the local farmer and delivered to markets in Brooklyn and Manhattan and The Bronx, getting a taste of that buzzing urban excitement. Being stuck behind that wheel and driving the same routes week after week stirred the desire for escape. During a few trips, I had to resist the urge to blast through the Lincoln Tunnel, plow through Jersey, and head west.

With the funeral parlor, the end was nigh, but I was happy for it. A lot of people began to favor cremation. Who can blame them? Cheaper, faster, smaller. Burn for the urn. No more six feet under, no more sucking blood and pumping chemicals. Eventually, that corporate offer did arrive, and I sold out faster than you could say necrophilia bake sale.

Except nobody says that shit. Only me. I'm being a goon. But I did feel as though I was selling off bodies.

The money from the sale saved me from total ruin. I kept driving the farm truck, and before I knew it, four or five years of my life flickered by. I was suddenly in my thirties. Most people my age had started families, popped out kids, so what was I doing still hanging around town?

I still slept in my childhood bedroom, which didn't help my psychic health, and one night I woke up, and there stood Mother, draped in her nightgown, skin translucent, jade eyes glowing.

She pinned me to the bed and plunged the knife into my chest, into the meat and muscle and sinew, over and over, night after night, until I started on the sleeping pills.

I'm not sure why it took her so long to show up, or why I endured the punishment for so long, but it was clearly time to leave town, to find Mother's body, or I would never sleep again.

I know. I'm slow to act. Don't judge.

I'd actually looked up the McKittrick family years ago, and there seemed to be a few still hanging around. There was a lector at the local church, Susan McKittrick, who I deduced, after some digging, was Quinn's aunt. I attended mass a few Sundays in a row, sat in the back pews, and after a few weeks, built up the courage to introduce myself.

As I walked up the aisle, her face gave off that fearful flicker of

Matthew Mercier

recognition that I would come to recognize in everyone who knew my double. I could almost see the name "Richard" on her lips, but when I extended my hand and said my last name, her face lit up with concern, a twisted knot that seemed to knock the wind from her chest. She let out a tiny, "oh," which said to me, *Oh, yes. Peabody. I know who you fuckers are.*

Thankfully she was quite polite and said, "Oh yes. Peabody. I know your family. How can I help you?"

Maybe I thought approaching her in a church would absolve me of whatever needed absolving, forgiveness by Catholic osmosis, but the peaceful setting of those stained-glass windows did allow me to cut to the chase.

"Are you related to Richard McKittrick?"

Her smile flattened, and she directed me to sit with her in the front pews. A few other folks lingered in the center aisle, but I had her full attention. I rambled for a bit, half apology, half-explanation, until she lifted a hand again and repeated, "How can I be of service to you?"

Finally, I said, "Ms. McKittrick, are you aware of what Richard took from us? Not metaphorically, I mean."

She looked over her shoulder, then back at me. She knew. She must. But she shook her head, so I lowered my voice and told her the unholy story in that holy place. After I finished, she said, "You are a liar. How dare you bear false witness."

"Ma'am, break out your Bible, and I'll swear on it." I slipped a leather-bound book from the pew and slapped my hand on it. "Here."

"That is a hymnal, young man." She shook her head. "Didn't you have a sister?"

"Yes."

"Where is she now?"

"Please. That's . . . I don't want to say. I just need to know. Where is Richard?"

She nodded, resigned, and then leaned into the darkness. "Richard was not well liked by our family. He was a strange bird. Even as a young boy. Even before his mother died. But after she died . . . "

She closed her eyes, made the sign of the cross, and placed a hand on mine. "We forgave your father a long time ago. But not Richard. He held on to his anger. We tried to include him in our

246

Poe & I

family gatherings after he lost his mother and brother in quick succession. But those losses, I think they warped his mind further. You said . . . he held up your sister at gunpoint?"

"Yes ma'am."

"Now that I believe. Richard, when he was a boy, had a plastic gun. Very realistic looking. A prop gun. I'm not sure where he found it or why my brother allowed him to wield it, but that little devil waved that thing around and pretended to shoot us . . . and oh . . . he was just so violent. More than other boys his age."

"When he was a teenager," I said, "he began visiting my mother."

"Yes. My brother got religion, decided forgiveness was best, and thought it might help Richard. But it only made him worse. And then my brother died, and that . . . " Here she paused and looked up at the cross again. "It never sat well with me. Or the family."

"I'm sorry? What didn't?"

"Peter's death. My brother. Richard's father." She took the hymnal from me and placed it on the pew, placed a hand on my knee. "We suspected Richard of foul play. Nobody could prove anything of course. But Richard. He inherited a fortune from my brother. You know that, right?"

"Oh yes . . . when he visited us years ago, his father had just died. I'm sorry, I don't mean to dredge up all old wounds."

"It's not old. It's still fresh. Did you know Richard changed his name?"

"No."

"Something odd. Anyway. He dropped off the face of the earth for a while . . . but I think . . . I know . . . he's down in the city. You see, that's where his cousin moved. My sister's daughter. Richard had an unhealthy obsession with her."

"His cousin?"

"Yes. Are you . . . what do you plan on doing?"

"I want to recover my mother's body. I want to give her a proper burial."

She shuddered, still not believing. "Cynthia works for a historical society. That's the only lead I have. She doesn't talk much to me. She's a bit odd herself." She stands and walks to the votary, takes a pen, and writes on a donation envelope. "That's her name. Cynthia McMullen."

Bless me, dear reader. It's been never since my last confession. I'm not used to telling the truth.

247

Chapter 27

Eureka

After Riverdale, nothing looks the same.

Richard is Quinn and Quinn is Richard. You saw what I saw. You heard what I heard. He's got my sister's book. He's got my pinkie. He's got Mother's face. He's got Ricky's Thurston's face. He's got Virginia's bones and Poe's tumor, and in all likelihood, he's got Mother's remains buried deep in the bowels of that enormous house after carting them around for close to eight years.

It can't be true, you say. You are out of your skull, Jonah.

Perhaps. But if we use the metric of Mother, if her ghost is the Geiger counter that will lead me to her bones, then I'm listening to her.

Right now, she's standing over me, reeking of earth, dripping in sweat, earthworms dangling from her ears, moss clumped in her hair, the tooth necklace draped between her fingers. All month, she's been trying to snap the molars back into her jawline. She can hold the teeth, but she can't hold scissors to clip the string, so she keeps trying to stuff the entire necklace in her gummy mouth, which just makes her frustrated, and so she wails even louder. Last week, Dupin got a hold of the necklace and began batting it around, a new cat toy, but Mother hissed and stomped and Dupin hissed and scratched.

My roommates are not getting along. I can only laugh. Never did I think it would all end this way.

My brain burns, my lungs burn hotter, and the black line of my mold scar is a searing live wire which is mainlining a river of fireworks into my cortex, popping, and exploding, flooding my

Poe & I

thoughts. I'm scratching and rubbing the skin of my forearm until it's volcanic red.

Mother is not oblivious to my pain. At night, when she appears, the look on her face is the motherly concern I never got when she was alive. She tries to touch me, but I keep my mouth shut and point to the knife.

You're not coming near me unless you put that down, Mother.
She's never ever listened to me—until now.

She rests the ghostly knife on the table, holds up her hands, and approaches slowly, her gummy lips green with attempted speech. I whimper and back up to the ship's ladder, ready to bolt, but the fact that she's put the knife down has me curious. She reaches out, her fingers the grayish tint of meat gone bad, and brushes the tips over my damaged forearm. She raises her eyebrows.

May I touch you, Jonah?

Not sure if she's speaking or if I'm filling in for her, but I nod, and she lays her hands on me—cold as steel, my veins hissing with steam like they are a blacksmith's tools dipped in water. Then she taps a rotten fingernail over my closed mouth, a cuticle falling into the well of my bottom lip. I blow air through my clenched teeth, so it flutters to the floor.

She wants inside.

Same old story. I shake my head, and we do the dance, back and forth until I realize what she's saying. She points to the scar, then to my chest, then curls her fingers and pulls her hand up and away from my body.

Let me take care of you, Jonah. Let me in, and I'll push out the sickness.

Ridiculous. It's a trick. Has to be. But then again, what have I got to lose? She's been slipping in and out of me for years now, and I've just been throwing her up, so what if this time it actually benefits my health?

"Fuck it," I croak. "Let's go."

She doesn't wait for me to change my mind.

She winnows into a ribbon and slides between my incisors as smoothly as a wet noodle, plunges into my gullet, rides the roller-coaster of my GI tract, bounces over my stomach acid—a lake of fire—and rattles up and down my rib cage as if it's a venetian blind.

She's never hurt so bad. At any moment, her razor-sharp

cheekbones are going to rip a hole in my stomach, and her head will rise up filthy with gore and scream "Tricked you, sucker!" But instead, I hear:

Trust me, Jonah. Just trust me.

Easier said than done. I run to the bathroom, lean over the toilet, heaving, ready to wretch her up in a gooey mess, but a piercing sharp pain—an arrow through my stomach—forces me to slump to the floor. I moan, rise to my feet, and hunchback it to the loveseat.

She won't let me go. Not this time. This was a mistake. She's worming her way through my chest, up my shoulder, and wiggling into my forearm, a sandworm chewing up mold and disease—at least, that's what I hope she's doing as I pass out from the pain.

I wake up hours later with a headache and green eyes. She's still in there. I sit on the toilet and shed twenty pounds with an epic dump. My mold scar is clammy, and I rub my chest.

"Okay, Ma. Let's give this a whirl."

So, I give the tours high on Mother. Poe history is streaming out of me while Poe himself is yammering in my head about Virginia and her bones. Dupin, my only comfort, won't cuddle with me. He can tell that I'm Mother. I try to pick him up and he nearly claws my eyes out, and when I exit the shed to clean up the trash, he bolts out into The Bronx. He'd rather take his chances on the streets.

My heart breaks three times over.

As we roll into December and the weather grows colder, so does my arm, which allows me a sharper focus, motivating me to watch the Ricky tapes again and again. How did Quinn get inside the basement? There has to be a secret door. Nobody was looking for one, because nobody was looking for a murderer, but if Lizzie is right and Quinn got in here . . .

I leap off the loveseat.

Forgive me. I'm no detective. I've been so wrapped up with my own shit, with fending off Mother and swallowing Mother and throwing up Mother that I've literally been sitting on the answer.

In all the shots of Ricky, he's sitting on the same loveseat, but I knew there was something off about the way the frame was composed, something missing, yet my monkey mind didn't see it until just now.

Poe & I

In Ricky's footage, there is no Poe Society safe. None. It should be crammed right between the arm of the loveseat and the red walls, where it sits now, but on camera, nothing.

I run the footage again, and there, in the final clip, Ricky is talking about how Poe Cottage is the best job he's ever had. When he finishes, he picks up the camera, and the lens drops for a split second. Before it cuts out, there it is—the blurry black edge of the Poe Society safe. Blink and you'll miss it.

Ricky positioned the camera on top of the safe, but that meant the safe had been in front of the loveseat, not next to it. It's been moved to its current position, squeezed in the corner, with a rug under it, and the loveseat crammed tight against it, hiding the obvious to the oblivious.

I yank the loveseat into the center of the room, bend down, and swipe a hand under the safe, across the rug. I'll have to move the safe, which thankfully is on wheels, but that doesn't make it easier. It takes me a full hour of pushing and heaving to move it off the rug.

Pull the rug up, and there, in the far corner, is a brown gromet, the color of the floor. The gromet clicks, and a square bit of floor pops up, relaxing on a pair of tightly sprung hinges. I peer into the hole that's just been created. It reeks of piss, rats, oil, and sewage. The iron rungs of a ladder are bolted into the gray throat of a chute, dropping into the darkness.

Smart thing to do would be to put the rug and safe back and never speak of this again. Except I'm not smart. I'm no longer myself.

I dig in my backpack for my headlamp and call Bradford and Lizzie. Neither one picks up. I leave messages for both, and then I try Oscar.

"Yo! Poe Presente!"

"Oscar, thank God. Listen."

I give him the score, and naturally he says, "White boy, that doesn't sound wise."

Yes, yes, yes, I know, I know, but who else is going to do this? Nobody. I can't ask anyone else to climb down here. Not Lizzie, not Bradford. Nobody but me, myself, and I. And Mother.

"My name is Jonah Peabody, and everything will be fine."

"What now?" Oscar says.

"If you don't hear from me in an hour, call me back."

Matthew Mercier

No guts, no glory, no regrets. I strap the headlamp over my third eye, slip onto the ladder, and descend into the dark, closing the door behind me.

I reach the bottom, and step on something that squishes and pops. Greasy water drips onto my neck, running down my back. Motor oil and roasted peanuts on the air. Above me is the grid of a ventilation grate. I'm under the street and begin to shuffle up a long, narrow corridor.

The pockmarked wall on my right falls away, and the gloom expands. I've been on enough hairpin mountain trails after midnight to feel invisible boundaries, the line where the cliff face drops off into the canyon, so I can feel the emptiness just two steps to the right. I pass a few staggered beams, evenly spaced. Between the beams is a bubbly yellow line and below are glistening train tracks—an abandoned subway platform.

Warm air pushing against my face, a faint rumbling, lights far off down the tunnel, and then, at the opposite end of the platform, a D express shooting by, heading south into the city, its florescent-lit collection of passengers either sleeping, reading, or staring into space, all stiff, blank, emotionless dolls. Then it's gone.

I hustle along the platform. The humps of rats skitter just out of sight. Soon, I hit another ladder, and, without pause, climb.

At the top, I feel the outline of another panel, find a deadbolt, tap it open, then push with my shoulder, hard. I hold onto a ladder rung with one hand and grunt, heaving. The panel shunts open with a loud click.

I poke my head into a carpeted, circular room with no windows and climb in, dizzy with discovery. Give my eyes a minute to adjust, but then I find portraits hanging on a curved wall. Jonas Bronck. Fiorello La Guardia. Lewis Morris. Colin Powell. Bella Abzug. Isaac Sidel. Ed Koch. All Bronx folks. And under Koch is a secretary desk, a small bookcase, a rotary phone, a file cabinet, and a tiny lamp.

My chest tightens as I turn off my light and sit in the gray hush. Car horns above, the screech of the subway below. The ceiling is all glitter, a brightness pressing down on my head. I drop onto my back, the carpet soft and fuzzy. My stomach yo-yos. I close my eyes, open them again, and find hundreds—no thousands—of pinpricks blinking back at me.

I stretch my spine and legs over the carpet, and the ceiling stretches with me. This isn't my third eye playing tricks. It's a fake

Poe & I

galaxy, a planetarium. Behold the universe, boys and girls. Try to fathom just how tiny you are.

Constellations now. Scorpio. Draco the Dragon. The Big Dipper. I reach out and try to touch Orion's belt. In the center sits a pulsing ball of light and the imprint of what looks to be a hand. I stare at the mass of dots and circles and spirals and cones. An illuminated inscription on the wall above the desk.

" . . . *I propose to show that this Oneness is a principle abundantly sufficient to account for the constitution, the existing phenomena and the plainly inevitable annihilation of at least the material universe.*"

It's Poe's *Eureka.*

Who built this? Didn't Quinn mention trying to construct an exhibit of *Eureka*? Where is the exit?

I stand too fast, blood rushing to my head, and stagger backwards, my hip hitting the trap door, which slams shut.

Cold panic surges into my veins as I claw the seams and surface of the door. All flat. No grommet, no discernable keyhole. I'm locked inside.

I scream, bellow, pound the floor, but how can I be upset? I knew where this tunnel would lead—well not exactly, but I knew it was a trap, and I still chose to be an idiot white boy. And why?

Mother.

As I collapse against the wall, she settles into my chest, regulates my heartbeat, and tells me to breathe, honey, breathe, breathe. You're not done yet. Not yet. Not today. You're not going to die inside this memorial. (Because that's what this Eureka Dome is, right? A memorial to lost Bronx history.) No, we're not done. Not today.

We pick up the rotatory phone, get a dial tone, and try to dial out. Nothing. We go through the rolltop desk. Empty. We try my cell. No reception. We bang on the curved concrete and yell.

We must be above ground or least on a level with Poe's Basement. We descended, walked due south, and then ascended again. We've buried ourselves alive. We've climbed into our own grave.

But no. Not a grave. There is a ventilation grate on the ceiling, air being pumped in from above. Stale recycled subway air, but still. Oxygen.

Jonah, I don't like the way Jonas Bronx is staring at us.

Mother's point is well taken. Jonas's severe 19th century visage

253

Matthew Mercier

is burning a hole in my brain. We walk over to him and take down his portrait, then go down the line and take all the portraits off their hooks, until we find what we are looking for behind Ed Koch.

A fisheye peephole. The kind you'd see in a door. We peep. All is dark. We push and push and bang and scream and eventually sink to the ground, weeping.

Then, above the air vent, we notice a camera looking down at our frustration. Quinn. He's watching. He must be. This is his weird private little office. I give the camera the finger. Mother clicks her tongue and tells me to be polite. I tell her to fuck off. Then I climb on the desk and try to send a text to Oscar, and by some miracle it goes through, so we can't be that far underground.

I didn't think to bring a sweatshirt, and now the cold of December is seeping through the stone, through my flimsy jacket. I curl up in the fetal position, chattering, praying for sleep, but it's impossible. Mother's mind is overlaying my own, a photo negative, and she's making a racket.

"Mother, go to sleep. We'll figure this out later."

I have a feeling it will resolve sooner, Jonah. He is watching.

Quinn. He must know, or he will know, that we've violated his sanctuary. Then my cell phone buzzes. A text. From Oscar. I leap onto the desk, the highest point in the room.

Where are U? Tried to call.

I'm underground.

No shit, Jonah. Where?

Across from the cottage.

What?

Then it hits me. The only structure directly south of the cottage.

Oscar, I'm inside the bandstand.

What?

I'm beneath the bandstand . . . I think.

Jonah . . .

The text cuts out. Nothing. I wait, holding my phone in the air. That's it. That's all I get. But I must be right, the curved walls give it away. There is a tiny concrete lip running the entire circumference of the bandstand, and I leave my phone on it, in case Oscar tries again. Then I hop off the desk, look up at the camera, spreading my arms wide.

"I'm here, Quinn. Give me call."

I then retreat to the floor, huddling and shivering.

Poe & I

I wake to the rotary phone ringing its retro music, a maddening shriek that bounces off the stone walls. I shuffle across to the desk and pick up.

"Is this Jonah Peabody?"

"Fuck you, Richard."

"Temper, temper. That's not even my name. Relax. Help is on the way."

"I don't need your help."

"Of course you do. Don't worry. This wasn't part of the plan, but so be it. I can be there in the morning."

"The morning? Fuck you, I . . . "

He hangs up. What time is it? My phone says eight. No text from Oscar. I slump to the ground, a passive, impotent lump. But no. Not passive. We started this, Mother. You and I and the whole damn family, and now we're going to finish it.

Sleep now, baby boy. Just go to sleep.

Chapter 28

April Fools

After that uncomfortable meeting with Aunty McKittrick, I got a lead on you, Richard, looked up your cousin, concocted a cover letter and resume, and mailed it off to one Cynthia McMullen, announcing my interest in a job with the Bronx Historical Society.

The least qualified person on earth soliciting a job with a prestigious historical society. What a hoax. What a red flag. But the point, of course, was to get your attention, to announce my presence to your cousin, who would surely recognize the name Peabody, after which she'd tell you the news—that I was back in town—and thus open a can of worms, which if we're talking graverobbing instead of fishing, takes on a whole different meaning.

That done, I started looking for apartments in The Bronx, but then I found that cheap deathtrap with Stavros the Greek and began requesting truck routes in the city and sleeping in the Queens apartment overnight, sometimes driving back upstate.

I could have built a life that way. Driving and hauling freight, not attached to anyone or any one place, but Mother was never far from my thoughts, and if I slept upstate, she was literally never far from me, standing right above my bed, trying to get inside me on a nightly basis, so much so that I had to begin sleeping in our barn, where she didn't seem to ghost.

Yes, I would have been happy to forget you, Quinn, but since we never resolved this shit in childhood, we needed to resolve it here in the tangled forest of maturity. I kept emailing Cynthia and

Poe & I

begging her to hire me, so it was only a matter of time before you found me, Richard, before you took the bait.

During one of my routes in the West Village, one of the farmer's market guys introduced me to Chumley's, and I started drinking there after work, got to know Ramses, made a few bets, plunged deep in the hole, but I was so nihilistic that I didn't care. And then I think either you or your private detective must have found me, because I saw you sitting in the shadows at Chumley's one night, a wraith among the vibrant college crowd.

Did I risk looking you in the eye? I may have. I really tried to stay in character, tried to play the innocent who just happened to stumble into your life again, but sending a letter to your cousin and begging her for a job—that gave the game away. We both knew what the other wanted, but still you performed and pretended, which I have to say was almost fun.

However, the moment I can't stop thinking about is that night back in April, when it was my turn to take the bait, when you gave Ramses the want ad, when he summoned me to Chumley's on that lonely Sunday night and offered me that plate of mushrooms. A new recipe, he called it.

What were you thinking, Quinn? You can't fool a country boy with mushrooms.

Poisoning me then didn't work, so you took my finger instead and now here I am, buried alive.

But not for long.

Chapter 29

Arnheim

I wake to the shunting of a deadbolt, the creak of hinges, a door opening. I'm in the attic of our childhood home, Father releasing Andy and I from prison.

Standing above me in the gloom is Quinn—gaunt and pale, drowning in a winter peacoat, twirling a ring of keys. "Good morning, sunshine. Ready to greet the day?"

I rub the crust from my eyes and stand.

Quinn tilts his head to the side, probing my face. "And good morning to you as well, Mrs. Peabody."

Mother stirs in my guts but remains quiet, advising me to play it cool. "I'm fine," I say. "I'm fine."

"Do you know your name?"

"Jonah Peabody," I say, standing up straight. "Get me out of here, Quinn."

He gestures to the open door, where there is a short ladder, climbing a mere eight feet into a blue winter sky. How ridiculous. How close to the surface I've been the whole time. Shuffling and stooped, bones aching and stiff, I steady myself on the ladder, and climb, emerging into the south end of Poe Park, the bandstand's greenish bronze molding rimmed with frost.

"Jonah!"

My name, being shouted from across the park. Oscar is on the opposite end of the oval, waving a gloved hand and running over to me in a puffy sports jacket, misty breath drifting in his wake.

"Damn bro. I was worried."

"When did I call you?"

258

Poe & I

"Came out here yesterday to try and find you, but then had to leave when they locked the park. Jesus, you look different. What's up with your eyes?"

"I'm sick," I say. "I . . . "

"Mr. Peabody requires medical attention, young man." Quinn emerges from the Eureka Dome and closes the faux concrete door behind him, locking it with a key in the shape of a rat's claw.

"Oh yeah. And who are you?"

"Arthur Quinn, at your service."

This takes the wind out of Oscar's bravado, although he tries to front. "Well, maybe we need to report you for locking him up."

"Mr. Peabody was trespassing. Weren't you, Jonah?"

I shiver and rub my arms. "It's fine, Oscar."

"Trespassing?" Oscar is incredulous. "Who are you fooling, old man. This is a public park."

Quinn holds up the keys. "True enough, but the bandstand belongs to the Society, and Jonah was in there after hours. He had no permission."

"Oscar, it's fine."

"No, this guy can't threaten you."

"I'm not going to press charges," Quinn says. "But Jonah and I have unfinished business."

"You can talk to him after he's had some breakfast." Oscar jerks his head to the side. "Let's go Jonah. Let's leave this loser behind."

Quinn is amused and stands there, crossing his arms. "Very well. I'll give you an hour to recover from your live burial, Jonah. But I'll be waiting at the cottage. In the parlor."

"I'll be there."

Quinn flicks his palm at us. "Run along now. I believe you are only going across the street."

This is what I was afraid of. Now Quinn knows where Oscar lives, although he may have known it all along. Oscar is unfazed. He and I turn our backs and walk across Kingsbridge to a tenement with a red door. We turn, and Quinn is still lingering by the bandstand, staring after us.

"Is that the creepy bastard everyone's been talking about?"

"Yes. Oscar, I'm sorry. He . . . "

"Get inside, white boy. Didn't I tell you this was a bad idea?"

"How did you know to be here, Oscar?"

Matthew Mercier

In the lobby of the apartment building, there is a baby stroller locked to the staircase with a bike lock. "I called Cynthia."

"Of course."

"What I always do in emergencies. I told her what you said, and she suggested I show up here this morning."

"Thank you. I—"

"You can explain later. We live on the fifth floor. You got the strength?"

We begin to climb. Behind the apartment doors, infants are crying, dogs are barking, televisions are blaring. Normal life soldiering on. The Garcia's door, 5F, is naturally blood red, and the knocker even more obvious—a raven's beak.

The entrance is a long hallway with framed maps of The Bronx. We pass a bathroom on the left, while on the right is a room stacked with books, and then it all opens up into a living room with a leather sofa and recliners all circling a faux wooden entertainment center. An older woman with crimson hair sits on the couch watching the morning news.

"Grandma, this is Jonah. The new Poe boy we were telling you about."

The woman reaches a wrinkled hand over the cushions. "Carmen Garcia. So nice to meet you. Sorry to not get up. Not as spry as I once was. Welcome to our home. Do you need something to eat? Oscar, has he eaten?"

The far wall is covered—and I mean covered—with framed pictures, an epic family tree arranged in a glorious triangle, a mosaic of life. "All my grandchildren," Carmen says, when she sees me staring. "Do you want some coffee? Get him some coffee, Oscar."

"Yes, yes. We're working on it, abuela."

"We sure are collecting people today."

"Collecting people?" I ask.

"You'll see," Oscar says.

He walks me deeper into the apartment, stopping outside another room. "You can chill in here. How do you like your coffee? I think we have blueberry muffins, too. You want a muffin?"

I nod, too dazed to speak, and push open the door. A room of file cabinets, books, portraits, manuscripts, and a printer. I step inside. In the printer feed is a title page:

The Truth of Arthur Quinn's Collection by Lizzie Borden.

Poe & I

Oscar returns with a steaming cup of joe and a muffin. "Sorry. All we had was bran raisin. Bathroom is by the door if this makes you poop fast. Don't suppose there was a bathroom in the bandstand."

I hold up the title page. "Oscar. Where is she?"

The kid jerks his chin at the ceiling. "Eat first."

I sip the coffee and gobble the muffin. "I need to be outside. Let's go now."

He shrugs, tosses me a jacket and hat, and we walk to the rear of the apartment, through a fully furnished kitchen, and climb out onto the fire escape. The cold is biting, but the view is fantastic. From here you can see Fordham University, the Metro North tracks, and the sprawling concrete mass of the East Bronx. On the roof, we're met with rows of raised beds and fruit trees, most now wrapped in burlap for the winter. There's a box of a greenhouse in the corner, one of those cheap pop-up jobs you can buy at Wal-Mart, and inside we find Carla and Lizzie, sorting seeds on a card table.

Carla smiles, lets out a huff, and puts her hands on her hips, as if to say, *Took you long enough.*

Lizzie does not look as cheerful, and when she sees me holding a copy of her pamphlet, her face sours even more.

"Lizzie, you're okay," I blurt.

"Of course she is!" Carla barks, throwing an arm around the archivist. "No way that goon is getting close to her."

"Except now," Lizzie looks at me, "Quinn knows where you all live."

"Meh," Oscar says. "He probably figured it out a long time ago. Let's see where he's at." He walks outside and climbs up the slope of the roof that looks over the park. Even from the greenhouse, you can see Poe Cottage.

"Eyes on the cottage," I say. "That's what you said."

"Literally. Twenty-four seven," Carla chirps. "We've even got little binoculars. We've been watching you the whole time, Jonah."

"That's creepy."

"Oh, come on! We're on your side."

"The question is," Lizzie says, "whose side are you on, Jonah?"

"Lizzie, I swear I didn't know Quinn would show up that night. You have to believe me. Look, I just spent nearly twenty-four hours locked inside the bandstand."

Matthew Mercier

"Yeah, I want to hear about this," Carla says.

Oscar re-enters the greenhouse, holding a tiny pair of binocs. "Looks as though Quinn walked back over to the cottage. I don't see him."

"Lizzie, how is your mother?" I ask.

"She's fine. She's safe. For now."

In the silence that follows, the unspoken questions are as heavy as lead. How dangerous is Quinn? Will he able to hurt Lizzie's mother? Oscar and Carla? How big is his reach, and how do we get him to stop?

"Jonah," Lizzie says, "your eyes. What did you do?"

Carla squints at me. "Oh damn. They're green. Yo! New contacts?"

"Yes," I say, taking the gift of an easy answer. Lizzie isn't fooled, but she stays quiet. I survey their tiny kingdom. "Don't y'all worry about theft up in here?"

"I'm more concerned about fire," Carla says. "But we got cameras, locks, sprinklers. Biggest thing is hungry people stealing vegetables in the summer, but I don't really care about that."

We circle back to business. I tell them about my foolish adventures underground, about Quinn's little office, about the secret entrance in the basement.

"I knew it!" Lizzie says. "I knew there was a goddamn underground entrance."

"But we still don't have any proof that he killed Ricky."

"No. No, we don't. But nice work Jonah."

"I'm on your side, Lizzie."

She says nothing.

"So, if you don't have evidence," Carla says, "then you need a confession."

"Good luck with that."

I look at my lap. "He'll confess to me."

"And why would he do that?" Oscar scoffs.

"Trust me. He will." I hold up Lizzie's pamphlet. "Is this why Ricky died? Is this why he's threatening you? Over a bunch of stolen artifacts?"

"We are soiling his already soiled reputation," Lizzie says. "It was the best I could do. Cynthia has some master plan. This is what she hired me to do, but she didn't tell me the fucker was insane."

262

Poe & I

"There is a lot she didn't tell you."

We head downstairs to the living room to warm up. Carmen insists on making us eggs and telling us all about her grandbabies, but before we get too comfortable the buzzer rings.

"It's him," I say. "I know it."

"Jonah, you don't have to go," Oscar says.

"Don't be foolish." I get off the sofa. "I'm the reason he's here. He won't hurt me. We have unfished business."

Lizzie reaches out for my hand.

"I'll see you at the party," I say.

"Jonah."

"It will be fine. It always is."

I'm sick of the past. I want to be in the moment, but I've got a bit more work to do before that can happen.

When I reach the bottom of the stairs, Quinn is nearly bursting out of his skin, giddy at the sight of me. He's got a leather satchel slung over his shoulder. "It's been over an hour, Jonah."

"Hello Richard."

He doesn't flinch at his real name, just smirks.

"Where is she, Richard?"

"Who's that? Lizzie?"

"My mother."

He sweeps his arm toward the busy street, to the park. "Let's go back to cottage, shall we?"

We walk through the cold morning sunshine. The park is empty. The trees are bare, and the grass sparkles with a sheen of frost. We pass the Eureka bandstand, which Quinn taps with his cane. "Thought about leaving you in there longer but figured it would be pointless."

I cover my mouth with a fist and cough.

"Sounds bad. You should take care of that. It's flu season."

I unlock the front gate and lead us into the museum, closing the door. We're alone in the parlor again.

"Home sweet home," Quinn says,

"No more games." I take off my jacket to show him the way the mold scar has worked its way up my arm. "You've won, Richard. I'm sick."

His face is glowing with suppressed glee. "Yes, both in body and mind." From the satchel he takes out a digital recorder and hits play. My voice floats into the parlor.

Matthew Mercier

"Mr. Poe. You're famous. Yes. Why don't you believe me? Look at you. You're the ghost; I'm flesh and blood. Get it? Here. Let me show you."

I bounce the heel of my foot. It's just my voice. No Poe.

Now I'm debating Eddie's poetry with Him. Then I'm telling Him I'll find Virginia. Then I'm telling tourists that Poe lives in the house with me, and that Virginia is out in the greenhouse. Then I'm telling Poe that I've found Virginia.

My speech is slurred, my tone aggressive. Then I'm raging to myself about the ciphers, about how I'm being stalked. Then I'm talking to Mother, weeping and screaming as she forces her way inside me.

Quinn raises a finger. "Here's the good part. Remember this conversation?"

Quinn's voice. *"Is that a gun, Mr. Peabody?"*

Me: *"It's not loaded."*

"I'll have to report this to Cynthia."

"No need to do that."

I sigh as he hits stop. "Okay, so I'm as crazy as you, Richard. I talk to ghosts. And that gun was plastic. Richard. You . . . "

"Stop calling me that." Quinn pulls an envelope from his coat and holds it up, waving it at me. "It gets better. You wrote this and sent it to the board."

"I didn't write anything."

Quinn reads: *"Dear board members. My name is Jonah Peabody. I am the caretaker for the last home of Edgar Allan Poe, and I live in the basement. But you already know this. I'm writing to you for a number of reasons. One, historical posterity.*

Two, protection against myself and my own mind. I don't know what the circumstances are at this moment. Maybe I'm already in jail. It's possible that I have committed a crime against somebody or against myself. No doubt I will try and convince you that Arthur Quinn is responsible for my troubles."

I press two fingers to my forehead.

"Whatever accusations I make against Quinn are a smokescreen, a way of deflecting the attention away from my own crimes. I've done horrible things, ladies and gentlemen. I once locked my sister in the attic of our home. I've stolen jewelry from corpses. I've slept with my own Mother's dead body. I've tortured animals, gambled away my college tuition, done prison

264

Poe & I

time for drugs, and even worse,"—Quinn clears his throat—"*I poisoned my own father.*"

The list keeps going.

"*I've lied, cheated, and deserted my family when they most needed me, especially my sister. I may have killed her, too.*"

Something bursts in my ear, a high-pitched ringing.

"*I've got anger, rage, a bit of madness inside me—an inherited sickness that I'm deeply ashamed of. No matter how much I try to convince you of my goodness, don't believe it. And no matter how much I try to convince you of Quinn's wrongdoing, don't believe it. I cannot be trusted. I am not well. Yours most sincerely, Jonah Peabody.*"

"Well," Quinn folds the letter, "that is a bit too much. I know that in the past, my character has been called into question, but I assure you that whatever wrongs I have committed in this life, I am no Jonah Peabody."

"Richard, this letter . . . you wrote that." I laugh. "You clearly know me."

Chunks of bile rise from my stomach. I cough, hack, beat my chest. Whatever is in there is coming up. I can't stop it, sliding up my throat and crawling into my mouth and dribbling over my lips. I finally spit what appears to be a cremini mushroom into my palm, slimy and wet.

"Brilliant move," I cough, placing the mushroom on the windowsill. "Throwing my own words back at me."

Quinn eyes the slimy fungus. "Mushrooms growing inside you? Your immune system must really have taken a hit."

I laugh so hard my third eye explodes in a supernova of purple and yellow dots. I stand and scream my head off for the hidden microphones. "Are you listening assholes? I hope I blow your eardrums out!"

Because that's how they did it, right? Hidden mics? Like a spy movie? I drum the walls with my fist and dig under the plaster, carving out bite-size chunks.

This finally gets a rise out of Quinn. "What are you doing, Jonah?"

My mold scar burns. My teeth chatter. Mushrooms ping-pong in my esophagus. I breathe, try to breathe. Everything will be fine. Slow down. You're not in trouble yet. You're just a person of interest. Nobody is coming to arrest you. You haven't been charged with a crime. Take a moment. Breathe. Let Poe breathe with you.

Matthew Mercier

"Jonah," Richard says, "you need to settle down."

I tap the flaking plaster next to Poe's desk, quoting *Landor's Cottage.* "This is an excellently constructed house. These walls are solidly put together."

"Jonah, stop hurting the cottage."

I break off a chunk the size of a potato chip. "You heard me. I'm unstable! I might hurt someone!"

"No need to shout."

"Why not? Are they extra powerful mics?" I sink my fist into the wall, sending a puffball of plaster into the air.

"Jonah, if you continue to threaten the integrity of this house, I will be forced to call the authorities."

My knuckles are bleeding. I've hit a stud. "Go ahead. And I'll tell them about the real bones in your house."

He blinks. "Then you won't get her back."

The veil has dropped. He's admitting it.

"Jonah, these recordings. You sent them to us."

"No, I didn't."

"And the letter, too. It's all from your email."

"Stop it, Richard. Stop it, stop it."

"You have a penchant for self-destruction, Jonah. You know this. It runs in your family."

There. Again. He slipped up. "You know my family?"

He shakes his head. "No. I'm assuming it runs in the family."

"Ah, but I'm just like you Quinn. A self-destructive liar and a cheat with a dubious past."

"Perhaps it's time for one more gift." He removes from the satchel a glossy, graphic novel with the density of a brick. Bigfoot is on the cover, sitting atop a mossy rock and staring out at a pine forest, with mountains and lakes in the background.

Beneath the title, *Memoirs of a Monster*, is a name:

Pamela Usher.

"This caught my eye. The illustrations are quite lovely and bear a remarkable similarity to the *Book of the Dead*, that tome you saw in my house. I'm currently trying to find Ms. Usher's contact information, but she seems to be a recluse. I believe she's somewhere in the Pacific Northwest. A good place to hide."

I'm ready to kill him, but Mother, seeing her name on the cover of the book, holds me back, and once more the veil drops from Quinn's words.

266

Poe & I

"Offer yourself to me on Poe's birthday, Jonah, and we'll see what we can arrange about these matters between us. Come to my party," he laughs, "with an open heart."

"Leave her alone," I croak.

"No, no I don't think so. Even if she's changed her name, she's still a Peabody." Quinn stands, leaning on his cane. "January 19th. I hope to see you." He pauses at the front door. "That resume you submitted to us, that's when it clicked. Very clever."

I close my eyes. Stupid. Of course he'd put it together. I sit there until he's gone. Mother cries inside me, then I walk downstairs, open the Poe safe. The gun is plastic, the teeth are Mother's, but the most precious thing I own is a stack of letters that I carry with me everywhere.

You will have questions, dear reader, but for now, this is what I will give you.

Chapter 30
Letters From the Dead

Dear Jonah,

I'm sorry. First and foremost, please know that. I'm crying as I write this. I never thought I'd be the one to break the promise. I mean, I knew I would leave town first, but I never thought I would betray our pinky promise. But you have to understand that I could not take being in that small petty town or in that house for one more minute. I had to cut ties, cold turkey, but I didn't think I would do it without saying good-bye. Consider this a temporary goodbye. We'll see each other again.

I'm on a Greyhound heading west. Don't tell anyone. I've got enough money to start over. It's all in traveler's checks. I'm not sure how I'll do it, but I will.

That bastard Richard . . . he's never going to leave us alone. I saw him in the town center a few weeks ago and he said—okay, he didn't say, but he implied— that he knew about my drug dealing, just like you said. He told me I was going to enjoy prison. He also said that I murdered Father, which I didn't Jonah, I didn't, but he was going to tell the police that I did and that he could prove it. It scared me so much that I decided to leave without my car. He could trace the plates. He could find me. So, I just grabbed what I could and fled.

I made such a mistake in giving Mother's body to him, but what could I do? I didn't want to die, and I honestly think he would have shot me. I don't think he cares. He's that cracked in

Poe & I

the head. *We needed to get rid of her body, but oh I made such a mistake. It's going to haunt my dreams forever.*

You can still report him. It's a felony, messing with a corpse. But if you do, I think he'll come after you, Jonah. I think that he will make your life worse. That's what he said. You need to get out of town, bro.

But please find Mother, please. Put her in the ground where she belongs. I know that it's my fuck up, I know, but please. It's the only way this will end.

I love you forever. I'll be in touch. Maybe under a different name.

Andy

Chapter 31

Operation Tamerlane

There you have it. My sister's confession. But sweet Jesus Mary mother of Carcosa, please ignore my "confession," the one Quinn wrote for me.

I'm not going to true-or-false that letter. You've come this far. Nobody can win with a dirty history like mine, and the more truth you tell the more people get scared. So, you hide the truth, but then people don't trust you because you're hiding something, and on and on it goes.

Mother knows the truth, and that's all that matters. She's in Quinn's house, and we're going to get her out.

Poe Cottage is closed for the holidays. I barely eat and lose five pounds. My wrists now fit inside mason jars. Mother is hurting *and* healing me. I'm coughing up mushrooms on a daily basis, collecting them in a brown paper bag, expunging the sickness. I crave sunlight and air. The winter daylight hours are so precious that I live in the parlor twenty-four seven.

One night, I reach for the candle lights on the mantlepiece, but the sleeve of my jacket catches the cord and pitches the plastic candle over the side. It falls and swings against the wall, smashing the bulb. The exposed fixture is fat and wide, room enough for two threads, one for the bulb and another for a tiny thing shaped like a pitchfork. Mother whispers, *Follow the wires.*

I obey and follow them into a sunken cabinet behind the mantle. Right before it plugs into the outlet, the wire splits, and a second line runs into the wall behind the cabinet. I remove some Dover editions of Poe's work and press my palm to the wall.

Poe & I

It shifts slightly, a tile that hasn't dried, and I feel around the edges until the bottom kicks out.

A fake panel. I pull it forward.

Behind the panel glows the box of a digital recorder.

I reach for the second candlelight switch and roll it. The recorder clicks to life. Clever. Plans within plans. I speak into the candle. "Hello Quinn. See you at the fundraiser."

The night before January 19th, I travel down to the sex shops in the West Village and purchase a pair of toy handcuffs. The night of, I break out cauldron-black hair dye and soak my unruly curls and bushy sideburns until all traces of my gingerness vanish. I paint my lips Rocky-Horror purple and eyebrows full moon white, wrap my neck in a kerchief, and paste on a fuzzy, caterpillar mustache.

Poe stares askance at me as I prep in the moonlit parlor, preening in his old mirror.

I hesitate to make inquiries about your motivations, Jonah Peabody. You do not seem at all well.

"Happy birthday, Eddie!"

Oh, is that today? I have no sense of time in here.

"As a birthday gift, I'm going to return Virginia to you. You sure you want her back?"

I wish for nothing more than to see my dear Sissy again.

"Your funeral, har har."

I ride a city bus and then walk to Quinn's mausoleum, attracting plenty of stares.

The mansion is a pulsing box of light and music. The marble lobby is glowing red. Cocktail glasses glisten, waiters dart, high heels click. The air is thick with reefer, cloves, burning leaves. A string quartet, arms plastered with black feathers, plays in the shadow of the staircase. The parade of costumes is outrageous. Kings and queens, goblins and gorillas, jesters and clowns, and oh, about two dozen versions of Poe.

In the main rooms off the lobby, chefs roll crab in seaweed, toss pasta with mushrooms, and carve roast chicken and glazed duck. Tables are full of vegetable and fruit, cheese and crackers, bubbling urns of tomato soup and corn chowder. Another room is devoted to just desserts—chocolate fountains with strawberries and pineapple for dipping, trays of custards and pies, licorice and gumball machines.

Matthew Mercier

Beyond the food, I find a cash bar and the auction hall—a narrow, low-ceilinged room. A projector sits in the middle of the aisle, ready to shine items on an enormous white screen. The bidding starts in fifteen minutes. I flip through the catalog of Poe artifacts. A lock of Edgar's hair. Cufflinks. Manuscripts. The West Point Cape. A wedge of his coffin. And finally, a rare first edition of '*Tamerlane and Other Poems: By a Bostonian*'.

"You bidding on anything, gingerbread?"

I turn, and there is Bradford in a tux. "No costume?"

"I don't like hiding my face."

"Didn't think you'd come."

"I wasn't going to, but Cynthia asked me to be MC for the auction. Seems like a pretty safe position to be in tonight."

"Safe. Right."

He puts a hand on my shoulder. "You're on your own tonight, Jonah. I can't be involved in whatever . . . damn . . . are your eyes green?"

"Yes. Good luck tonight. We understand."

"We?"

"Mother and I."

"Okay."

I leave him and wander into the rainbow tunnel, scanning for familiar faces under the devils, ghosts, and sexy surgeons, pupils flickering behind cheap plastic masks. There is a rotund jester in the corner sizing me up, then he grins and waves.

Oh Jesus.

I wave my pinkie nub at Ramses, who gets up and vanishes into the crowd.

I move through the blue room, the yellow, the red, and finally the Poe room, where Virginia's bones are being gawked at.

Another Poe is standing in front of the case, lecturing to partygoers in a mournful Southern accent. "My poor wife is encased in this glass tomb. Not buried alive, I grant you, but something far, far worse—buried above ground. Her soul is not at rest. It wanders the Earth when it deserves the release of ascension. The only way it can do that is if these remains are allowed to join me in Baltimore."

This Poe whips out Lizzie's pamphlet from her back pocket, but only a few people seem to be interested. I snag one from a disinterested devil.

Poe & I

"The Horrible Truth of Arthur Quinn's Museum."

It's a corrective to Quinn's collection. This indigenous clay pot is filched from a sacred Navajo site. That rare book is lifted from a private collection in France. This display of artifacts from the Antebellum South glorifies racism and sensationalizes history. On and on. The text is fully cited and sourced. It calls out Quinn's questionable practices, undermines what people are looking at, if they actually care. I notice the flyer in dozens of hands but also in the trash bins. After the crowd wanders off, I say to Poe "Nice job, Edgar."

Lizzie takes a moment, scanning me up and down, and says, "Thank you, Junior. Nice duds. Great minds think alike."

I hold up the pamphlet. "Where is he?"

"He's around. I'm trying to avoid him."

"You don't seem that concerned."

"Cynthia is going to protect me." She takes me by the hand. "Jonah, you should leave. Now. I think Cynthia . . . "

"We're not leaving without her bones."

"We?"

"Mother and I."

Lizzie recoils. "Jonah, you need to . . . "

Her gaze wanders to the hooded Red Death, who is a little early, but making the rounds and greeting everyone—it's Cynthia, whose Irish eyes smile at us briefly. Lizzie grabs my emaciated wrist. "Jonah, she doesn't want you here."

"Everything will be fine."

I follow Death into the Eureka Dome, a flashing rave that nearly sends my third eye into seizures. A pulsing purple dot—an infinite orb—tracks across the ceiling, growing bigger and bigger with each pulse until it finally explodes, shooting out dozens of spears, spirals, and daggers that splatter over our heads. A hip-hop tune blares in time with the supernovas.

The statues are now actors. Grandmaster Flash is a real DJ, spinning records, conducting the party. Colin Powell marches in step on his podium. Bella Abzug shimmies her generous booty. Isaac Sidel slow jams in his rumpled detective duds. And Jonas Bronck, the bearded founder, twirls a walking stick, as if he's grand marshal in a damn parade.

No Anne Hutchinson. And Andromeda's book is missing.

Matthew Mercier

The web of bodies moves in a herky-jerky throb under the strobe lights, and the crowd cheers as smoke hisses from the ceiling. Death is standing across the throng, gesturing for me to follow.

She leads me outside to a flagstone path that curves toward a tiny greenhouse. Seedlings stretched end to end, potted geraniums and herbs, serpentine orchids reaching for the ceiling, a familiar purple flower in a trio of terracotta pots. Wolfsbane.

"Don't touch," I mumble.

Cactus and aloe, explosions of green, purple, and pink—a hothouse rainbow that rustles and quivers, the plants whispering to each other about the strangers in their midst.

My head swims, my skin breaths, and I half-expect a portal to split open above me.

The Red Death is bent over the plants, spritzing them with a tiny bottle.

"Where is he, boss?"

Without a word, she exits the greenhouse, and we follow the flagstone path to a pair of double doors at the rear of the house. Inside, she leads me down a long hallway of antique gaslights and crimson wallpaper to an armless couch, where a visitor can sit and gaze at the sole exhibit—two framed drawings, two women. No placards needed. Mother Peabody on the left, a cross dangling over a tattered orange sweater, and on the right, Quinn's mother, a pearl necklace draped over a powder blue blouse. Mother looks down on me with that gap-toothed grin while Quinn's mom flashes a Kennedy smile, a brick wall of pearly whites.

The Red Death slips away. Then a cane taps the floor, and Richard sits next to me, staring at his mother. "Beautiful, isn't she?"

Present tense. Same as my father. Keeping the dead alive with sentimental grammar. "They both were," I say.

"Oh, I don't know. Yours is a bit homely."

It's all I can do to stop Mother from ripping his throat out. "What was she like, your mother?"

"You deserve to know nothing."

"One thing."

He rubs his kneecaps. "Oh, fine. She plays the flute. First chair."

"What does that mean?"

Poe & I

"Such a philistine, Jonah. First chair. It means she's the best."

"Oh." In my pocket, I slip my stumpy hand into one of the cuffs.

"I'm surprised you came tonight. I thought for sure you'd run. Like your sister."

"No," I sigh. "No, I don't run."

I whip out the cuffs and slap the second around Quinn's left wrist, which gets the requisite reaction. He bolts upward, pulling me with him. "Oh, well done, Tony Curtis. What's that's going to get you?"

"Take me to her, Quinn. Now."

"No need to be rude. That was our next stop."

We crabwalk to a staircase, leading down into another goddamn basement. More dirt, more dampness. The party noise fades as we clump sideways down the planks. At the bottom, only the hum of a boiler and a hot water heater, glowing in the corner. Smooth concrete floor, no ventilation or light or windows. And just ahead, another line of doors, three of them, evenly spaced apart. Two shut, one open. We enter the open cell—low ceiling, flimsy cot, bedpan, a nightstand with a tiny lamp.

"Hey there, Professor." The reverb of his voice box is loud against the four walls.

My own voice box fails. My mouth goes dry, and my right knee trembles.

Ramses as the jester, sitting in a chair and flipping through a book of Poe. "I don't get this guy. Too brainy. This story. *The Man That Was All Used Up.* Cynthia says it's about me. Soldier comes back from war all in pieces, missing body parts. They try to put him back together, like that giant egg from the fairy tales." His voice crackles with static. "He starts telling stories about himself. Some real, some not."

"Mr. Ramses?" Quinn is clearly surprised. "What are you?"

The Red Death walks in behind us, and Ramses steps forward, grabbing Quinn by the shoulders. Quinn's alabaster face jellies in shock as Ramses looks down at the handcuffs. "You two getting kinky? Unlock him, Jonah."

I slip from the toy handcuffs quite easily—thin wrists and a missing pinkie help with that—and then I unlock Quinn, even as Ramses snaps real handcuffs onto his other wrist.

"Help your bookie, Jonah," says the Red Death.

I shake my head.

Matthew Mercier

Cynthia huffs, pushes past me, and grabs Quinn's struggling ankles. She and the fireman lift him onto the bed. His bones look sharp as glass, his skin fishy and slick. Ramses secures his other wrist, takes out another pair of cuffs, and locks his ankles to the lower posts. Quinn is now spread eagle across the mattress, his skinny body stretched to the limit.

"Unlock me!" he screams. "Do you know what she's done, Jonah? Your precious boss? Do you know what she's capable of? She's done her own dirty work! She killed Mason, not—"

Cynthia slaps Quinn across the face. Everyone jumps, even Ramses. Quinn starts to speak, but she puts a hand over his mouth. The boss speaks to me but is looking at him.

"Do you believe that, Jonah?"

I don't know what to believe any more. Quinn's face is my face, pleading. His eyes are my eyes, begging. He's a boy again, trapped inside the car, watching his mother crumble to the ground. Cynthia takes her hand away as Ramses hands her a rag.

"Look, I've done bad things," Quinn bellows. "I've done awful things. But."

"Bad things?" I say. "Such as?"

He bites his lip, opens his mouth, bites it again, and shakes his head. He thrashes and screams, his ribs pushing through tissue paper skin. His U scar flushes pink. Cynthia stuffs the rag in his mouth.

"Time to go, Jonah," Cynthia says. "Unless you'd like to watch."

I rub my throat. "Watch?"

She scans the length of Quinn's body. "Withdrawal. From the heroin."

"Drugs? That's true?"

"Of course. He's our very own William Burroughs. A functional addict. Oh, it won't be pretty. Fluids will exit the body. Snot, shit, sweat. It can last for days. He actually might end up looking like poor Mr. Valdemar. A rotting liquid mass of loathsome—of detestable putrescence."

Quinn's eyes are streaming tears.

"Arthur has been good at covering his tracks all these years," she rubs her cousin's forehead, "but that's all over."

"Wait," I say. "Are you going to nail him for Ricky?"

"Did you find any evidence?"

"No, I . . ."

Poe & I

"Even if we did, I don't think he'd stand trial for anything. With his money, he could avoid justice forever."

Quinn's pale body glows nuclear. His eyes are pleading with me, and a pit opens in my stomach. Then, behind the bed, inside the rippling red walls of the cottage, a body begins to form.

"I know what you're thinking, Jonah." She looks at the wall behind Quinn, following my gaze. "But I'm doing this because I care about Arthur, or Richard, if that's what you want to call him. His addiction was getting out of hand, we had to intervene. I didn't want you to witness this, but you're a stubborn mule. However, you've also been a useful distraction. And hooking me up with the fireman here was a brilliant idea." She winks at Ramses, who winks back. "He's as damaged as me, which is how I like them, but all of this is to say you're now an accomplice."

The wall behind Quinn is pulsing. A black arm pushes out, thick with purple bruises. A wrinkled torso, the hint of a beat-up face, and the glowing white iris of a dead eye. The good eye drops to look at Quinn, curious. It reaches out a knobby hand and brushes Quinn's forehead, leaving dark smudges. Quinn screams behind the rag.

"Let's go, kid," the fireman flicks his chin at me. "Play time is over. I'll be looking after the tweaker here."

"How much is she paying you, Ramses?"

"Don't worry about it."

I wiggle my stump in his face. "If the price is right, huh? Some hero."

Cynthia snorts a laugh. "I did a little detective work on our Ground Zero worker, Jonah. I wouldn't put too much faith in his stories."

Ramses shrugs. "I might have exaggerated a bit."

A cold shiver runs through me. I guess a bullshitter attracts bullshit. Ricky Thurston is now fully formed in the wall behind Quinn. Ramses pushes a palm against my chest. "Time to go, Professor."

Ricky Thurston is holding two flickering hands on either side of Quinn's head, pressing hard. My gut is ice. Now Thurston has a hand on Richard's neck, who gurgles, eyes rolling back in his head.

Suddenly, I want to rip the sock from Richard's mouth and free him from his ghosts. Cynthia's neck is twitching. She's a raw nerve.

"Boss . . . did Quinn kill Ricky?"

Matthew Mercier

"Of course."

"Where's your evidence?"

"I don't have any." Cynthia sighs. "But I've suspected Quinn for a long time."

"So, you're just going to leave him locked up?"

"I take issue with your pronoun. The correct combo is 'You and I'. We. We are just going to leave him locked up. There is no clean way out of this, Jonah. Yes, we'll leave him there until the drugs are out of his system. And then he'll need time to recuperate, but who knows. He could easily have a relapse. You seem to think I don't have my cou . . . that I don't have Quinn's best interests at heart."

There. She almost said it. Cousin.

"Cynthia, we agreed to help each other."

"Did we? There's no written contract, right? No legal conditions. You distrusted me so much you changed the locks."

"What about Quinn's money? That collection? All of Lizzie's work?"

"Ms. Borden's efforts will not be wasted."

"But you can't just . . . "

"Mr. Peabody, correct me if I'm wrong, but you've got more than one drug count on your record, right? At least two? A third would be three strikes. Under Rockefeller law, that could mean some serious jail time."

"Yes."

"Very well. So, for now Quinn will stay locked up . . . "

"With Ricky's ghost?"

" . . . and I expect you to keep your mouth shut and give the tours this weekend. We must keep up the front of a respectable business. No ghosts. Understood?"

"Understood."

"Very good. Now, begone. Before I lock you up, too."

Ricky Thurston is hovering inside the wall, sitting cross-legged, his charcoal flesh mixing with the red brick. He's holding the cat o' nine tails from Quinn's collection. Bits of flesh are dripping off its hooks. Deep gashes now run across Quinn's shoulders and down his chest.

Ricky stares at me from inside the wall with his one good eye. Cold. Indifferent.

"Wait," I say. "I've got something to tell you, Richard."

Poe & I

Quinn tilts his head, as if listening to a faint echo. His chest rises and falls, up and down.

"I'm sorry my family caused you so much pain. I'm sorry we took your mother from you."

Then I lean closer and whisper in his ear.

He doesn't move. He considers what I've said for half a minute, then laughs so hard I think his ribs might break. I stand and back out of the room, into the dank cellar with Cynthia, as pale as her cousin. I curl my lips over my teeth and say, "Where is my mother?"

Cynthia gestures to a room across the hall. My heart is beating against Mother's heart, and I'm afraid I'll be overcome before I can reach the doorknob, since Mother is screaming like crazy inside me. She knows.

I open the door. There is the hemp coffin, a patina of green fuzz coating its lid. I step forward, knees wobbling in their sockets, and reach for the lid. The latch is gone. I flip it open. The lid breaks off the rotten hinges and falls to the cement floor.

There she is. No. There *it* is. A full skeleton. Flesh melted off. A fan of sooty gray hair screaming off the crown of the skull. Teeth ripped out. Ribcage picked apart. Mother wails, and I give in to the lead weights in my knees, falling to the ground and weeping the way I never wept for her, as Cynthia rubs my back. It's not comforting. She's trying to play a role, and it doesn't suit her.

"I'm taking her out of here," I say. "Tonight."

She hands me a large backpack and a pair of latex gloves, as if she knew I would demand this. "Please do."

I pack Mother up, bone by bone, leaving the skull for last, not caring how much it will get banged up or scratched. With each piece, Mother whimpers and coos.

"What . . . what did he do with her Cynthia? With her body? All these years?"

Cynthia shudders and turns away from me, the darkness of the basement pressing down on us. "Use your imagination."

I block out the images, my gut heaving. The poor bastard. The poor, sick bastard.

"What did you whisper to Richard?" she asks.

"That," I wheeze, "is on a need-to-know basis."

She directs me to the rear exit, and then I run from that madhouse, my Mother in my chest and on my back.

279

Chapter 32
Living History

Two weeks after the party, I meet Bradford and Lizzie at the Empire to debrief and discuss the obit in the *New York Times*.

Arthur Quinn, noted philanthropist and reclusive billionaire, died in his Riverdale home last week from an apparent heroin overdose. Mr. Quinn made his fortune on Wall Street in the late eighties and spent most of his later life traveling the world, collecting art, and donating to museums anonymously. He famously did not wish for his name to be associated with any organizations, save for The Bronx Historical Society, of which he was the president and an active board member for many years. Allegations of blackmail and extortion around Mr. Quinn's private collection had recently surfaced, and an investigation has clouded the proceedings around his death.

"Overdose," Bradford taps the paper. "Best way to murder an addict."

"No," Lizzie says. "No. He shot those drugs up his arm. Not Cynthia."

"Don't kid yourself." I rub the stub of my pinkie. "Although I think Ramses did the deed, for a song. Not Cynthia."

I've told them everything. They asked, and I confessed. The creepiness of it all has bonded us together, here at the end of all things. We feel used.

Quinn's death has come under investigation, and although his body was discovered with needles and raw product, detectives found Cynthia's story questionable, so it all blew up into a supernova scandal. The press hyperventilated. The Historical

280

Poe & I

Society disavowed any association with Quinn. His name was removed from all records and plaques. Even the state attorney got involved to handle the mess of Quinn's estate.

It will take Cynthia months to climb out of the legal quagmire. Quinn's home-made mausoleum is a crime scene.

We demand a meeting and pummel her with questions. Did Quinn murder Ricky and Mason? Who buried Ricky's interview? And who planted the mics in the cottage?

"Those mics were all Quinn," Cynthia says, "but I assure you those recordings of you will be destroyed, Jonah. As for Mason and Ricky, there are some secrets which do not permit themselves to—"

"Enough Poe," I snap. "You can't tell us anything?"

"Any answers I give would be just speculation."

"Speculate," Lizzie hisses. "We insist. That tunnel into the cottage . . . "

"Proves nothing."

"Did you know it was there?"

"Oh, yes. But again. What does it prove?"

"We talked about this, Cynthia. You believed Quinn murdered Ricky."

"I know, dear. But how?"

"I don't know." Lizzie is near tears. "I found everything but that."

"There we go." Cynthia asks if we want anything from the collection. Once the state is done with the investigation, she'll probably have to sell some of it to pay her legal bills. But she can give some of it away.

Bradford perks up. "That first pressing of *The Message*."

"Done. Lizzie? What do you want?"

"Justice for Ricky."

"We've achieved that."

"No, you haven't."

"Jonah?" the boss says. "How about you? I presume you want your sister's book?" She says this with the weight of a threat that only I can hear. The only thing I haven't told everyone is her familial connection to Quinn.

"Yes. I presume my finger is a lost cause."

"I'm not sure what he did with that."

"And we want Virginia."

"Ah, the fake bones."

Matthew Mercier

"Fake?"

"Oh, God yes. Plastic crap. You didn't believe all that, did you?"

We did. Except Bradford. He says he never bought it. Nonetheless, we take the fake bones and invite Oscar and Carla to the cottage for a ceremony. We symbolically bury a few slivers of fake Virginia in the garden and then create a makeshift altar in the parlor.

"I can't believe I'm doing this with y'all," Bradford shivers. "This really isn't my thing."

"Settle down, big man," Carla chirps. "It's justice for the spirits."

"Exactly. This is just symbolic," Lizzie says. "Right, Jonah?"

"Symbolism up the wazoo."

We say a few words, read *Annabel Lee* while the hairs on the back of my neck tingle. I cough, scratch, rub my chest. Mother is still inside me. Her bones are in the armoire, waiting for a proper burial. I feel like a spirit myself these days. One foot in this world and in the next.

Poe drifts out of the bust. He looks at us, puzzled, but then He sees the bones, and His face warps with understanding. He drifts towards the altar, brushes His hands over the faux remains of His wife, and looks out at the shell of the greenhouse, where Virginia's orbs are gathering. I pretend to see nothing. But with Mother, I now have double the third eye.

Bradford swears. Oscar looks as if he's going to pee. Lizzie and Carla are holding hands.

Poe looks as though He might weep as Virginia drifts through the walls, fully formed, frail and cracked. She looks at Her "bones" on the altar, then raises Her eyes to Poe, stern and unhappy. They stand on either side of the altar, and it sounds as if they're talking, but we can't hear a word. Poe is smiling, but not Virginia. By the end of their conversation, She looks more at peace than Poe, whose smile is now tempered, resigned. She does take His hand in Hers, and He bows His head. She kisses Him on His brow, then looks at us, faintly nods, and raises Her hands to the sky, evaporating and leaving Poe behind.

Till death do us part. I realize that if Poe Cottage does something to people, then it follows that it's most famous occupant would be also haunted by His ghosts. I have Mom. Ricky, his Uncle. Poe, Virginia.

Eddie glares in my direction.

Do not pity me, Jonah Peabody. If I am entirely truthful, it

Poe & I

feels wonderful to be free from earthly desire. I think . . . I think it may be what I have always wanted.

He looks down at His body, which is slowly beginning to fade.

I suddenly have a dozen questions about France and Alexander Dumas, but I don't want to ask them in front of everyone. The case is now closed. He turns and floats into the bust, His face mixing with the dust motes.

The parlor is empty.

"Holy shit, did you feel that?" Oscar says. "That was deep. They were here! I have to change my underwear."

Carla yanks his belt. "Way to ruin a sacred moment, bonehead."

Lizzie smiles at me and winks. Bradford whistles. "Y'all crazy. I didn't see anything."

After Virginia's "burial," Bradford, Lizzie, and I hit the road for a Poe field trip. Cynthia is still creeping us out with her foggy motivations, so we use the trip to decompress and debrief.

Bradford has finished his thesis (*The Unbearable Horror of Whiteness: Black History in a Post-Racial World*) and is headed back to Vermont that summer for a research fellowship at the Washburn Library. It might lead to a teaching job, or he might move out west, overseas, wherever his research takes him, as long as it's not The Bronx.

"Your Uncle will miss you," I say.

"Happy ending there. He's off the streets. Found an SRO that won't make him pray or get off the sauce. Program called Housing First."

"Your uncle?" Lizzie asks.

"Alabama," I tell her. "He popped in for my first tour. That's great, Bradford."

"We'll see. We've been down this road before."

We make a stop in Baltimore and tour their Poe Museum, where the resident expert, Jeff Jerome, tells us the tumor theory of Poe's death carries weight, but the tumor itself never left the coffin, so whatever Quinn had was just one more hoax.

We hit the other Poe hot spots—his grave and the building on East Lombard where "a gentleman, rather worse for wear", was found, "in great distress" at Ryan's 4th ward polling site.

I figure we've done a complete tour, but as we start to drive back north, Bradford pulls off the highway. "One more stop."

"Poe-related?" Lizzie asks.

Matthew Mercier

"Thesis-related."

"American horror?"

"The worst."

We hop over to the "nice" part of Charm City—all brick townhouses—and find a green space across from the state house, one of those parks with bronze statues of local heroes stained with pigeon shit. We feed a meter and walk the length of the park, gazing at historical men whose names I don't recognize. (There's even a Peabody. Always one in the crowd.) At the southern tip, we find a guy sitting in a chair at a sharp angle, draped in robes.

ROGER B. TANEY OF MARYLAND
CHIEF JUSTICE

"A judge? What's his deal?"

Bradford hawks a goober into the man's lap.

"Taney signed off on the Dred Scott decision. Slaves could never be considered citizens, only inhuman pieces of property. One swipe of his pen, and he turned them into monsters." He spits again. "And people wonder why Baltimore is such a horror show. Post-racial my ass. This city is cursed. Long as this judge is presiding."

Lizzie and I decide that when Bradford starts teaching history classes, we're going to audit them. Online if need be. After the trip, we say our goodbyes. Nothing sentimental. Bradford, for all his talk of uncovering history's shadowy secrets, admits he could have done without knowing Cynthia's. But no regrets.

"You both take care of Poe," he says. "And each other. Stay weird." Stay weird. My new mantra.

Back in The Bronx, I find a cheap apartment, and we cleanse the basement for Ricky's sake. Oscar and Carla give the cottage tours now. I fill in every now and then, but the team effort feels right. The kids keep pestering me about Quinn and the party, but I tell them, in that horrible way that adults have, to not ask too many questions. It's still a rift between us, all these secrets, but when we tell them it might endanger their future, they get it. Bad enough their boss may be a murderer.

Dupin comes back to us, and we buy him a black kitten, name her Muddy. They're both indoor cats now and live with me offsite.

284

Poe & I

I take a part-time job at a soup kitchen on Webster Avenue, which gets me out of the house and myself. Lizzie starts an oral history of Poe Cottage caretakers, the better to ensure that Ricky Thurston won't be erased from history. She's also started writing a post-apocalyptic, punk rock young adult series called *Teenage Wasteland*, in which teens try to restore rock and roll to their barren world, with help from the spirits of Deborah Harry, Chuck Berry, David Hackney, Kim Deal, Peter Frampton, and Keith Moon. They fight internet trolls and corporate thugs with re-outfitted woofers and tweeters.

The other big news is that the cops finally bust the drug ring, which just means they've chased that horse to another track, but it's nice to have our streets returned to us.

Eventually Cynthia tells us they're going to phase out the caretaker job. With the Garcia siblings and Arnheim across the street, there's no more need for the basement apartment. Lizzie and I ask if we can spend one more night. Cynthia agrees to this. She shows up that Saturday as we're locking up. We ask her how the investigation is going.

"Oh, there is a lot to deal with," she sighs, "but it's my burden to carry. Quinn's estate has been left to the Society, but the detectives may have something to say about that."

"So, Quinn named you in his will, too?" Lizzie asks.

"He named the Society."

"Convenient."

"How's the book?" I ask.

We've heard that she's broken bread with Peggy Mason and agreed to finish Lloyd's work. Or rather, her work.

"Oh, too many facts to pin down, too many sources missing. I don't know what Mason was thinking. I don't know what I was thinking. Poe as a French spy? My God. I'm going to turn it into a novel. Historical espionage. Fiction is really my first love."

"What's the title?"

"*A Spy in The House of Usher.*"

"Sounds trashy."

"Doesn't it? Speaking of writing, I understand you wrote a lot of this down, Jonah."

"I took a few notes."

"Well, I hope I don't have to say it too loudly—"

"For my eyes only. I got it, boss."

Matthew Mercier

"I'm not your boss anymore." She extends a hand. "Thank you both for everything."

As we stroll out to the porch, Lizzie can't help but take pride in the garden, which she and Carla have been designing according to Poe's texts. Tulips, hyacinthine, star of Bethlehem. They've gone off script too, ordering a couple of mushroom logs.

"Mushrooms?" Cynthia says. "What kind?"

"Tippler's bane!" I say. "AKA Inky Cap. I noticed some growing in Quinn's greenhouse."

Lizzie holds up a log of withered, bell-shaped fungus. "They're a perfect Bronx mushroom. You can find them growing in abandoned lots, disturbed areas. But don't use them in cooking."

"No?"

"Poisonous," I say. "But only if you combine them with alcohol. A lot. Alcoholic levels of alcohol. Legend has it the KGB used them, right Lizzie? A little mushroom gravy, plus long Siberian nights, plus vodka, and presto—heart attack. Untraceable. Your victim just drank themselves to death, and it was their own fault. Easy!"

"Intriguing," Cynthia says. "Poe would certainly appreciate such morbid knowledge. Well, carry on."

She walks to the front gate, a dark cloud hovering above her shoulders. Hard to say what I feel any more for her—pity, empathy, fear—but if Lizzie and I are carrying shadows in our souls after all this, I imagine the boss is, too.

"That was a little mean, I guess."

"She deserved it," Lizzie says.

"You think she did Mason?"

"Peggy said they ate mushrooms that night. And Mason and Ricky were both big drinkers."

So was my father.

Fill in the blanks. Make your best guess. We've made ours. If you don't want to make a criminal out of Cynthia, I understand. But you see how she handled the ending. Not that I can stand on the moral high ground. If police want my full confession, I'll give it, but not just yet. A few more doors to shut.

Chapter 33

Choose Your Own Adventurous Past

This next part I'm only sharing with you, dear reader, my fellow watcher from afar.

After Quinn's death, I travel back home to visit Susan McKittrick and tell her everything. She doesn't take it well. The consequences of Cynthia's actions are going to have a ripple effect. Eventually it will come out that Cynthia and Richard were cousins, and who knows how that will play out for the rest of the family. More unwanted attention. She tells me I should pray for forgiveness and mercy. I tell her that instead of praying, I might just go the police, consequences be damned, and I remind her what Richard did with my mother's body. She tells me to please leave her alone.

I make a stop at the old homestead. It's falling apart, a house of death as deathtrap. The porch is tilted at a dangerous angle, and a number of windows are broken. The foundation is cracked after a rough winter. It's not worth selling or fixing. I should just pull an Usher and let the earth swallow it whole.

I bury Mother's remains in the backyard, and she drifts out of me that night, although a clump lodges in my throat and sinks back into my chest, where it stays no matter how much I heave and holler.

Then, one more walk in the graveyard. I sit in the shade of a maple tree and nod off to grackles chattering in the treetops. I wake in full sun and float out of my body, above the graveyard—a green chessboard of gray and black tombstones. I float higher, the sun tugging at my belt. Maybe I have been telling you this story from another dimension. It's nicer up here, cleaner than The Bronx.

287

Matthew Mercier

Maybe I'll stay here forever. I'd make a good ghost—angry, guilty, melancholy, stubborn, lily-white.

As I hover here inside my third eye, looking down at myself, the sun begins to slip away, and the stars come out. I see Andromeda's freckles mixing with the Milky Way, her big smile in the last streak of purple sunset.

From up here I can see the past, and I can see the afternoon that Richard visited us. I can hear the conversation he and Andy were having in kitchen before I arrived, discussing the best way to cook a certain type of mushroom for Father's next meal.

Andromeda is nodding and listening, and then she's preparing that meal for Father. I see him eating that meal and dying a few days later. The same way Ricky and Mason died. Heart attack.

Afterward, I call her, which I've always been able to do, folks. No apologies. I was protecting my sister, and I always will.

The first thing I say when she picks up is, "He's gone." The second is, "Congrats on the book, sis. I'm proud of you."

"You going to come visit me?"

"Maybe," I say. "I might have to go to the police. About Richard. I mean."

"Why Jonah?"

"It's the right thing to do. I'm an accomplice."

"But you don't know anything for certain. You have to go live your life, Jonah."

"I will. Just not yet. I enjoy living vicariously through you."

"Stop it, bro."

You see how this works? I've been receiving Andy's letters all these years. She's the one who's been canning salmon in Alaska. Shooting kangaroos in Australia. She's the one who went to college and had all those great teachers. She lived all those adventures, she wrote the thesis on Poe, which is how I know so much about him. Her life is my resume. We swore to protect each other until the end, and I meant it.

My name is Jonah Peabody, and everything will be fine.

Chapter 34

The Center of the Universe

I now have a favor to ask of you, my co-conspirators, (the definition of a reader) sitting in your easy chairs or on public transport, or in a city park. I have one more secret for you to keep.

Please, if you visit Poe Cottage, don't bother the current docent for stories. There isn't a caretaker anymore. Whoever gives you a tour won't know about Jonah Peabody or Ricky Thurston. Names have been changed to protect the guilty. The basement is now just that—a regular basement with a boiler and hot water heater.

Lizzie and I settle in for our last night. It's peaceful and calm. Above us, the rats skitter in the ceiling. Below, the D train rumbles. Outside, the Bronx hums along, all systems normal. We're at the center of everything, and everything is in its place.

After Lizzie falls asleep, Mother tugs at my chest. My arm is healing, my lungs are clean, but she's still lingering, crammed inside a ventricle, close to my heart.

Listen, she whispers.

The wind chimes, tinkling in the spider oak. You can only hear them at night, after the Bronx falls asleep.

Dark lightning flashes in my chest. I roll away from Lizzie, hurry into the shed, and pull on my boots. Outside, Poe is standing on the back lawn, staring into the oak.

He points, *Your Mother . . .*

"I know."

Would you care for a leaping contest, Jonah Peabody? Before I depart this plane?

I indulge Him for a few leaps across the lawn, and with each

Matthew Mercier

lunge He flies higher and higher, His coattails flapping against the starless dome of night until His final leap lifts Him over the crown of the oak tree, over the roofs of the tenements, and into the endless expanse of Bronx sky.

Then I'm alone on the lawn, a crazy white boy hopping around by himself.

I approach the spider oak, stand on my tiptoes, and grab the lowest limb, sucking down cold spring air as I haul myself into its branches. Halfway up, I stop and crane my neck.

Two limbs above me, in plain sight, is the wind chime—five metal tubes knocking together with their ivory doppelgangers. Five white pieces of fluted and polished bone. Mother. The last remaining pieces of her rib cage.

The waterworks come fast, heaving sobs for Father, Mother, Ricky, Mason, even Quinn and Cynthia. Mother streams up my esophagus and over my lips, a moist fog breaking over my face, kissing and caressing me without malice.

Thank you, son. Thank you, thank you, thank you.

I keep climbing, dodging the telephone wires, until I'm above the bone chime, climbing toward the sky, that gaping dark matter that waits to swallow the earth. If I listen hard enough, I can hear the fires of hell crackling, the ice of the Milky Way creaking, and the entire planet groaning on its axis, spinning and tilting us all towards our mutual, delicious oblivion.

I'll make a poet yet.

I reach the top, bracing my feet in the crook of two limbs and leaning my palms above me on two more, so that I'm hanging, suspended, and with the Bronx below and the heavens above, I lean back my head and howl.

Acknowledgements

This book is pure fiction—a hoax—from top to bottom.

Normally I would never state so obvious a point, however Poe Cottage is quite real, and still sits at the intersection of Kingsbridge Road and the Grand Concourse in The Bronx, nestled safely inside Poe Park. I was employed there from January 2002 to December of 2005, proudly serving as caretaker and head docent, and clocking roughly 150 weekends, 300 days, and 500 hours giving tours, answering questions, and debunking myths about Edgar Allan Poe.

Absolutely nothing in this book should be taken as a reflection of my time working for The Bronx Historical Society, a crew of wonderful Bronxites who maintain and care for Poe Cottage. A big thanks to my former boss Kathleen McAuley, who entrusted me with the coolest once-in-a-lifetime gig a young man could ask for.

Thank you to the whisper network which led me to Poe in the first place: Joe DeSanto, Tim Kantz (a former caretaker himself) and Bob Roberts. Thanks also to Siobhan O'Neil, who took over docent duties immediately after I left.

I must also thank the fabulous storytelling group *The Moth* where I began sharing TRUE stories about my time with Edgar. Many thanks to the producers who listened, coached, and cheered me on through numerous live performances, including Jenifer Hixson, Sarah Austin Jenness, Kate Tellers, Meg Bowles, Catherine Burns and Lea Thau.

All this performative storytelling led to fellowship with a whole crew of raconteurs, including a pair of scoundrels, Terence Mickey and Eddie Gavagan. Love you guys.

Thank you to all my teachers, past and present, who endured my early attempts. Going in reverse: at the Hunter College MFA program, Colum McCann and Peter Carey; in undergraduate, Stephen Geller and Karen Mankovich; and, in 9th grade at Norwich Free Academy, Wally Lamb, for being my first example of a writer living the life.

A version of *Poe & I* was revised at the Constance Saltonstall Colony for the Arts in Ithaca, so thank you to the foundation and its wonderful executive director Lesley Williamson for providing the gift of time and space.

For crucial beta reads: James McCloskey, Stephen Black and Patrick Wynne. I'm especially grateful for the friendship of Concetta Ceriello, who generously read this manuscript early and often, and then talked me down from a metaphorical ledge more times than I care to count.

Thanks to Victor LaValle who allowed me to plant an easter egg in here from his own fictional universe—it's stamped inside the front cover of another *fictional* book authored by a *fictional* author, a one Mr. Kilgore Trout, himself a creation of the late great Kurt Vonnegut. Thank you, Victor and Vonnegut.

Jerome Charyn gave me permission to reference Isaac Sidel, the best damn detective in The Bronx. If you've not read Charyn, I recommend The Isacc Quartet, starting with *Blue Eyes*.

There is also a blink-and-you'll-miss-it homage to the great film *Adult World*, written by Andy Cochran, directed by Scott Coffey, and staring John Cusack. Please watch the movie. (I'll leave it up you to make the Poe connection.)

Many thanks and praise are due to Joe Mynhardt and the crew at Crystal Lake for believing in this book and putting it into your hands; to Theresa Derwin for passing the manuscript on to Joe; to Jaime Powell for editing; to Ben Baldwin for the great cover and putting up with my various requests for tweaks.

Eternal love and gratitude for my family, including my parents, John and Doreen Mercier, for creating a beautiful home and encouraging my creative side; for my musical brother Steve, who did a stint at the cottage when I needed a break; for Aunt Donna and Uncle Louie and all the baked ziti; for my fairy godmother Kathy McGlade, who was always—and still is—a constant loving presence in my life.

And finally, I don't have enough words to praise my wife Claudia, who's supported and believed in me from the start, who's always teaching me to dream big even when it scares me, who puts up with all my quirks and foibles, and who climbed the fence of Poe Park to visit me in the early days of our relationship. After you did that, Claudia, I knew you were the woman for me. I love you so much.

The End?

Not if you want to dive into more of Crystal Lake Publishing's Tales from the Darkest Depths!

Check out our amazing website and online store
or download our latest catalog here.
https://geni.us/CLPCatalog

Looking for award-winning Dark Fiction?
Download our latest catalog.

Includes our anthologies, novels, novellas, collections, poetry, non-fiction, and specialty projects.

WHERE STORIES COME ALIVE!

We always have great new projects and content on the website to dive into, as well as a newsletter, behind the scenes options, social media platforms, our own dark fiction shared-world series and our very own webstore. Our webstore even has categories specifically for KU books, non-fiction, anthologies, and of course more novels and novellas.

About the Author

Matthew Mercier is a writer and storyteller living in the woods of the Hudson Valley. He's worked as a tour guide at the Mystic Aquarium, run a youth hostel in Albuquerque, been slimed as a salmon packer in Naknek, Alaska, provided showers for homeless men on the Bowery, and proudly served three years as head docent and caretaker for the Edgar Allan Poe Cottage in The Bronx. He earned an MFA from Hunter College where he taught writing and children's literature. His work has appeared *The Brooklyn Rail, Mississippi Review, Glimmer Train, Rosebud Magazine, Creative Nonfiction, The Fairy Tale Review, Shotgun Honey, and Mystery Tribune*. He's told stories live on stage with **The Moth** and been heard on NPR's *The Moth Radio Hour,* as well *The Story Collider, RISK* and *The Truth* podcasts. He's been awarded the Leon B. Burstein scholarship from the New York chapter of the Mystery Writers of America, and a residency from the Saltonstall Foundation. Currently, he is writing and producing radio dramas for Radio Free Rhinecliff in Rhinecliff, NY. For more information, visit him at matthewmercier.com.

Readers . . .

Thank you for reading *Poe & I*. We hope you enjoyed this novel.

If you have a moment, please review *Poe & I* at the store where you bought it.

Help other readers by telling them why you enjoyed this book. No need to write an in-depth discussion. Even a single sentence will be greatly appreciated. Reviews go a long way to helping a book sell, and is great for an author's career. It'll also help us to continue publishing quality books.

Thank you again for taking the time to journey with Crystal Lake Publishing.

Visit our Linktree page for a list of our social media platforms.
https://linktr.ee/CrystalLakePublishing

Follow us on Amazon:

Our Mission Statement:

Since its founding in August 2012, Crystal Lake Publishing has quickly become one of the world's leading publishers of Dark Fiction and Horror books. In 2023, Crystal Lake Publishing formed a part of Crystal Lake Entertainment, joining several other divisions, including Torrid Waters, Crystal Lake Comics, Crystal Lake Kids, and many more.

While we strive to present only the highest quality fiction and entertainment, we also endeavour to support authors along their writing journey. We offer our time and experience in non-fiction projects, as well as author mentoring and services, at competitive prices.

With several Bram Stoker Award wins and many other wins and nominations (including the HWA's Specialty Press Award), Crystal Lake Publishing puts integrity, honor, and respect at the forefront of our publishing operations.

We strive for each book and outreach program we spearhead to not only entertain and touch or comment on issues that affect our readers, but also to strengthen and support the Dark Fiction field and its authors.

Not only do we find and publish authors we believe are destined for greatness, but we strive to work with men and women who endeavour to be decent human beings who care more for others than themselves, while still being hard working, driven, and passionate artists and storytellers.

Crystal Lake Publishing is and will always be a beacon of what passion and dedication, combined with overwhelming teamwork and respect, can accomplish. We endeavour to know each and every one of our readers, while building personal relationships with our authors, reviewers, bloggers, podcasters, bookstores, and libraries.

We will be as trustworthy, forthright, and transparent as any business can be, while also keeping most of the headaches away from our authors, since it's our job to solve the problems so they can stay in a creative mind. Which of course also means paying our authors.

We do not just publish books, we present to you worlds within your world, doors within your mind, from talented authors who sacrifice so much for a moment of your time.

There are some amazing small presses out there, and through collaboration and open forums we will continue to support other presses in the goal of helping authors and showing the world what quality small presses are capable of accomplishing. No one wins when a small press goes down, so we will always be there to support hardworking, legitimate presses and their authors. We don't see Crystal Lake as the best press out there, but we will always strive to be the best, strive to be the most interactive and grateful, and even blessed press around. No matter what happens over time, we will also take our mission very seriously while appreciating where we are and enjoying the journey.

What do we offer our authors that they can't do for themselves through self-publishing?

We are big supporters of self-publishing (especially hybrid publishing), if done with care, patience, and planning. However, not every author has the time or inclination to do market research, advertise, and set up book launch strategies. Although a lot of authors are successful in doing it all, strong small presses will always be there for the authors who just want to do what they do best: write.

What we offer is experience, industry knowledge, contacts and trust built up over years. And due to our strong brand and trusting fanbase, every Crystal Lake Publishing book comes with weight of respect. In time our fans begin to trust our judgment and will try a new author purely based on our support of said author.

With each launch we strive to fine-tune our approach, learn from our mistakes, and increase our reach. We continue to assure our authors that we're here for them and that we'll carry the weight of the launch and dealing with third parties while they focus on their strengths—be it writing, interviews, blogs, signings, etc.

We also offer several mentoring packages to authors that include knowledge and skills they can use in both traditional and self-publishing endeavours.

We look forward to launching many new careers.

This is what we believe in. What we stand for. This will be our legacy.

Welcome to Crystal Lake Publishing— Tales from the Darkest Depths.

www.ingramcontent.com/pod-product-compliance
Lightning Source LLC
LaVergne TN
LVHW021741111224
798873LV00004B/464